Disordered Minds

MINETTE WALTERS

Disordered Minds

MACMILLAN

First published 2003 by Macmillan
an imprint of Pan Macmillan Ltd
Pan Macmillan, 20 New Wharf Road, London N1 9RR
Basingstoke and Oxford
Associated companies throughout the world
www.panmacmillan.com

ISBN 1 4050 3416 5 HB
ISBN 1 4050 3417 3 TPB

1 3 5 7 9 8 6 4 2

A CIP catalogue record for this book is available from
the British Library.

Typeset by SetSystems Ltd, Saffron Walden, Essex
Printed and bound in Great Britain by
Mackays of Chatham plc, Chatham, Kent

For Benson & Hedges

No man is so good as to be free from all evil,
nor so bad as to be worth nothing.

MICHAEL CRICHTON

One

Colliton Park, Highdown, Bournemouth
Monday, 4 May 1970, 1.30 p.m.

IT WASN'T MUCH of a park, barely half an acre of wilted grass off Colliton Way where local people walked their dogs in the mornings and evenings. During the day it was hardly frequented at all, except by truants who hung around the trees that lined the fences. The police rarely visited it and, anyway, there was a hundred yards of open space between the only entrance and the offenders. In the time it took two overweight coppers to lumber across, the teens were long gone, vaulting the low fences into the gardens that formed the rear perimeter. As complaints came in thick and fast from homeowners whenever this happened, the police, preferring an easy life, tended to leave the youngsters alone.

The logic ran that while they were in the park they weren't thieving, and it was better to turn a blind eye and concentrate official efforts in the city centre. To the cynical police mind, truanting came low on their list of criminal behaviour.

Situated at the poorer end of Highdown, Colliton Way had little going for it. Unemployment was high, school attendance poor, and the proposed new buildings on the acres of waste ground behind it, which had promised jobs and houses, had faltered to a halt. The only site under construction was the Brackham & Wright tool factory, which was a planned replacement for the present, antiquated building in Glazeborough Road. This was no consolation to its workers, many of whom lived in Colliton Way, because up-to-date technology and automation always brought redundancies.

The most persistent truants were three boys. They were charismatic and generous as long as their leadership wasn't challenged, dangerously violent when it was. It made them a magnet for unhappy children who misinterpreted generosity for affection and cruelty for regard, and none of the children understood how damaged the boys were. How could they, when the boys didn't know it themselves? Barely able to read or write, only interested in immediate gratification and with no rein over their aggressive impulses, they thought they were in control of their lives.

That May Monday followed the aimless pattern of the many before. So entrenched was the boys' truancy that their mothers no longer bothered to get them out of bed. Better to let sleeping dogs lie, was the women's thinking, than face a beating because their overgrown sons were angry at being woken. The boys were incapable of getting up. None of them came home before the early hours – if they came home at all – and they were always so drunk their sleep was stupor. All three mothers had asked for them to be taken into care at one time or another, but their resolve had never lasted very long. Fear of reprisal, and misguided love for their absent first-borns, had always effected a change of mind. It might have been different if there had been men around, but there weren't, so the women did what their sons told them.

The boys had picked up a couple of thirteen-year-old girls in the centre of town and brought them to the park. The skinny one, who had her ten-year-old brother in tow, held no interest for them; the other, a well-developed girl with flirtatious eyes, did. The girls sat opposite each other on a bench seat with their knees drawn up to their chins and toes touching while the four boys sprawled on the grass at their feet, staring at their knickers. Wearing knee-high boots, miniskirts and crocheted see-through tops with black bras underneath, the girls understood exactly where their power lay and it amused them. They spoke to each other about sex, and pointedly ignored the boys.

The response was lacklustre. The boys passed round a bottle of stolen vodka but showed no interest in the crude flirting and, without an endgame, all sport grows tedious, even cock-teasing. The skinny girl, annoyed by the boys' lack of interest in her, teased them for being virgins, but the taller girl, Cill, swung her legs to the ground and shuffled her skirt down her bum. 'This is silly,' she said. 'C'mon, Lou. We're going back down town.'

Her friend, a small undernourished clone with smudged black eyes and pale pink lips, performed her own skirt-wriggling act and stood up. They both aped the fashion sense of Cathy McGowan from their favourite pop show, *Ready, Steady, Go!*, with belts worn at hip level and hair ironed straight to fall in heavy fringes over their forehead. It suited Cill, whose face was strong enough to take it, but Lou, who was tiny, like Twiggy, wanted to cut her hair in an urchin style. Cill wouldn't allow it. It was part of their friendship pact that they looked alike, or as near alike as was possible for a well-developed teenager and one who had to stuff Kleenex down her bra.

'You coming, or what?' Cill demanded of Lou's ten-year-old brother, nudging him with her toe. 'Your dad'll string you up if the bizzies catch you, Billy. You see if he don't.'

'Leave me alone,' the child mumbled tipsily.

'*Jee-sus!*' The drink had made her quarrelsome and she cast a scornful eye over the prone bodies. 'Blokes are so fucking pathetic. Me and Lou's had the same as you, but we ain't passed out.'

'Don't push your luck,' said one of the boys. He wasn't the tallest, but he was dark-haired and dark-eyed, and to her immature mind he looked like Paul McCartney.

Another, a freckle-faced redhead, reached a hand up Lou's thigh. 'Slag,' he jeered, squeezing hard.

She squeaked and pulled away, smacking at him. 'Virgin, virgin, virgin!' she chanted. 'You ain't never gonna get it, you're too fucking ugly.' He made a grab for her foot and she wailed at Cill to get him off. 'He's gonna pull me over.'

The taller girl put a boot on his chest. 'Let her go!'

He relaxed his hold with a grin. 'What d'you expect? You're a coupla tarts, ain't you?'

She manoeuvred a stiletto heel over his nipple. 'You wanna say that again?'

He was visibly pubescent, with hair above his lip and acne crowding his neck, and he was too drunk to be intimidated. 'You're a fat tart,' he slurred lazily, ''n' you've been laid so often I could park a car up yer cunt. Want me to try?'

His two friends rolled onto their fronts and watched the tableau with a gleam in their eye. To a girl with more experience, it would have been a warning sign, but Cill was a novice. She brought her full weight down on her heel as she stepped over him, dancing away before he could catch her. ''N' don't never call me fat again or I'll put my heel on your cock next time.'

The redhead clutched at his chest. 'That bloody hurt!'

'It was supposed to, dickhead.' She jerked her chin at the other girl as she started to walk away.

But there was no such easy escape for Lou. She was trapped against the bench and lost her balance when the dark-haired boy made a lunge for her. He grabbed her arms as she fell and spreadeagled her on the grass, and her wails of fear brought Cill running back. Their mothers should have warned them about the dangers of whipping up testosterone, but the only advice either had been given was: if you dress like a tart, you'll get yourself raped, and it'll be your own fault when it happens.

Believing she was streetwise, it was Cill who was the more naive. With animal instinct, Lou became catatonic immediately and held no attraction for the aroused adolescents. Cill fought back determinedly and took the full brunt of the assault. She kept calling on Billy to run for help but, at ten and drunk, all he could do was bury his head in his arms.

It was when they pulled her by her hair into the lee of the trees that Cill gave up. The pain was indescribable and sent tears coursing down her made-up cheeks. It masked all the other pains she experienced. All three wanted her – she was the dominatrix – and they took it in turns to have her. The dark one raped her twice. She was too young to understand psychological trauma, but the ripping of her clothes – so loved and so longed for – the sweat, heat and filth of a prolonged gang bang and their leering, triumphant faces as they repeatedly violated her destroyed her in a way that their overexcited, briefly sustained penetrations could not.

'That's the last time anyone calls me a virgin,' said the redhead, standing over her and zipping himself with a flourish.

The dark boy kicked her. 'Bitch! If you run to the cops, you'll get more of the same. Understood?'

With a belated sense of self-preservation, Cill closed her eyes and shut him out. She could name each one, although she never would. Her dad would kill her if he knew she'd been raped, and the police wouldn't believe her anyway. *It was broad daylight in a park in Bournemouth, and no one had done a thing to help her.* Part of her brain wondered if the road was too far away for passers-by to see what was happening, the other part reproached her for dressing sexy. Her mum was right – she *had* brought it on herself – but all Cill had ever wanted was for people to say she was pretty.

Lou crawled across the grass to lie beside her. 'They've gone,' she whispered, stealing her small hand into Cill's. 'You OK?'

No-oo-oo! It was a scream that would reverberate in her head for days. 'Yeah. What about you?'

The child curled into a fetal ball with her head on Cill's chest. 'Your dad'll tan your hide when he finds out.'

'I ain't telling him.'

'What if you get pregnant?'

'I'll kill it.'

'Billy'll tell our mum.'

'Then I'll fucking kill him, too.' She pushed Lou off and sat up. 'Where is he?'

'Over there.' She jerked her head towards the bench. 'You

shouldn't've stood on him, Cill. Ma says it's always the girl's fault when a man gets angry.'

Cill tugged her torn top over her exposed breasts and stared at the hymenal blood on her thighs. She didn't need a lecture on blame, she needed to get home without being seen. With a vicious grab she caught Lou's hair and twisted it round her fist. 'I wouldn't've 'ad to if you hadn't called him a virgin. Now, are you gonna help me, or you gonna drop me in it again?'

Tears sprouted in the other child's eyes. 'You're hurting me,' she pleaded.

'Yeah,' said Cill unemotionally.

'It weren't my fault it happened.'

'Bloody was. It was you called them virgins. You're a fucking stupid bitch, Lou, and you didn't do nothing to stop it.'

'I was scared.'

'So was I . . . but I came back.'

Lou gave an uneasy wiggle of her shoulders. 'There weren't no sense us both getting done.'

'No,' said Cill, taking another twist of hair and digging her knuckles into the smaller girl's scalp. 'But you fucking well will be if you or Billy ever tell on me.' She stared into Lou's eyes, her own full of tears. 'You got that? Because if my dad has a go at me again, I'm off . . . and I ain't never coming back.'

*

The cooling between the two girls was noticed by their families and their teachers. Once or twice Louise Burton's father tried to find out what had caused it, but Lou, who kept pestering to have her hair cut in the urchin style she so craved, shrugged and said Cill had found another friend. Billy slipped out of the room each time, but it didn't occur to either of his parents that he knew anything. Nor were they interested enough to pursue it. Free of Cill's influence, Louise reverted to dressing appropriately for a thirteen-year-old, and the brief flurry of truanting that had brought her to the unwelcome attention of her headmistress ceased abruptly.

For Priscilla Trevelyan's parents, the break was equally welcome. Their daughter had become wayward in puberty, but Louise Burton's unquestioning subservience had exacerbated it. Mr Trevelyan, disappointed by Cill's unwillingness to apply herself and troubled by her early maturity, had exercised a tough, physical discipline to control her, and the sudden loss of affection between the two girls was acknowledged with relief but never mentioned. He was worried that talking about it would rekindle the dependence and he forbade his wife to show sympathy. He put Cill's bad temper down to the broken friendship, but overlooked it because of her new-found commitment to attending school.

The girls' teachers were less sanguine after a fight broke out between them during a PE lesson on Friday, 29 May. There had been three weeks of hostile silence before Louise said something that prompted Priscilla to react. It was a cat-fight of teeth and claws with the smaller child taking the brunt of it before the pair were finally pulled apart by a furious games teacher and marched in front of the headmistress. Priscilla stood in stony-faced silence, refusing to speak, while Louise sobbed about having her hair pulled and Cill trying to persuade her to truant again. The headmistress, who didn't believe her, nevertheless made the decision, in the absence of apology or explanation, that Priscilla should be punished with a week's suspension while Louise was let off with a caution.

Predictably, Cill's father took out his disapproval in a thrashing and, as she had threatened, she ran away some time during the early hours of Saturday, 30 May. Mr Trevelyan described the punishment as 'a couple of smacks' when the police asked if there was a reason for his daughter absconding, but otherwise he could not account for the out-of-character behaviour. She had never done it before, she had a good home and was doing well academically. Yes, there had been a few truancy problems in the past, but that was the fault of the secondary-modern system. Priscilla was easily bored by lessons that were geared to the less intelligent.

Louise, under questioning by a sympathetic policewoman, began by saying that Cill would kill her if she told the truth, then confessed the rape. She couldn't name the boys, but her description led to them being rounded up and their homes searched for any sign of the missing girl. They denied any knowledge of rape, Priscilla Trevelyan or Louise Burton, and nothing was found to connect them with an assault or the girls. It didn't help that Louise hadn't known their names, could only give vague descriptions, couldn't remember how they were dressed, and that Cill's crocheted top, miniskirt and knickers had been thrown away. Nor, when Louise tearfully insisted that Cill had brought it on herself by getting drunk and talking sexy, did the police believe an assault had taken place. Heavy petting, perhaps, but not full-on gang rape.

However, as the major stumbling block was the alleged victim's absence, the boys were released after token questioning at 13.23 on Monday, 1 June. Rape was taken less seriously in 1970.

*The following is a single-chapter excerpt
from Dr Jonathan Hughes's*
Disordered Minds

DR JONATHAN HUGHES

DISORDERED MINDS

DISORDERED MINDS

'An important study into judicial blunder' – Jeremy Crossley

Jonathan Hughes, 34, was born in London where he now lives. He graduated with a first-class honours degree from Oxford University in 1992 and has made a particular study of the Middle East. He lectures widely on comparative religion and internecine conflicts. His first two books, *Racial Stereotyping*, 1995, and *Banishment*, 1997, explore the problems of ghettoization and social exile. In *Disordered Minds* he re-examines some infamous twentieth-century miscarriages of justice, where the rights of vulnerable defendants were exploited by the system. He is critical of Western democracies that take their morality and virtue for granted.

Dr Hughes is a research fellow in European anthropology at London University.

12

Howard Stamp – victim or murderer?

Many would argue that the brutal murder of fifty-seven-year-old Grace Jefferies in June 1970 in Bournemouth, Dorset, was another case where public pressure influenced police handling of an investigation. Press outrage over the slashing and stabbing of shy, disabled Grace whipped the public into a frenzy, and pressure was on the police to find a culprit. The headlines of Saturday, 6 June 1970 drew parallels with the Manson family's killing of Sharon Tate less than a year earlier.[1]

'Police fear copycat murder as Manson trial approaches'; 'Grandmother tortured in California-style bloodletting'; 'Orgy of bloodlust'; 'Walls daubed with blood'. We must assume that these ideas came from the police, because there's too much unanimity to lay the blame on journalists. If so, it was criminally misleading. Grace was alone when she was murdered, unlike Sharon Tate whose five guests were slaughtered with her, and 'daubed' was a fanciful description for the arterial splatters of blood on Grace's wall. It gave the impression that Bournemouth police had found something similar to the 'Pig' scrawled in blood on Sharon Tate's front door.

Not unreasonably, the public was terrified. The 'Tate murders' in Los Angeles on 9 August 1969, followed twenty-four hours later by the 'La Bianca murders', had shocked the world. Newspapers obsessed on 'drug-induced cult horror' after details of the

---

1. The trial of Charles Manson, Susan Atkins, Leslie Van Houten and Patricia Krenwinkel began six weeks later on 24 July 1970.

massacres emerged. The Beatles were in the dock for their song 'Helter Skelter', along with the Vietnam War, Californian 'flower power', Woodstock, long hair, pot-smoking and free love. The idea that these American diseases had crossed the Atlantic to erupt in savage murder in respectable Bournemouth was so shocking that there was a collective sigh of relief on Sunday, 7 June when Howard Stamp confessed.

There was no gang involvement. It was a 'domestic'. Stamp, a retarded twenty-year-old with a noticeable harelip, was Grace's grandson. He had a history of truancy, bizarre behaviour, refusal to work and an unhealthy obsession with the rock group Cream, particularly the drummer, Ginger Baker. He was held for questioning for thirty-six hours and finally admitted the murder at four o'clock on the Sunday morning. There was no solicitor present, and because he was illiterate his statement was written for him. It was an open-and-shut case and the accused was duly sent to trial and convicted in August 1971.

Disturbing parallels

Open-and-shut cases had similarly led to the convictions of Timothy Evans and Derek Bentley in the 1950s, and the later convictions of Stephen Downing for the murder of Wendy Sewell in 1973 and Stefan Kiszko for the murder of Lesley Molseed in 1975. Like Stamp, all four were illiterate or semi-literate with physical or mental disabilities, and all were highly vulnerable to police suggestion.

Timothy Evans, twenty-six at the time of his conviction, was retarded and illiterate; Derek Bentley, nineteen, was mentally handicapped; Downing, a physically immature seventeen-year-old, had a reading age of eleven; and Kiszko, twenty-four, who suffered from XYY syndrome, hypogonadism, had undeveloped testes and was described as 'a child in a man's body'. Three of these men were denied the services of a solicitor and made confessions that they later retracted, claiming the police had used coercion to obtain the statements or had written the statements themselves; the fourth, Derek Bentley, who was under arrest when his sixteen-year-old co-defendant, Christopher Craig, shot PC Sidney Miles, accused the police of lying when they claimed he shouted an order at Craig to commit the murder and was therefore guilty of 'joint enterprise'.

Police and prosecution confidence in each man's guilt resulted in botched investigations and the suppression of evidence. Although it was recognized at the time that all four men were emotionally immature with learning difficulties, these factors were not taken into account during their interrogations or at their trials. Indeed, many would argue the opposite: their vulnerability was exploited to secure a quick indictment. It has taken years to exonerate them – in Bentley's case nearly half a century – but they are now known to have been victims of four of the twentieth century's most notorious miscarriages of justice.

Reforms of the system

Two pieces of legislation, PACE (the Police and Criminal Evidence Act), 1984, and CPIA (the Criminal Procedure and Investigations Act), 1996, belatedly addressed many of the issues raised by both the Downing and Kiszko interrogations, although neither man's case had been reviewed at the time of the 1984 Act. The mainspring for that reform was almost certainly 'Operation Countryman', an internal police investigation during the 1970s, which revealed terrifying levels of corruption in the Metropolitan Police. In its wake, Chief Superintendent Ken Drury of the Flying Squad was jailed, along with twelve other Scotland Yard detectives, for accepting bribes to falsify evidence.

Public confidence in the police was irreparably damaged and discontent with the whole criminal-justice system grew as doubts were raised about the safety of individual convictions. Prominent campaigns, claiming miscarriages of justice, centred around the Guildford Four – released in 1989; the Birmingham Six – released in 1991; and the Bridgwater Four – released in 1997. Other notable releases were the Cardiff Three and the M25 Three. In 1999 thirty convictions were quashed when it was revealed that the West Midlands Serious Crime Squad had fabricated evidence, tortured suspects and concocted false confessions. At the time of writing, dozens of appeals are still in the pipeline.

Stephen Downing

Stephen Downing served twenty-eight years before the Court of Appeal freed him in 2002. A small, shy seventeen-year-old with learning difficulties, he was interrogated by detectives for nine hours before, near to exhaustion, he agreed to sign a statement in which he admitted battering a young woman with a pickaxe handle in the cemetery in Bakewell, Derbyshire, where he worked. No solicitor was present to advise the teenager, nor was his father allowed to see him. At the time he signed the statement the victim, Wendy Sewell, was unconscious but still alive, and detectives assured the youngster that if he wasn't guilty Wendy would exonerate him when she came round. She died two days later and Downing was charged with her murder.

He retracted his statement immediately but his confession became the mainstay of the prosecution's case at Nottingham Crown Court the following year. He was found guilty and sentenced to life, with a recommendation that he serve seventeen years. This would have made him eligible for release in 1989, but, because he consistently denied his guilt, his applications were refused. It is a cornerstone of the UK penal system that remorse is a precondition for parole, so an IDOM (in denial of murder) prisoner will not be considered. To innocent men and women who are prepared to put their good name above a lifetime in prison, this rule is a catch-22.

Nearly three decades after Wendy Sewell's murder, the presiding appeal judge, Lord Justice Pill, acknowledged that errors had been made in Downing's interrogation. The court could not be sure, he said, that Mr Downing's initial confessions to the police were reliable and it followed that his conviction was 'unsafe'. Downing's freedom and good name were returned to him but warning shots were fired across the Court of Appeal's bows. Don Hale, a crusading journalist who had worked for seven years to bring Downing's plight to public attention, said, 'What worries me is how many similar cases lie buried in the prison system.'

Stefan Kiszko

One such was Stefan Kiszko who was interrogated by police in 1975 for the murder of eleven-year-old Lesley Molseed in Rochdale. Convinced of Kiszko's guilt, police ignored the immaturity and social backwardness that had led to a lifetime's bullying, failed to tell him of his right to have a solicitor present, refused to allow him to see his mother (his only friend) and did not caution him until long after they had decided he was the prime suspect. When he finally confessed, he did so because police told him he would be allowed home as soon as he said what they wanted to hear.

Like Downing, he retracted his confession immediately but, again, the confession became the main plank of the prosecution case. Part of Kiszko's statement was a false admission that he had exposed himself some weeks earlier to two teenage girls who had named and identified him. Sixteen years later, when Kiszko was released by the Court of Appeal, these two girls, now grown women, admitted they had invented the story after seeing a taxi driver urinating behind a bush. More criminally, police withheld semen evidence at the trial which they knew would exculpate Kiszko.

As a sufferer of XYY syndrome, Kiszko was sterile. This was known to the police in 1975 because a sample of Kiszko's semen taken during the investigation contained no sperm. Yet the pathol-ogist who examined Lesley Molseed's clothing had found sperm in the semen stains on her underwear. The police kept this evi-dence from the defence and the court, and it was only discovered when an enquiry into the case was ordered in 1990. Two years later, when an application on behalf of Kiszko was heard by the Court of Appeal, Lord Chief Justice Lane said, 'It has been shown that this man cannot produce sperm. This man cannot have been responsible for . . . [the semen found on] . . . the girl's knickers and skirt, and consequently cannot have been her murderer.'

Kiszko was released immediately. However, his brutal treatment at the hands of other prisoners, who had frequently beaten him, had driven him into a world of delusion where conspiracies abounded. Convinced that his mother – a lonely and steadfast voice on the outside claiming his innocence – had been part of the conspiracy to condemn him, he needed nine months' rehabili-tation before he could return home to her care. He died after eighteen months, his physical and mental health destroyed, fol-lowed six months later by Mrs Kiszko herself.

Public outrage at Kiszko's treatment was immense, although few recognized that by baying for blood in the wake of a child's murder they had added to the pressure on the police to find a culprit.

Howard Stamp

Bullied mercilessly at school for his harelip and defective speech, Stamp had a miserable attendance record. Described as 'work-shy' at his trial, he had withdrawn into self-imposed isolation, too frightened to go out. 'He was teased every time he left the house,' said his mother in his defence. 'He looked funny and he couldn't read or write.'

Today he would have been dubbed a self-abuser. Not only is it clear that he suffered from an eating disorder – he was painfully thin with an immature physique – he made a habit of cutting his arms with razors. His mother, unable to understand or cope with behavioural difficulties that were barely recognized in the 1960s, begged her GP to certify him before he 'used the razor on some-body else'.

It was this request that convinced police he was guilty of the brutal murder of his fifty-seven-year-old grandmother, Grace Jefferies, on Wednesday, 3 June 1970. Found in a 'bloodbath' at her home in Mullin Street, Highdown, on the border between Bournemouth and Poole, Grace had been stabbed and slashed thirty-three times. The press dubbed it 'murder by a thousand cuts' because most of the non-fatal injuries were to her arms and legs, suggesting she had been tortured for some time before her throat was slit. The inescapable conclusion, according to the pathologist, was that she had staggered upstairs to her bedroom while her tormentor slashed at her arms and legs with a carving knife.

Suspicion focused on Stamp when witnesses came forward to say they'd seen him running from Grace's house on Wednesday, 3 June, two days before her body was discovered on Friday, 5 June. Bloodstains on his clothes seemed to confirm his guilt, and after thirty-six hours of interrogation he confessed to the murder. As with Downing and Kiszko, he had no solicitor present and retracted his confession shortly afterwards. He admitted running from Grace's house, but claimed that his grandmother was already dead when he entered with his duplicate key. Horrified by what he had found, he fled home and locked himself in his bedroom, too shocked to tell anyone what he'd seen. It was another forty-eight hours before a postman reported that Grace's curtains had been drawn for several days.

It seemed a straightforward case, yet there were many inconsist-encies in the evidence. The pathologist's first estimate suggested Grace had been dead four days before her body was found. This was later amended to forty-eight hours to tie in with the witness statements. At the trial, the pathologist explained the mistake as a 'slip of the pen' and the defence failed to press him. In a similar volte-face, the postman who alerted police to Grace's drawn curtains told the court that when he'd said 'several days' he had meant 'two at the most'. Again, the defence did not press the issue.

The flakes of dried blood on Stamp's trouser knees and shirt cuffs are consistent with his second statement: that he knelt beside his grandmother's body (two days after the murder if the pathologist's initial estimate was correct) to see if she was dead. They are less consistent with police and prosecution claims that he took a bath to wash off Grace's blood, then, dressed in fresh clothes, brushed against a blood-spattered wall on his departure. If this were true, some of the blood would still have been viscous enough to be absorbed by the fibres, and Stamp's back, behind, shoulders or thighs would have been the contact points, not his knees and cuffs.

The defence made some attempt to challenge the forensic evidence, most of which centred on hair and dried scum taken from the sides and plughole of the bathtub. The prosecution alleged that Stamp had immersed himself in water after the murder in order to clean himself. Both sides agreed that whoever killed Grace would have been covered in blood. The prosecution case was that Stamp had either committed the murder naked or removed bloodstained clothes from the property. This latter suggestion gained credibility after a witness said Stamp was carrying a black polythene bag when he ran from the house. (This bag was never recovered despite an intensive police search.)

The scum showed traces of Grace's blood group, and the hairs were identified as Stamp's. In addition, Stamp's fingerprints were found on the bathroom door and lavatory seat. Adam Fanshaw QC, counsel for the defence, succeeded in striking out the fingerprint evidence by arguing that Stamp was a regular visitor to the house. However, he was hampered over the hair evidence by Stamp's own insistence that he had never taken a bath in Grace's house.

The pathologist for the defence, Dr John Foyle, put up a strong argument against the hairs being Stamp's by quoting Professor

Keith Simpson, the noted Home Office pathologist, in a comment made during the 1943 Leckey trial.[2]

The word 'identical' does not mean the hairs necessarily came from the same person, only that they *could* have. That is the most one can ever say about hairs. Identical hairs are not compelling evidence like fingerprints, for they carry so much less detail.

Unfortunately, Dr Foyle crumpled under cross-examination when Fanshaw failed to protect him against prosecution jibes of inexperience and publicity seeking. In a damaging about-face which implied the hairs were Stamp's, he said it was just as probable that 'the hairs had been deposited in the bath on a previous occasion'.

Stamp's mother, Wynne, made a poor witness for her son and should never have been called. Timid and of low intelligence, she stammered through her evidence, misunderstanding many of the questions that were put to her. She used her day in court to highlight her own problems – 'I've had a terrible time because of Howard's physical and mental troubles . . . no one knows what I've had to put up with . . . there ought to be help for people like me . . .' She could give no explanation for why Howard had been at Grace's house on the Wednesday when he'd been due to start a job at Jannerway & Co (a local dairy) that afternoon, except to say that he was 'lazy'. Nevertheless, she held firmly to her belief that Howard would never have hurt his grandmother. 'He always went to her when he was depressed. She understood him because she had a cleft palate too. It runs in the family.'

Grace's disability (an untreated cleft palate had left her with a severe speech impediment) had made her as reclusive as her

2. Gunner Dennis Leckey was tried for the murder of Caroline Traylor in 1943. Although found guilty and sentenced to death, Leckey was acquitted by the Court of Criminal Appeal on a technicality and allowed to walk free. Although Professor Simpson's comments referred to a 1943 case, they were still true thirty-five years later when he repeated them in *Professor Keith Simpson: An Autobiography*, published by Harrap Limited in 1978.

grandson. Sent into service in 1928 at the age of fifteen, she gave birth to Wynne a year later. Nothing was known about the father, although the fact that she continued to be employed by the same family, and was allowed to keep her child, suggests that she may have been raped by a member of the household. Ten years later, aged twenty-six, she married Arthur Jefferies, forty-three, a merchant seaman who adopted Wynne and provided the home in Highdown, Bournemouth, where Grace lived for the rest of her life.

Tragically for Grace, Arthur was killed in 1942 during an attack on a North Sea convoy, and she became a widow before she was thirty. Three years later, aged just sixteen, Wynne met, and subsequently married, Fred Stamp, a farm worker from Bere Regis in Dorset. The marriage was of short duration – Wynne blamed their baby's 'ugliness' for the break-up – and mother and son returned to Bournemouth to live in council accommodation in Colliton Way, half a mile from Grace's home in Mullin Street. While there is no evidence that Grace and Wynne did not get on, it seems there was little communication between the two women.

Grace was variously described by neighbours as 'odd', 'eccentric', 'a bit of a recluse', 'shy', 'not very friendly'. She was probably all of these things because, like her grandson, she would have found social interaction difficult. Certainly she had few callers, although a more likely reason for Wynne's failure to visit was that she didn't have a car and worked full-time as a packer at Brackham & Wright's tool factory in Glazeborough Road.

There is some evidence that Stamp went to his grandmother's house whenever he bunked off school. Neighbours mentioned seeing a child in the garden during the summers of the 1950s. If so, Grace never reported it to his mother or the truancy officer, and this would have persuaded Stamp that his grandmother was a safe refuge from bullies. Certainly, as he grew older he became a more frequent visitor, which is why he was identified so easily by the witnesses who saw him running away. 'It was that skinny grandson,' said one. 'He used to hide with Grace instead of signing-on [for work].'

The prosecution argued at trial that Stamp's instability and self-abuse had increased to such a point that Grace had become afraid of him. As proof they quoted a letter to Wynne in which she said, 'Howard's started shouting again even though he knows it frightens me. I've told him I'll put the police on to him if it goes on.' Further on in the letter, and not quoted by the prosecution, she added, 'I said if only he could meet a nice girl he'd start to feel better about things but he told me to shut up. You should have had words with the police when they laughed at him about the bullying. That's what did for him. He says it's a waste of time, but I got Arthur, didn't I?'

The defence failed to pick up on this, yet there are two reasons why they should have done. First, Grace's meaning was surely this: Howard's been shouting again and it frightens me because I don't know how to help him. I've persuaded him to stop by threatening him with the police. We both know he's scared of them. They made fun of him when he told them he was being bullied, and he hasn't trusted them since. Second, if Stamp found the police intimidating, then nothing he said during his interrogation was reliable. Indeed his confession suggests that shocking them by admitting to a brutal murder was preferable to being jeered at for locking himself in his bedroom out of terror.

Stamp's case was never re-opened because he hanged himself in 1973. However, even the most cursory comparison between Wynne Stamp's evidence and the prosecution case reveals alarming disparities. Wynne described her son as 'not interested in cash because he hated going to the shops'. The prosecution said, 'every drawer in Grace's house had been pulled out, either in a search for money and valuables or suggesting that Grace had disturbed a burglar'. Wynne claimed she wasn't 'a good housekeeper' and her son was always 'tidying up' after her. The prosecution described Grace's house as 'thoroughly vandalized'. Wynne said her son was ashamed of his cut arms and wore long-sleeved jumpers and shirts to hide them from her. The prosecution said that 'a man who revelled in using a razor on himself would take *pleasure* in slashing at a woman who was afraid of him'.

There's no question that Stamp was badly let down by his defence team, and the inescapable conclusion is that they were as convinced of his guilt as the police and prosecution were. It's hard to understand why. However inadequate his social skills, however unattractive his appearance, he was clearly a vulnerable young man of low self-esteem and serious emotional difficulties. One theory that would fit the prosecution case is that Stamp was an undiagnosed paranoid schizophrenic who erupted one day in a fit of delusional violence against a woman who loved him.

There is no evidence to support this. He was examined by two psychiatrists to establish if he was fit to plead, and neither diagnosed schizophrenia. The verdict of the prosecution psychiatrist was that Stamp was 'self-absorbed and introverted, but otherwise normal'. The defence psychiatrist found him 'depressed and suicidal'.

Howard is illiterate with a low IQ which means he has difficulty under-standing simple instructions . . . He is deeply reserved, particularly when speaking about himself, refuses to look his interlocutor in the eye and covers the lower half of his face with his hands. This self-consciousness, amounting to obsession, is attributable to a poorly reconstructed harelip . . . Howard shows symptoms of agoraphobia and regularly betrays a sense of worthlessness . . . These emotional difficulties are not helped by being on remand, as he is fearful of interacting with officers and other inmates . . . these feelings of inadequacy are making him depressed and suicidal.

I am concerned by his lack of confidence both in himself and in his relations with others. He has no amour propre and seems to feel he deserves punishment. It is for this reason that he made a habit of cutting his arms during and post-adolescence and is now refusing to eat in prison. I am confident that he is, and has been for some time, suffering from anorexia nervosa, an eating disorder, which is rare in young men but not unknown. This disorder is triggered when an individual persuades himself he is unattractive . . . In Howard's case, the deformity of his lip is clearly the major contributory cause.

. . . I consider him unfit to stand trial because he is incapable of taking a necessarily objective view if the charges are to be countered. In addition, he will be so distressed by his public display in court that he will be unable to function successfully.[3]

The defence psychiatrist's recommendations were ignored and Stamp was ruled competent to plead.

With the knowledge that we now have about eating disorders, it is more likely that the young man was suffering from body dysmorphic disorder. BDD is associated with obsessive–compulsive disorder and is not a variant of anorexia nervosa or bulimia nervosa, although self-harm and a refusal to eat are typical symptoms as the condition worsens. In most cases, an individual's obsession relates to facial features – defects can be real, imagined or exaggerated – and the sufferer comes to fear ridicule in social situations. The disorder usually begins in adolescence, becomes chronic and, if untreated, can lead to loneliness, isolation, severe depression and even suicide.

If this is indeed what Stamp was suffering from, then it becomes less probable that he killed his grandmother. She was the one person he could feel comfortable with, because she shared his disability. She may not have had a harelip, but her speech impediment was more severe than his, her friends as few and her dislike of going out as great. They were two of a kind, both preferring isolation to ridicule, and it stretches belief that Stamp's personality could alter so radically that he would move outside his self-harming, self-obsessive, self-hating introversion to slash and stab the one person who protected him.

Even if Grace had attempted to jolt him out of depression by suggesting he 'find a nice girl' because things had improved for her after she 'got Arthur', and Stamp had become angry, it seems that shouting was the worst he did. Perhaps Wynne had tried making the same suggestion with the same result. She said at the

---

3. Taken from *Clinical Studies* by Dr Andrew Lawson (Random House, US, 1975).

trial, 'He liked ladies better than men, but they didn't like him. It made him angry.'

This was interpreted by the prosecution as 'anger against women – one woman, his grandmother, Grace Jefferies, who had become frightened of him', but a more credible explanation is that Stamp voiced frustration when his mother and grandmother urged him to trawl for a date because he knew how painful and futile the exercise would be. Certainly, his suicide three years later is testimony that he found making friends of either sex difficult. A prison officer said at the inquest, 'He was very timid. The other inmates picked on him because of it. He wouldn't come out of his cell unless he was ordered.'

One can only imagine how lonely and desperate Stamp must have felt when even his mother believed in his guilt. 'I stopped visiting when they moved him to Dartmoor,' Wynne said at the inquest. 'We had nothing to say to each other and it was a long way to go.' The coroner, presumably wanting to rule out any suggestion of murder by other prisoners, asked Wynne if she thought Howard was the type to kill himself. She answered, 'He had a lot on his conscience.'

But did he?

Police pay lip service to re-opening cases, but the constraints of limited budgets and the time pressures of rising crime rates mean there is no realistic chance of anyone else facing charges. There is too little data on file, and precious little physical evidence, to indict a second individual a quarter of a century after the event. It's axiomatic – hence the reforms in PACE and CPIA – that if police believe a man to be guilty, they do not waste time looking for evidence that will exonerate him. In addition, and this is pertinent to a trial, the memories of witnesses who failed to come forward at the time or were never followed up will be deemed 'unreliable' twenty or thirty years later.

Nevertheless, since DNA fingerprinting was first introduced in evidence in England in 1987,[4] the balance has swung against murderers who've 'got away with it'. While, to date, no prominent miscarriage of justice has been satisfactorily rectified by this technique, belated convictions have been achieved in a number of unsolved murders.

In 1970, DNA fingerprinting was a distant dream, yet inferences from press coverage of the trial in April 1971 suggest police did collect physical evidence from Grace's house that could even now exonerate Stamp.

'The prosecution alleges that a T-shirt found in the house belonged to Stamp. This was denied by the defence although Wynne Stamp later admitted that her son had owned one "like it".' (*The Times*, Tuesday, 13 April 1971) 'Discarded gloves linked to orgy of blood-letting' (Headline – *Sun*, Wednesday, 14 April 1971) 'A pair of bloodstained gloves thought to belong to the victim was found in a litter bin near the home of Grace Jefferies. Police believe they were worn by her murderer and then discarded.' (*Daily Telegraph*, Wednesday, 14 April 1971) 'The ace in the prosecution case is that hair found in Grace Jefferies' bath has been identified as the defendant's. Dr James Studeley (Home Office pathologist) said the hairs were identical with Stamp's.' (*The Times*, Wednesday, 14 April 1971)

'Adam Fanshaw, counsel for the defence, denied that hair recovered from Grace's bath could have belonged to Stamp. "The defendant has never taken a bath in his grandmother's house," he said, "therefore any similarities shown by Dr Studeley (Home Office pathologist) between the defendant's hair and hair retrieved from the bath must be coincidence."' (*Daily Telegraph*, Thursday, 15 April 1971). 'In his summing up, Adam Fanshaw QC said, "Dr Foyle (pathologist for the defence) has shown that the defendant's hair is comparable in character, colour and form to his mother's hair, yet no one is suggesting Wynne Stamp committed this murder. The prosecution has failed to prove that the hairs found in the bath are the defendant's, merely that they are similar. Any ginger-haired

---

4. Robert Melias in the UK was the first man in history to be convicted on DNA evidence.

person could have committed this crime ... However, it is equally probable that hair from the defendant may have dropped into the bathtub during a previous visit."' (*The Times*, Friday, 16 April 1971)

This indecisiveness was damaging to Stamp's cause. Fanshaw, later to become a High Court judge, ran an inconsistent defence. On the horns of a dilemma because his client insisted he had never taken a bath in his grandmother's house, he offered alternative explanations to the jury. The hairs weren't Stamp's but, if the jury decided they were, then they must have dropped into the bath by accident. However, Wynne Stamp gave evidence that her son had not visited his grandmother's house between Thursday, 28 May and Wednesday, 3 June. As she also insisted that her mother was too house-proud to leave her bath dirty, that left Wednesday as the only day for Howard's hairs to drop in 'accidentally'. Not unreasonably, the jury preferred prosecution claims that there was too much hair for this to have happened. The quantity was only consistent with someone immersing his head in water and rubbing it with shampoo.

If the pathologist's second estimate is to be believed, the crime took place between 12.00 and 14.00 on Wednesday, 3 June 1970. From the pattern of blood on the stairs, walls and floors, it was estimated that Grace had taken between one and two hours to die, and this fitted conveniently with sightings of Stamp. He was known to have left his mother's house at 11.45 when he was seen by a neighbour. She described him as 'looking normal' although she was unable to say what he was wearing. All the witnesses who saw him leaving his grandmother's house put the time at between 14.00 and 14.30 and their descriptions of his clothing were similar: 'white shirt, not tucked in, and blue jeans', 'shirt and trousers', 'white T-shirt and Levi's'. They all agreed his behaviour was 'peculiar'. One said he was 'running like a bat out of hell'. Another: 'He wasn't looking where he was going and bumped into the back of a parked car'. A third: 'He tried to hide his face but I saw it before he turned away. His eyes were mad and staring'.

None said his hair was wet, nor that it looked different from normal. But they should have done if the prosecution was correct in its assumptions. In appearance, Stamp aped his hero, Ginger Baker, the legendary drummer with the 1960s rock group Cream. A photograph of Stamp taken by his mother three months before the murder shows him with a pale, pinched face, straggly moustache and beard, and a tangled mat of wiry hair hanging over his face and down to his shoulders. Wynne said he rarely washed it because it 'frizzed up when it dried and stuck out round his head'. She also claimed he 'put vaseline on it to make it heavier'. In his summing-up Adam Fanshaw drew attention to these discrepancies – 'if the defendant shampooed his hair, it must have been wet or sticking out when he left the house . . . there were no residues of vaseline on the hairs in the bath'. But the jury wasn't impressed.

Perhaps they thought frizzy hair and matted hair looked much the same. Perhaps they found Stamp's clean-cut appearance at trial – he had been persuaded to shave and accept a short-back-and-sides to present a boyish appearance – inconsistent with his mother's descriptions of him as 'always plastering his hair over his face to hide his lip'. They certainly accepted the prosecution's claim that shampoo, a detergent, dissolves vaseline, a petroleum-based product, despite the defence's attempts to prove that vaseline-residues would have remained on the sides of the bath.

In one last twist, Stamp's mugshot, taken four days after he was said to have had a bath, presents an identical appearance to the photograph taken three months earlier. Pale, pinched face, straggly moustache and beard, and a tangled mat of *vaselined* hair to his shoulders.

Irreconcilable evidence

The earliest Stamp could have reached Grace's house was 12.00, and the latest he could have left it was 14.30. This would have given him two and a half hours in which to work up a rage, slash and stab his grandmother before cutting her throat, take a bath, wipe his fingerprints from the bath taps (they were clean), vandalize her house to cast the blame elsewhere, pull the curtains and secure the windows.

Even assuming all this were possible in so comparatively short a time, he also had to remember to dispose of a pair of gloves in a litter bin after he left. Yet witnesses described him as behaving peculiarly, running like a bat out of hell, bumping into things and having mad, staring eyes. In other words, he was a man in a panic.

It's difficult to see how this mad flight in the middle of a summer afternoon can be reconciled with the thoughtful way he appears to have acted in the wake of the murder. Why draw attention to himself after leaving the scene if he'd made an attempt – however poor – to cover his tracks? Indeed why was it necessary to leave the house in such a hurry? Wynne said he rarely returned from visits to his grandmother until the early hours – 'they watched telly together' – so why didn't he do the same that day? Not only would it have given him longer to lay a false trail, it would also have allowed him to slip out under cover of darkness.

The more obvious explanation for his flight is that his second statement was true. He let himself into his grandmother's house and was so shocked by what he discovered that he ran home in terror to lock himself in his bedroom.

When was Grace Jefferies killed?

The pathologist's first estimate, later dismissed as a 'slip of the pen', suggested Grace died on Monday, 1 June 1970. The postman's statement, amended at trial, referred to her curtains having been drawn for *several* days before he decided to report his concerns to police on Friday, 5 June. The blood deposits on Stamp's clothes were described as 'flakes', which implies *dried* blood. In his second statement Stamp said, 'I knew Nan was dead the minute

I pushed her hand. It was cold and her fingers fell open. When I touched her shoulder it felt stiff.'

This gives us the beginnings of a time frame. Rigor mortis starts after three to four hours in the small muscles of the face, hands and feet, before affecting the larger muscles. As it wears off, it follows the same pattern. Stamp's description implies rigor was still present in the major muscle of the shoulder, but had started to disappear in the smaller ones of the hand.

Because it's a chemical process, rigor can be affected by a number of variables: environmental temperature, body temperature, illness, activity before death, the physical conditions in which the corpse is left. Typically, a body that is described as cold and stiff has been dead between twelve and thirty-six hours, and one that is described as cold but *not* stiff may have been dead up to seventy-two hours. Cool environments and obesity delay onset, thereby extending the overall time frame. Warm environments and high metabolic activity before death advance it, thereby shortening the time frame.

Because of these variables, rigor is a poor indication of time of death. In Grace's case, there are conflicting factors. She was a large lady, but her metabolic rate must have been high in the hour before her death as she tried to avoid her tormentor. It was summer and the ambient temperature outside was warm; however, her curtains had been pulled to shut out the sunlight and police described the house as 'chilly' when they entered. Loss of blood would have lowered blood pressure, while fear would have heightened metabolic activity.

The only records we now have of Dr Studeley's findings come from newspapers:

'The pathologist detailed the post-mortem results and said they were consistent with Mrs Jefferies having been dead some forty-eight hours before he examined the body . . . In cross-examination, counsel for the defence challenged some of his conclusions. "Isn't it true," he asked, "that the staining of the abdomen suggests decomposition was of longer duration than two days?" Dr Studeley denied this. "The process is faster when a body is exposed to air." Fanshaw then asked why he'd found no evidence of rigor mortis. "Grace Jefferies was a heavy woman. Wouldn't you have expected lingering stiffness in the larger muscles?" "By no means," said Dr Studeley. "The weather was warm and Mrs Jefferies suffered horribly before she died. In such circumstances the onset and completion of rigor would be comparatively quick."' (*Daily Telegraph*, Tuesday, 13 April 1971) 'After taking into account various factors, Dr James Studeley said the post-mortem results accorded with Mrs Jefferies meeting her death during the morning or afternoon of 3 June. He rejected defence claims that some of his conclusions were questionable.' (*The Times*, Tuesday, 13 April 1971)

Dr Foyle's testimony for the defence put the death twenty-four to thirty-six hours earlier. However he faltered under cross-examination.

'The pathologist for the defence argued that putrefaction was too advanced for the forty-eight-hour estimate. "Green staining appears on the right side of the abdomen in the first couple of days. Thereafter the discolouration spreads and the abdomen begins to swell with gas." He pointed out that Dr Studeley's notes from the post mortem mentioned "pervasive staining and some bloating". "This is more consistent with three to four days," he concluded. When asked by prosecuting counsel if he'd examined the body himself, Dr Foyle admitted he hadn't.' (*Daily Telegraph*, Wednesday, 14 April 1971) 'Dr Foyle said he believed the defendant's statement "had the ring of truth". "Mr Stamp's description suggests the process of rigor mortis wasn't complete at the time he found the body. This would agree with my estimate that Mrs Jefferies died during the night of 1 June or by the evening of 2 June at the latest." Asked under cross-examination if he'd seen the body, he said he hadn't. "It's a matter of interpretation," he said. "Assuming Dr Studeley recorded his findings accurately, then I cannot support his conclusions. In cases like this, time of death is always difficult to establish, but there's no doubt in my mind that Mrs Jefferies was killed much earlier than is being suggested." However, when pressed by prosecution counsel, Dr Foyle agreed that Dr Studeley's conclusions were "not beyond the bounds of possibility".' (*The Times*, Wednesday, 14 April 1971)

Interestingly, it was the prosecuting counsel, Robert Tring QC, who referred to Dr Studeley's 'slip of the pen'.

'Robert Tring asked the witness why he had written four days in his post-mortem notes if he was now claiming that Mrs Jefferies had been dead only two days. Dr Studeley said it was "a slip of the pen" which he corrected on the official report.' (*The Times*, Wednesday, 14 April 1971)

It's hard to understand why Adam Fanshaw didn't challenge this error when his own pathologist was arguing that 3–4 days was a more likely estimate. One explanation is that he planned to recall Studeley after his own pathologist had successfully established the night of 1 June/day of 2 June as a possibility, and/or use the mistake as the main focus of his summing-up. Another explanation is that he didn't want to alienate the jury by badgering an elderly pathologist for a lapse of concentration, and intended to infer that Studeley had changed his mind under pressure from the police. In either event, the ground was cut from under his feet when Dr Foyle agreed that Studeley's findings were 'not beyond the bounds of possibility'.

There was no reason why Foyle should have examined the body. Cause of death wasn't the issue; it was *time* of death that was in dispute. Stamp had alibis for 1 and 2 June – Wynne had taken a two-day 'sickie' in order to 'make him look for a job' – and 3 June was his first opportunity to visit Grace. Nevertheless, even had the defence insisted on their own post mortem, which was their right, it wouldn't have been helpful.

The significant factors in establishing time of death – ambient temperature, rigor mortis, algor mortis (body temperature), livor mortis (settling of the blood), autolysis and putrefaction (indicators of decomposition) – are useful only when the body is first examined, not after a week's refrigeration. Nor was there any reason to assume Studeley's data was wrong. An important fact brought out at the trial was the reference to 'pervasive staining and bloating' of the abdomen. If, as Foyle claimed, this was more consistent with three to four days of decomposition, then the algor-mortis readings were important[5] and may explain why he was confident Grace had died 'much earlier'. In simple terms, if hourly readings showed an increase, then Grace's body had already cooled to the ambient temperature and was on the rise again.

Without more information, we can only guess what the debate was about, but the fact that it took place at all does seem to indicate the data was open to interpretation.

Who killed Grace Jefferies? And why?

Despite prosecution claims that Stamp rifled his grandmother's drawers for money, or set out to pretend someone else had, there's no evidence that Grace had anything worth stealing. Wynne thought she 'kept some cash in a shoe box', but couldn't suggest anything else that might have been stolen. The obvious person to ask was Stamp himself, since he knew Grace's house better than anyone, but as he was the main suspect, asking him was never on the cards.

The house was described as 'vandalized' and a brief description was given by the policeman who broke in through the front door.

'"I knew something was wrong when I saw the downstairs rooms. The place was a mess. Everything was broken: chairs, mirrors, even the plants had been torn out of their pots. It looked as if a kid had had a tantrum. I became alarmed when I saw blood on the stairs."' (*The Times*, Monday, 12 April 1971)

The prosecution alleged that Stamp lost his temper and started breaking things, and when his grandmother remonstrated with him he pursued her upstairs with a carving knife from the kitchen.

---

5. After death, body temperature cools until it reaches the level of its surroundings. This process takes between eight and twelve hours on the skin, and twenty-four to thirty-six hours in the centre of the body. Once putrefaction begins (about two days after death) the temperature rises again due to the metabolic activity of bacteria.

But if Stamp was innocent, then what does the destruction in the house tell us? Was it done for fun? Out of frustration? Anger? What kind of person vandalizes other people's property?

Research suggests he will be a young male with a history of truancy who associates with other delinquent youngsters. He will be living in a family with multiple problems, where there is little or no discipline and negligible supervision. Among his character traits will be aggressiveness, impulsiveness, self-centredness, an inability to see another's point of view and a lack of forward-thinking, all of which will make it difficult for him to understand the consequences of his actions and lead him to act on emotion and whim.

This is reflected in the policeman's remark: 'It looked as if a kid had had a tantrum.' Stamp certainly conformed to one of the above rules. He was a persistent truant, but he displayed the opposite character traits to a delinquent. He was too frightened to go out, too conscious of other people's opinions to forget his deformity, too aware of the consequences of his actions to attempt dating. Indeed, his vandalism was directed against himself. The more likely scenario if he'd killed his grandmother was that the police would have found two bodies when they broke in: Grace with a slit throat; Howard with multiple cuts on his arms before a last remorseful slice to his wrist brought peace.

Both prosecution and defence agreed that someone with frizzy or kinked ginger hair took a bath after the murder. The defence drew similarities between Wynne's hair and her son's hair not to suggest that Wynne murdered Grace but to demonstrate that hair was an unreliable method of identification in 1970.[6]

If either Grace or Wynne had had siblings, it would be tempting to look in their direction, but Wynne was an only child and there is no record that Grace had brothers or sisters. The kinked gene may have come from Wynne's unknown father, but any links with him seem to have been severed very quickly and it's unlikely

---

6. Since DNA fingerprinting was introduced in 1987 it has become one of the *most* reliable methods.

that he or his subsequent children would have sought out Grace to murder her.

More likely, Stamp was the victim of malign coincidence. Ginger hair is a characteristic shared by a significant number of British people and is frequently kinked – it appears to be one of its properties. Some past and present celebrities who've had it are Henry VIII, Queen Elizabeth I, Vincent Van Gogh, Ginger Baker, Art Garfunkel, Bette Midler, Mick Hucknall. To recognize how such a coincidence might happen, it's important to recall the words of Professor Simpson: 'Identical hairs are not compelling evidence like fingerprints, for they carry so much less detail.'

In the end, the most convincing evidence for Stamp's innocence of this crime are the pristine bath taps and the bloodstained gloves in the litter bin. These point unfailingly to someone else being in Grace's house. The gloves were used to search her drawers, vandalize her house and take up a knife to stab her, and the taps had to be cleaned because her murderer removed the gloves when he got into the bath.

The prosecution painted Howard Stamp as an angry young man of low intelligence who erupted one day in a fit of violence against the loving grandmother who protected him. In order to get away with it he donned a pair of gloves, took a bath, wiped his fingerprints from the taps but failed to remove them from any other surface. Why? His prints were found elsewhere in the bathroom, even on the lavatory seat, but if, in the wake of the crime, he recognized that to leave them on the bath taps would be harmful, why go on to insist that he'd never used the bath?

His detractors would argue that he wasn't bright enough to do anything else. Having confessed to everything at the beginning, he then rushed to denial. Indeed, the prosecution inferred that his denial was a tacit admission of guilt.

'In his summing-up, Robert Tring . . . drew the jury's attention to the evidence from the bathtub. "The defendant claims he never used it," he said, "yet we have shown that he did. You must ask yourselves why he lied when only a guilty man would have been afraid to admit he'd taken a bath in Grace Jefferies' house."' (*Daily Telegraph*, Friday, 16 April 1971)

Unfortunately for Stamp the jury accepted this at face value instead of questioning why, if he was willing to say his confession had been coerced, he wasn't equally willing to 'remember' a recent bath. While it would have been wrong for his barrister to suggest such a thing, there is no doubt Fanshaw would have discussed the evidential conflicts his client faced in such a way that the implications were clear. 'My job would be a great deal easier if you'd used your grandma's tub, Howard. Are you *sure* you never did?' Wouldn't a guilty man have jumped at a way out?

In light of the Evans, Bentley, Kiszko and Downing miscarriages of justice, it's impossible to examine Stamp's case without having similar misgivings. He was an immature man with learning difficulties who was convicted on a retracted confession and disputed evidence. It's arguable if he even understood the case against him, let alone had the clarity of thought to present a viable defence.

Less than three years after his trial Howard Stamp was dead, driven to suicide by loneliness and despair. In his comparatively short life he had been teased and bullied for his harelip, mocked for his stupidity, accused and convicted of murdering the one person who protected him, then abandoned to fend for himself in the harsh environment of prison. Most would say it was a fitting punishment if he had murdered his grandmother. All would raise their hands in horror if DNA evidence proved tomorrow that he did not.[7]

---

7. Anyone who has information relating to the murder of Grace Jefferies and/or the conviction of Howard Stamp can contact Dr Jonathan Hughes, c/o Spicer & Hardy, Authors' Agents, 25 Blundell St, London W4 9TP.

Appendix

When I consulted Michael Williams, professor of behavioural science at Durham University, he suggested a profile of Grace Jefferies' murderer. 'I have drawn some general conclusions, based on limited facts. Normally, I would visit the scene and study all available evidence. This is clearly impossible when the event happened thirty years ago, therefore much of this offender profile is informed guesswork. Victim-profiling has gained in importance in the last decade since it was recognized that a victim's pattern of behaviour can also give clues to his/her murderer. Without more information about Grace Jefferies' character and lifestyle, my deductions are again guesswork.'

This murder was an isolated event and not part of a series. As there was no evidence of a break-in, and Grace was described as 'reclusive', it's reasonable to assume she knew her killer. This persuaded her to open her door. Because she was protective of her grandson, we can also assume she was protective of herself, which means her visitor was a regular caller or someone she recognized from the neighbourhood. The murderer may not have intended to kill when he entered the house but, once inside, he lost his temper. He wreaked destruction out of frustration, possibly when he realized there was nothing worth stealing. Grace's speech impediment may have been the trigger for torture. He slashed at her to make her 'talk' (either because it amused him or because he wanted her to tell him where her money was hidden). Oblivious both to the passage of time and the consequences of being caught on the premises, he took a bath to wash off her blood.

If we absolve Howard Stamp,[1] then the crime took place earlier than midday on 3 June 1970. This would expand the time frame during which the killer was able to operate. A significant factor was the closing of the curtains, which suggests he was in the house during the hours of darkness and feared being seen. It also explains why he was able to come and go without being noticed. Nevertheless, Grace was unlikely to open her door after dark unless she thought her visitor was 'safe', and this implies an accomplice, almost certainly a girl, who was known to Grace and had a good excuse for being there. If this girl stayed to witness the crime, it is certain she experienced the same terror that Grace experienced; if she left after her boyfriend gained entry, then she was easily persuaded of his innocence and/or terrified into silence. In either case, she would not have spoken to the police.

Significant features of the crime are: an expectation that there was something worth stealing; limited knowledge of forensic techniques (he left evidence of himself behind); sudden uncontrollable anger (he started destroying furniture); cruelty (he tortured his victim); a lack of forward thinking (he killed her regardless of the consequences); inexperience (he didn't expect to be covered in blood); no concern about being caught in the act (he took a bath afterwards).

The killer was an immature person with a disorganized mind and anger/emotional problems. He may have been high on drugs, drink or glue. He believed Grace would be an easy 'score' and was unnaturally confident about getting away with it. He was used to making threats – 'land me in trouble and you're dead' – and he expected to be obeyed. This suggests a disdain for people in general, a disdain for the police in particular and a history of criminal behaviour. There was no prior planning – he'd heard rumours that Grace kept cash in the house but he didn't bother to find out whether they were true. He was used to having his own way and became violent when he was thwarted.

Today he will be in his late forties and he may have a drink or drug

---

1. Professor Williams added a caveat: 'It was not unreasonable for the police to fix on Stamp as the prime suspect. He was Grace's only regular visitor, she thought of him as safe, he was frustrated with himself and his life and he was known to lose his temper. There remains a question mark over his guilt, although I agree with Jonathan Hughes that (1) the time frame appears to have been distorted and (2) Stamp would have reacted differently if he'd committed the murder.

problem. He has, or had, ginger hair and will have spent time in prison. While in his teens he lived in or around Mullin Street in Highdown, Bournemouth. He was part of a deadbeat family who were disliked by their neighbours. He rarely attended school and regularly ran into trouble with the police. He was charismatic enough to attract a girlfriend (probably because he ran with a charismatic gang). He was the dominant partner in the relationship, although she was probably brighter. Because he is illiterate or semi-literate, he is unemployed or works as an unskilled labourer. He is easily roused to anger. If he lives with a partner and children they will be terrified of him; if he doesn't, then there are women and children in hiding who know him.

A selection of the 100-plus letters
received by Jonathan Hughes

Tithe Cottage
West Staington
Dorset DT2 UVY

Sunday, 12 August 2001

Dear Dr Hughes

I have just finished your book 'Disordered Minds'. I was
particularly interested by the chapter on the Grace Jefferies
murder as my wife and I were living in Bournemouth at the time.
As you know, it was a cause célèbre which filled many column
inches in the national press. Indeed nothing so dreadful had
happened in the town since Neville Heath's atrocious murder of
Doreen Marshall in 1946.

With respect, I cannot accept your proposition that Howard
Stamp was innocent. My wife and I were personally acquainted
with one of his schoolteachers at St David's Primary School, and
she said he was a 'wrong-un' from the age of six. While I accept
that this is hardly evidence of guilt, I do believe that teachers
have a feel for these things.

I fear you have fallen into the fashionable trap of looking to
excuse sin, either by laying the blame at someone else's door or
by portraying the sinner as a victim of circumstance.

Yours sincerely

Brendan Mcconnell.

Replied 15.09.01, asking for name of teacher. Followed up on 3.10.01
and 14.11.01.

No response.

The man you're looking for is Barry Morton.
He's got red hair and lives at
3 Springhill Close, Christchurch, nr Bournemouth.
He regularly beats his wife and kids.

Received on 15.09.01. No address or signature. Checked out Barry
Morton – too young (2 yrs old in 1970).

Bournemouth

Dear Dr Hughes,

I was at school with Howard Stamp. He was bullied all the time.
Not that he turned up very often. Sometimes his mother dragged
him in by his ear when the school inspectors got on to her. She
wasn't a nice woman, she was always hitting him. I felt badly
about the way he was treated. He was called terrible names. Even
the teachers were nasty to him. I never believed he killed his nan
but I don't know who did.

Yours sincerely,

[signature]

Unable to reply without a full name and address.

COUNCILLOR G. GARDENER

25 Mullin Street, Highdown, Bournemouth, Dorset BH15 6VX

Dr Jonathan Hughes
c/o Spicer & Hardy Authors' Agents
25 Blundell Street
London W4 9TP

17 December 2002

Dear Jonathan Hughes

After hearing an interview with you on Radio 4 some weeks ago, I was prompted to buy your book *Disordered Minds*. You will have noted that I live in the street where Grace Jefferies was murdered although, as I'm sure you're aware, her house and the two on either side were pulled down in 1972 to make way for a block of flats. I moved here from London in 1985 and by then her story was forgotten. I became aware of it after a spate of burglaries in the road when a neighbour mentioned that she hadn't seen so many police since Grace's body was found. Naturally, I was curious and she gave me the details.

For over a century, Bournemouth has been depicted as a tranquil place of substantial villas, beautiful beaches and conservative (with both small and big Cs) inclinations, where the wealthy middle classes choose to retire. In some ways that is still what it represents, but an influx of service industries – finance, insurance, tourism – plus the inauguration of the university in 1992 and the success of the international airport, has brought a multitude of job opportunities to the town. It is now regarded as one of the 'buzz' cities on the south coast.

With that in mind, it's difficult to imagine the 'ghetto' that Highdown was in the 1960s. Trapped between the borders of Poole and Bournemouth, it was a dumping ground for difficult families where two, and sometimes three, generations were dependent on the dole. Most lived in council accommodation, while the 35% who owned their homes were widows or retired couples surviving on small pensions. The crime rate was disproportionately high compared with more affluent wards, although it tended to be opportunist thieving from property and gratuitous vandalism rather than the mugging and stealing of cars which is prevalent in other cities today.

This may go some way to explaining the shock that local people experienced when Grace was murdered. There was always concern amongst homeowners about the 'deadbeat' families on their doorsteps, but they had learnt to lock their doors and protect their possessions. A 'California-style' killing was a different matter altogether, particularly when the victim was a shy widow with few friends. You make some reference to that in the book, but by no means enough. The local panic engendered by press headlines on the Saturday after the body was found was enormous.

The police in all parts of Bournemouth were besieged by terrified women convinced they were going to be next. There was a mass exodus from Highdown as widowed ladies went to live with their sons or daughters rather than face a madman. Most remembered the murder of Doreen Marshall by Neville Heath, who was an early 'serial killer'. The convictions of Ian Brady and Myra Hindley for the Moors murders in April 1966 were still fresh in the mind. Charles Manson and his family were about to go on trial in America. It seemed as if the world was turning to multiple murder.

You mention the 'collective sigh of relief' when Howard Stamp was arrested and charged, but it wasn't until the evidence was heard at trial that local people felt able to relax. My neighbour said they all thought the police had arrested the wrong person. She described Stamp as 'someone who wouldn't say boo to a goose let alone murder anyone'. In fact it was widely believed that the police had frightened him into making his confession, especially as none of the witnesses who saw him running away remembered seeing any blood on his clothes. There was a continuing fear that the real murderer was still at large.

As you make clear in your book, it was the forensic evidence that not only swung the jury against Stamp but also persuaded local people that he must be guilty. One detail you omitted was that Dr James Studeley for the prosecution had trained under Sir Bernard Spilsbury – the 'father' of forensic medicine – in the 1930s. Much was made of this by the prosecution during their cross-examination of Dr Foyle, whose qualifications were 'pedestrian by comparison', since he had trained in Australia under an 'unknown'. At one point, Robert Tring QC asked him to name a pathologist with whom he'd worked that a member of the jury might have heard of. He was unable to do so, and could only claim to have read their work. As this came after a similar question to Studeley, who cited not just Spilsbury but also Sir Sydney Smith, Professor Keith Simpson, Dr Francis Camps and Dr Donald Teare, who between them had founded the 'Association of Forensic Medicine' in the late 1940s, Foyle appeared to be a lightweight.

In particular, his quoting of Keith Simpson's comments on 'identical hairs' lost credibility when Studeley was able to counter with remarks made by Simpson at another trial. 'The supporting evidence of identical hair is useful when everything else is pointing in the same direction.' In Stamp's case, of course, the 'everything else' was his confession.

I applaud your efforts to bring Stamp's case to public attention, although I gather from your Radio 4 interview that you've had little success to date. From my own research I support your view that he was convicted on a coerced confession and unreliable evidence. However, in the absence of another suspect, it will be hard to prove. Sadly, my only neighbour who was here in 1970 died five years ago and, while I believe Wynne Stamp is still alive, I have never been able to find out where she went. Rumour had it she changed her name to escape publicity, but I have no firm evidence of that.

If I can be of any further assistance, please feel free to write.

Yours sincerely

George Gardener

George Gardener

Replied 05.01.03. During subsequent correspondence arranged a meeting for 13.02.03 at the Crown and Feathers pub in Highdown.

Two

Heathrow Airport, London
Wednesday, 12 February 2003, 11.00 p.m.

THE NEWS that evening was bleak. The government had ordered a ring of steel around Heathrow Airport. Scimitar light-weight reconnaissance tanks were parked menacingly along the perimeter walls, soldiers and armed policemen patrolled the terminals. London felt ominous. Even leaderless. The threat of looming war with Iraq – an unstoppable war if the BBC and the broadsheets were to be believed – depressed and worried its inhabitants. For many, the argument for a pre-emptive strike against a crippled country and a broken-backed dictator hadn't been made, and few understood why it was necessary to rattle sabres at Saddam Hussein when for fifteen months the enemy had been Al Qaeda.

There were rumours of splits in the Cabinet, and the Prime Minister's popularity had reached an all-time low. The Government had looked weak since a negotiating shambles had persuaded the firefighters to go on national strike, sucking soldiers away from the front line in order to man the pumps at home. People talked gloomily of a return to the 'British disease' of the 1970s, when strikes had been commonplace. Patriotism was quoted as a reason why firefighters should remain at their stations. The air was thick with recrimination as the country took sides . . .

It was felt by every returning traveller to Heathrow that

47

evening. They were warned to expect tanks and troops, but the reality of hard-faced soldiers and armed policemen in and around the terminals was shocking. It smacked of the military dictatorships they were being urged to mobilize against, and the more sceptical amongst them questioned the political convenience of unspecified terrorist threats so close to war. It was clever propaganda if it meant a reluctant population was frightened into accepting the necessity of pre-emptive strikes.

This was certainly Dr Jonathan Hughes's position as he emerged, tired and angry, from Terminal 4 at eleven o'clock that night and lit a much-needed cigarette outside the exit doors. He was a tall, good-looking man with close-cropped dark hair and gold-rimmed spectacles, but that night he looked ill and drawn. He'd had trouble at both ends of the journey: four hours of checking-in at JFK airport and a tailback of queues at Heathrow's passport control. Depression swamped him as he looked at the tanks and thought how easy it was for demagogues to whip up religious and racist hatred.

New York had been bad, but this was worse. He watched a woman wearing hijab cross the pavement towards him with lowered head, her tight shoulders betraying her fear. Airports were uneasy places since 9/11, and it wasn't just police and immigration officers who looked with suspicion at anyone with Arab features or Islamic dress.

Perhaps the Muslim woman felt Jonathan's gaze because she glanced up as she approached. The hijab, a pale green scarf wrapped like a nun's wimple round her forehead, cheeks and neck, performed its intended job of stripping her of her allure, and not for the first time Jonathan wondered why so many women were prepared to cover themselves rather than put the onus on men to behave with decency. At times like these the hijab bore such obvious witness to a woman's faith that it was dangerous. He felt his usual contempt for Muslim men. Not only did they want their wives to take responsibility for their own chastity – *'a woman should be concealed, for when she goes out the devil looks at her'* –

they were too cowardly to advertise their own belief. Where was the male equivalent of the veil?

The woman scurried by, dropping her eyes the minute she met his angry ones. If she expected sympathy, she was out of luck. Jonathan studied comparative religions, but only for academic reasons. He didn't admire or approve of any of them. For him, the world was a godless desert where belief systems clashed because man's aggression was untameable. God was just an excuse for conflict, like capitalism or communism, and he found it laughable when leaders quoted morality as justification for their actions. There was no morality in killing people – a peasant's genes were as valuable to the species as a president's – merely expediency.

He dropped his cigarette and crushed it underfoot, the expression on his face showing his irritation as he stared after the woman. He deeply resented the implication behind the hijab, that every man was a potential rapist. Jet-lagged and cynical from a week in New York where reasoned discussion on a Palestinian state and the problems of Islamic fundamentalism had been impossible, Jonathan found his homecoming deeply dispiriting. It might have been Hiram Johnson who said the first casualty of war was truth, but to Jonathan's jaundiced eyes the first casualty was tolerance. As far as he was concerned, the world had gone mad since the attacks on the World Trade Center and the Pentagon.

Three

HE WAS IN no better frame of mind by the morning. If anything, another sleepless night had made his depression worse. He should be using the day to recover instead of flogging himself to death to meet George Gardener. His interest in Howard Stamp was intellectual – a careless judicial system was indicative of a tired democracy – but he had no real desire to launch a crusade to clear one individual's name. He was a man of letters, not a man of action. He stared impassively out of the train window and wondered why he'd left it too late to cancel.

Sleet driving in on an icy east wind rattled the panes every time the train slowed. The other passengers, wary of meeting Jonathan's eyes, pointedly read their newspapers. He was an unsmiling man whose spectacles made him look older than his thirty-four years. The spectacles were cosmetic, his eyesight was perfect, but he wore them because he disliked not being taken seriously as an academic. He was dismissive of poor teaching and lazy thinking and had a reputation for departmental infighting. It won him few friends but it meant his intellectual authority was recognized. Certainly his fellow travellers found the brooding, introspective stare intimidating.

'For God's sake, Jon, everyone takes you seriously . . . they wouldn't dare do anything else . . .'

50

In the gardens and parks on the outskirts of town, thick layers of ice had formed on lakes and fish ponds, but when Jonathan finally disembarked at Branksome Station, after a cold wait at Bournemouth Central for a local train, the sleet was turning to water on the pavements. Shopkeepers, already suffering the knock-on effects of war-jitters and plunging stockmarkets, stared despondently out of their windows as the wind-chill factor persuaded customers to stay at home. The weather would make the headlines on the local news that evening when Age Concern made a plea for help with pensioners' heating bills. Zero temperatures were a rarity in Dorset, which was why so many elderly chose to live there.

'Blair orders in tanks' read a stand outside a newsagent halfway up Highdown Road. It was a solitary shop, a tiny trading-post in a run of shabby terraced housing. Jonathan glanced at the front pages of the newspapers on the racks inside the door. It was old news about the tanks at Heathrow. The war was still phoney. He crossed a side road and sheltered in the lee of a house to consult his map, cursing himself for coming. A jet-lagged body was unequal to the task of providing warmth, and his lightweight raincoat was about as waterproof as a piece of gauze. Worse, he had stomach cramps because he hadn't eaten since eight o'clock last night.

He screwed his eyes against the wind and sleet to read the street sign and wished he'd had the sense to look at a weather forecast. Irritation bubbled briefly against George Gardener. The councillor's last letter had said the Crown and Feathers was within easy walking distance of Branksome Station, but the man probably belonged to the Ramblers' Association and hiked twenty miles for pleasure every weekend. Easy walking distance to Jonathan was a couple of blocks, not a trek through a snowstorm. His fingers were numb, his shoes were leaking, and he didn't believe this wild goose chase would lead to anything. His depression rode him like a black dog.

He took out a cigarette and cupped his hand round the flame of his lighter. The wind blew it out immediately. It was symptomatic of the day. Walking in Howard Stamp's footsteps thirty years after his death in order to talk to someone who'd never met him was pointless. He flicked the lighter again with the same result and blamed himself for ever allowing Andrew Spicer to include a contact address in the book. 'If you believe what you write, then do something about it,' Andrew had said. 'If you don't, then stop lecturing the rest of us on injustice.' Jonathan tossed the cigarette into the gutter and clamped down on his simmering anger.

What did Andrew know about injustice? Jonathan should have taken him to New York and introduced him to some of his black and Islamic friends who were too frightened to go out. Hate crimes were increasing as troops were dispatched to the Gulf. If the whites weren't worried about war, they were worried about their investments. It was not a good time to be an American Arab or American Muslim. Even Jews were being targeted because of Israel's perceived intransigence towards a Palestinian state. At the bottom of the heap were north Africans on educational scholarships. As Jonathan knew well. He'd flown out to attend the funeral of Jean-Baptiste Kamil, a twenty-three-year-old student of his, who'd asked directions of the wrong man.

Divorced old Etonian Andrew Spicer, whose mouth had been stuffed with shiny white silver on the day he was born, was never going to suffer that kind of discrimination. Instead, he needled Jonathan. 'It's time you left your ivory tower and got your hands dirty,' he told him after reading Gardener's letter. 'It'll make a good follow-up if you can prove your theory, and I won't have trouble getting an advance either.'

Jonathan was reluctant. 'It'll be time-consuming.'

'You need the money.'

It was true . . . 'Not that badly.' Certainly not badly enough to have another book 'spiced up' by Andrew's editing. It had turned a thoughtful study on injustice into an unashamedly commercial book. 'You ruined the last one.'

'It wouldn't have sold if you'd done it your way. As it is, you made a nice little profit. You'll stand to make a bigger one if you mount a campaign for Howard. Look at Ludovic Kennedy's *10 Rillington Place*. It was made into a film.' Andrew folded his fat little hands on his desk. 'You need the money, Jon. You can't buy Paul Smith suits and go to the opera every night on an academic's salary.'

Money. With it, a man could lock his resentments in a box and be the person he wanted to be. Without it, he was nobody. Jonathan checked his map, saw with relief that Friar Road was the next on the left and battled on, head down. He didn't notice the BMW that drew quietly into the kerb behind him.

The Crown and Feathers was on the corner, a dark Victorian building with pebble-dashed walls and signs in the windows advertising live music on Saturdays and discounted meals for senior citizens on Mondays, Wednesdays and Fridays. Jonathan's misery deepened. He loathed cheap and cheerful. No doubt the pub was a pit stop for coachloads of old-age pensioners on day trips to the coast. Or, worse, a drop-in centre for the ones who lived there. There would be piped Vera Lynn singing 'The White Cliffs of Dover' and 'We'll Meet Again', the food would be inedible and the wine, if it was offered at all, would be vinegar. He should have stuck to his guns and insisted on a restaurant in town, but he might have had to foot the bill. With a sigh he shouldered open the door to the lounge bar and was surprised to find it almost deserted.

An elderly man sat on a bar stool, supping beer and staring into space. A middle-aged couple were tucked away in a corner, heads together, sharing secrets. All three looked in Jonathan's direction when he entered, but the lack of response told him neither of the men was George Gardener. There was no one serving. He peered through a doorway marked 'saloon', but it was empty except for a snooker table. The only food on offer appeared to be a list of sandwiches tacked to a wooden post; the only wine a couple of bottles beside the till with their corks pushed in. It was a place of cheap ale and no frills, and he wondered what sort of man would choose it for a meeting. Old Labour, Jonathan decided gloomily, and still fighting the class war.

Cold and wet, he shrugged off his raincoat and parked himself beside the bar. As an afterthought he took off his spectacles and tucked them into his breast pocket. Looking like an academic was the least of his problems. It was sporting the designer suit and shirt that was the mistake. He looked like a peacock in a chicken run, as out of place in the Crown and Feathers as the ancient beer drinker beside him would have been at Covent Garden. He felt the old man slide off his stool to move closer and studiously avoided his gaze. He was never in the mood for small talk – it was a talent he didn't possess – and especially not with a stranger who looked as if beer was his staple diet. The marbled hands were shaking so much that the decrepit Methuselah needed both of them to lift his glass.

'Don't get many of your sort in here.'

Jonathan ignored him. It didn't take any deep intellect to guess what he meant by 'your sort' and he wondered why it was always the elderly who came out with such statements.

A bony finger poked his arm. 'I'm talking to you.'

Jonathan lowered his leather briefcase to the floor and retrieved his cigarette pack from his raincoat pocket. 'What sort is that?' he asked, ducking his head to the lighter. 'Men who wear suits?' He shifted his glance to stare pointedly at the jabbing finger. 'Or men on *very* short fuses?' He made a fist of his right hand and rested it on the bar.

The old man, perhaps mistaking the signet ring for a knuckle-duster, put some space between them. 'Landlord's out back,' he said. 'Keep telling him he's losing customers, but he don't pay no heed. There's been a couple come and gone before you walked in.'

'Mm.'

'You should help yourself. Roy won't mind . . . long as you pay, of course.'

'Mm.'

'Maybe you don't go for ale? Not used to it, eh?'

'Mm.'

'Don't say much, do you? Cat got your tongue?'

Jonathan made an effort. It wasn't the old man's fault he was overdressed for the occasion. He should have built in time to go home and change before a night with Verdi at the Royal Opera. 'I'm in no hurry. I'm meeting a man called George Gardener. Do you know him? He's a local councillor.'

The rheumy eyes gave a flicker of amusement, presumably anticipating that an Old Labour dinosaur and a peacock would make uneasy bedfellows. 'Maybe.'

'Is he a regular?'

'Comes in a couple of times a week. Sits over there to listen to the moaners.' He nodded towards a window table. 'Calls it a surgery or some such nonsense. Bloody waste of time *I* call it. How's a councillor going to increase benefits, eh? That's the government's job.'

Jonathan gave a non-committal nod.

'They should get off their arses and look for work,' the old man grumbled. 'No sense bellyaching to someone who can't do nothing.'

'No.'

'What you want with George, then? Looking for somewhere to live?'

'No.'

'Good thing, too. Them as can afford it buy off the council . . . them like me what ain't got two farthings to rub together get down on bended knee and pray we don't get turned out.' He stared into his beer. 'It isn't right.'

'No.'

Belligerence sparked abruptly as if the repeated monosyllables annoyed him. Or perhaps it was the chill in the air – there didn't appear to be any heating in the room. 'What would you know about it?' he snapped. 'Where you from?'

'London.'

The old man gave a derisive snort. 'Timbuctoo, more like.'

'It's only two hours by train,' said Jonathan mildly. 'I did the trip this morning. It wasn't that difficult.'

He was rewarded with a suspicious glare. 'You making fun of me?'

'No.'

'You'd better not be. I fought in the war so the likes of you could make something of yourselves. I got medals for it.'

Jonathan took a thoughtful puff of his cigarette. The sensible thing would be to move to one of the tables, but he was damned if he'd give the old brute the satisfaction. He loathed senility with a passion. It was rude, it was self-absorbed and it contributed nothing to man's advancement. Rather the opposite, in fact. It was a destructive force, both in families and in society, because of the insatiable demands it made on the next generation.

The finger started jabbing again. 'You listening to me?'

Jonathan took a deep breath through his nose before whipping up his hand and grasping the frail wrist. 'You don't want to do this,' he said, lowering his hand to the counter. 'I'm cold, I'm wet, I'm tired and I am not in the best of moods.' He relaxed his grip. 'I sympathize with your housing problems but they are not my responsibility. I suggest you take them up with your MP, although he'll probably tell you to be grateful to taxpayers like me if you've been living on benefit all your life.'

'Don't you lecture *me*,' the old man snapped. 'I got rights. More'n you'll ever have. I'm a Christian, I am, and it's a Christian country . . . or would be if we didn't keep opening our doors to heathens.'

'This man bothering you?' asked a burly, dark-haired man, appearing through the saloon door.

Jonathan shook his head.

'I wasn't talking to you, mate. I was talking to my regular. I don't tolerate assaults on old guys. Certainly not by jumped-up wogs in fancy dress.'

It was like a punch to the midriff. Jonathan hadn't been called a wog for years.

'That's a bit strong,' said the old man. 'He'll have you in court if you're not careful, Roy.'

'What did he have hold of your hand for? Was he hurting you?'

'No,' Jim admitted fairly. 'Didn't like me poking him.'

'Then I apologize. No insult intended,' Roy said, raising a trap in the counter and moving behind the bar. 'Should have called you a black.' He stood with his arms crossed, eyes narrowed aggressively, as if pulling a pint for this customer was the last thing he wanted to do. 'What can I get you?'

'Nothing.' Jonathan squashed his cigarette into the ashtray with a shaking hand and reached for his raincoat. 'I'd rather take my chances in town.' He took a card from his pocket and flicked it onto the bar. 'If George Gardener comes in, tell him he can reach me on that mobile number. I'll give him the time it takes me to eat lunch, then I'll leave.'

The landlord's expression changed. 'Christ! Are you Jonathan Hughes? Listen, mate, I'm sorry. You should have said.'

'What?'

'Who you were, for Christ's sake. I've been expecting a white bloke. Does *George* know you're a darkie?'

Jonathan took another calming breath. 'Don't worry about it,' he said, shrugging into the sodden coat and lifting his briefcase. 'I'll chalk it down to experience.' He retrieved his card and tucked it into his pocket. 'On reflection, you can tell your friend I've changed my mind about meeting him. I don't like the company he keeps.' He headed for the exit.

The landlord called after him, 'Hang on, mate . . .' But his words were lost in the wind as Jonathan flung open the door.

*

After two hundred yards his furious pace slackened as a sense of proportion returned. He told himself to follow his own advice and chalk it down to experience. It wasn't the first time it had happened and it wouldn't be the last. His passport was scrutinized by zealous immigration officers every time he entered the country. He'd learnt to bite his tongue, particularly since the events of 9/11, but it still maddened him. As a child his brain had churned with hatred every time he was slighted – *ignorant racists . . . low-grade trash . . . foul-mouthed illiterates* – but he had never said the words out loud.

If Andrew was to be believed, he should have done. Holding back anger during adolescence had led to repression.

'You never stood up to your bullies, pal. You'll argue a point to death in an article or a letter, but you won't do it face to face. Christ knows why. You're aggressive enough . . . on paper, anyway.'

'I confront my colleagues and students every day.'

'Where it's safe. It's not as if your students are ever going to hit you. You're two different people, Jon. A Rottweiler inside your department, an obedient whippet outside.'

'They're dogs.'

'Don't split hairs. You'll write damning critiques of your colleagues – it's made you a hero with your students – but you shy away from confrontation on the street. You spend a fortune on flashy suits to get yourself noticed, then hunch your shoulders and wear old men's glasses in case you are. You go to the opera, but you always go alone because you think an invitation might commit you to a relationship. It's a pity you didn't deck a skinhead when you were fifteen. You've been suppressing your feelings for so long you don't have any any more.'

'What makes you think it was whites who were the only problem? The Jamaicans and the Chinese were just as bad, and they ran in bigger gangs.' Jonathan's face hardened at some distant memory. 'They were illiterate and stupid, and none of them could speak English well enough to be understood.' He gave a cynical shrug. 'You try being half Iranian, half Libyan in that kind of environment . . . with a dark skin, Caucasian features and an English name that no one believes you're entitled to. Trust me, you keep your head down and work like crazy to get yourself out of it. The last thing you do is take a swing at anyone.'

'For an anthropologist, you have a great dislike of people, Jon.'

'It has nothing to do with anthropology. Abstract science doesn't generate hate.'

'Then what does?'

War, thought Jonathan. His anger and aggression had increased by leaps and bounds since his passport had started being questioned. At the back of his mind was a constant fear that if he lost it, he would lose everything. As always, he patted his breast pocket to reassure himself it was there. The gesture was so automatic it had become a nervous tic.

A car drew into the pavement beside him. It was an ancient Mini Cooper with its back seat piled high with books and files. 'Excuse me . . . excuse me!' a woman called in a shrill voice as she wound down her window. 'Are you Jonathan Hughes?' The voice rose to hideous vowel-strangled stridency. '*Excuse* me . . . *excuse* me!'

Jonathan ignored her.

He heard the gears crunch as she set off in pursuit on the wrong side of the road. '*Please* stop!' she shouted, pulling round a parked car to draw ahead of him. 'Oh, *help*!' Her wail reached him as a van appeared out of the sleet in front of her and she slammed on her brakes.

Jonathan screwed up his eyes in pained disbelief and waited for the inevitable to happen. She was lucky. The reactions of the van driver were as quick as hers and he stopped his vehicle a yard from her bumper. His views on women drivers, mouthed through his windscreen with his finger pointing skywards, were inaudible but intelligible, and none of it was complimentary. In particular, he didn't like *fat* women drivers. With a shake of his fist, he reversed up and pulled away.

Jonathan bent down to look through the window. 'You'd better pull over before anyone else comes,' he said. 'I'll wait.'

She was red-faced and shaking, but she had the presence of mind to do as he said. 'God, that was stupid,' she said, opening her door and climbing out. 'I am so, so sorry. What must you be thinking?' She was zipped into a padded red coat with wellingtons on her feet and a lime green woollen hat clamped to her head like a Roman helmet, none of which did anything for her figure or her complexion. She looked like a squat garden gnome and Jonathan wondered if she ever bothered to consult a mirror. He put her age at about sixty.

'What do you want?' he asked.

'I'm George Gardener.' She offered an apologetic hand which he shook reluctantly. 'I can't tell you how embarrassed I am about this. I could murder Roy and Jim for being so crass. I'm not going to make excuses for Jim – he's rude to everybody – but I'm afraid Roy thought you were a crack-cocaine dealer.' She pulled a wry face. 'The police keep warning us about London-based gangs moving in and he thought you were one of them.'

'Is that supposed to make me feel better?'

The colour deepened in her roughened cheeks. 'I'm just trying to explain why he said what he did.'

'I thought crack-cocaine dealers were Jamaican Yardies. Do I look like a Jamaican?'

'No, but . . . well, you have a very English name and you don't look like an Englishman either,' she said in a rush.

Jonathan was unimpressed. 'And you have a very male name, Mrs Gardener, but I didn't insult women because I was expecting to meet a man.' His mouth twisted cynically. 'Does your friend assume all *white* men who enter his pub are drug dealers?'

She hesitated, considering the wisdom of answering. 'As long as you don't mind my quoting him, then yes, he would . . . if they were flash bastards in smart suits . . . and the police had told him the gangs were white. People like that don't go into his pub.' She wrung her hands. '*Please* don't be offended. Roy wasn't being racist, he was just trying to explain why he hadn't recognized you. He works very hard to keep drugs out of that pub, which is why most of his customers are elderly and he doesn't make any money. It's not a trendy place. The young wouldn't be seen dead in it.'

Jonathan could well believe that. He wouldn't frequent the Crown and Feathers if he were paid. But he wondered at her naivety and was tempted to repeat the conversation from his point of view. There was no question in his mind that Roy was as racist as they came, but there was little point arguing about it. 'All right,' he said with a curt nod. 'I am not offended.'

'Then you'll come back?' she asked eagerly.

'No. I'm freezing to death and I'm not a beer and sandwiches man, Mrs Gardener. I'll find somewhere with a more substantial menu.'

She sighed. 'It's Miss actually, but I can't stand being called Ms. I'd rather you called me George.'

Why wasn't he surprised? No man in his right mind would want this earnest little bumpkin with her terrible fashion sense and bulky body.

'Roy made a hotpot specially,' she told him. 'He's a good chef – *truly* – and he's given us one of the private rooms. There's a *fire* going. The only reason I chose the Crown and Feathers was because Roy knew Howard Stamp.' She placed a small, pleading hand on his arm. 'It all went wrong because my car wouldn't start. It's the cold. I should have put newspaper under the bonnet last night, but I wasn't expecting a freeze. *You* wait: statistics say that at least two of my constituents will have broken a hip by this evening and fifty per cent of the rest will be shivering in blankets to avoid upping their heating bills. Those are the pensioners like Jim.'

Jonathan might have said that Bournemouth was holding fewer and fewer attractions for him, but he hesitated when she mentioned Howard Stamp, and she saw the interest in his face.

'Oh, *brilliant*!' she said, clapping her hands like a born-again Christian. 'Hop in and I'll drive.'

He almost abandoned it there and then. 'I'd rather walk, thank you.'

'Oh, come *on*,' she said, shepherding him round the bonnet. 'I need Roy to charge the battery for me, so there's no point leaving the car here. You don't want to pay any attention to what that van driver said. My eyesight's fine and I've had a licence for years. Also, I don't usually drive on the wrong side of the road.'

She didn't seem to understand 'no' and, with resignation, he folded his tall frame into the cramped passenger seat. She was sorry she couldn't adjust the seat, but the Mini doubled as a filing cabinet and there wasn't enough room. Jonathan's knees were almost touching his chin and he smiled rather sourly. The only thing he was grateful for was that none of his students could see him. Slumming it wasn't Dr Hughes's style at all. George chattered like a little bird back to the pub, parked in a courtyard at the back, then solicitously helped him unfurl in order to march him upstairs to the private room where he was forced to accept the landlord's apologies.

It didn't go as well as she'd hoped. Roy Trent wasn't the type to eat humble pie, and Jonathan, who struggled with his own racism in a way that whites would never understand, was immediately re-offended to be called black. Despite his dark skin, he never thought of himself as black, only as an Arab. His irritation increased as George urged him forward, butting against his back with a large plastic carrier bag that she'd retrieved from the back of her car. *She* looked like a tramp, the landlord – the *chef* – looked as if he hadn't washed his hands in weeks, and Jonathan's fastidious nature recoiled at the whole idea of breaking bread with them.

'I could probably take the racism ... I don't agree with it, but I suppose I understand the history. It's the snobbery I hate. You have such an inflated opinion of your intelligence, Jon. You think it puts you above everybody else ... but clever people do not set out to patronize everyone they meet ...'

Four

INSIDE, the two men eyed each other like a couple of silverback gorillas preparing to fight over a ripe female. Roy Trent, at a disadvantage because he was on his knees trying to bring the fire to life, or because he genuinely cared for the fat little gnome behind Jonathan, capitulated first. 'Listen, mate, I'm sorry,' he said, shovelling coal into the grate. 'I saw this big black geezer gripping old Jim's hand and giving him the evil eye, and I thought, shit, he's dressed up like a dog's dinner and he's talking like Lawrence bloody Olivier. I mean, it's not normal, is it? We all know Jim's a miserable old sod, but we tend to switch off and let him get on with it. It's George's fault really. All she told me was that an author was coming – some fellow who'd written about poor old Howard – so I was expecting a puny little critter in an anorak. I mean, Howard's hardly front-page news, is he?' He flicked Jonathan an assessing gaze. 'The real trouble is, you don't have a foreign name. I mean, Jonathan Hughes – what could be more English than that? Now, if you'd been called Mohammed or Ali, there wouldn't have been a problem.' He stood up, wiping his coal-blackened hands on his trousers. 'Apology accepted?' he asked, proffering his right.

Jonathan, well aware that he'd been purposely maligned, grasped the hand firmly in his and bore down heavily on the man's metacarpal bones. 'As long as you accept mine.'

There was a flicker of irritation in Roy's eyes but he answered pleasantly enough. 'OK. What do you want to apologize for?'

'Making wrong-headed judgements about whites,' said Jonathan. 'It's a bad habit of mine. You all look the same to me.'

'Go on, I can take it. What's the punchline?'

'Germans are well educated, the French are well dressed, the Irish have talent and Americans are polite.' He shrugged. 'As the British are none of these things, I invariably make mistakes in my dealings with them.' He removed his raincoat and hung it on a hook beside the door before smoothing his jacket and hoping the shiny patches on the elbows wouldn't be noticed. 'I apologize for the suit. I wore it as a courtesy to the person I was meeting – ' he felt George stir uncomfortably behind him – 'but I should have realized how inappropriate it would be. Of course, if your pub had been called the Pig and Wallow, there wouldn't have been a problem – I'd have had an idea what to expect – but the Crown and Feathers suggested a classier establishment.'

There was a long pause while Roy thoughtfully massaged his fist. 'Just for the record, so you don't get it wrong another time, you can't tell a pub by its name, mate. The Pig and Wallow could be the best inn you'll ever come across.'

Jonathan smiled slightly. 'Thank you for enlightening me,' he murmured. 'Being black and foreign does make the vagaries of English naming traditions very difficult to understand.'

Roy jutted his chin aggressively. 'You left out our good qualities. We don't take life as seriously as the Germans . . . we don't bellyache like the French . . . we don't emigrate at the drop of a hat like the Irish . . . and we don't worship money like the Americans.' He tugged his old jumper over his beer gut. 'I'll concede the bad dressing, though. So what nationality are you?'

'As British as you, Mr Trent.'

'Except I'm English.'

The room was a small one with a table laid for two and a couple of leather armchairs on either side of the fire. Jonathan motioned to one of the chairs, inviting George to sit down. 'May I take your coat?'

She clamped her arms over her chest. 'No, I'm fine.'

He wondered what she was wearing underneath. *Pyjamas?* It wouldn't surprise him. Nothing would surprise him today. 'Do you mind if I sit down?'

'Please.'

He crossed one elegant leg over the other and put on his spectacles. 'If you're asking what my racial roots are, Mr Trent, then my father's family is Iranian and my mother's family is north African. I have an English name courtesy of my paternal great-grandfather, who was called Robert Hughes, and the reason I'm British is because I was born here and hold a UK passport. I attended a London comprehensive school, won a place at Oxford and am now a research fellow in European anthropology at the University of London. I speak English, French and Farsi fluently and can get by in German and Spanish.' He steepled his hands under his chin. 'So what are your racial roots? I'd say there's a lot of Welsh in you.'

'None at all,' said the burly man suspiciously. 'My parents are both Dorset folk.'

'Interesting. Yet your Celtic genes are so strong.'

'How do you make that out?'

'Body shape, stature, eye colour, facial type. A true Englishman would have Anglo-Saxon characteristics. He'd be taller and fairer, with blue or grey eyes and a finer bone structure. You have strong Celtic features – wiry dark hair and brown eyes – and your body shape is endomorphic. It's why the Norsemen called the Welsh trolls, because they were short, dark, hairy men with big bellies.' He glanced at George as she made small tut-tutting noises. 'I'd say you're at least seventy-five per cent Welsh, Mr Trent.'

'That's rubbish,' said the other man crossly. 'You can't tell an Englishman just by looking at him. I'm fat because I eat too much. It doesn't make me bloody Welsh.'

Jonathan touched his hands to his forehead in obeisance. 'I do apologize. I hadn't realized being Welsh was such a problem for you. It's another area of the English psyche that I've never understood. I thought it was the Scots and Irish you didn't like.'

'I am *not* Welsh.'

George gave a nervous little wave. 'He's teasing you, Roy. The Angles and Saxons were Germanic peoples who invaded England in the fourth century . . . at the same time as the Jutes and Vikings. The Jutes were Danes, the Vikings were Norwegian. Prior to that we were conquered by the Romans – who were *Italians* – and seven centuries later we were taken over by the Normans who were *French*.' She squeezed her eyes at Jonathan in painful pleading. 'Dr Hughes was joking about endomorphs – *I'm* one, *you're* one – an *Iranian* could be one. It's got nothing do with nationality, any more than colour has. For most of us nationality's a *choice*, Roy . . . not a birthright.'

'Not for me it isn't,' he said stubbornly. 'I was born here. It's the asylum seekers who look around for something better that choose.'

George gave a disheartened shrug as if his xenophobia was not new to her. 'At least recognize that it was the whites who invented economic migration, Roy. Everyone who went to America was looking for a better life.'

Jonathan watched the man's mouth set into even more obstinate lines. He was tempted to tell him they both belonged to the same racial group, Caucasian – the non-Negroid peoples of Europe, the Middle East, north Africa and western Asia – including the Welsh – but it would only offend him. Instead he took pity on George's red face and extended a hand. 'Shall we start again? I'm afraid I've been very ill-tempered since last night when I flew in from New York and was put through the wringer by an immigration officer. He asked me my views on Osama bin Laden. When I refused to answer, he kept me hanging around for an hour while he checked to see if my passport was genuine.'

Roy accepted the olive branch. 'Why did you refuse?'

'Because there was only one answer. Even bin Laden's most fanatical supporters are hardly likely to admit it to an immigration officer.'

Roy appreciated the point. 'Did he ask the whites the same question?'

'What do you think?'

'No.'

Jonathan nodded. 'You learn to live with it, Mr Trent. At times like this, when people are frightened, there's always a presumption of guilt if your face doesn't fit. It's depressing. It happened to the Irish living in England every time an IRA bomb went off. It happened to Howard Stamp when people thought a Manson-style killer was roaming Highdown.'

But mention of Howard Stamp brought an immediate cooling. Roy glanced at his watch. 'I'd better see what's going on downstairs. Can I get you something to drink? Are you allowed alcohol? George suggested a Gevrey-Chambertin to go with the hotpot but perhaps you'd prefer something else? Wouldn't want to offend your religion or anything.'

'I'm an atheist,' said Jonathan, watching him, 'and the Gevrey-Chambertin sounds excellent. Thank you.'

'I'll be back shortly.' He patted George's arm as he passed. 'If you don't take that coat off soon, girl,' he murmured, loud enough to carry, 'you'll spontaneously combust . . . and the hat's not doing you any favours either, trust me. If you're going to be judged on your looks, you might as well get it over and done with as quickly as possible.'

*

Trent closed the door behind him, but listened for a minute or two before he walked away. His first remark to Hughes had been accurate. 'A jumped-up wog in fancy dress.' The man was certainly doing himself no favours with George. Apart from anything else, he was insisting on calling her Miss Gardener. With an amused smile he walked down the stairs and pushed open the kitchen door, only for his amusement to turn to anger when he saw his ex-wife watching the CCTV monitor in the corner.

'What the hell are you doing here?' he asked angrily. 'I told you to stay away.'

She glanced at him. 'I fancied a look at the famous author.'

'Why?'

'So I'd recognize him again. I don't trust you, Roy, never have. When were you planning to tell me he was black?'

'I didn't know myself.' He stared at her for a moment before taking a couple of wine glasses from a cupboard and transferring them to a tray. Age had been kind to her, whereas George looked every one of her years. The difference was character. George was ugly, unassuming and kind; his ex was a good-looking bitch.

She flicked the fringes of her cashmere scarf. 'A sad little anorak, you said, who doesn't know shit except what he's got from old newspapers. Instead Denzel Washington turns up.'

'He says he's an Iranian.'

'Who cares? He's black enough to be a nigger.' The woman's pale eyes narrowed aggressively. 'Your girlfriend's going to bust a gut to help him whatever he is. She's a do-gooder, for Christ's sake, and it's PC to be nice to wogs.'

'Yeah, well this one's an arrogant bastard. I don't think George likes him much.' He grinned suddenly. 'You can thank me for that. I put his back up before she even arrived, and now she's having to grovel.'

The woman looked interested. 'Did you do it on purpose?'

He nodded towards the monitor. 'Seemed worth a shot. I watched that old fool Jim Longhurst needle him for ten minutes, then went out and added to his grief. He's easily offended . . . but it doesn't stop him looking down his nose at proles. He's treating poor old George like something the cat brought in.'

'I watched her go after him. She'd have licked his black arse if he'd given her half a chance.'

Roy gave a contemptuous snort. 'You might . . . she wouldn't.'

'He's not bad looking.'

'Looks like a woofter to me,' said Roy, wiping his hand on his trousers as if it had been contaminated. 'It won't cut any ice with George. She's only interested in what he can do for Howard.'

'You sure she doesn't know anything?'

Roy shrugged as he reached for the Gevrey-Chambertin. 'What's to know? If it wasn't Howard who killed Grace, then it was some other kid with ginger hair. The best either of them can do is clear the little sod's name.' He placed the bottle on the tray with a corkscrew. 'But there isn't a chance in hell they'll put anyone else in the frame – ' he flicked her a speculative glance – 'unless you know something I don't, Cill.'

'Don't call me that,' she snarled. 'What about DNA? He mentions it in the book.'

He could feel the heat of her impatience. 'There's nothing to test it against,' he said calmly. 'All the evidence was destroyed after Harold died. George pestered the police for years until they told her it was incinerated.' He hefted the tray and pushed past her. 'Now get lost before someone sees you.'

*

'I suppose you heard that,' said George with a sigh as the door closed behind Roy.

Jonathan nodded.

'Oh, well.' She tugged off her hat and sent her stubbly grey hair shooting skyward with static electricity. 'I had an argument with the hairdresser,' she explained apologetically, before discarding her coat to reveal an old yellow jumper with car oil down the front and a pair of equally grubby grey leggings tucked into her boots. 'And I'm on nights at the moment so I didn't wake up till eleven. I thought I'd check the car before I put on my glad rags and, when it wouldn't start . . .' She gave a self-deprecating shrug. 'I agree with you about it being courteous to dress up, Dr Hughes, but I ran out of time to change. I rather hoped you'd be an elderly, short-sighted professor . . . and wouldn't notice.'

Her hair looked more like the after-effects of chemotherapy, and he wondered if the glad rags included a wig. He rose to his feet and pulled the other chair forward. 'The only reason I'm wearing a suit, Miss Gardener, is because I'm going to Verdi's *Falstaff* tonight.' He smiled as he sat down again, but it was a mechanical civility rather than an expression of friendship. 'Let's just agree that first impressions aren't always right . . . and take it from there.'

Her enthusiasm returned immediately. 'Oh, thank goodness,' she said with feeling, dropping into the other chair. 'I was beginning to wonder how we'd get through this meal if I had to watch my p's and q's for hours. Putting on airs isn't my strong point – as you've probably noticed.' Her voice had no accent until her pitch rose and the vowels betrayed London roots. 'My poor mother despaired of me. She wanted a dainty, well-behaved daughter and she got a bull in a china shop.'

'Is she still alive?'

'No. Died of breast cancer when I was fourteen.' She pulled another face as if screwing her eyes and lips into gargoyle twists was a nervous mannerism, and Jonathan thought how astonishingly ugly she was. 'She was ill for a long time before that so I was effectively brought up by my father. He had no airs and graces either, which is why I never learnt them.'

'What did he do?'

She smiled affectionately, bobbing forward to sit on the edge of her seat. 'He was a postman.'

Jonathan stretched his feet towards the fire and leaned back to put distance between them. 'Is he still alive?'

She shook her head. 'Heart attack fifteen years ago. That's when I upped stumps and came to Bournemouth. I'm afraid the genes aren't healthy on either side. If I make old bones it'll be a miracle, though it won't upset me hugely if I don't,' she said matter-of-factly. 'There's a lot of misery in old age.'

'Jim being the perfect example,' Jonathan said dryly.

Her eyes twinkled mischievously. 'You can't blame old age for that. According to Roy, he's always been miserable. Did he tell you about his medals?'

Jonathan nodded.

'You have to feel sorry for him. He has flat feet so he spent the war emptying dustbins. He's told the medal story so often that I think he believes it now, but it's sad when someone has to invent a history because their lives have been such a disappointment.' The eyes, a bright blue, examined him closely. 'My father always said the hardest cross to bear was a chip on the shoulder. The more you resent it, the heavier it gets.'

He wondered if she was having a dig at him. 'How come the night shifts? What do you do?'

'Nothing very grand. I work in a nursing home.'

'As a nurse?'

'Just a care assistant. I used to be a tax inspector when I lived in London.' She smiled at his expression. 'We don't all have horns, you know. Some of us are quite nice.'

'Why give up? Couldn't you have transferred to a tax office down here?'

'It seemed like the right time to reassess priorities. In any case, I enjoy working with dementia. All my patients have amazing imaginations, none of which bears any relation to logic or reality. I have one old lady who's convinced her husband was murdered. She tells everyone he was bludgeoned to death by angry neighbours.'

Jonathan looked doubtful. 'Doesn't it upset her?'

'Only when she's told it's not true. It's her fifteen minutes of fame to produce a conversation-stopper while a naive young nurse is trying to feed her. She sulks if people point out that her memory's at fault. It's like telling Michael Jackson he's black.' She squeezed her eyes shut. 'Oh lord! Foot in mouth. Didn't mean to use the b-word. Sorry!'

'Just don't use the w-word,' Jonathan said, hiding his irritation.

'What's that?'

'Welsh.'

She gave a squeak of laughter. 'Oh dear! That was quite funny, wasn't it? What's wrong with the *Welsh*, for goodness sake?'

'King Offa built a dyke in the eighth century to keep them in Wales,' he said ironically. 'I expect it has something to do with that.'

Another giggle. 'How did you know Roy would react the way he did?'

'Because he wants to be thought of as English. If I'd accused him of being Scottish or Irish, he'd have been just as angry. He probably doesn't like Lancastrians or Yorkshiremen either, so his Englishness is very much West Country-based.' He raised an eyebrow. 'If you scratched him hard enough, his preferred passport would say Dorset. That's the only tribe he wants to belong to.'

She examined his face for a moment. 'And you, Dr Hughes? What tribe do you want to belong to?'

It was a question he couldn't answer. Indeed, it was easier to list the tribes he didn't want to join – blacks, whites, yellows, browns, mulattos – than to name the one he did. His father wanted him to acknowledge his paternal roots, his mother hers, and all he could do was make the best of being British. And that wasn't easy. *Easy* would have been for his warring parents to have remained in their own countries, rather than emigrate to England, produce a single child and wait eighteen years to declare their hatred for each other. Had Jonathan been born in the homeland of either of his parents, he might have felt he belonged. Instead they'd left him rudderless, with only a flimsy passport to prove who, and what, he was.

He reached for his briefcase. 'Shall we talk about Howard Stamp? I thought you might be interested in some of the letters I've received.'

'If you like,' George agreed.

'He's the reason we're here,' Jonathan reminded her.

'Oh, I doubt it,' she said. 'I can't think of a single occasion when I've had just one reason for doing anything. Can you?'

He snapped the catches on his briefcase. He had no intention of discussing philosophy with her. 'There's a woman who was at school with him – Jan – but she didn't give me an address or surname. Roy might be able to identify her. Another correspondent mentioned a schoolteacher. It would be useful to find her if she's still alive.' He extracted the letters and handed them over.

George didn't read them immediately. 'Have you ever thought that Howard's only purpose in life was to be a scapegoat? That's rather sad, don't you think?'

Jonathan flicked through the remaining letters. She'd be telling him God moved in mysterious ways next. 'I'm more interested in the shortcomings of the police and judicial systems,' he said patronizingly, 'particularly when they have to deal with inadequate personalities or accused from different cultures who don't have a facility with language.'

'I see,' was all she said, before bending her head to the first piece of paper.

Five

THE GEVREY-CHAMBERTIN made George's face even redder, a fact remarked on by Roy when he reappeared with their lunch. 'You want to watch it,' he warned her. 'You'll be done for drink-driving if you're not careful.'

He was solicitous of her in a ham-fisted way, and Jonathan wondered about the exact nature of their relationship. She certainly took Trent's comments in better spirit than he would have done, but then friendship for him meant mutual respect. Anything less wasn't friendship. 'You'll die a lonely old man,' Andrew had warned once. 'Loyalty is worth more than respect.'

'Same difference.'

'Hardly. Your sycophantic friends wouldn't dream of pointing out your flaws.'

'What makes you think they're sycophants?'

'Because you choose them carefully. You need to be admired, Jon. It's a gaping flaw in your character.'

'So what does that make you?'

'A loyal friend from Oxford days – your *only* friend from Oxford. You should think about that. It may be my easy-going personality, though I suspect it has more to do with the fact that I'm eight inches shorter than you, took over the family business and cheated on my wife.'

'Meaning what?'

'That you can look down on me, literally and figuratively, so I've never threatened your self-esteem. My business success, such as it is, is transparently inherited, and my failed marriage means

74

I'm no better at keeping women than you are. It's an interesting paradox in your character. You demand respect for yourself, but you can't give it. The minute you decide you're being eclipsed, you move on. I assume it's fear of perceived failure and not jealousy of another's good fortune that makes you do it, but it's a damned odd way to conduct your life.'

Jonathan watched George use a letter to fan her face and tamped down a sudden rush of contempt. He looked away to hide it, questioning quite seriously whether there was something wrong with him. He felt divorced from the room, from the people in it, even from himself – this level of detachment wasn't a normal symptom of jet lag. He wondered if the wine was to blame. Strange tremors, like electric shocks, shot up his arm every time he lifted the glass to his lips, although only he seemed aware of them.

'You can't go on like this . . . you should see a doctor . . .'

The room was too warm. He took out a handkerchief and wiped a bead of sweat from his upper lip. 'I gather you knew Howard Stamp,' he said to Roy as the man laid the table.

'Depends what you mean by "know", mate. He used to pop into my dad's shop once in a while to pick up stuff for his gran but, as he never said much, we weren't exactly close.'

'Where was the shop?'

'You'll have passed it on your way here. It's the newsagent in Highdown Road.'

Jonathan remembered. 'Was he older than you? He'd be in his mid-fifties if he was still alive.'

'Yup,' Roy agreed unhelpfully, retrieving salt and pepper pots from a cupboard. 'You wouldn't have thought it at the time, though. He managed to grow a bit of a moustache and a scrappy little beard, but he never looked his age. He was a right little wimp . . . even his voice failed to develop. My dad called him "sparrow chest" and told him to get a Bullworker . . . but he never did.' He paused, thinking back. 'He should've done. He'd have had more confidence with a muscle or two.'

'You called him "poor old Howard" earlier. I assumed you had some sympathy for him.'

'In retrospect I do – he was bullied rotten – but at the time . . .' He broke off with a shake of his head. 'A bloke couldn't afford to feel sympathy then. The kids today think they invented street cred but it's been around for decades. Only a loser would have admitted friendship with Howard.'

'Classic torture tactics,' murmured Jonathan mildly. 'The Scylla of isolation and the Charybdis of fear.'

Roy paused in what he was doing. 'Scylla' – *Cill?* – at least, had struck a chord. 'If you spoke English,' he said carefully, 'I'd know what you were talking about.'

'Scylla and Charybdis were six-headed monsters who inhabited rocks in the Mediterranean,' said George. 'Ulysses had to steer his ship between them without being snared by either in Homer's *Odyssey*.'

Roy relaxed noticeably. 'I expect you're right,' he drawled, 'but it still isn't English.'

'Howard was between a rock and a hard place,' Jonathan explained, 'bullied because he was friendless, and friendless because he was bullied. He had nowhere to go except inside himself. The outward sign of his distress was cutting his arms.'

Roy shrugged. 'Not my fault, mate. You can't hold the rest of us responsible because Howard didn't have the bottle to stand up for himself. We all got teased, but most of us learnt to deal with it.' He removed the casserole dish from a hotplate on the sideboard and placed it on a mat in the middle of the table. 'Good eating,' he said, before vanishing again.

'Was he one of the bullies?' Jonathan asked, clenching his fist involuntarily on the arm of his chair.

George noticed it and heard the edge to his voice. 'Probably,' she answered honestly, 'but then all the children were. I don't think it would be right to single Roy out as an aggressor. He was five or six years younger than Howard, so he wasn't at school with him, and the school bullies were the worst.' She heaved her bottom out of the chair and moved to the table. 'Perhaps scape-goat was the wrong description. Whipping boy might have been better. The first had the sins of the Jews laid on his back before he was chased into the wilderness, the second was flogged for the failings of others. In either case, the guilty escaped punishment. It's a very twisted concept.'

'But an old one.' Jonathan pulled out the other chair. 'Jesus died on the cross to take the sins of the world on himself. Or have I got that wrong?'

She smiled slightly. 'You know you haven't,' she said, unfolding her napkin, 'but there's a difference between the son of God absolving the world and some poor goat being expected to do it.' She took his plate and spooned lamb hotpot onto it. 'Here's another animal sacrifice,' she joked, handing it to him. 'Help yourself to vegetables. As far as I know, they've never had to atone for anyone's sins. Or am I wrong, Dr Hughes?'

There was more of the same during the meal. Serious remarks interspersed with teasing darts. She seemed intent on proving her general knowledge to him, and he let her do most of the talking while he struggled to eat the lamb hotpot. His appetite, as usual, was negligible and after five minutes he pushed his half-finished plate away and lit a cigarette without asking permission in case she refused. He wanted to remove his jacket, but he was worried she'd notice his fraying shirt cuffs.

Every so often he tried to break her garrulous flow. His questions were factual. Was Howard's primary school still in existence? Would they have records? Which secondary school did he attend? Was *that* still in existence? Would *they* have records? She answered readily enough, only to go off on a tangent immediately, and his frustration grew. He wanted to remind her that this was a fact-sharing meeting, instigated at her invitation, but he didn't know how to do it because he wasn't used to voluble middle-aged women who pulled faces and giggled under the influence of drink.

After half an hour she pushed her plate aside and propped her chubby elbows on the table. 'Do you mind if *I* ask some questions now?'

'What about?'

'You.' She shook her head as his expression closed immediately. 'Not personal questions, Dr Hughes, questions about why you became interested in Howard's case. For example, how did you come across it and where did you research it? Downing and Kiszko's cases were fairly well known even before their convictions were quashed, but interest in Howard died with him. He's not mentioned in books or on the Internet and, as I said in my first letter, the story was dead long before I moved to Mullin Street. So what brought you to him?'

'A *book*,' said Jonathan with unnecessary emphasis, 'although, admittedly, it's only available in academic libraries – *Clinical Studies* by Dr Andrew Lawson. It was published in 1975 and has been out of print for years. It's a collection of psychiatric assessments, one of which was Stamp's. I quote it in *Disordered Minds* . . . the attribution is in a footnote.' He smiled the mechanical smile again. 'I always assume readers share my interest in bibliographic references, but obviously I'm wrong.'

George's cheeks turned a brighter crimson. 'I hadn't realized that's what sparked your interest. May I ask why it did?'

He shrugged. 'I thought I made it clear in what I wrote. There were parallels between Stamp's case and the other cases I detailed. It seemed obvious to me that, had he lived, his conviction would have been quashed.'

She nodded. 'Most of your information comes from newspaper coverage. Is that the only research you did?'

He saw a criticism immediately. 'It's a common enough resource tool, Miss Gardener . . . but, no, I also had some correspondence with Adam Fanshaw, who in turn put me in touch with Stamp's solicitor. They're both retired now, but they were able to fill in some of the gaps, particularly about Grace's history. The solicitor sent me a copy of a letter that was quoted at the trial, but it contained some rather more interesting information that I referred to in my book. I also consulted a psychological profiler.'

She toyed with the edge of her plate. 'Do you ever consider the advantages your dark skin gives you?' she asked abruptly.

He frowned. 'I'm sorry?'

'Most decent people would hate to be thought of as racist. Surely that works in your favour some of the time?'

It was another tangent, but he didn't understand where it was leading. 'I don't follow.'

She held his gaze for a moment. 'Presumably most educated whites, meeting you for the first time, make a point of expressing interest in what you say . . . even if it bores them. Isn't that an advantage of being dark-skinned? They wouldn't show the same courtesy to an overweight, middle-aged white woman.' She smiled slightly. 'But then being fat is a lifestyle choice – and being coloured isn't.'

'I wouldn't know, Miss Gardener. You're the first person who's accused me of being boring. I don't see how it relates to Howard.'

'I was wondering how far he contributed to his own bullying,' she mused. 'How far does *anyone* contribute to their own bullying?'

'They don't. Howard became a target because of his harelip. He couldn't help it, any more than blacks and Asians can help having dark skin. Bullying's a form of terror – and terrorists always choose the easiest targets.'

She reverted to the subject of research. 'Were documents your only tool? Did you never think of coming down to Bournemouth to find people who knew Howard?'

It was another criticism. 'Not until today, no. But neither did I go to Rochdale to research the Kiszko case, nor Bakewell to research the Downing case.'

'Didn't you think it was important?'

'My expertise lies in examining and analysing available records, not in hammering on doors looking for long-lost witnesses. The

Stamp case was one chapter in a long book that took over a year to write. I felt there was enough documentary evidence to posit the possibility of a mistrial, and you clearly agreed, otherwise you wouldn't have written to me. The idea now is to take the case further.'

'I'm not trying to offend you,' she said. 'I'm just interested in how an academic approaches a subject like this. I'd love to have gone to an established university myself, but it wasn't easy for a postman's daughter at the tail end of the sixties.'

Oh, please! Did she think it was any easier for a half-breed from a sink estate to win a place at Oxford at the tail end of the eighties? 'It's precisely because I thought it was important to find people who knew Howard that I included a contact address in the book,' he said patiently. 'It's also why I'm here today – ' he took out another cigarette – 'although I don't seem to be making much progress.'

'Only because you think your agenda's more important than mine.'

He flicked his lighter to the tip. 'What makes you say that?'

'Body language.'

'For Christ's sake, stop being so bloody stuffy. You look as if someone's rammed a broomstick up your backside.'

He forced a smile to his face. 'Do you mind if I take off my jacket?'

She noticed he was sweating. 'Be my guest.' She watched him stand up and meticulously empty his pockets before carefully draping the fine wool over the back of the chair. He tucked his wallet, passport and a couple of pens into his briefcase, then unbuttoned his shirtsleeves and folded them back. It was an interesting routine, she thought – very Pavlovian. 'The reason I'm asking these questions,' she went on as he took his seat at the table again, 'is because, unlike you, I *have* done the legwork . . . on and off since I first heard Howard's story.' She took a folder from the carrier bag she'd brought with her. 'These are my notes.'

The file was a good two inches thick. 'May I see them?'

'Not yet,' she said with surprising firmness. 'First I'd like you to tell me what you plan to do with them.'

'Assuming they add to the knowledge I already have – and with your permission of course – I'll include them in a new book.'

'About what? Howard . . . or the iniquities of the judicial system?'

'Both, but Howard principally.'

'May I ask why?'

Jonathan saw no reason not to be honest. 'My agent's impressed by the number of letters I've received – not all of them sympathetic – but there does seem to be considerable interest in Howard.'

'And your agent thinks the book will sell?'

He nodded.

'That's good.' She propped her chin in her hands. 'Now let me tell you why I'm interested in the case. As I said in my first letter, my introduction to it was through one of my neighbours who knew Grace by sight. They had a nodding acquaintance, but they weren't friends and they didn't socialize. Whenever my neighbour talked about the murder she always concentrated on the horror of it and the impact it had on the street. She said it was months before she dared go out and years before she opened her door without worrying about being murdered . . . in other words, long after Howard was convicted.' She fell into a brief silence while she marshalled her thoughts.

'I asked her if she believed they'd caught the right man,' she went on after a moment, 'and she said no. Others were persuaded by his confession and the evidence, but she wasn't.' She placed a hand on the folder. 'She was one of the witnesses who came forward to say she'd seen Howard on the day of the murder, but she wasn't called at trial. At the time she was relieved, because she'd never been in court before and she'd found the police questioning intimidating. *Afterwards* she questioned why her evidence had been excluded. She even wrote to her MP about it, although she never received an answer.' She pulled a face. 'It's not untypical, but considering what she had to say it should have been taken up.' She fell silent again.

'What was it?'

'That she'd seen Howard's *arrival* and not his departure. She was cleaning her sitting-room window when she watched him let himself into his grandmother's house with his key. She had the radio on and she was listening to the lunchtime news on the Home Service. The presenter signed off just after Howard closed the door.' George smiled impatiently at his lack of understanding. 'In 1970 Radio 4 was called the Home Service, and the lunchtime news finished at two o'clock. It was followed by *The Archers*, and my father tuned in every day.' She rapped her knuckles on the edge of the table. 'There really is *no way* that Howard could have done everything he was accused of in half an hour.'

Jonathan felt a stirring of excitement. 'Did this woman make a statement?'

'Yes. I used my contacts on the police committee to try to get hold of the original, but we didn't have any success. If the file's still in existence, no one knows where it is – the best guess is that it was destroyed after Howard died. However, I do have a copy that my neighbour dictated to me from memory in 1997. It won't be exactly the same, of course, but she signed it and we had it officially notarized.' She heaved a sigh. 'Poor woman. She died shortly afterwards, riddled with guilt that she hadn't made more of an effort to keep him out of prison.'

He dropped ash onto his plate. 'Why didn't she?'

'Because she was a humble little person who had absolute faith in the police. Before the trial she assumed her evidence wasn't important enough to call her as a witness; afterwards she started to worry about it. She said she spoke to the local bobby, and he told her it was done and dusted. She made an attempt to contact Wynne, but Wynne had already been rehoused because of the furore . . . then Howard hanged himself.'

'And she gave up?'

'Yes.'

'When did she write to the MP?'

'Three days before Howard died. She assumed that's why she never had a reply. Then I came along and stirred her up again.' She paused. 'I still don't know if it was the right thing to do. She'd managed to persuade herself he wouldn't have confessed if he hadn't done it, and her conscience would have been easier if she could have gone on believing that.'

'You can't blame yourself.'

She gave a small laugh. 'You'd be surprised what I can blame myself for, Dr Hughes. At the moment I'm beating myself up because the car wouldn't start. They say a good beginning makes a good ending, so the reverse must be equally true . . . start badly and it goes downhill from then on.'

Jonathan ignored the comment. From his perspective, things had improved considerably since she'd started taking the meeting seriously, and he wondered how long she intended to make excuses. It was a peculiarly English characteristic to keep worrying at the vomit. He took a notepad and pen from his briefcase. 'What was your neighbour's name?'

Her blue eyes searched his black ones for a moment before, with obvious regret, she screwed her face into pained apology. 'Oh dear, this is where we hit the buffers at the bottom of the slope. I'm afraid I'm not going to tell you, Dr Hughes, nor will I allow you to read my notes. I've made free with one piece of information that points to Howard's innocence because I'm embarrassed to have brought you all the way down here only to send you away empty-handed. However, if you want to write this book, then you'll have to put in the hours yourself – as I have done.'

He stared at her with contempt, saying nothing, and she wiggled her shoulders uncomfortably. 'I'm sure you'll believe it's a racist thing, but it isn't. I've spent fifteen years researching Howard's case, the last ten trying to bring it to public attention.

I was so optimistic when I heard your interview on Radio 4 and read your book, but now . . .' She broke off with a shake of her head.

He gave a cynical laugh. 'But now that you know *Disordered Minds* has raised the interest to a commercial level,' he finished for her, 'you'll try to write the book yourself. Have you ever written anything before, Miss Gardener? It's not easy, you know.'

She tucked the folder back into its carrier bag and stood up, reaching for her coat. 'You misunderstood me. The reason I won't share my information with you, Dr Hughes, is because I don't like you.' She shrugged. 'You exploit your colour to intimidate people, and in my book that's a form of abuse. You might not have treated me like dirt if I'd been better dressed or hadn't arrived late, but I doubt it. As my father was fond of saying, what can you expect from a pig but a grunt?'

Six

THERE WAS no sign of George when Jonathan followed her downstairs five minutes later, but her Mini was still parked where she'd left it in the yard, with a wire trailing from a battery charger under the bonnet to a plug inside the kitchen. The sleet had turned to rain and he stood irresolutely by the back door, wondering what to do. Leave? Seek her out to apologize? If so, what for? He didn't understand the accusation of abuse at all. He'd taken Roy's slights, even accepted his apology with the best grace he could muster. What more could he have done? He certainly hadn't inflicted his colour on George over lunch.

Nevertheless, he'd clearly said something to make her angry, although he had no idea what it was. It certainly wasn't his reference to her writing the book, because she'd made up her mind by then. Nor had he challenged any of her theories – which was the reason his colleagues usually took umbrage. Perhaps she'd been offended that the flaring pain in his gut had prevented him eating Trent's lard-filled hotpot? His natural inclination was to pin her down and argue the logic of her position. If she wanted publicity for Howard, then whether she liked Jonathan or not was immaterial as long as he was able to generate it. But hers had been an emotional response and he didn't think she'd appreciate a lesson in logic.

The sound of rising voices came from the kitchen. '. . . sake, woman. Keep the volume down,' said Roy firmly. 'You'll have Jim quoting you all over the shop if you're not careful.'

'What does it matter if he does?'

'You'll be done for slander.'

'I couldn't give a damn. He's not even very *bright*, Roy, just a miserable little oik who's taught himself to speak properly. I don't believe a word he says. I'll eat my bloody hat if he ever went to Oxford – a polytechnic more like. God *knows* how he got a doctorate.'

'Jesus! Will you calm *down*, girl!'

'Why should I? He never once asked if I had any qualifications, just wrote me off as a postman's daughter. You should have seen his reaction when I told him what Dad did, he couldn't put enough distance between us.'

'What makes you think he's an oik? He sounds like a right ponce to me.'

'Only because you've never lived in London. You can take the man out of the city, Roy, but you can never take the city out of the man. I should *know*, I was born and brought up in the blasted place. His accent's all over the shop. He's a fake, a bloody little con man who'd rather exploit other people than do the work himself. He's not interested in justice, he just wants to make money. I'm so *angry*, Roy.'

'Disappointed, more like.' There was the sound of chair legs scraping across the floor. 'Buck up, girl. There'll be others. Like you say, it took fifty years before Derek Bentley got his pardon.'

'But I haven't *got* fifty years, Roy.'

'Then you'll have to prove the doctors wrong, darlin'. Stay put. I'll get rid of him, then I'll take a look at your battery. It's had over an hour so it ought to be charged.'

There was a click as a door swung open, and Jonathan turned towards it, his face unusually apprehensive. The pain in his abdomen was like an acid burn eating through his stomach wall, and he wished to God he'd brought some indigestion tablets with him. He swallowed bile, blaming the hotpot for his problems, and Roy grinned, seeing only discomfort at George's trashing of his character.

'You're all right, mate,' he said, closing the kitchen door behind him. 'I'm not going to bite you. It's pissing with rain, so I came to find out if you want a taxi to the station. If I ring now, it'll take ten minutes or thereabouts. You can wait in the bar or hop back upstairs.' His grin broadened. 'You're safe as long as I keep George in the kitchen.'

Jonathan made a feeble attempt to regain the moral high ground. 'I don't know what I did to upset her.'

'Then you'll have something to puzzle over on the train ride home. So . . . shall I call a taxi or would you rather walk?'

'Why did she write to me if she wasn't willing to pool information?'

'Because she's been trying for years to get someone interested. She was pleased as punch when she heard you on the radio. Thought you were the guy to get things moving.'

'I am.'

'George doesn't think so. As far as she's concerned, you're just after the credit. Howard can go hang himself – excuse the pun – if you can make money out of it. That's not George's way. Never has been.'

'I'm happy to acknowledge her input. I'll pay her a percentage of the royalties if her information leads to something.'

Roy shook his head. 'You really don't get it, do you? She spent half an hour apologizing for my big mouth, then she realized you're more of a bigot than I am. For the record, she has two Open University degrees – one in psychology and one in criminology – also an external PhD from Sussex in behavioural science.' The amusement returned to his voice. 'You shouldn't make assumptions, mate. George is far too modest to call herself a doctor – unlike you – but she's *just* as entitled. The difference is, she earned her qualifications the hard way: in the evenings while she held down a full-time job. You got yours the easy way: *free* – paid for by the likes of George. That's where being the token black pays dividends.'

'You're wrong,' said Jonathan flatly.

'Not according to George. You shouldn't look down your nose

at people, mate, not if you want their cooperation. She's a good old girl, she'll bust a gut for anyone, but she doesn't like bullies, she doesn't like people who take advantage and she doesn't like snobs.' He pointed a thumb at the floor. 'And you're all three. *Now* . . . do you wanna taxi or do you wanna walk?'

*

It was the accusation of bullying that gave Jonathan most pause for thought as he retraced his steps along Highdown Road. Anger had always simmered behind his insecurity, erupting sometimes in uncontrollable tantrums against his mother and his demented grandfather, but he had never thought of himself as a bully. That was a title he reserved for his father, whose frustration could explode into violence with terrifying speed. There had been no joy in Clarence Hughes's life, merely a daily grind of menial toil for the local council that had stultified his intellect and driven him to rage against the only people who were safe – his family.

From early childhood Jonathan had understood what fuelled his father's resentment even though he hated him for it. Clarence had wanted to amount to something in life, but immigration to Britain – far from offering him the opportunity to shine – had been a soul-destroying move. He wasn't a stupid man, but his heavily accented English, and his lack of recognized qualifications, had closed the door to jobs that would have given him status. Instead, he laboured at menial tasks and hid his contempt for the people he worked with. The victims of so much repressed emotion were his family, in particular his only child, on whom all hopes of a better future were placed.

Such weighty expectations had taught Jonathan to compartmentalize his life early, hiding his secrets as fearfully as a thief. To his mother, he was a popular boy whose late returns from school were due to visits to friends. To his father, he was an intelligent, hard-working student who stayed on after hours to work in the school library. To his teachers, he was the son of an Indian lawyer and Ugandan doctor who'd been expelled by Idi Amin in the

1970s and had their wealth confiscated. To his bullies, he was invisible.

The truth – that he'd hidden in the school lavatories because he was too frightened to walk home, and had invented a background for his parents because he was ashamed of them – became obscured even in his own mind. It was easier to embroider fantasies of popularity and forced exile than to question his own timidity and his yearning to be respected. He'd even grown comfortable in the role of victim, gaining strength from it by logging each new slight on his tally stick of revenge.

At what point he decided to convert fantasy to fact, he didn't know. When he gained the place at Oxford? When he started aping the long vowels and clear diction of the upper middle class? When he realized that an appearance of wealth was almost as valuable as wealth itself? Or that the myth of good breeding was easily established by the simple expedient of cutting his family out of his life? Perhaps there was no defining moment, perhaps his descent into pathological deceit had been so gradual that no lie had ever seemed shocking enough to call a halt.

'Why do you push people away? Are you afraid they're going to see your flaws? What's the big deal, anyway? No one's perfect . . .'

He read the new placard outside the newsagent as he passed: 'US accused of bully-boy diplomacy'. The pedant in him questioned the juxtaposition of 'bully-boy' and 'diplomacy'. The two were irreconcilable . . . or should be. The one suggested brute ignorance, the other deft intelligence, though in a phoney war the rattling sabre was a powerful propaganda tool for friend and foe alike.

Jonathan couldn't count the number of times his father had wept for the man he had become, but it hadn't changed his behaviour. Fear of his heavy hand – a more potent weapon than the hand itself – had been the dominant discipline in both his marriage and his only child's upbringing. The injustice had been Jonathan's demented grandfather's regularly mistaking his growing grandson for his hated son-in-law. With a courage he'd never possessed, even in his prime, the old man had belaboured the adolescent for the sins of the father while his mother held her finger to her lips and begged him with her eyes to let her Abba vent his spleen. 'It's good medicine,' she would say. 'Now he'll sleep.'

As he trudged on, contempt for his mother wound like a snake about Jonathan's heart. She was an ill-educated peasant who had fawned over her idiot father and paid lip service to her responsibilities to her son. *What can I do? I'm just a woman. Clarence won't allow it . . . Clarence will lose his temper . . . Clarence has problems . . . Clarence will hit me . . . Clarence . . . Clarence . . . Clarence . . .*

'Women make you so angry, Jon . . . one day you'll cross the line and you won't know you've done it until it's too late . . .'

*

Trains came and went at Branksome Station, but Jonathan felt too ill to take any notice. He stood under cover, leaning against a wall, loose-limbed and swaying slightly, clutching his briefcase to his midriff and staring into the middle distance. As they left, several passengers reported an Arab-looking man, sweating profusely and behaving strangely. The acting station master assessed him carefully through a window and wondered what to do. He couldn't imagine that a suicide bomber would choose Branksome Station as a target, but he reminded himself that Palestinian bombers blew themselves up on buses; trains were just a different mode of transport. He was about to call the transport police when another passenger, a woman, approached the man and shook him by the hand.

*

'Are you all right?' the dark-haired woman asked Jonathan kindly as she reached for his right hand and clasped it warmly. She wore an expensive overcoat with the collar turned up and a cashmere scarf looped around her neck, obscuring the lower part of her face. 'You look as if you're about to fall over. Do you want some help?'

He glanced at her briefly, then reverted to staring across the track. Nausea threatened every time he moved his eyes. He'd persuaded himself it was weeks of sleepless nights followed by jet lag. It would pass, he'd been telling himself for nearly an hour. Everything passed eventually. But the gnawing pain in his stomach said it was something worse.

The woman moved in front of him. 'You need to talk to me,' she encouraged him. 'There are two policemen watching you.' She was pretty in a manufactured way – most of it was paint – but she looked genuinely concerned. Jonathan, who had seen the way everyone else had been giving him a wide berth, wondered why she was bothering with him.

Policemen . . .? He wedged his back more firmly against the wall. 'I'm all right,' he managed.

She laughed and touched a gloved hand to his arm as if she were greeting an old friend. 'You need to smile and play up a bit,' she said. 'They're very suspicious of you.' She tilted her head towards the platform entrance. 'They're behind the wall over there and they're afraid there's a bomb in your briefcase.'

A bomb . . .? The absurdity of the concept struck Jonathan forcibly even as he felt something give way inside his head – the first of the retaining walls that held his emotions in check. There was nothing in his briefcase except his wallet, letters about Howard Stamp, his ticket to the Royal Opera House and his passport. *If a single lie unravelled* . . . 'Why would they think that?'

'You're black,' she said bluntly, 'you're sweating like a pig and you look shit-scared. It doesn't take much these days to get the cops excited.'

Another wall collapsed. *Why did everyone keep calling him black? Why did everyone keep likening him to a pig?* Hysteria rocketed round his gut, searching for an exit, before converting into painful tears behind his eyes. He was scared and sweating because he didn't know what was happening to him. He tried to bolster the myth of jet lag. No one this tired could take the funeral of a murdered boy, anti-Arab bigotry, hostile immigration officers, tanks, soldiers, critical spinsters, dirty landlords . . . *war* . . . without suffering an emotional backlash. But he knew it wasn't true. The truth was that his fabricated personality was disintegrating in front of a total stranger because someone at last was showing him a little kindness.

The woman moved closer and he caught a waft of her scent. 'I guess you've had too much to drink, but if you don't want the cops poking their noses in, then talk to me, pretend we know each other . . . even better, give me your briefcase.' She held out a hand. 'That's what's got them twitched. They'll go away if you let me open it.'

He handed it to her, suddenly dizzy. 'I'm not drunk.'

'You're giving a damn good impression.' She rested the case on her knee and flicked the latches, pulling the leather flap open so any watcher could see. Her scurrying fingers rummaged through the letters before she took them all out and handed them to him. 'Look at me,' she told him. 'Make out we've met on purpose. Select something and give it to me.'

He steeled himself to look down, quelling the sickness that rose in his throat. 'Who are you?'

'It doesn't matter. Just give me a piece of paper. Good.' She took the page and scanned it. 'Talk to me. Say rhubarb if you want, but at least give the impression that we're having a conversation.'

How did she know the police thought he had a bomb in his briefcase? 'Rhubarb?'

'Again.'

'Rhubarb . . . rhubarb . . . rhubarb.'

She pointed to something in the letter and flicked him a smile. 'Now laugh. People who laugh don't blow up trains.'

'I don't want to blow up a train. I'm a British academic. My passport's in the case. All I have to do is show it to them.'

'They'll still question you. Everyone's been reporting a mad-looking Arab on the platform. I slipped round the back; otherwise they wouldn't have let me through.'

'Why aren't you afraid?'

'I know who you are. I saw you at the Crown and Feathers.'

Jonathan groped through his memory. There had been a couple in the bar, he recalled, but he didn't think the woman had been this one. 'I don't remember you.'

She stuffed the letters into the briefcase and tucked it under one arm. 'It's a big place,' she said cryptically, glancing towards the platform entrance. 'You're all right now, I think. They seem to have gone. Come on, there's a seat down here.' She put her other hand under his elbow and urged him along the platform. 'You'll feel better if you sit down. You're so wet already, a little more water on your bum won't matter.' She lowered him to the metal bench and sat beside him. 'Did Roy say something to upset you? He can be a right jerk at times.'

Jonathan leaned back to stare at the sky and felt the nausea begin to subside. The rain had eased off and a weak sun had broken through the clouds although it was still very cold. Her scent, an attractive one, filled his nostrils, and, for the first time in months, he found the closeness of a woman comforting. He couldn't account for it, nor did he bother to try, he was just grateful for the human contact. 'Is he a friend of yours?'

'Not really. I know his ex-wife, so I get to hear about his faults. He's famous for opening mouth before engaging brain. Did he say something insulting?'

'*That's where being the token black pays dividends*...' Was the truth ever an insult? Perversely, Jonathan found himself defending the man. 'If he did, it probably wasn't intentional.'

'I wouldn't bet on it,' she said with an easy laugh. 'He may not be the brightest thing on two legs but he knows how to get under people's skin. You don't want to dwell on it. It gives him a buzz if he thinks one of his jibes has hit the spot.'

Despite her expensive clothes, he didn't think she'd been born to wealth. Her voice had a rough Dorset burr, much like Roy Trent's. 'Does he do it to you?'

'He does it to everyone. That's why he has so few customers.'

It was a different explanation from George's, but it appealed to Jonathan rather more. 'Do you know Councillor Gardener?'

'Roy's girlfriend? Only by sight.' She turned to look at him. 'Don't tell me *she* upset you? She got religion after the cancer – wants the world to accept Jesus and all that cr—' She broke off. 'I'm being a bitch. Forget I said that. She's very well-meaning . . . crusades for the poor. I can't believe she'd say anything unkind.'

Fleetingly, Jonathan wondered why she was so intent on blaming someone else for his problems. 'It's just exhaustion,' he said. 'I flew in from the States last night and didn't sleep. I'd have done better to stay at home.'

'Was the trip worth the effort?'

'To the States?'

'No . . . today's . . . down here.'

He shook his head.

'Will you come back?'

He glanced at her. The question wasn't overly intrusive, but somewhere in the recesses of his mind her persistence struck a suspicious chord. 'Did Roy send you after me?'

'Hardly,' she said with a small laugh. 'He'll have forgotten all about you by now.' She nestled her chin into her scarf. 'To be honest, I was surprised to find you here. You left the pub a long time before I did. So . . . are you feeling better?'

'I am, yes.' He was surprised. The nausea had gone, and even the tremors in his arms had ceased. 'You've been very kind.'

'I'm in a charitable mood.' She looked along the track. 'Your train's coming. I'll see you onto it, then all you have to do is make the connection at Bournemouth Central. Can you manage that?'

He pushed himself to the edge of the seat. 'What about you?'

'I'm going the other way,' she said, standing up and offering him his briefcase as the train drew in. She'd relocked it at some point, and he took it gratefully.

'Then why are you on this platform?'

'I could see you were in trouble.'

He shook his head. 'I don't even know who you are.'

'A good Samaritan,' was all she said, as she opened a carriage door and urged him inside.

His last view of her was muffled in her scarf with a gloved hand raised in farewell but, as he waved back, it occurred to him that he wouldn't recognize her again. All he had seen was a pair of painted eyes beneath a dark fringe. It wasn't important until he opened his briefcase at Bournemouth Central and discovered that she'd stolen everything that mattered to him. She'd taken his wallet, his train ticket, his opera ticket, and worst of all she'd left him with nothing to prove who he was. His passport was gone.

After that he lost it. He ran about the station, barging into people and shouting at them. Some thought he was a pathetic lunatic. Some thought he was dangerous. When two transport policemen tackled him to the ground, he called them fascist scum and struck at them with the briefcase until one of them wrenched it from his grasp and kneed him in the gut.

Seven

Central police station, Bournemouth
Thursday, 13 February 2003, 8.30 p.m.

ANDREW SPICER was not amused to be summoned from his office in London at five o'clock that evening to drive to Bournemouth to vouch for his friend. The most basic checks on Jonathan's identity had revealed that a man with his name had had his passport queried the night before when he flew in from America, and police, unimpressed by his behaviour after he was arrested for running amok at Bournemouth's main station, insisted on proof of who he was before they would consider releasing him.

It was the opinion of the doctor summoned to test Jonathan Hughes for drugs and excessive alcohol – both of which proved negative – that further tests were required. The man was clearly ill. Jonathan was advised of his right to go to hospital, but as he retreated into silence, refusing both medical assistance and a solicitor, there was little to be done except approach Andrew Spicer, literary agent, whose name and address were on several letters in Jonathan's briefcase. An attempt was made to contact Councillor George Gardener, whose correspondence suggested a lunch appointment at the Crown and Feathers, but every call was intercepted by an answerphone. There was a similarly negative response from the pub itself, which wasn't due to open again until five thirty.

How seriously ill was he? At death's door? Mental, rather than physical, said the doctor, so hardly an emergency. Once Andrew was persuaded to drive from London, the police lost interest. They had other fish to fry, and a safely contained, tearful Arab posed less of a threat than impatient drivers on freezing roads.

When Andrew finally arrived at eight thirty, tired and hungry after sitting in gridlock on the M3, he was shown Jonathan through a two-way mirror. 'Do you know this man?' he was asked by a uniformed sergeant who introduced himself as Fred Lovatt.

'Yes.'

'Who is he?'

'Jonathan Hughes.'

'What's your relationship with him?'

'I'm his literary agent.'

'How long have you known him?'

Andrew unbuttoned his jacket and pointed to a chair. 'Am I allowed to sit down? I haven't eaten since breakfast and I'm dead on my feet.' He slumped onto it when the sergeant nodded. 'What's he done?'

'Just answer the question, please, Mr Spicer.'

'Twelve years . . . thirteen years. We were at Oxford together, but I didn't get to know him well until he brought his first manuscript to me in 'ninety-two. We've been friends ever since.'

'What's his profession?'

'Academic. He's a lecturer and research fellow in European anthropology at London University. Rather a good one, as a matter of fact . . . and much appreciated by his students because he takes the trouble to make the subject interesting.'

The sergeant pulled out another chair. 'Is there a reason why he wouldn't tell us that? Why would he have a problem if his university was approached for verification?'

Andrew studied his friend's face through the window. 'What are you charging him with?'

'Nothing at the moment.'

'Then why are you holding him?'

'Because he's committed an offence and he's refusing to answer questions on it. He won't be released until we're satisfied it's safe to do so.'

'What offence?'

Sergeant Lovatt consulted a piece of paper. 'Running amok at Bournemouth Central. He collided with passengers and screamed about being – ' he arched an eyebrow – 'assuming this is right . . . *fall* staff? Possibly *full* staff? He's refusing to explain what it means. Do you have any ideas, sir?'

Andrew frowned. 'It's a Verdi opera. It's on at Covent Garden tonight. *Falstaff* . . . Sir John Falstaff. He's a comic character from Shakespeare's *Merry Wives of Windsor*, also *Henry IV Parts 1 and 2* and *Henry V*. He's a big fat man with large appetites.'

The sergeant looked doubtfully towards Jonathan, whose shirt was hanging off his thin shoulders. 'Why would Mr Hughes claim to be this man?'

'He wouldn't have said *being* Falstaff, but he might have said *going*. He's opera-mad. He told me he had a ticket for it . . . that's why he flew home last night. Otherwise he'd have cancelled today's appointment and waited for a cheaper flight.'

Lovatt read the paper again. 'According to the witnesses, he said, "I am Falstaff." One of them claims he also said, "The devil's a woman." Is he married? Does he have problems at home?'

Andrew shook his head. 'He had a steady girlfriend for a while, but they split up after Christmas. I don't think it affected him much; he never gave the impression it was serious.'

'Is he a Muslim?'

'No.' The fat little man smiled slightly. 'Nor is that question sequential on "the devil's a woman", Sergeant. As far as I'm aware, it is not Islamic doctrine that Satan wears a dress. They believe the opposite: it's the devil in men – the trouser snake – that's the problem. That's why their women cover themselves.'

The sergeant was unmoved. 'Does this Falstaff character have problems with women?'

Andrew looked interested suddenly. 'He certainly does in the opera. Verdi took the story from Shakespeare's *Merry Wives*, where

Falstaff is portrayed as a figure of fun. He loses all his money and comes up with a plan to improve his finances by seducing the rich wives of Windsor. When the women find out about it, they devise humiliating punishments for him.'

'What kind of punishments?'

'Slapstick stuff. I haven't seen it for a while but, as far as I recall, they dump him in a river, then make him parade around in fancy dress. It's the trouser-snake theme. The women lead him on by pretending to like him – get him excited, in other words – then slap him down when he thinks he's about to score. It's a tale of male mockery by feisty ladies. The lesson is that women are intellectually and ethically superior to men.'

The sergeant gave a grunt of disapproval, as if the lesson didn't appeal to him. 'Pretty topical then. That's all anything's about these days.'

Andrew didn't disagree. 'It always has been. It's the battle of the sexes . . . men are from Mars and women from Venus. Human nature never changes. We can analyse our DNA, email each other across the world, transplant hearts . . . but the fundamentals remain the same. Men hunt, and women control the family. Simple as that. Shakespeare's perceptions are as true now as they were when he recorded them four hundred years ago. He was a behavioural scientist before behavioural science was invented – ' he ticked the air – 'a genius of a psychologist, with a very real understanding of the dynamics of relationships – particularly male–female relationships.'

'Mm.'

'Sorry,' said Andrew. 'I'm a fan . . . tend to get carried away.'

'I've only ever seen *Hamlet*. Someone told me the whole play could be reduced down to the speech about suicide. "To be or not to be". Is that right?'

'He's certainly a man who explores his own tormented identity. In that respect, it's a precursor of modern theatre.'

Sergeant Lovatt studied Jonathan through the window. 'Does Mr Hughes have a tormented identity?'

Andrew followed his gaze. 'Don't we all?'

'Some more than others, I suspect,' the other said blandly. 'Has he ever displayed any mental problems that you're aware of?'

Too many to count, Andrew thought. *Envy ... resentment ... insecurity ... self-loathing ... just like his agent and every other poor sod on the planet who didn't measure up to expectation.* 'No,' he said. 'What makes you ask?'

'Your friend resisted arrest and refuses to explain himself. We're interested why.'

'Presumably because he doesn't believe he's done anything wrong. He writes books about the pitfalls of social stereotyping and the failings of the criminal justice system when it treats the stereotype and ignores the individual. I imagine he's working on the principle that if you haven't charged him, then he shouldn't have been arrested in the first place.'

The sergeant shook his head. 'There was nothing wrong with the arrest, sir. Mr Hughes was detained under stop-and-search powers after going berserk in a public place. When he was taken into custody, he tried to hit an officer with his briefcase.'

'Did he make contact?'

'Barely. If he wasn't such a big girl's blouse, he'd be facing a charge of assault, and that's a serious offence.' A muscle twitched at the side of his mouth. 'He's not much of a fighter, your friend. The transport policeman who detained him said it was like wrestling with a stick insect.'

'What about the people he bumped into?'

'They were willing to let it go.'

'So what's left, other than refusing to answer questions? I thought that was a right, not a crime.'

'Unless you make a habit of it. He flew in from America last night and was detained for an hour for the same reason.'

'Oh, for Christ's sake!' said Andrew impatiently. 'It happens every time. If it's not his views on bin Laden, it's which bloody cricket team he supports. I'm never asked questions like that, and if I were I'd say Osama was a splendid fellow just to see what reaction I got.' He leaned forward. 'If no one else wants to pursue it, you've no reason to hold him.'

'We still want an explanation, Mr Spicer. Heathrow's on heightened alert because of terrorist threats, and the same applies in the major conurbations. Unusual behaviour is taken seriously.'

'More so when the suspect looks like an Arab, I suppose.'

The man didn't say anything.

'If you have his passport, then you know he's British. It *used* to mean something.'

'He isn't carrying anything that can identify him, sir. That's why we asked you to drive down here.'

Andrew looked surprised. 'He must have his passport. He's irrational about the damn thing . . . so terrified of losing it he pats his breastpocket all the time.'

The sergeant shook his head. 'No passport.'

'What about his wallet?'

'No wallet. No money. No credit cards. No train ticket. Certainly no opera ticket to Verdi's *Falstaff*. He's a bit of a mystery, your friend. All he has in his briefcase are a pay-as-you-go mobile telephone – with a rundown battery – and some letters addressed to him care of Spicer & Hardy – ' he eyed Andrew thoughtfully – 'which makes his refusal to cooperate rather surprising. You'd think he'd be falling over himself to prove who he is.'

'Or explains it,' Andrew countered. 'When was the last time you had your identity questioned twice in twenty-four hours? You haven't questioned mine. How come I'm squeaky clean without a passport, but Jonathan isn't? Is he right? Are you a non-person if you're paperless and dark-skinned in this country?'

'You came voluntarily, sir, and Mr Hughes did not. He was detained legitimately and asked to account for himself. When he refused, he was arrested and brought here. Had he been willing to answer a few straightforward questions, he would have been released as soon as we had confirmation that his answers were true.'

'What sort of questions?'

'Address, job, next-of-kin details, what took him to America. Nothing out of the ordinary . . . and nothing we wouldn't ask a white man in the same circumstances.'

'I've told you his job, so to be strictly accurate it's *Dr* Hughes, not Mr Hughes. He lives in a flat in West Kensington – off the top of my head it's 2b Columbia Street or Road – and his next of kin are his parents, though he hasn't seen them for years. They divorced shortly before he went up to Oxford, and I believe his mother repatriated. He doesn't know – or care – what happened to his father. As for the trip to America, he was attending the funeral of one of his students who was killed in a racist attack on the streets of New York.' He glanced at the window again. 'Jon's the one who pulled strings to win him an educational scholarship, so I shouldn't think he's feeling too happy that the lad was murdered.'

'How does he afford it on an academic's salary?'

'What?'

'Trips to America, Paul Smith suits, Versace shirts, tickets to the opera, Armani glasses. What kind of books does he write? Bestsellers?'

Andrew hesitated before he answered. 'Not exactly. He's a single man with no dependents.'

'It's an expensive lifestyle, Mr Spicer. Does he own his flat?'

'I've no idea.'

'Does he have any other income that you know of?'

'No.' He studied the sergeant's deadpan face for several moments. 'What are you suggesting?'

'These are uncertain times, Mr Spicer.'

Andrew laughed. 'If you're thinking he's some sort of terrorist, you're way off-beam. He hates violence.'

The sergeant allowed himself a small smile. 'Does he live alone, sir?'

'I believe so, yes.'

'Rent and mortgages in Kensington don't come cheap, Mr Spicer.'

This was a policeman with a great capacity for taking in knowledge, Andrew thought, as he watched Jonathan take off his designer specs and polish them on the end of his tie, revealing how red his eyes were. In repose and under the bright lights, his face looked gaunt, while his shoulders had the skinny rigidity of a clothes hanger. Andrew's feelings for Jon had always been ambivalent. Their friendship was based on mutual liking and a shared interest in literature and good wine; however, Andrew despised Jonathan's adopted accent, he despised the snobbery, and, very particularly, he despised the lies. Until today he had never had reason to believe they were anything but a cloak for insecurity, but now he wondered. It was certainly true that the cloak had become increasingly transparent in the last few months.

He turned back to the policeman. 'That suit's come out so often you could check your face in the elbows, and the specs are purely for show. I'm not his bank manager so I don't know how he conducts his finances, but it wouldn't surprise me if he's up to his eyes in debt. Money talks loudly, and to someone like Jon a place in Kensington and tickets to the opera are probably worth the interest on a loan.'

'Meaning what?'

'Some people need to promote a false image of themselves. You can flaunt a trip to Verdi's *Falstaff*, but you can't flaunt an empty fridge.' He saw the scepticism in the other man's eyes, although whether it was for Jonathan's stupidity in wasting money on the opera or disbelief of Andrew's analysis, it was impossible to say. 'I know very little about how terrorists work, but I assume the first rule is, don't draw attention to yourself. Is running amok normal behaviour?'

The sergeant shrugged. 'We had a doctor check him for drugs and alcohol. His view is that Mr Hughes is close to breakdown. I'm no expert in terrorists either, Mr Spicer, but I imagine it wreaks havoc with the mind . . . particularly if your own death is part of the process.'

Andrew couldn't disagree with that. 'It's more likely his house of cards is collapsing. Maybe the split with his girlfriend caused it . . . maybe he was more serious about her than I thought.' He paused, recalling a remark Jon had made in the wake of Emma's departure. '*I couldn't love her the way she wanted . . .*' 'He's not an easy man to read. Most of what he thinks and feels stays locked inside his head.'

'Go on.'

'I'm guessing it started at Oxford. I didn't know him so well then, he moved in a smarter circle than I did. It's a precious place . . . or can be,' he corrected himself. 'The mythology of dreaming spires and gilded youth. To a cynic like me, it's pretentious nonsense – even corrupting – but to someone who comes from the wrong side of the tracks, it's seductive.'

'He doesn't sound like someone from the wrong side of the tracks.'

'That's part of the fiction. He bought into the idea that image was everything – if you can pass yourself off as one of the elite, then you're made. The problem is, you have to support the lifestyle – and if you can't afford it, you lose your friends.' Andrew shrugged. 'I think he's afraid he's about to be exposed as a fraud. Which probably answers your question about why he didn't ask one of his colleagues at the university to vouch for him.'

The sergeant looked thoughtful. 'It's an offence to misrepresent yourself in a job application.'

Andrew shook his head. 'There's nothing wrong with his qualifications,' he said with a wry smile. 'It's his breeding he's worried about. The man's an anthropologist. It won't be easy admitting he's the unlikely product of a Jamaican road sweeper and a Hong Kong maid when he's made a habit of passing himself off as a dark-skinned Caucasian.'

*

Andrew, given half an hour to persuade his friend to answer questions, eschewed sympathy in favour of brutal honesty. He listed the options. Assuming Jonathan had nothing criminal to hide, he had a choice of explaining himself and hitching a ride home with Andrew that evening, or keeping up the silence and spending a night in the cells while police made enquiries of his friends and colleagues in London. If he chose the latter, his detention would become public knowledge and he would have to make his own way home if and when he was released. As the police had found no credit cards, cash or return ticket in his pockets or in his briefcase, that could prove difficult.

If Jonathan could not afford his own lawyer, there was a duty paralegal kicking her heels in the waiting room. However, unless he wanted to prolong his agony by explaining his actions to a stranger – bearing in mind the potential charges were minimal – he'd be mad to waste time on a bored young woman who hadn't taken her exams yet. The police doctor who'd tested his urine had hinted at depression, and if Jon persisted in silence there was a strong possibility his next stop would be the psychiatric department at the local hospital. The knock-on effects of this, when an explanation for his absence reached the university, would be rather more serious than a quiet consultation with a GP in London.

Finally, his agent, who knew more about his author than his author realized, had already blown the gaffe on Jonathan's financial situation, self-esteem problems and inability to sustain relationships . . . so it was pointless continuing to save face.

'You could lend me some money to get home,' Jonathan muttered, staring at the floor.

'I could, but I'm not going to. What happened to yours?'

'It was stolen.'

'Why didn't you tell the police?'

'Because they're fascists, and they only arrested me because I'm black.'

There was some truth in that, thought Andrew, but now wasn't the time to say it. 'Grow up, Jon!' he said curtly. 'Football hooligans are regularly arrested for running amok, and ninety-nine point nine per cent of them are white. Your colour didn't come into it. In any case, you are where you are. You can either keep licking your wounds, or you can show some sense. Rightly or wrongly, you're banged up in a provincial nick with question marks over your behaviour. God knows what's been going on, but you can either tell me about it . . . or you can tell the sergeant. Either way, you need to tell someone.'

Jonathan dropped his head into his hands but didn't answer.

'What happened with Councillor Gardener? How did that go?'

'She called me a pig.'

'She? I thought it was a man.'

'Short, fat and bossy. A bit like you, except she's a hideously ugly middle-aged spinster who spends most of her time gurning.'

Andrew lined up a chair beside him and sat down. 'Why did she call you a pig?'

Jonathan ground his knuckles into his eyes. 'She didn't like me. Accused me of bullying her and said, "What you can expect from a pig but a grunt?"'

'What did you do?'

'I left.'

'I meant, how did you bully her?'

'I didn't ask her what her flaming qualifications were.'

It wasn't much of an explanation but Andrew made a reasonable guess at what had happened. 'By which I presume you patronized her . . . and she didn't like it.'

Jonathan gave an indifferent shrug which Andrew took for assent.

'Who stole your wallet?'

More knuckle-grinding. 'I think it was the woman at the station, but it could have been any of them.'

'What woman?'

'The one who helped me.'

'What was her name?'

'I don't know, she wouldn't tell me.'

'Was this before or after you ran amok?'

'Before.'

'Why did you need help?'

'The police thought I had a bomb in my briefcase so she opened it to prove I was harmless.' Jonathan gave a stifled laugh. 'She said she was being charitable . . . and I believed her. That's how stupid I was. Since when did a woman do anything for free?'

Wondering if that was an oblique reference to Emma, Andrew filed the statement away. The minutes were ticking away and he couldn't afford to be sidetracked. 'The sergeant didn't mention a bomb. He said you bumped into other passengers and shouted about being Falstaff.'

'It was a different station. They were watching me from the entrance because I was sweating.'

'Which station?'

'Branksome.'

'It's been freezing all day. Why were you sweating?'

'I felt ill. You can't be ill in this country if you're black. It frightens the natives.'

'Don't talk crap, Jon! We have our ups and downs but, by and large, we're pretty peaceful.'

'Then why are we going to war?'

Andrew turned to look at him. 'Is that what this is about? Were you given a hard time in the States?'

His friend gave a hollow laugh. 'It's an Arab thing. We're all potential terrorists.'

Andrew shook his head. 'Except you're not an Arab. You're half Jamaican, half Chinese and by some freak of genetics you ended up looking like a Bedouin.'

Jonathan's jaw set in a hard line. 'How do you know what my parentage is?'

'You got rat-arsed the week after Emma left. I couldn't follow most of it but I had the Caribbean–Asian conflict rammed down my throat.' A confused loathing of his parents mixed with racist hatred of anyone of Afro-Caribbean or Chinese descent because of the vicious gangs who had terrorized him as a child.

'Why haven't you mentioned it before? Why let me go on pretending?'

'It wasn't my business. If you want to be an Arab or an Iranian, then so be it. I don't see it matters very much unless it causes problems for you. Does it?'

Nationality's a choice, not a birthright . . . 'No.'

'Then why are you here? Why were you feeling ill at the station?'

'It was jet lag. I just needed a bit of time, so I leaned against a wall.'

'How long for?'

'I can't remember.'

'Then this woman appeared and went through your briefcase?'

'Yes.'

'Didn't you think that was a bit peculiar?'

Jonathan glanced at him, showing eyes bloodshot with exhaustion. 'I do now,' he muttered. 'At the time I believed her. I even thanked her for her kindness. You can't get much stupider than that . . . allowing a woman to make a fool of you, then thanking her for doing it.'

It explained the Falstaff reference, Andrew thought. 'Oh, come on, pal, you were conned. It sounds like a professional scam . . . look for people in trouble, then rip them off while you're pretending to help them. You should have told the police. She's probably well known to them.'

Jonathan didn't say anything.

'All right, *I'll* tell them. What did she look like? What sort of age?'

'I don't know.'

'You must have some idea.'

He went back to staring at the floor. 'I felt sick every time I moved my eyes, so I never really looked at her.'

Andrew shook his head. The whole story was becoming more and more bizarre, and he found himself sympathizing with the sergeant's view that Jon was suffering mental problems. 'This isn't a figment of your imagination, is it?' he asked bluntly. 'Does this woman actually exist?'

'Why would I invent her?'

'Because you're up shit creek without a paddle, mate. You've lost your passport, your money and your return ticket. You've alienated the only useful contact for a book on Howard Stamp and had yourself arrested for behaving like a maniac. What the *hell's* been going on?'

No answer.

Andrew stood up. 'This is crazy. I'll ask them to phone George Gardener. At least she can tell us what happened at the pub.'

'She said she knew Roy Trent and saw me at the Crown and Feathers.'

'George Gardener?'

'The woman. She had a dark fringe and spoke with a Dorset accent.'

'Who's Roy Trent?'

'The landlord.' There was a long pause. 'He's the bully, Andrew. He pretends to be helping her, but he does it in a cruel way. He called me a wog and a darkie and said I only got the place at Oxford because I was the token black.'

'Ri-i-ight.' Andrew watched him for a moment before turning the door handle. 'When did you last have a decent night's sleep, Jon?'

His friend gave another muted laugh. 'I think too much,' he answered cryptically.

Eight

THE SERGEANT agreed to telephone the Crown and Feathers but, rather than throwing any light on Jonathan's story, Roy Trent said the pub had been virtually empty at lunchtime and he didn't remember a dark-haired woman. He knew a number of brunettes and auburns but, without a name, he couldn't be any more helpful. In any case, he'd found Jonathan's wallet and passport on the floor of the upstairs room when he'd come to clean it. He'd assumed Jonathan would phone as soon as he realized they were missing but, as he hadn't, he was planning to ask George Gardener to return them because she knew his address. 'What's with the dark-haired woman?' he finished curiously.

'A female of that description gave Dr Hughes assistance at Branksome Station. She claimed to know you.'

'So?'

'Dr Hughes says she went through his briefcase.'

'And he thought she'd stolen his wallet?'

'Yes.'

'How come it's taken you so long to call? It's hours since he left.'

'He didn't tell us anything was missing until a few minutes ago, sir.'

Roy gave a surprised laugh. 'He's got real problems, that fellow. Why didn't he phone? The first place you'd check is where you took your jacket off. I'd've put his mind at rest quick as winking.'

The sergeant caught Andrew's eye and looked away. 'What sort of problems?'

'The whole-world's-out-to-get-me sort. He's just the type to jump to the conclusion his stuff's been stolen instead of thinking it might have been his fault. Mind, he'd've found out he'd dropped it a damn sight sooner if he'd let me call a taxi. But he wouldn't have one. Insisted on walking, even though it was bucketing down. Why did he need assistance?'

'We're not sure. Was he drunk when he left your pub?'

'Couldn't have been, not on what he had here . . . couple of glasses of wine, maximum. He might have been drinking before he arrived, of course, but he didn't look like it. He was sweating when he left, but that was because he'd blotted his copybook with George and she was rabbiting on at full blast about what a jerk he was. He couldn't get out fast enough, which probably explains why he didn't check his pockets properly.'

'Do you have George Gardener's number?'

'Sure. She's on nights this week so you'll have to call her at work. Hang on, I'll find it for you.' He came back with a nursing-home number a few seconds later. 'It's the Birches,' he said when the sergeant asked which one it was.

'The Birches,' repeated the sergeant, writing the number on his notepad. 'Is that the big place in Hathaway Avenue?'

'Yup.'

'How easy will it be to get hold of Ms Gardener?'

'Not difficult. She carries a pager.'

'Right. Thank you, Mr Trent.'

'Hang on! What about this bloody wallet and passport? Does Hughes want to pick them up or should I post them?'

'I'll send a car.'

A wary note crept into Roy's voice. 'This isn't some sort of insurance scam, is it? There's not much in the wallet, you know . . . just a couple of twenties and some tickets. I assumed, as he didn't come back for it, he keeps his credit cards somewhere else. I'll be bloody angry if he tries to accuse me of stealing from him.'

'He's not accusing anyone of anything at the moment, sir.'

'Then what's the story? It all seems mighty peculiar to me.'

You and me both, thought the sergeant, as he avoided the question by thanking the landlord again and cutting the line. He tapped his pen on his desk for a moment, then asked Andrew to find out from Jonathan what was in the wallet. 'It's important, Mr Spicer. If you think you're being lied to, please tell me.'

While Andrew was out of the room, he consulted with the Transport Police, then checked for any call-outs of the regular force to Branksome Station that afternoon. Both came up negative. There was no response at Branksome, which had closed for the night, but an operative at Bournemouth Central said the only information logged on the line about an Arab acting suspiciously was the 'running amok' episode for which Jonathan had been arrested.

Andrew listened to the tail end of the conversation when he returned. 'Do you think he imagined this woman?'

The sergeant shrugged. 'Not necessarily, but he may have embroidered the encounter when he found his wallet was missing. He seems to like painting himself as a victim of injustice.'

'Is that what the landlord said?'

The other man ignored the question. 'I'm not unsympathetic, Mr Spicer. It can't be easy for any dark-skinned person with all the anti-Muslim feeling that's in the world at the moment. What does he say was in the wallet?'

'Nothing worth stealing . . . except to him: a return ticket which he needed to get back in time for the opera, the *Falstaff* seat and forty-odd quid. He wasn't asked to show his ticket at Branksome, which is why he didn't discover it was missing till he reached Bournemouth Central. He says he should have just got on the train and blagged his way back to London, but he was too tired to think of it.'

'What about credit cards?'

Andrew shrugged. 'He wouldn't say where they were, but he's not claiming they were in the wallet.'

George Gardener was as surprised as Roy to be answering police questions about Dr Hughes six hours after she thought she'd seen the back of him. She knew nothing about the missing wallet and passport, but she'd left the pub shortly after Jonathan. Like Roy, she had no recollection of a dark-haired woman. 'There was hardly anyone there,' she told the sergeant. 'I only remember seeing Jim Longhurst. I suppose people may have come in while Dr Hughes and I were upstairs, but he left by the back door, and that's not visible from the bar.'

'Mr Trent said you had a row with Dr Hughes. May I ask what it was about?'

'We didn't row,' she said. 'Roy's probably talking about me voicing my opinions in the kitchen. I believe Dr Hughes heard me, which is why he refused to wait for a taxi.'

'Did he come by taxi?'

She hesitated. 'I don't know . . . no, I don't think so. His raincoat was very wet when he got into my car, too wet for the few minutes before I caught up with him.'

'Was this before or after you voiced your opinions?'

'Before. I was late for our meeting and there was a misunderstanding between him and Roy. I went after him in my car.'

'What sort of misunderstanding?'

She sighed. 'Roy made a remark that Dr Hughes interpreted as racist. We were both expecting a white man – it's not a foreign name, you see, which is how the misunderstanding occurred.' She paused. 'Has he lodged a complaint against Roy?'

'Not that I'm aware of.'

'Then what's this about?'

'That's what I'm trying to find out, Ms Gardener. It would help if you gave me a summary – *brief*, if possible – of this meeting. What was the reason for it? What happened to make you voice opinions about Dr Hughes?'

'Oh dear! It all seems very petty now.'

'Please.'

Sergeant Lovatt was expecting a rambling account but, in the event, it was surprisingly concise. George explained their common interest in Howard Stamp and referred to the differences between

113

herself and Jonathan as a 'personality clash'. Their dislike had been mutual, and she'd recognized very early that she'd be walking on eggshells if she tried to work with him. Their attitudes to life were diametrically opposed – possibly because she was a generation older and Dr Hughes aspired to more sophisticated standards than she cared about or was capable of achieving – so she had found it impossible to take the meeting further.

'I'm sorry if he's offended,' she finished, 'but I did explain that it wasn't a racist issue. Sometimes chemistry works and sometimes it doesn't. Sadly, in this case it didn't . . . and I wasn't prepared to hand my notes to someone whose motives I distrusted.'

'Mm.'

'Does that help, Sergeant?'

Not really . . . 'Did he say he was feeling ill while he was with you, Ms Gardener?'

'No.'

'Did he *look* ill?'

Another hesitation. 'If you'll forgive what appears to be another racist remark . . . his skin was too dark to tell. I know when white people are ill – even strangers – but I'm not well enough acquainted with black faces to recognize symptoms. He mopped his brow fairly regularly and didn't eat much – but there was a fire in the room and I assumed he didn't like Roy's food.' Her concern sounded in her voice. 'Now I feel awful. *Is* he ill? Is that why you've called?'

'He appears to have left his wallet and passport at the Crown and Feathers, Ms Gardener. It upset him. Without a return ticket, he had no means of getting back to London in time for the opera.'

'I see,' she said, although the lack of conviction in her voice suggested the opposite. 'Why didn't he phone Roy?'

The sergeant stared across his desk at Andrew. 'Perhaps he was embarrassed. There seem to have been some very unfortunate remarks made at this meeting. Thank you for your help.'

He replaced the receiver. 'I need verifiable contact details before he leaves, Mr Spicer. However, I see no reason to detain him any longer tonight. I believe your assessment of your friend is right – that he has money difficulties and that the loss of his wallet pushed him off balance. It can be retrieved from the Crown and Feathers where he left it. I'll give you directions there, although I suggest you leave Dr Hughes in the car and collect it from Mr Trent yourself. If your friend gets himself into any more trouble tonight, he will not go back to London. Understood?'

Andrew nodded. 'Is this the end of it?'

Lovatt's expression was unreadable. 'I've no idea, Mr Spicer. I shall submit a report but I can't say whether any further action will be taken.' He stood up. 'If your reading of your friend is accurate, then you should encourage him to seek professional help. I repeat, unusual behaviour is taken seriously these days . . . whatever the reasons for it.'

*

Andrew checked his watch as he shut the passenger door on Jonathan. It was after ten o'clock and he was desperately hungry. He toyed with the idea of finding something to eat before driving to Highdown, but he didn't think he could do it and reach the Crown and Feathers before closing time. It made him irritable, and he slammed his own door with unnecessary force as he climbed in behind the wheel.

'I'm sorry,' said Jonathan quietly. 'I'd have chucked those letters in a bin if I'd known they were going to call you.'

Andrew fired the engine and reversed out of the police car park. 'Not your fault,' he said with commendable control. 'Better someone who knows you than someone who doesn't.'

Jonathan clamped his hands between his knees. 'Better no one at all. I should have taken the first train.'

Andrew never held grudges. 'You were a breakdown waiting to happen, pal. All you'd have done is postpone it.' In an uncharac- teristic gesture of affection he punched Jonathan lightly on the shoulder. 'Be grateful it didn't happen at the opera. You'd have gone to pieces watching poor old Falstaff being pilloried – and that would have been horribly public.'

'You can't get more public than Bournemouth Central.'

'Certainly not if you're Jamaican. The brothers don't seem to have found Dorset yet.'

Jonathan turned away to stare out of the window.

'You're black, Jon, and it's tearing you apart. However much you don't want to admit it, you have to address it at some point.'

'What do you want me to say? I'm black and I'm proud?'

'Why not? It's my mantra. I say it all the time. I'm a short, fat, ugly white bloke so I tell myself, "I'm black and I'm proud" and I go out and strut my stuff. It doesn't mean anyone sees anything except a short, fat, ugly white bloke, but it gives me a hell of a buzz. I'd swap with you any day.'

'No, you wouldn't. It's hell being black.'

'Would *you* swap with me?'

'Yes.'

Andrew laughed. 'Like hell you would! It's no fun being five foot five. I can't even reach the pedals on this blasted car without jamming the seat against the steering wheel. You need a big personality to be a midget.'

'At least you've *got* a car.'

Andrew refused to rise and a silence fell. He wanted more explanation than Jonathan had given but he was wary of provoking further self-indulgent misery. Whether Jon was genuinely depressive, or simply depressed by a combination of circumstances, he was in no mood to view his situation objectively. And that was a pity because his best opportunity to learn how to do it was now. Objectivity was a talent Andrew had in spades, and not for the first time he wondered what Jonathan would say if he knew the truth about his agent.

Jonathan watched Andrew follow two signs to Highdown before he spoke. 'Where are we going?'

'You dropped your wallet and passport at the Crown and Feathers. We're stopping off for them on the way.'

'Who says?'

'The sergeant phoned the landlord. He found them after you left.'

Jonathan leaned his head back and closed his eyes. 'He can't have done,' he murmured. 'I took everything out of my breast pocket and put it in my briefcase when I removed my jacket. George Gardener watched me do it. I put the passport in the wallet and the wallet in the flapped pocket.'

'Then it fell out,' said Andrew reasonably.

'No. I checked when I put the correspondence back in the case. It's habit. The last wallet I had was stolen at a party when I left my jacket lying around. Now I always remove it and put it somewhere safe. And I never go anywhere without my passport.'

'OK.'

The corners of Jonathan's mouth lifted in a faint smile. 'Don't you believe me?'

'I'm too tired to care,' Andrew said bluntly, drawing up behind a black BMW. 'It doesn't make any difference anyway. The sergeant told me to pick the damn stuff up from the Crown and Feathers, and that's what I'm going to do . . . the emphasis being on *I*, Jon. You can wait in the car while I go inside.'

*

There were a few more customers in the bar than when Jonathan had been there but Andrew's impressions were no more favourable than his friend's. He approached a young woman behind the bar. 'Is Roy Trent around?' he asked.

'He's at the back. Can I help?'

'A friend of mine left his wallet here at lunchtime. I believe Roy's expecting someone to call for it.'

'Oh, yes.' She looked doubtful. 'He told me it'd be a policeman.'

'The man he spoke to was Sergeant Lovatt. He said he would send a car . . . but he didn't specify who would be in it. I was volunteered.' He took out a card. 'My name's Andrew Spicer and I'm a literary agent. The wallet belongs to one of my authors, Jonathan Hughes. Would you mind asking Roy to bring it out?'

'I guess it's OK.' She raised the hatch in the counter. 'If you go through that door over there, it takes you past the saloon and into the kitchen. It's a white door. He's in there.'

Andrew questioned the business's viability as he negotiated the walkway behind the counter of the darkened, empty saloon. Overheads alone must have been crippling, and to keep a room that size unoccupied was financial suicide. Nor did it make any sense. All the manager had to do was recruit a decent chef and build a reputation for good eating. He crossed the hall where Jonathan had stood listening to George's outburst, tapped on the white door opposite and pushed it open.

A man was sitting at the table watching a couple of television monitors in the corner. He switched one off as Andrew came in, then rose aggressively to his feet. 'You're in the wrong room, mate. This is private.'

'The barmaid told me to come through. Are you Roy Trent?'

'Yes.'

Andrew proffered his card. 'My name's Andrew Spicer. I'm Jonathan Hughes's agent. Sergeant Lovatt asked me to pick up his wallet and passport from you.'

Trent glanced at the card, then used his bulk to shepherd Andrew out of the room. 'She's a complete dipstick, that girl,' he said with irritation. 'I left them behind the till in the bar and told her to hand them over when the car arrived. If you retrace your steps and tell her I said you could have them, you'll be fine.' He looked up the stairs as footsteps sounded on the landing.

Andrew followed his gaze. 'It wasn't her fault. She was expecting a policeman.'

A woman appeared on the landing and started down the steps, only to pause when she saw Roy had company. The light was dim but Andrew had a glimpse of a pale face beneath a dark fringe before the landlord thrust against him and forced him to step backwards. 'I'll come with you,' he said affably. 'Knowing Tracey, she probably won't be able to find them. You know the saying the lights are on but there's no one at home – it was written for her. She's pretty enough – decorates the bar nicely – but that's about all.'

Andrew, annoyed by the shoving, recognized that Trent was talking for the sake of talking and decided to dig his heels in. 'Is that the woman who helped Jonathan at the station?' he asked, coming to an abrupt halt and turning round. 'If so, I'd like to thank her.'

Trent shook his head. 'No.'

'No what? No, it wasn't her . . . or no, I can't thank her?'

'It wasn't her.'

Andrew showed surprise. 'How do you know without asking? She matches the description Jon gave, and the woman said she knew you.'

Trent's smile didn't reach his eyes. 'A lot of people know me, mate, but that's not the lady that helped your friend. This one's just arrived.' He gestured impatiently to Andrew to proceed. 'Now . . . do you want this wallet or not?'

Andrew led the way back into the lounge bar and watched Trent retrieve a slim black leather holder from behind the till with a passport tucked between its folds. 'Check it by all means,' he said, 'but, like I told the copper who phoned, there's very little in it. If anything's missing, it went missing before Dr Hughes got here.'

Andrew opened it and flicked through the contents. 'Nothing's missing,' he agreed. 'The only thing unaccounted for is how it came to drop out of his briefcase. It's the old-fashioned upright sort and it doesn't fall over very easily. Even if it did, it wouldn't lose its contents.'

There was a lull in the conversation on the other side of the bar as curiosity drew the customers to listen. Suddenly, Trent had time on his hands. 'Listen, mate, I'm just the guy who found it,' he said good-humouredly. 'If it wasn't in his briefcase then it was in his jacket pocket. I don't see it matters one way or the other – long as he gets it back. You just tell him I'm glad it worked out for the best.'

Andrew smiled. 'Ms Gardener watched him transfer it from his jacket to the case . . . and Dr Hughes checked that it was still there before he left the pub.'

Trent shrugged. 'Then he made a mistake. What's the big deal, anyway? You said yourself there's nothing missing.' He caught the eye of one of his customers and pulled a comical face. 'What's the world coming to, eh, Tom? You keep a guy's wallet safe, and the next thing you know you're being hauled over the coals for it. Me, I was expecting thanks . . . but I might as well have been pissing in the wind. Forget gratitude – ' he shifted his attention back to Andrew – 'it's all about compensation these days.'

Andrew chuckled as he tucked the wallet into his own breast pocket. 'At least be honest – er – *mate*. The police have already told you there's no question of compensation.' His eyes snapped in challenge. 'I'm sure you know as well as anyone that truth is in the detail . . . and I'm one of those boring people who finds detail interesting.' He extended an open palm. 'Thank you. Jon will be very grateful to have everything back intact.' He gripped Trent's hand, very much as Jonathan had done earlier, crunching the metacarpals in a surprisingly strong grasp for a small man. 'It's been interesting seeing the way you do business.'

Nine

ANDREW FOLDED himself into the car and leaned across Jonathan to retrieve his mobile from the dashboard pocket. He punched in the numbers for directory enquiries. 'Yes, please, Bournemouth. The Birches, Hathaway Avenue . . . it's a nursing home.' The sergeant wasn't the only one with a retentive memory, he thought, as he clicked onto the nursing home number. 'Yes, hello, I'm sorry to bother you at such a late hour but I was wondering if I could have a quick word with George Gardener . . . no, it's not personal . . . it's a follow-up on the call she had earlier from Sergeant Lovatt.' He absorbed the irritation from the other end. 'I do apologize. You have my guarantee I'll only keep her for a minute or two. Yes, I'll wait . . . thank you.'

He plugged the mobile into the car microphone, then took out Jonathan's wallet and handed it to him. 'Trent's a bastard,' he said cheerfully, 'and I think I've just seen your dark-haired thief.'

Jonathan looked at him in surprise. 'You don't know what she looks like.'

'No,' Andrew agreed, 'but she had a dark fringe and Trent didn't want me anywhere near her. He frogmarched me away.'

A breathy voice came through the car speakers. 'Hello. This is George Gardener.'

'Andrew Spicer, Ms Gardener. Jonathan's agent. You contacted him through my office, if you remember.'

'They said it was the sergeant again.'

'It's the same matter. I was with Sergeant Lovatt when you spoke to him earlier. I wonder if you'd be kind enough to confirm one small detail for me. Jon tells me you watched him take off his jacket and put his wallet and passport in his briefcase. Is that right?'

'Yes,' she said without hesitation. 'He was very meticulous about it.'

'Did he take it out again at any point?'

'No . . . well, not when I was in the room with him at least. He may have done so after I left.' There was a beat of silence. 'I don't understand what's going on. Why all these questions? What's happened to Dr Hughes?'

Andrew stared through the windscreen. *What the hell . . . ?* There'd almost certainly be a piece about it in the local newspaper tomorrow. 'He became distressed after his wallet was stolen,' he said curtly, 'and, unfortunately – the way things are at the moment – a dark-skinned Arab who shows visible agitation is viewed as a threat. He's been under arrest for six hours and was only released after I drove down from London to vouch for him.'

She sounded baffled. 'I thought Roy found the wallet at the pub.'

'Let's just say it was in his possession, Ms Gardener. I picked it up from there ten minutes ago. Whether Dr Hughes dropped it is another matter altogether.'

'I still don't understand.'

'No,' agreed Andrew, 'neither do we, so I suggest you ask Mr Trent for an explanation. It's not as though the wallet was even worth stealing.'

'Was anything missing?'

'No.'

'Is Dr Hughes saying Roy stole it?'

'No,' said Andrew again. 'He believes it was a dark-haired woman on Branksome Station who helped him when he wasn't feeling well.'

She took time to assimilate this information. 'Well, I'm sorry he was ill, but I still don't understand what it has to do with Roy.'

'The woman claimed to be a friend of Mr Trent's . . . and she clearly must be, Ms Gardener, otherwise he wouldn't have been able to return the wallet to me.'

'She said she was a friend of his ex-wife's,' corrected Jonathan in an undertone.

'Did you hear that, Ms Gardener?'

'Was that Dr Hughes speaking?'

'Yes.'

'Oh dear, I'm so sorry. I can't help feeling partly to blame. None of this would have happened if I hadn't been late.'

Jonathan shook his head but didn't say anything.

'He said the woman claimed to be a friend of Mr Trent's ex-wife,' Andrew prompted her. 'She has a dark fringe and speaks with a Dorset accent. Does that ring any bells?'

'I'm afraid not. I've never met his wife, and certainly none of her friends. Perhaps she was lying?'

'Then how did Mr Trent get the wallet back?'

Another silence while she considered the conundrum. 'Perhaps Dr Hughes is mistaken,' she said unhappily. 'Perhaps he took it out again after I left. We were both rather rattled.' She waited for Andrew to respond, and when he didn't: 'It all seems very strange,' she finished lamely.

'I agree. If Mr Trent provides you with an explanation, I'll be interested to hear it.'

She didn't answer immediately. 'If nothing's missing, he'll say it's a storm in a teacup.'

'Of course he will,' Andrew acknowledged. 'He's obviously more used to lying than telling the truth.'

She tut-tutted indignantly. 'That's a terrible accusation to make against a man you don't know.'

'Surely not,' said Andrew ironically. 'As the saying goes: what can you expect from a pig but a grunt?'

*

Cill lit a cigarette and blew the smoke into Roy's face. He'd backed her into a corner of the kitchen and his thrashing finger had been lambasting her for what seemed like hours. It reminded her of their tempestuous marriage before she left him for Nick. 'Give it a rest,' she said sulkily. 'There's no harm done. I got the sodding thing back to you quick enough, didn't I? How was I to know he'd go running to the cops instead of making a phone call?'

'He's a wog, you stupid bitch. They always go to the police. Why the fuck did you do it?'

'Because it seemed like a good idea at the time.' She whooshed out another cloud of smoke to force him into retreat. 'I wanted his address, and the letters only had his agent's address.'

'Why?'

'In case you've been lying to me.'

His eyes narrowed. 'About what?'

'How much you've told the fat spinster. You're too damn friendly with her. I thought maybe she's been pricking your conscience. Nick thinks you've gone soft, Roy – there was a time when the only thing a bleeding heart liberal was worth was a damn good kicking.'

He gave a snort of angry laughter. '*Nick* thinks!' He turned to the CCTV monitor. 'You're married to a gorilla, Cill. All he thinks about is sex and food. You made a bad bargain there, darlin'.'

She ignored him. 'All right, *I* think you've gone soft. What difference does it make? Nick always agrees with me if I give him what he wants.'

'Jesus, you're so thick! What were you planning to do if you did get his address? Kill him? Thanks to me, he was away and done with. George didn't want anything more to do with him.' He jabbed the finger in her face again. 'He's a jessie – no fucking guts; I knew the minute I clapped eyes on him he'd be a pushover. *I* riled *him*, so *he* riled George . . . happens every time. Then you have to stick your nose in and land me with his sodding agent.'

She smacked his finger away. 'What's he going to do?' she demanded crossly. 'The wog's got his wallet back intact. If you stick to your story, there won't be a problem.'

'I know blokes like Spicer. Once they get the bit between their teeth, they never stop. He knows damn well Hughes didn't drop his wallet here.'

'He's a midget,' she said dismissively. 'Since when were you frightened of midgets?'

'Since I was taught some sense. It's a pity you never learnt any, darlin'. Small guys use their brains . . . big guys like your brain-dead husband put all their energy into getting atop the nearest available tart.'

'What's he gonna do?' she repeated sulkily.

'Talk to George,' Roy said grimly. 'I'll put money on it.'

'So?'

'She'll be at me with the questions again.' He brought his fist up and rested it under her chin. 'If you'd let it alone, Cill, she'd've gone on with her research and got precisely nowhere because I was the only source she had.' He moved his knuckles up her soft skin, caressing it gently, before pressing them against her cheekbone. 'Now she'll come looking for you, and if you drop me in it one more time – ' he spread his lips in an evil smile – 'I'll use this in such a way that even the gorilla you married won't recognize you.'

Cill ignored him again. Roy's threats were never more than bluster. 'Nick's getting worse, you know. He's been dropping things, but he won't go near the doctors. I think the paralysis is spreading.'

Roy lowered his fist and turned away. 'Well, you won't be shedding any tears over it. He's worth more to you dead than alive.'

'Maybe I have feelings for him.'

'Don't talk crap,' said Roy dismissively. 'The only feelings you have are for his money. You're getting quite a taste for the high life one way and another.'

'Someone had to look after him.'

He gave an angry laugh. 'You're so full of it, darlin'. You thought you'd get a pussy cat . . . instead you get a drooling lunatic whose anger control mechanism's shot to pieces.'

Her pale eyes glittered malevolently. 'He adores me,' she said, 'always has. I make him feel better about himself.'

'Only because he doesn't know who you are.'

It was true, but she was damned if she'd admit it. Half of Nick's brain had been scrambled seven years ago in London when two Metropolitan coppers ran him head first into a lamp-post before taking their boots to him. They claimed they mistook him for a drug baron who was known to carry a gun. The fact that a gun was never found, the only drugs he had on him were class-C tranquillizers and he was held in a cell for three hours before he was given medical attention meant compensation of two hundred thousand for brain damage, wrongful arrest and imprisonment. It had taken his solicitors five years to win it through the courts, but Cill had thought dumping Roy to play Florence Nightingale to a cripple was a gamble worth taking.

'You won't be shedding tears neither, darlin',' she said, running a soft hand up between Roy's shoulder blades. 'I always said I'd share it, and I will.' She dug her fingernails into the nape of his neck. 'In any case, it was you told me to do it.'

He pressed his fingers into his eye sockets. 'I'll swing for you one of these days, Cill.'

She touched her lips to his cheek. 'Don't be silly, darlin'. I'm the only girl you've ever loved.'

*

It wasn't until Andrew turned onto the A31 and put his foot down that Jonathan roused himself to speak. 'Thanks.'

'Pleasure. We'll stop at the first service station and get something to eat. There's one on the M27.'

'I'm OK. Don't worry about me.'

'I'm not. I'm worrying about myself. I haven't eaten since breakfast.' He glanced at Jonathan's tired face. 'You'll be eating, too, pal, whether you like it or not. You can't go on starving yourself . . . not if you want to remain sane.'

'I'm not starving myself.'

'Then why are your clothes hanging off you?' He flicked the indicator and pulled out into the fast lane of the dual carriageway. 'You can stay with me tonight, then tomorrow I'm taking you to my doctor.'

'I can't. I have a tutorial at eleven.'

'I'll phone your department and say you won't be in till Monday.'

'I really—'

'Cut the crap,' Andrew said sharply. 'I've hauled my arse halfway across the country to bail you out. The least you can do is humour me. If nothing else, the doc will give you some knock-out pills to help you sleep.'

Jonathan hunched his shoulders. 'They don't work. I've tried . . . nothing works when your brain won't switch off.'

'Is it Emma?'

His friend gave a mirthless laugh. 'No.'

'Then what's the problem?'

It was a moment before Jonathan answered. 'The usual,' he said with sudden resignation, as if recognizing that Andrew needed something for his trouble. 'Rueing the day I was born into this bloody awful country . . . wishing I was white and rich. It's an apartheid thing. Either you belong or you don't.'

He spoke with such bitterness that Andrew didn't doubt he believed what he was saying. Perhaps it was true. 'Who said you don't belong?'

Another humourless laugh. 'You mean apart from immigration officials, policemen, Dorset landlords and anyone else who fancies a swipe?'

'Apart from them,' Andrew agreed calmly.

'Everyone's prejudiced – it's been worse since the attack on the Trade Center.'

'That was eighteen months ago, and you've only been twitched since Emma left.'

Anger sparked briefly in Jonathan's eyes. 'Drop it, OK. If it makes you feel comfortable, then go ahead, blame my problems on a failed relationship – it's how you excuse yours.'

'I don't recall ever discussing my problems with you, Jon. We usually pore over yours for hours on end.'

'Yes, well, stop blaming Emma. The truth is what happened today. Strangers don't see *me*, they see someone who isn't a member of their cosy club. You try dealing with that day after day and then tell me you sleep soundly at night.'

'We're all in the same boat. When strangers look at me, they see a bald short-arse with zero status. It's just as painful . . . particularly when women do it. I watch their eyes skate over my head while they look around for a big, handsome fellow with a full head of hair – ' he gave an amused chuckle – 'and I wouldn't mind if I didn't have a preference for tall women. That's life. You have to recognize it's going to happen and be willing to make a few compromises.'

'Like what?'

'Don't wear your heart on your sleeve. People react badly if you show you care. They either take advantage or leg it as fast as they can.' He slowed as they approached a roundabout. 'Calling the police fascists wasn't the best idea you've ever had.'

Jonathan stared grimly through the windscreen. 'Do you know how many times I've been stopped and searched in the last six months? Four, including last night. How many times has it happened to you?'

'In the last six months? Not at all. In my life? Once, when a fight broke out as I left a pub.'

'Point made then. As a kid, I was stopped every other week.'

'Only because you were expecting to be. If you flag a prophecy, it'll fulfil itself immediately. I'm not saying it's fair, but suspicion breeds suspicion.'

'And which came first?' Jonathan growled. 'Police suspicion of me or mine of them. Try applying your simplistic rules to that little conundrum. I was hoping for some sympathy, not another damn lecture on the dangers of alienation. I'd tolerate it if I thought you'd ever experienced it, but you haven't. A broken marriage hardly counts, not when your wife still invites you to dinner and your girls stay weekends.'

'You'll be telling me next how lucky I am,' said Andrew mildly. 'All the joys of family life without the irritation of living with any of them. Despite their age, the parents are fit and independent – courtesy of a share in a thriving little agency – the wife and kids are safely parked with a man who appreciates them – courtesy of a generous divorce settlement – and I can dedicate myself to what I really enjoy doing: working to support them all.'

'Considering the divorce was your fault, you're damn lucky Jenny didn't break off all contact.'

'Mm . . . except she was having an affair too. It's easier to maintain relationships when both parties feel guilty.'

Jonathan looked at him. This was something he hadn't known. 'I thought it was only you.'

'I know you did.'

'You should have told me.'

'Why?'

'I always thought what an idiot you were to chuck Jenny over for a woman who only lasted a few months. I can't even remember her name now. Claire? Carol?'

'Claire,' said Andrew, 'a blonde, blue-eyed bombshell, just like Jenny. They say men are always attracted to the same type of woman, but it doesn't seem to work the other way. Greg – Jenny's lover – is ten feet tall and looks like Brad Pitt. I can see exactly why she was attracted to him. The girls, too. They adore him as much as she does.'

Something in his tone caused Jonathan to frown. 'If Jenny was equally to blame, how come she did so well out of the divorce?'

Andrew glanced at him. 'I made it easy for her.'

'Then you're a fool. She got the house, the bloke and the

kids – ' he made a dismissive gesture – 'and you got a miserable two-up, two-down in Peckham. What kind of trade was that, for Christ's sake? No wonder Claire buggered off.'

Andrew gave a small laugh. 'I'll take that as a compliment. Obviously, I mistook my profession.'

'What does that mean?'

'I'm a better actor than Greg.'

There was a short silence.

'I don't understand.'

'Claire never existed. The only blonde, blue-eyed bombshells I've ever had relationships with are Jenny and the girls. You don't have a monopoly on pride, Jon. What did you expect me to do? Get down on my knees and beg? I was happy as a sandboy – beautiful wife, beautiful children, house, secure job, good social life – then, *wham*, the wife hits me between the eyes with the muscled actor from next door who's been shafting her for months. The irony was, I really liked him . . . still do, as a matter of fact.'

'You're mad,' said Jonathan in disbelief. 'Why would you lie about a thing like that? It's cost you a fortune in guilt money.'

'It depends what you value. As long as the business isn't threatened, I'd rather be thought of as a bit of a dog than an embarrassing burden on my wife's conscience. Do you think Jenny would be on the phone all the time, or Greg would invite me to dinner, if they thought I was a sad, lonely git who still hankered after his ex-wife? Would the girls be happy to stay overnight if I'd slagged off their mother for two-timing me?' He spoke matter-of-factly without any attempt at sympathy. 'More importantly, the parents see their grandchildren whenever they want. They castigate me regularly for causing the break-up but go on treating Jenny as their daughter-in-law. All in all, I'd say it was cheap at the price.'

Jonathan's incredulity deepened. What did a man have to gain by turning himself into a whipping boy for an errant wife and critical parents? '*They were flogged for the failings of others . . . it's a very twisted concept . . .*' 'Why let Jenny off scot-free? She bad-mouthed you enough at the time. I remember her telling me what a shit you were.'

'I hope you agreed with her. I was never too sure she totally believed in Claire.'

'I did as a matter of fact. I said you'd married too young, and the marriage was bound to fail.' He thought back. 'She wasn't very happy about it.'

'Her pride was dented. She thought she was the only woman in my life.'

'What about your pride?'

'Shot to pieces till I invented Claire. She was a great restorative.'

'I'd have wanted revenge.'

Andrew shrugged. 'I couldn't see the point of going to war over something I couldn't control. You can't force people to love you . . . you can't force them to be loyal. All you can do is keep affection alive and hope for the best.'

He was living in cloud cuckoo land, thought Jonathan. 'Are you expecting Jenny to come back?'

'No.'

'Then I don't get it. What's the quid pro quo for acting honourably if no one knows you're doing it?'

'I don't have to walk around with a neon sign on my forehead, saying "loser".'

Jonathan felt the familiar anger knot inside his jaw. 'Meaning that I do, I suppose?'

''Fraid so. You're a sitting duck for the Roy Trents of this world.'

COUNCILLOR G. GARDENER

25 Mullin Street, Highdown, Bournemouth, Dorset BH15 6VX

Andrew Spicer
Spicer & Hardy Authors' Agents
25 Blundell Street
London W4 9TP

2 April 2003

Dear Mr Spicer

I hesitate to write to Dr Hughes as he may not wish to correspond with me, but I would be grateful if you could pass on my apologies to him and my best wishes for his recovery. I have had a long conversation with Sergeant Lovatt and, though he refused to go into details, he did say that Dr Hughes had been unwell.

The circumstances of our meeting were unfortunate, and I take much of the blame. I have some experience of illness, and I should have realized that Dr Hughes's reticence was physiologically based. He was clearly exhausted, but I made no allowances for poor health, jet lag or even the severity of the weather that day. My only excuse is blind dedication to exculpating Howard Stamp, and a long history of disappointment in the attempts I've made to do so. I am now so programmed for failure that I see it before I need to.

Re. our short phone call on the evening of 13 February. Roy Trent stands by his story that Dr Hughes left his wallet at the pub. However, after Sergeant Lovatt gave me the details of Dr Hughes's arrest, I made enquiries at Branksome Station. The clerk in the ticket office remembers Dr Hughes well because some passengers expressed concern about his behaviour. The gist of the clerk's story is as follows:

He thought Dr Hughes was drunk as he was swaying and trying to focus on the other platform to keep his balance. His face was wet – the clerk thought it was rain until he realized Dr Hughes was sweating – and he was clutching his briefcase to his chest. Several trains went through but he didn't take them. At least two people thought he was a suicide bomber trying to pluck up the courage to go through with it. The clerk was worried enough to consider phoning the police. However, a woman approached Dr Hughes for what appeared to be a pre-arranged meeting. They smiled and talked and Dr Hughes gave her his briefcase from which she removed some papers. The clerk remembered seeing the woman earlier in the ticket hall, and assumed Dr Hughes had misunderstood where the meeting was to take place. He admitted he wouldn't have been worried if Dr Hughes hadn't been an Arab – he would have dismissed him as a drunk. He was relieved when the woman helped him onto a train and took the problem out of his hands. She had dark hair and held a scarf to her mouth, but he couldn't remember anything else about her except that she left in a black BMW that had been parked for forty-five minutes in the 'drop-off only' zone.

Because this seemed to validate Dr Hughes's version of events, I made some discreet enquiries about Roy Trent's ex-wife. Her name is Priscilla Fletcher, formerly known as Cill Trent. I was unable to discover her maiden name, but she has been described to me as mid-forties, medium height, slim, dark hair cut in a straight fringe, light-coloured eyes (possibly blue) and attractive. Her current husband, Nicholas Fletcher, is in 'business' – there's some mystery over exactly what he does – and they live in Sandbanks, an expensive part of Poole. She had a child by Roy – a son, now in his thirties (!) – but none by Fletcher. Because of the son, she and Roy remain on good terms. While there is no evidence that this is the woman who approached Dr Hughes, the description seems to fit.

Nevertheless, I remained puzzled as to why Priscilla Fletcher, an apparently wealthy woman (or indeed one of her friends) would have taken the wallet. For this reason I related the clerk's story to Roy Trent, embroidering the description of the woman to more closely resemble Priscilla Fletcher, and asked him what he made of it in view of Dr Hughes's certainty that she was the thief. Roy's reaction was interesting. He treated it as a joke and said if Dr Hughes was right, the woman must have returned to the pub after it closed for the afternoon in order to leave the wallet on the floor of the room where Dr Hughes and I had lunch. And that hadn't happened. I agreed the story was absurd, pointing out that she must also have known where the lunch took place, which would suggest someone very familiar with the running of the pub. Therefore, unless Roy recognized the woman's description, Dr Hughes must be mistaken. Roy agreed that he did *not* recognize the woman's description.

I should say at this point that I've never had reason to disbelieve anything Roy has told me in the past. Our relationship is an informal one, based on two years of friendship after he gave me permission to use his pub as a 'surgery'. I don't claim to know him well – he is not a forthcoming man – but I've always found him pleasant and supportive, particularly with the help he's given me in unearthing information about Howard Stamp. Of course I was intrigued by the lie, particularly as I could see no reason for it. He might easily have said, 'I know several women who match that description, my ex-wife being one, but none of them came to the pub that day.' I was, after all, agreeing with him that Dr Hughes was mistaken.

I was interested enough to do some further research and began by making a number of assumptions, any one of which might have been false, but which seemed worth testing. These are the assumptions I made:

1. Roy's ex-wife stole the wallet.
2. She did so because she: (a) is an opportunist thief; or (b) was told to; or (c) was interested in Dr Hughes; or (d) a combination of the three.
3. If it was an opportunistic theft, how did she know: (a) to return the wallet to Roy; (b) that he would protect her?
4. Because she returned it, she must have known: (a) that Dr Hughes had been at the pub earlier; (b) what he looked like.
5. She knew these facts because: (a) she had been at the pub herself; or (b) they had been given to her by someone else.
6. Apart from myself, Roy Trent is the only other person who knew when, where and why I was meeting with Dr Hughes.
7. The only way Priscilla Fletcher could have known these details is if Roy told her.
8. If theft of money wasn't her motivation, then she wanted to know more about Dr Hughes.
9. She did not ask Roy for details because: (a) she didn't think he would tell her; or (b) he didn't know the answers; or (c) it was he who told her to commit the theft.
10. If (b) or (c), Roy did not want to display undue interest in Dr Hughes by quizzing me about him.

11. Dr Hughes's only reason for coming to Bournemouth was his interest in Howard Stamp.

I already knew that Roy Trent was acquainted with Howard Stamp, if only 'by sight' (Roy's words), but it seemed reasonable to infer that Priscilla Fletcher was also connected with him in some way. Out of curiosity, I went back to the newspaper coverage at the time of Grace Jefferies' murder to see if there was anything I'd overlooked. I came across an unrelated story about a thirteen-year-old called Priscilla 'Cill' Trevelyan who went missing from her home in Highdown a week before Grace's body was found. As yet, I have been unable to establish whether Cill Trevelyan and Priscilla Fletcher are one and the same. However, there are similarities between the photograph of the missing girl and the one I've managed to track down of Priscilla Fletcher/ Trent, taken five years ago at a Crown and Feathers barbecue, courtesy of Jim Longhurst. I hope Dr Hughes will appreciate the irony! (Copies enclosed.)

While I am reluctant to jump to conclusions at this stage, it seems that Cill was subjected to a gang rape before she ran away and this would accord with Priscilla Fletcher (mid-forties) having a son in his thirties. I attach photocopies of the newspaper clippings which might be of interest to Dr Hughes when he's well enough to read them. He will, of course, note immediately that Cill Trevelyan had shoulder-length dark hair. He will also note the descriptions of her assailants – none of whom was named and none of whom was charged through lack of evidence. Interestingly, the story of this missing thirteen-year-old never made it into the national press, presumably because she was posted immediately as a 'runaway'.

There is nothing to link Cill's story with Howard's except the coincidences of time and place and some thought-provoking descriptions. However, the synchronicity of events, coupled with the unnecessary theft of a wallet thirty years later, does raise questions. At the moment I have no idea what the linkage might be, but I am left with the suspicion that Priscilla Fletcher feels she has something to lose if Howard's case is resurrected. I am willing to forward further information that comes my way, if you think Dr Hughes would be interested. I will, of course, understand if he prefers to wash his hands of it.

In conclusion, Roy Trent is not party to this information and, for the foreseeable future, I intend to remain on good terms with him. I would be grateful if you and Dr Hughes would avoid doing anything to prejudice that position. Thanking you in advance,

Yours sincerely

George Gardener

Encs.

Bournemouth Evening News – *Saturday, 30 May 1970*

CONCERN FOR MISSING GIRL

Bournemouth Police today asked for help in the search for Priscilla Trevelyan, 13, who went missing from her home in Highdown during the early hours of this morning. She is 5′ 5″ tall, weighing approximately 8 stone, with shoulder-length dark hair, possibly dressed in blue jeans and a long-sleeved white T-shirt. Known as Cill, the youngster is believed to have run away after an argument with her father.

Mrs Jean Trevelyan, 35, blamed her daughter's school. 'Her father was upset because she was given a week's suspension for fighting. But it takes two to make a fight and the other girl wasn't punished at all. Cill's bright and she knew that wasn't fair.' She broke down as she made a plea for her daughter to come home. 'We love her and we want her back. No one's going to be angry.'

Police are following various lines of enquiry. 'She's mature for her age,' said a spokesman, 'and she was in the company of some older boys three weeks ago. There's a possibility she may be with one of them now. Two were described as dark-haired and of medium build, the third as tall and thin with ginger hair. We are asking these boys to come forward. They have nothing to fear if they know where Cill is. The imperative is her safe return.'

Police have not ruled out abduction. 'Runaways of this age are vulnerable. They may accept offers of help from people who seek only to exploit them.' The Metropolitan Police has been alerted. 'London is a magnet for unhappy children,' said the spokesman.

Bournemouth Evening News – *Monday, 1 June 1970*

HUNT FOR 13-YEAR-OLD CONTINUES

Three teenage boys were released without charge today after being questioned by police over the disappearance of Priscilla Trevelyan. They matched descriptions given by one of her school friends, but all three denied knowing Priscilla or having any knowledge of her disappearance. A police spokesman says there is no evidence to link them with the missing girl.

Priscilla's father, David Trevelyan, 37, was also questioned after neighbours mentioned constant rows between the two. 'They didn't get on,' said one. 'He was worried about her truanting.' Police denied that Trevelyan was a suspect. 'Parents are always questioned in these circumstances,' said a spokesman, 'but we are satisfied Mr and Mrs Trevelyan know nothing of their daughter's disappearance.'

He admitted that the authorities are baffled. 'Several sightings of a girl matching Cill's description have come to nothing, and we are no further forward. After leaving her house she appears to have vanished.' They have made a fresh appeal to the public by issuing a series of photographs of the girl in the hope of jogging memories.

MINETTE WALTERS

Bournemouth Evening News – *Saturday, 25 July 1970*

MOTHER'S ANGUISH OVER MISSING TEEN

It's just two months since 13-year-old Priscilla Trevelyan left home after an argument with her father, yet her file has been shelved and the team looking into her disappearance disbanded. In simple terms, a runaway does not command the same level of police attention as a child who's been abducted, and Priscilla has joined the frightening statistic of 75,000 children under 16 who run away from homes or institutions in this country every year.

While most of these children return after one night away, some 1,000 will still be missing months later. They are in danger of physical and sexual assault, and many of them resort to crime and prostitution to stay alive. 'Cases like these are always difficult,' said PC Gary Prentice who holds a watching brief over Priscilla's file. 'If a runaway doesn't want to be found, there's little the police can do. We've circulated her photograph to other forces and we hope someone will recognize her. Many children return home at Christmas when memories of family are strong. I hope this happens in Cill's case.'

Priscilla's mother, Jean Trevelyan, is heartbroken. She acknowledges that trouble at home was a contributory factor but she insists it's out of character for her daughter not to have telephoned. 'The police say there's no evidence of abduction, but little girls don't vanish into thin air. I wish I'd never mentioned the row with her father. He was trying to support the school's punishment, but it gave the police an excuse to stop looking for her.'

PC Prentice denies this. 'We pursued every lead we were given. Sadly, Cill was a disturbed adolescent with complications at home and at school. She'd been truanting for some time before she decided to run away. There's always concern when a 13-year-old goes missing, but we're optimistic that Cill is bright enough to survive. Her friends described her as "street-smart", which is an American expression she taught them after reading it in a magazine. She used it to describe herself.'

Jean Trevelyan remembers it differently. 'Cill was always in trouble. People expected her to behave responsibly because she was well-developed for her age, but at heart she was like any other 13-year-old. One of her friends told the police she was gang raped before she ran away, but they were less interested in that than they were in the argument she had with her father.'

PC Prentice admits the rape allegation but says there was no evidence to support it. 'If it happened, then it's tragic that Cill was too ashamed to tell anyone about it.' He agreed that the stigma of rape is a disincentive to reporting it. 'Police forces are working on ways to encourage women and girls to come forward,' he said, 'but there's still a long way to go.'

This is no consolation for Jean Trevelyan who sits by her window, praying for Priscilla to come home. 'We've lost more than our daughter,' she weeps, 'we've lost our good name. People say we were unkind, but she was our only child and we wanted the best for her. The police claim to be sympathetic, but they've never once portrayed us as loving parents.'

The photographs of Priscilla that line the room endorse Jean's love for her daughter, but she admits they've only been on display since Priscilla vanished. Like so many mothers, she found the balance between disciplin-ing an errant adolescent and continuing to show love a difficult one. 'We were strict because we worried about her, but we didn't know what worry was until she left. David is devastated by it all. It's a terrible way to learn that the time to show your child affection is when you're most angry. We disciplined her because we loved her, yet she must have believed it was done out of hate or she wouldn't have run away.'

Her greatest anguish is that Priscilla felt unable to tell anyone she'd been raped. 'Her friend said she thought people would say it was her fault because she was wearing a mini-skirt, but we live in a terrible society if a 13-year-old thinks she'll be blamed for what happens to her. The police have cast doubt on the rape, but I know it happened because Cill threw her skirt away. She saved up for it and it was her favourite. She wouldn't have done that if she had nothing to feel ashamed about.'

One is left with a sense of enormous tragedy. A grieving mother, indefinitely confined to her house for fear her daughter comes back to find no one at home. A father crippled by guilt because he upheld a school punishment. A house empty of laughter. A child missing because there was no one she could ask for help.

Bronwen Sherrard

S P I C E R & H A R D Y

AUTHORS' AGENTS 25 BLUNDELL STREET LONDON W4 9TP

Cllr George Gardener
25 Mullin Street
Highdown
Bournemouth
DORSET BH15 6VX

Monday, 7 April 2003

Dear George Gardener,

Thank you for your letter of 2 April, and your kind wishes for
Jonathan's recovery. Prior to your meeting he had been suffering
for some time from severe stomach cramps and nausea which he
foolishly put down to stress and overwork when the problem was
a bleeding ulcer. His trip to the US only exacerbated the problem
and he developed complications on the day he visited you.
Fortunately, it was caught in time and he's now well on the road
to recovery. No thanks to him! I am telling you this because he
won't tell you himself as he feels there are no excuses for his
behaviour. My own view, as I understand from Sergeant Lovatt
that you are not well yourself, is that it was a clash of illnesses
and is best forgotten. May I return the compliment you paid Jon,
and send you my good wishes for *your* speedy recovery.

I enclose a letter from Jonathan re. Priscilla Fletcher/Cill
Trevelyan. However, I wish to stress: (a) his willingness to be
involved in your project; and (b) the expertise he can bring to it.

Jon has many strong points but self-promotion isn't one of them. When he tries, he sounds patronizing. When he doesn't, he looks smug. Both traits are deeply infuriating, but they're easier to ignore if you view them as a disability.

Yours sincerely,

Andrew Spicer

Andrew Spicer
Enc.

DR JONATHAN HUGHES
Flat 2b Columbia Road
West Kensington
London W14 2DD
Email: jon.hughes@london.ac.uk

Saturday, 5 April

Dear George

I'm embarrassed to think how badly I behaved the day we met,
so please don't feel you have anything to apologize for. My trip
to Bournemouth was a salutory lesson in my own stupidity. They
say every cloud has a silver lining, and mine certainly has. I
won't bore you with the Damascene conversion – you probably
hate the cliché as much as I do – suffice it to say that I have
taken Andrew's advice to live at peace with myself.

I was fascinated by your letter and the enclosures. You may by
now have validated or refuted your assumptions. However, I
draw your attention to the following:

• Having studied the photograph of Priscilla Fletcher, I believe
  she may have been the woman who approached me on
  Branksome Station.
• While there is a similarity between the photographs of Priscilla
  Fletcher and Cill Trevelyan, it appears superficial. It may be a
  result of the child having lost puppy fat, or the fact that her
  picture is in black and white, but to my eyes the bone structure
  of the faces is very different. Cill has a heavier jaw and more
  pronounced cheekbone than Priscilla's rather delicate

equivalents. Cill's eyes look darker, although this may be due to the monochrome.

- Priscilla is extremely fair-skinned, giving her a 'Snow White' look – dark hair, pale face. While it's a common enough combination, fair skin is more usually associated with red or blonde hair, except in the Irish and Welsh(!!). Interestingly, my impression of the woman at Branksome Station was that her look was a manufactured one. The photograph gives the same impression. (Painted eyes, reshaped eyebrows, dyed [?] hair.)
- If these are the same person, then there are some interesting discrepancies.
- If they are two different people, then the similarity is striking, particularly as they are both called Priscilla, and Cill Trevelyan would now be in her mid-forties.

I imagine you have already scoured the newspaper archives for any information on Cill Trevelyan's return. You may even have located her parents, assuming they remained in the Bournemouth area. But if, as I suspect, you've found no evidence that she ever came back – (I'm guessing you did this research before you wrote to Andrew) – then the obvious question is: if Priscilla is *not* Cill, then why would she want to adopt the name and looks of a girl who vanished thirty-plus years ago?

Here are some other details that struck me as I read the newspaper clippings:

- Compare: 'Three teenage boys . . . matched descriptions given by one of her [Cill's] school friends . . .' with Jean Trevelyan's claim: 'One of her friends told the police she was gang raped . . .' There are various inferences to be drawn from these two statements: the friend either witnessed the incident or was told about it afterwards; the friend only revealed what had happened after Cill went missing.

- Compare: 'the youngster is believed to have run away after an argument with her father . . .'; 'neighbours mentioned constant rows between the two . . .'; '[her father] was worried about her truanting . . .'; 'Cill was always in trouble . . .'; '[Jean Trevelyan's] greatest anguish is that Priscilla felt unable to tell anyone she'd been raped . . . [Cill] thought people would say it was her fault . . .' The strong presumption in all these statements is that David Trevelyan would *not* have been sympathetic if Cill had admitted to being raped.

- 'It takes two to make a fight and the other girl wasn't punished at all.' Again, there are various inferences to be drawn from this. The commonest reason for children to fall out is when one says, 'I'll tell on you.' If 'the friend' was also 'the other girl', then the rape was the secret they shared and a threat to reveal it may have been the cause of the fight. If it was a different girl, then either Cill lost her temper over anything and everything *or* the secret was out. The fact that Cill was punished and the other girl wasn't suggests Cill started it and/or was the more violent and/or refused to give a reason.

- From all of the above references, it is reasonable to accept PC Prentice's analysis: 'Cill was a disturbed adolescent with complications at home and at school.' (There was an unusual amount of aggression in her life – hitting out at school suggests she was no stranger to being hit at home.) While a child like that may well abscond – research suggests that most runaways have suffered physical or sexual abuse – she was unlikely to keep her name. Indeed, if she hadn't been found in two months, and was still alive, she *must* have been calling herself something else. I believe that's the name she would continue to go by – *even if she returned home* – because it would have been a demonstration to her father that the rules had changed and a new 'she' was setting the agenda.

I don't pretend to know any better than you which assumptions are correct. However, I do believe it might be worth trying to put a name to Cill Trevelyan's school friend. Presumably she was the same age as Cill, and a 13-year-old would have been deeply traumatized by the rape (more so if she witnessed it and did nothing to help), closely followed by the guilt of not speaking out, a spiteful threat to 'tell' and Cill's disappearance.

I am no psychologist so I'll rely on your expertise to boot this idea into touch if it's too far-fetched. *The schoolfriend seems a more likely contender for Priscilla Fletcher than Cill Trevelyan.* (Transference reaction? Mitigation of guilt by 'resurrecting' the wronged person? Envy/hero-worship – Cill got away and she didn't?) Are any of these credible? Can trauma in childhood define behaviour through to middle age?

I have failed dismally to make a connection between Cill's story and Howard's, although I have noted the skinny, ginger-haired 'rapist'. (Also the medium-build dark-haired duo, one of whom may have been Roy [?] Is that your thinking?) All I can say re. the boys is that it would require considerable chutzpah to leave a police station following questioning about a rape, only to break in on a vulnerable woman a few hours later and torture her to death. Again, I rely on you for an analysis of juvenile behaviour.

Finally – unless you come back with evidence that Cill resurfaced – my strongest suspicion from reading the newspaper reports is that she never ran away at all, but was killed by her father. According to one of the articles, David Trevelyan was exonerated after being questioned by police, but I would need some very

strong evidence to believe that. Statistics don't lie. Children who
vanish into 'thin air' are usually dead, and children who 'vanish'
are usually victims of their parents. David Trevelyan was a
violent man, and I fear Cill may have made the mistake of trying
to excuse 'the fight' by telling him about her rape.

I look forward to hearing from you again.

Yours sincerely

From: George Gardener [geo.gar@mullinst.co.uk]
Sent: Tues 08/04/03 19:20
To: jon.hughes@london.ac.uk
Subject: Cill Trevelyan

Dear Jonathan, You are absolutely right. I can find no record that
Cill Trevelyan ever resurfaced. David & Jean Trevelyan left
Highdown in the 80s but I have no forwarding address as yet. My
new friend (!) Sergeant Lovatt is looking into it for me. He is also
trying to locate the file on Howard. Apparently records from all the
divisions were collected together in a central archive 20+ years ago.
However, as redundant files are usually destroyed, he isn't holding
out much hope. I'm keeping my fingers crossed.

Re: the schoolfriend and transference. Transference is commonly
an emotional response – often experienced during therapy – where
people transfer personality characteristics of parents/partners/
friends to someone else. It's an immature reaction, where neurotic
patterns of behaviour, often formed in childhood, colour subsequent
relationships – e.g. in very simple terms, a child who grows up
afraid of a stern father will fear all men in authority. Clearly, it's more
complicated than that but, generally, transference relates to an
imbalance, or perceived imbalance, of power within a relationship,
which is taken forward to other relationships and will *certainly
persist into middle age*. [NB: It's not necessarily a negative
response. If a child grows up admiring his father, he will look up to
men in authority.]

If you're right that Priscilla Fletcher is the school friend, then it's
highly likely that trauma at 13 has lingered into adult life. However
the most obvious contender for that is Cill herself as she's the one
who experienced the abusive relationships! In some ways, I'd say
idolatry or hero-worship is closer to what you're looking for.

Interestingly, Howard was a case study in hero-worship. You made the point yourself when you said he aped his hero, Ginger Baker. He wanted to look like Baker, wanted to have the courage to rebel in the same way, wanted to be admired in the way Baker was. It was a displacement of his unloved self to a more acceptable substitute. I shall have to do more research, but it's not inconceivable that Cill became a 'totem' to a traumatized child, particularly if her disappearance meant the loss of a best friend. I question how long those feelings would have lasted, however.

I shall certainly follow your advice to track down the friend. If nothing else, she will be able to tell us something about Highdown in 1970. Fred Lovatt suggested that one of the reasons Cill's disappearance dropped out of the headlines so quickly was because attention shifted within days to Grace's murder and Howard's arrest. The coincidences of time and place continue to fascinate me, however. It seems so unlikely that two unrelated events should happen within such a short period in the same area, although I take your point about the boys and chutzpah. It's not unknown, of course. Jack the Ripper killed two women within half an hour of each other, even though he'd been disturbed performing the first murder and the hue and cry was up. Adrenalin does strange things to the mind as well as the body.

Best wishes, George

Ten

9 Galway Road, Boscombe, Bournemouth
Friday, 11 April 2003, 6.30 p.m.

GEORGE DREW UP in front of a smart semi-detached house and left the motor running while she listened to the end of a dispatch from Baghdad. The news was still dominated by the fall of the Iraqi capital, although reports of rampant looting now took precedence over correspondents' and politicians' surprise at the lack of opposition to the US army. For George, a long-time peace campaigner, the three weeks of over-the-top war coverage had been depressing. State-sponsored killing had become a showpiece for technology – smart bombs, laser-guided missiles, embedded journalists with videophones – when the reality on the ground was chaos and death.

She sighed as she switched off the engine. Ideas and words were being twisted to distance sensitive Western consciences from what was being done on their behalf. The killing of Iraqi civilians was 'collateral damage'; the deaths of British servicemen at the hands of their own side were 'friendly fire' or 'blue on blue'; questions about the failure to find weapons of mass destruction – the excuse for war – the *only* excuse – were brushed aside with 'we know they exist'. How? In the same way the police had 'known' that Howard Stamp was a murderer?

Justice demanded honesty, and there was no honesty in validating war through euphemism and vague suspicion. She particularly disliked assertions that the aim of invasion was to bring democracy to the Iraqi people. You have no vote, was the overbearing message. Do as we say because we know what's good for you. It was the same sanctimonious self-righteousness that had caused every miscarriage of justice in every democracy in the world.

I accuse you because I dislike you . . . I accuse you because I can . . .

J'accuse . . .

*

It had been easier to obtain the name of Priscilla Trevelyan's school friend than George had feared. A request to the *Bournemouth Evening News* to find out whether Bronwen Sherrard, the byline on the piece 'Mother's anguish over missing teen', was still on the staff had come up with a negative. However, the name was uncommon enough to prompt a not very hopeful look in the local telephone directory. Even when she found an entry and dialled the number, she wasn't optimistic it would be the same woman. Or if it was, that she'd remember details from an article she'd written in 1970.

However, it was indeed the same woman, now retired, and though she couldn't recall the information off the top of her head, she had kept meticulous files of all her work. George explained her interest by saying she was researching Highdown of the 1960s and 1970s, and Bronwen phoned back the next day with the name Louise Burton and the additional bonus that the family had been rehoused in Galway Road, Boscombe. 'I never spoke to her or her parents,' she finished. 'When I went to the house, her mother called the police.'

'Why?'

'I imagine they'd had enough of doorstepping journalists,' said the woman with a laugh, 'so let's hope you have better luck than I did.'

'Do you know where they lived when they were in Highdown?'

There was rustle of paper. 'Number 18, Mullin Street,' said

Bronwen helpfully, completely unaware of the extraordinary face that George Gardener was pulling at the other end of the line.

*

A check of the electoral register had shown that a Mr William Burton and a Mrs Rachel Burton were still living at 9 Galway Road, and George rang the bell in the full expectation that she was about to meet Louise's parents. But it was a man of around forty who answered the door. 'Mr Burton?'

'Yes.' He was tall and broad-shouldered, with rolled-up shirt-sleeves and tattoos on his muscular arms. Behind him, somewhere down the corridor, a television blared at full blast, overlayed by the sound of girls arguing. He wiped his hands on a towel and smiled enquiringly. 'Sorry about the row. What can I do for you?'

George pulled one of her faces. 'If they're killing each other, I can always come back later.'

He listened for a moment. 'Nn-nn. It's fairly mild tonight. They only get really het-up when they find the other one's nicked their clothes.'

'Your daughters?'

He nodded. 'Identical twins with fiery hair and fiery tempers.' He grinned amiably. 'You can have them if you like. We'll pay good money to be rid . . . the wife's close to strangling them.'

George laughed. 'How old?'

'Sixteen. I keep telling them they're old enough to marry but they won't take the hint.' He flicked the towel over his shoulder and started to unroll his sleeves. 'To be honest, I'm not sure there'd be any takers. The lads can hear 'em coming a mile off and they do a runner immediately.' He chuckled. 'How can I help?'

He was too nice to be related to Priscilla Fletcher, George thought, raising a clipboard with a photocopied page from the electoral register. 'Are you William Burton?'

'That's me.'

She offered a hand. 'My name's George Gardener. I'm a councillor. I'm canvassing for the local elections on 1 May.' It had

153

seemed a reasonable cover story to detain him long enough to ask a few questions – the elections were certainly happening – but she realized it was a mistake when his face closed immediately.

He released her hand and started to close the door. 'Sorry, not interested. We won't be voting.'

'May I ask why not?'

'I'm a fireman,' he said, nodding to a cap and uniform jacket hanging on a hook in his hallway, 'and I'm sick to death of politicians telling me I'm unpatriotic because they chose to declare war while I was trying to strike for a decent salary. How does that make me unpatriotic?'

'Oh dear,' said George, pulling a face. The withdrawal of labour had been very divisive. 'The only answer I can give you is that I'm against both the war and the strikes. I've always believed that negotiation is the only way to solve problems.'

'Yes, well, war was declared in our names without anyone asking our permission to do it.' He obviously felt strongly enough to elevate George to the position of Prime Minister because he glared at her as if she were responsible for sending the troops in. 'Over a million people said no, and that was just the tip of the iceberg. For every *one* who slogged up to the peace march in London, there were another *ten* who couldn't make it.'

'Were you on it, Mr Burton?'

'Mm. Fat lot of good it did.'

'Me, too.' She put a hand on the door to prevent him closing it. 'Were your daughters with you?'

'Yes.'

'Then that's the good it did, Mr Burton,' she said earnestly. 'Youth's been quiet for too long, but it found a voice over this. I've been campaigning for nuclear disarmament for thirty years but I've never seen anything like that march.' She lowered her clipboard but kept her other hand on the door. 'You can't vote for me because this isn't my ward – and I'm an independent, so I have no clout at Westminster. My view is that abstention is a perfectly honourable tradition, so I won't waste your time trying to persuade you out of it.'

He exerted mild pressure against her hand and came up against resistance. 'But?'

'The person I really want to speak to is Louise Burton. I assumed the Mr and Mrs Burton in this house were her parents, but obviously not. You must be her brother, unless it's pure coincidence that Burtons have been registered here since the seventies.'

The question was clearly one he'd answered before, because he didn't seem put out by it. 'It's getting on for thirty years since Lou left. The folks bought the house off the council at the end of the 1980s and I took it over seven years ago when they retired to Cornwall. I don't think Lou's been back once in all that time.'

'Do you know where she is now?'

He shook his head. 'We lost track of her after she got married.'

'Do you know what she's calling herself?'

Billy didn't answer immediately. 'Are you a private detective?'

'No,' she said in surprise. 'I'm what I said I was – a councillor . . . for Highdown ward. Also a care worker at the Birches in Hathaway Avenue. I live in Mullin Street, where you and your family used to live before you were transferred here.' She paused. 'Do you have many private detectives looking for your sister?'

'I presume it's Cill Trevelyan you're interested in – it was Lou's only fifteen minutes of fame.' She nodded. 'OK, well, the Trevelyan parents pay up every so often to see if a private agency can track her down. The last one came about three years ago. They always get to Lou eventually – at least to the fact that she used to live here – but it doesn't help them. Apart from the fact we don't know where she is, she had no more idea than the rest of us what happened to Cill.' He shrugged apologetically. 'Sorry.'

'What about your parents? Have they kept in touch with her?'

'No.' He seemed to feel his parents needed defending. 'It wasn't their fault. They did their best, but she always thought the grass was greener somewhere else. She left school at sixteen, became a hairdresser and got married almost immediately . . . then we lost track. There was a rumour she went to Australia, but I don't know if that's true.'

George looked crestfallen. 'Oh dear! I was so hopeful of being able to speak to her when I found that Burtons were still registered here.'

'Sorry,' he said again, stepping back to end the conversation.

She kept her hand on the door. 'What was the name of her husband?'

He smiled rather cynically. 'No idea. We weren't invited to the wedding. As far as I remember, she referred to him as Mike when I managed to track her down for the folks, but he was in jail so I didn't meet him.' He shook his head at her expression. 'It happens,' he said. 'I was luckier. I married a gem.'

George nodded. 'I know it's a terribly personal question, but did she have a baby when she was fourteen or fifteen?'

He hesitated. 'Not that I'm aware of.'

It was a strangely evasive answer. 'Surely you'd have noticed,' said George with a smile.

'I was a lot younger than she was, so I probably wouldn't have understood what was going on. Put it this way: I don't recall a baby suddenly arriving in the family.'

'Was she ever married to a man called Roy Trent who runs the Crown and Feathers pub in Highdown?'

His eyes held hers for a moment and she thought she saw a flicker of indecision. 'Not that I'm aware of,' he repeated, 'but, like I say, we lost track of her.'

Perhaps it was his hesitations, or the fact that he didn't give a firm negative, that prompted George to pose her next question. 'Was Louise raped at the same time as Cill?' she asked bluntly. 'Is that why the family was rehoused?'

'No.' He was back on firm ground. 'She saw it happen but she wasn't involved. Look, there's no mystery about it. We were moved because she was frightened out of her wits – first the rape, then Cill running away, then the police questions. My parents put her in a different school so she wouldn't keep being reminded about it.'

'Would she have told your parents if she'd been raped? Cill didn't tell hers.'

'It was a different time. Mini-teens today wear crop tops, but if they did it then they were accused of being tarts. Cill's dad went ape-shit every time she put on a miniskirt.'

'And *your* parents?'

'The same.' Another shrug. 'Me, too, if it comes to that. I'm shotgun Dad. I hate it when my kids prance around half naked . . . it's an open-invitation to the first predator to have a go.'

'Then Louise may have been raped as well, but never admitted to it,' George said reasonably.

'She wasn't raped,' he said bluntly, 'and she didn't get pregnant as a result . . . which I assume is the point you're trying to make.' His eyes hardened suddenly. 'Look, there was enough damn gossip at the time. None of us needs it resurrected.'

George dropped her hand. 'I'm sorry. I didn't mean to upset you. It's just that – ' she broke off on a sigh. 'Does the name Priscilla Fletcher mean anything to you?'

'No.'

She thought he was going to slam the door in her face, but he didn't. He waited, as if he expected her to go on. 'Priscilla lives in Sandbanks,' she said. 'She's in her mid-forties and looks like an older version of Cill Trevelyan. She used to be married to Roy Trent and had a son by him when she was in her early teens. At that time, she was calling herself Cill. Do you know if your sister named Roy Trent to the police as one of the rapists?'

Billy avoided the question. 'Half a minute ago you were making out this woman was Lou, now you're saying she's Cill Trevelyan. Who is she?'

'I don't know, Mr Burton. That's what I'm trying to find out.'

She flipped over the top page on the clipboard and turned the pad towards him. 'This photograph was taken five years ago. Do you recognize her?'

His expression was unreadable. 'No.'

'Does it remind you of Cill Trevelyan?'

He shook his head. 'I barely remember her. I was ten years old when she left.'

George flipped to the next page. 'This is the picture of her that was in the newspapers.'

Billy stared at it for several seconds and his expression was genuinely appalled. 'Christ! She's so *young*!'

'She was only thirteen, Mr Burton, just a child still.'

'Yes, but . . . I've always had it in my head she was quite grown-up. Christ!' he said again, taking the board and staring at the image. 'She still has her puppy fat. My two looked older than this at thirteen.' With an abrupt movement he flipped back to the photograph of Priscilla Fletcher. 'Maybe you should tell the Trevelyans . . . give 'em a chance to talk to this woman. Far as I know, they've never come close to finding a match.'

'Do you have an address or a phone number for them?'

He shook his head. 'No, but I think I kept the card of the last agency that came looking. They'd know.' He glanced at his watch. 'I can't look for it now – I'm on shift in an hour – but if you give me a contact number I'll see what I can do tomorrow.'

George took back the clipboard and wrote her name and number on the back of the electoral register duplicate. 'Why do you remember Cill as quite grown-up?' she asked curiously as she handed the page to him.

'She was a bit of a tart . . . liked talking sexy. It's what got her raped.'

'How do you know?'

Billy's expression blanked immediately. 'Guesswork,' he said, before nodding a curt farewell and closing the door.

*

George would have put money on him trying to avoid any future contact so she was surprised to receive a call the following morning. He was briskly matter of fact, quoting the name and details of a Bristol-based detective agency. 'You need to be careful how you go about it,' he warned. 'I talked it over with my wife last night and she said it would be cruel to raise the Trevelyans' hopes if it isn't Cill.'

Privately, George agreed with him. She was back on night shifts and she'd mulled the problem over during her quiet periods. Without any expectation of William Burton coming through with the name of the detective agency, she had considered hiring one herself to find out who Priscilla Fletcher was. A quick browse on the Internet on her return home gave promises of 'confidentiality', 'discretion' and 'caution', with hourly prices and flat fees not entirely beyond her bank balance.

Even so, there were too many ethical dilemmas for someone of George's sensibilities. Whoever Priscilla Fletcher was, she had the same right to privacy as anyone else – unless she'd committed a crime – and George could hardly argue that the theft of a wallet was justifiable grounds for breaking her cover. If she was Cill Trevelyan or Louise Burton, then it was a moral minefield. Both women had chosen to distance themselves from their families, and George had no entitlement to expose them. Yet that would be the inevitable outcome if a detective agency made a link with Cill, for George had no confidence that the Trevelyans' long search for their daughter wouldn't prompt a sympathetic – but *discreet* – approach in return for a fee.

Nor, from a selfish point of view, could George see what use the information would be to her. If the woman turned out to be Cill or Louise, George would still have to persuade her to tell her story; and what leverage could she use except threats of exposure? '*Tell me what I want to know or I'll give this information to your parents.*' Apart from the absurdly childish nature of the menace, George wouldn't be able to carry it through. It rubbed against the grain of all her principles – namely the inalienable right of every individual to life, liberty and the pursuit of happiness.

In the early hours she'd recognized how much easier it would be if she could approach the Trevelyans' detective agency as a concerned citizen who'd spotted a similarity between Cill and a woman living in Sandbanks. Whatever the outcome, they'd feel obliged to tell her something, if only to stop her pursuing the search herself. Nevertheless, she appreciated as soon as William Burton gave her the agency's details that one avenue had been closed. George didn't believe he'd have given them to her if he thought Priscilla Fletcher was his sister. *Or would he?* Was it a double bluff? 'Perhaps I should just abandon it,' she said with a disingenuous sigh. 'If it is Cill Trevelyan, then she obviously doesn't want to be found.'

He didn't answer immediately. 'That's what I thought until my wife asked me how I'd feel if one of the twins went missing. You'd never get over it, particularly if you found out she'd been raped and hadn't told you. I've been thinking about it all night and I reckon the parents have rights, too, even if just to know she's still alive.' He paused again. 'If it's any help, I made the point about Cill not wanting to be found to this Bristol agency, and they said she couldn't be forced to see her parents if she didn't want to.'

'What's changed your mind, Mr Burton?' George asked curiously.

'About what?'

'You've lived with this for thirty years but you're suddenly taking it personally. Why?'

'No one bothered to show me a photograph before,' he said flatly. 'They were looking for Lou, so it wasn't necessary . . . but it made me realize how young Cill was. My dad always said she was a flighty piece who was too forward for her own good and, once you get an idea into your head, it's difficult to shift. There wasn't much sympathy for her in our house, not after Lou started refusing to go out. The folks blamed Cill for everything. "If only

Louise had never met that bloody girl . . ." – that was all they could say for months.' He fell silent.

'Cill seemed to have suffered a lot of abuse,' George said unemotionally. 'Reading between the lines of the newspaper articles, I got the impression her father didn't think twice about hitting her.'

'He was always taking his belt to her. It didn't stop her acting up, though, just made her run away rather than face another larruping.'

'Because of the fight with Louise?'

'Yes.'

George made a pencil tick on a notepad in front of her. 'It seems odd the school only punished Cill for it,' she said mildly. 'You'd think they'd both be suspended.'

'Lou said Cill wouldn't explain, so the head gave her her marching orders. That's how it worked in those days.'

'What was Lou's explanation?'

'Probably what she told our folks – that Cill had tried to persuade her to truant again.'

'It doesn't sound like the truth, though, does it? It's more likely she was teasing Cill about the rape . . . maybe even threatening her. Something along the lines of: do what I want in this relationship or I'll tell on you.' She waited through a brief silence. 'It takes a lot of imagination to understand how devastating rape can be to the victim, particularly gang rape. It's as much a violation of the mind as it is of the body. The poor child was probably scrubbing herself raw every day in order to wash off their filth. Would Louise have understood how badly her friend had been damaged?'

'No.'

'Which is why she did nothing to help her?'

'She was too scared. They dragged Cill by her hair, then kicked the shit out of her. There was blood all over her legs . . . that's why Lou went back for some trousers.' His voice took on a sudden urgency. 'You don't think about psychological stuff when you're a kid . . . you *can't* . . . most of the time you're struggling to understand why your parents never stop arguing. It might have been different if Cill hadn't launched in on us. She kept saying she'd kill us if we blabbed—' He broke off abruptly.

George let the admission ride. 'She must have been very frightened of her father. Have you never asked yourself *why* she talked sexy? How did she know so much about it? Physical and sexual abuse often go hand in hand.'

There was a long silence. 'Why does he keep sending people to look for her?'

'Any number of reasons. Guilt . . . love . . . obsession. A friend of mine's convinced he went too far and killed her, so perhaps he's trying to pretend she's still alive.'

'That's what my folks thought at the time – lots of people did – but I remember Dad saying he'd been questioned and let go because there was nothing in the house to show Cill had died. Plus, they never found a body.'

'And when they did find one, Cill was promptly forgotten,' said George with deliberate flippancy.

'I don't get you.'

'Grace Jefferies. She was murdered in Mullin Street a few days after Cill went missing. I've been wondering if the two events were connected.'

He sounded surprised. 'It was Howard Stamp did that. I remember Dad telling me what a miserable little tosser he was.'

George took a breath to calm her irritation. 'If they'd had DNA testing in 1970, Mr Burton, Howard wouldn't even have been charged, let alone sent for trial. It was someone else who killed Grace, but in those days no one gave a damn if a miserable little *tosser* got sent down for something he didn't do. It was par for the course.'

'What makes you think Cill's disappearance was linked to the murder?'

'Statistics,' said George bluntly. 'Lightning never strikes in the same place twice . . . or if it does, there's a reason. Louise said one of the rapists was ginger-haired. Do you know what his name was?'

'What's ginger hair got to do with it?'

'Grace's murderer had ginger hair.'

This time the silence was interminable, as if the man at the other end was putting together pieces of a jigsaw. 'I knew them by sight,' he said at last, 'but the only name I remember was Roy. He's the one kept kicking Cill.'

Eleven

THE SPICER & HARDY offices were on the third floor of a converted townhouse in a smart Victorian terrace in west London. Courtesy of Andrew's ex-wife, who made a living as an interior designer, it had been revamped six years previously to reflect a more modern taste than Mr Spicer and Mr Hardy's (deceased without issue) penchant for a donnish library-look of dark walls, heavy leather furniture and mahogany bookcases. Andrew, who had loved the old style and still recalled the happiness of childhood days curled in an armchair in his father's office reading whatever was available, had never come to terms with the acres of space that Jenny had created using glass, colour and artificial lighting. However, no one shared his feelings. To everybody else, the frequently photographed decor was a triumph.

George Gardener was no exception. 'Goodness!' she said admiringly as Andrew escorted her up a flight of unremarkable stairs into the reception area, where a trompe l'œil reflection converted a quadrant of glass and chrome into a sweeping semicircular desk. 'It's huge.'

'Smoke and mirrors,' said Andrew, opening another door. 'Be careful you don't walk into a pane of glass by mistake.'

She caught a glimpse of her reflection and hastily buttoned her jacket. 'You must have a very confident receptionist. I'm not sure I'd want to be looking at myself all day long.'

Andrew chuckled. 'We're not big enough to afford one, so the phones are all inside. It was my wife's least good idea. She was either planning for a future that was never going to happen, or she got it into her head that agents' offices are like doctors' waiting rooms, and people drop in off the street clutching manuscripts to their chests.' He invited her to go in front of him. 'It makes a good quiet room for reading or one-on-one meetings, so it isn't entirely wasted.'

The next room was open plan with three desks, isolated from each other by glass screens, foliage plants and pools of artificial light. There were no drawers below the L-shaped ebony table tops, and only computers and telephones stood on them. 'Goodness!' said George again, astonished by so much neatness. 'Isn't this room used either?'

'It certainly is. This is the hub of the whole operation. All the paperwork's done in here . . . correspondence, contracts, payments, manuscript returns.' He nodded to the first desk. 'That's where my rights manager sits. She works on a stack of files every day.'

'Where are they?'

He stooped to release a catch under the table top, and a mirrored panel swung back to reveal shelves of papers. 'The doors are set at a slight angle to reflect the carpet but the illusion vanishes the minute you open them. Personally I think it's awful, but then I'm boring and old-fashioned. The staff love it. It's about creating space, even imaginary space. I'm told it's good for stress levels.'

'It makes sense,' said George, thinking of the tiresome clutter in her Mini, 'but it wouldn't do to put me in here. I'm far too untidy. I'd never be bothered to clear away at the end of the day and that would spoil the impression for everyone else.'

'Me neither,' said Andrew, leading her down a short corridor to a room at the end, 'so you'll feel at home in here. This is where I drew the line.'

The room wasn't exactly as his father had left it, but it was close enough for comfort. The leather armchair, double-sided partners' desk and mahogany bookcases remained, but it was lighter and cleaner than when Mr Spicer Snr had dropped cigarette ash on the floor, coated the books and ceiling with nicotine and allowed a single walkway through the piles of manuscripts that littered the floor. Secretly, Andrew still hankered after the old man's eccentricity, but Jenny had convinced him that image was everything. Visitors viewed a man's surroundings as a reflection of his professionalism.

He hadn't seen the truth of that until she left him for the actor. There was a tragic irony that he'd allowed her virtually free rein with his business premises while failing to appreciate that 'image is everything' was a coded message for him. Occasionally he indulged in depressive navel-gazing, when he wondered whether she'd have stuck by him if he'd lost weight, worn lifts in his shoes and bought a toupee. There was no argument that the business had perked up since the refurbishments, which was a good indication that superficiality worked.

As if to prove the point, George gazed about the room with approval. 'If you drew the line, does that mean your wife didn't have a say in what was done?'

'No, but we agreed I could keep the antiques and make it a mirror-free zone.' He gestured for her to sit down and placed himself in his ergonomic swivel seat. 'To be strictly accurate, she's my ex-wife, but don't let it worry you. We parted on amicable terms.' He watched her settle herself in the worn armchair and wondered why she and Jon had come to blows. She was smartly dressed in a navy blue suit, make-up had toned down the ruddiness of her cheeks and soft grey hair lay in fluffy curls on her forehead. She reminded Andrew of one of his aunts – a favourite of his – and he was predisposed to like her. 'I'd have invited you to my house, but it's in south London and difficult to find, so I thought this would be easier for both of you.'

'Is Jonathan coming?'

Andrew nodded. 'I told him twelve thirty so that you and I could have a quick chat before he arrived.' He put his elbows on the desk and leaned forward. 'He's placed himself under a self-denying ordinance, George – keeps telling me this is your story, not his. He's happy to assist, but he wants you to write it and take the credit.' He lifted an eyebrow. 'How do you feel about that? If you have a facility with words you can make some money as well as highlighting the injustice against Howard. Jon's keen for me to act for you, and I'm willing to do so if you want to give it a shot.'

She watched him closely. 'Shouldn't you argue against that if you're his agent?'

'Not if he instructs me otherwise. In any case, he's not an easy man to argue with.'

'It sounds as if there's a "but" coming.'

Andrew smiled. 'The book will be much easier to sell if Jon's the author. He's the one who put Howard on the map, and his publisher will be interested in a follow-up if there's good evidence that Howard was innocent.'

George shrugged. 'I didn't expect anything else. I only know how to write dissertations.' She flipped open the small case that she'd brought with her and removed a pile of notes. 'I'm quite happy for Jonathan to take what he can from these . . . although I'm starting to question how valuable they are. I have a feeling I've been steered away from anything important, which is why I asked for this meeting. I hoped if we put our heads together we might come up with some fruitful leads.'

'Mm.' Andrew folded his hands under his chin. 'The trouble is, Jon wants to play the martyr at the moment. It's a very tedious side to his character. He beats himself up every time he falls short of whatever unachievable standard he's set himself. If he wasn't an atheist I'd sign him into a monastery and give myself a break.' He watched her face screw into a sympathetic twist. 'What I'd like to suggest is a joint enterprise, with Jon's name at the top because he'll be writing the book and your name underneath because you'll be providing the bulk of the research. You can negotiate percentages between yourselves, or I can give you the name of an arbiter. Either way, you should end up with a fair return for your work. Does that appeal to you?'

'Not at all,' she protested. 'I wasn't expecting to be paid when I first approached Jonathan, and I certainly wouldn't have proposed a second meeting if I thought it was going to be a discussion about property rights and money. I was hoping to do what we should have done the first time – pool information and see where it takes us.'

'Gre-eat!' said Andrew with mild irony. 'Now I have two martyrs on my hands. We have the potential for a book that can exonerate a man's name . . . and no one to write it. What do you suggest I do? Postpone this meeting until I can find a ghostwriter to sit in on it and take notes? Offer the idea to another agent?'

George was a sensible woman whose only affectations were comical expressions and an inclination to giggle. 'I misunderstood,' she said. 'Do I gather the joint enterprise was less a suggestion than an order? Am I to insist on my name on the cover in order to make your friend feel comfortable?'

Andrew tipped a finger at her. 'The more insistent you are the better, as far as I'm concerned. Self-denying ordinances don't suit him. He's easier to live with when he's battling for his rights, a pain in the neck when he turns himself into a doormat.'

She looked amused. 'How's his blood pressure? Perhaps being a doormat is better for his health.'

'No chance. Sitting around twiddling his thumbs is sending it way up.'

'I'm no actress,' George warned. 'If you're expecting me to be angry, I won't be able to do it. I'm a negotiator, not a table-thumper.'

'Is that a yes?'

She shrugged. 'I suppose so . . . as long as you ask him in front of me if he's still refusing to run with the project himself. I'd like to hear him say no for myself.'

'Agreed. If he does, are you willing for me to act as agent in the joint enterprise?'

'Do I have a choice?'

'Most certainly. I'm sure any agent would be willing to represent you – I can even recommend the better ones. The difficulty will be if Jon prefers to stay with me.'

'Then it'll have to be you.'

'Excellent!' He stood up and reached across the desk to shake her warmly by the hand. 'I'll have a contract drawn up tomorrow, but in the meantime you've given me authority to fight for your best interests . . . which means I'd rather you said nothing until I ask for your agreement on a deal. Can you do that?'

'As long as you don't misrepresent anything I've said.'

'Other than emphasizing your insistence on a joint enterprise, there's nothing to misrepresent,' said Andrew. 'As part of the Spicer & Hardy stable, you're as valuable to me now as Jon is.'

*

When she looked back on it, George could only admire Andrew's skilful manipulation of his friend. As predicted, Jonathan arrived in metaphorical (*and* literal) sackcloth and ashes, having taken the trouble to dress down for the meeting while George had put on her glad rags, but he wasn't so crass as to draw attention to either. He merely complimented George on the work she'd done on the Cill Trevelyan story, then refused outright to take on the project when Andrew asked the question. His arguments were persuasive.

He had come across Howard by accident after reading *Clinical Studies* and most of his theories about the case were guesswork. To prepare a compelling rebuttal would require more definitive research, including interviews and legwork, and he couldn't commit the necessary time or energy. Andrew had worked with first-time authors before and was perfectly capable of editing an amateur up to publishable standard, or paying a mentor to help George achieve it herself. While Jonathan had a known interest in miscarriages of justice, his real commitment was to the mistakes made in the areas of asylum-seeking and economic migration. By contrast, George's known commitment was to Howard Stamp, and Howard's interests were best served by someone who had absolute faith in his innocence – which Jonathan didn't have.

Andrew showed his impatience. 'I explained all this to George before you arrived,' he said, 'and it doesn't pass the so-what test, pal. I'm starting to question whether this book's worth anyone's time . . . *mine* included.' He levelled an accusing finger at Jonathan. '*You* are having second thoughts about Howard's innocence and *George* – ' he swivelled the finger towards her – 'supects her research is compromised. I'm willing to act for either of you if you offer me something solid, but I'm not interested in half-measures. Any editor worth his salt will throw it straight back at me if the case for miscarriage isn't proven.'

Jonathan turned a surprised face towards George. 'How is your research compromised?'

She looked at Andrew.

'If you're not interested in the project then it's none of your business,' Andrew answered for her. 'George was hoping to negotiate a fifty–fifty split, but as you're not keen I suggested we approach Jeremy Crossley.'

Jonathan's eyes narrowed immediately. 'Why him?'

'He's an historian, and it's the sort of project he enjoys.' He raised a calming hand. 'I know, I know . . . he slated *Disordered Minds*, but that should work in George's favour, especially when I tell him you've changed your mind about Howard's innocence.' He grinned. 'He'll bust a gut to prove you wrong.'

'You're doing this on purpose,' said Jonathan curtly.

'What?'

'Riling me. You know bloody well what I think of Jeremy Crossley. I wouldn't wish him on my worst enemy, let alone someone like George. He'll take every piece of research she can give him, then cut her out of the equation. That's how he works.'

'Don't be an idiot,' said Andrew dismissively. 'I'm acting for

George, so no one will have access to her information until we've agreed a contract. She won't get a fifty–fifty split with Crossley, of course, but she'll get something, as long as her research has demonstrable value.' He tapped the desk with the tip of his forefinger. 'But that's the issue, I'm afraid. The message I'm getting from both of you is that there are major flaws in your analyses . . . so the scheme looks dead in the water before we even start.'

'I see you've learnt Crossley's review by heart,' said Jonathan sarcastically.

'I can't even remember it,' said Andrew indifferently.

'Like hell you can't. Every other sentence referred to "flawed analysis" of data. It was a hatchet job by a second-rate academic who thinks he can write.' He turned abruptly to George. 'Don't let Andrew railroad you into this. It's a bad idea. Write it yourself . . . you're perfectly capable.'

'You know that's not true,' said Andrew firmly. He nodded to a pile of manuscripts beside his desk. 'That's my slush pile,' he told George. 'If there's one halfway reasonable script in there, I'll be surprised. Writing's a craft – no one can expect to master it the first time they put pen to paper – and Jon knows that as well as I do.'

'There are other authors,' said Jonathan. 'It doesn't have to be Crossley.'

'Agreed. What about that fellow you work with . . . published by Hodder? Henry Carr. He might be interested. I was talking to his editor the other day and she said he's green with envy . . . wants to find any idea that will outclass *Disordered Minds*.'

Jonathan bared his teeth. 'Even you wouldn't stoop that low.'

'You'd better believe it,' Andrew warned. 'I'm after the best deal for George, and Evans will agree to a sixty–forty split if it means he can get one over on you.'

'You're being ridiculous. There are plenty of good young authors on your list who'd jump at this chance. Why aren't you offering it to one of them?'

'Because the advance will be higher with an established name, and that's to George's advantage, particularly if she can earn the money before a word's been written.'

Jonathan considered for a moment, then shifted his attention back to George. 'Are you sure this is the route you want to go, because I'd be happy to advise you if you think you can do it yourself.'

She opened her mouth to say something.

'Jon's not the best person to do that,' Andrew warned her. 'You want someone who believes in Howard's innocence.'

'Stop putting words in my mouth,' said Jonathan irritably. 'The expression I used was "absolute faith". It's important to keep an open mind when looking at issues like this. You can't ignore contrary evidence just because it doesn't suit your theory. You have to examine it even more rigorously.'

'Which is the opposite of what you said earlier. Now you're advocating healthy scepticism in George's co-author. I wish you'd make up your mind.' He looked at his watch. 'To be honest, I can't see the point of this . . . we're just going round in circles. If you're not interested, then you might as well leave so that George can convince me she's got something worth selling. It's a waste of time arguing over co-authors if there isn't enough proof even to get them excited.'

'Is there a link with the Cill Trevelyan story?' Jonathan asked.

George spoke before Andrew could. 'I'm not sure,' she said. 'That's why I wanted to talk to you. You were right about the school friend – her name was Louise Burton. I've managed to locate her brother and he—'

Andrew broke in. 'You're doing this against my advice, George. Jon should only be party to this information if you've agreed a contract with him.'

She gave a guilty sigh. 'I'm sorry, but it's obvious he doesn't want one . . . and we *are* going round in circles. I told you half an hour ago that I'd like to work with Dr Hughes, but he's not obliged to return the favour if he doesn't want to. I'm no writer – '

she smiled apologetically at Jonathan – 'and I'm not much of an academic either . . . so I quite understand your reluctance. The trouble is, if what William Burton told me is true, then Roy Trent was one of Cill's rapists. I rather hoped . . .' She petered into an unhappy silence.

Jonathan hunched his shoulders. 'I'll go with fifty–fifty.'

Clever girl, thought Andrew, staring at his hands.

*

'I know it's tempting to see linkage in synchronicity,' said Jonathan, 'but it's very dangerous. Coincidences happen. It's why PACE and CPIA were introduced, and why DNA has become the major plank in police investigations. Everyone's looking to eliminate malign chance.'

'But if Howard was innocent then malign chance is precisely what convicted him,' George protested. 'It was the hair in the bath that persuaded the jury, but the prosecution proved it could only have come from the murderer. Yet Howard wasn't the murderer.'

'All the more reason not to fixate on another ginger-haired suspect. A goodly percentage of the population carries the gene.' He smiled to take the sting from the words. 'Which isn't to say we'll ignore your rapist – he certainly fits the profile – just be wary. The real pity is that the only name William Burton remembers is Roy . . . it was a popular name in the fifties and sixties so there were probably quite a few of them.'

'Not *that* popular,' said George. 'Surely it's Roy Trent?'

'Roy Rogers . . . Roy Orbison . . . Roy of the Rovers . . . Roy Castle . . .'

'At least one of those was a comic-book character,' said Andrew.

'So? Bill Clinton and David Beckham named their children after places. All I'm saying is we can't assume Roy Trent from Roy.'

'It's a reasonable guess, though,' said Andrew. 'The man's an ape.'

'That doesn't make him a rapist. Or let me put it another way – which of you is willing to go in and suggest it to him with no evidence to back it up . . . and what do you think his answer is going to be?' He glanced from one to the other. 'Right! We need to find Louise or, even better, the Burton parents. They might be able to give us a surname.'

'Assuming they'll talk to us,' said George doubtfully. 'I got the impression from William that they're extremely reluctant to be involved.'

Jonathan flicked to the end of the transcript. 'Did you tape these conversations or make notes?'

'I made notes in the car after the first one and used shorthand for the telephone call. I typed them up immediately afterwards so I'm confident they're accurate.'

He read the description of William Burton that she'd added at the end. 'Forties, six foot approx, well-built, tattoos on his arms, thinning sandy hair, grey eyes, pleasant smiling face, fireman. Married with twin daughters.' 'You liked him,' he said more in statement than question.

'Yes. He was very upfront and friendly at the beginning. We talked about his daughters who were arguing inside the house, and he was very amusing. He only tightened up when I mentioned his sister. He kept saying he hadn't heard from her for years, but I didn't entirely believe him.'

'You say here that he "looked troubled" after you asked him if Louise had had a baby when she was fourteen,' remarked Andrew, tapping a page of the transcript copy that she'd given him. 'He answered: "Not that I'm aware of." You've put "evasive" with a question mark. Is that how it struck you at the time?'

George nodded. 'He went on to say he was a lot younger than she was and wouldn't have understood what was going on – it's a couple of lines down. I thought that was a very strange response . . . as if something *had* happened and he didn't want to lie about it. I've also put a question mark beside the "lot younger". Louise would be forty-five or forty-six now, and William looked a good forty plus.'

Jonathan drew her attention to some notes that came after William Burton's description. '(1) He wouldn't have phoned if he'd recognized Priscilla Fletcher as Louise. [Double bluff?] (2) Did he recognize her as Cill Trevelyan? (3) Why does he feel so "connected" suddenly? [Because of Cill's photo? Because of his daughters? Because Priscilla F. is Cill and he knows it?]'

'What's the significance of his daughters?' he asked.

'It's at the beginning of the telephone transcript. He said his wife had asked him how he'd have felt if one of them had gone missing at thirteen. Also, he was very struck by how young Cill looked. He remembers her as quite adult and was shocked to see she still had her puppy fat.' She paused. 'It's as if he saw her as a person for the first time . . . and I'm wondering if that was because he recognized her in Priscilla Fletcher.'

'I should think it's more likely your first statement was correct. Thirty years after the event, he saw Cill for what she really was – a vulnerable child – and it shocked him.'

'He said his parents blamed her for everything that went wrong. They called her "that bloody girl" and made out she was a tart.'

'What sort of things?'

She shrugged. 'The rape . . . Louise becoming agoraphobic . . . the police questioning. Those are the ones he mentioned, but he said it went on for months.'

'The agoraphobia?'

'Presumably.'

'Interesting,' Jonathan said slowly. 'What was she frightened of? The boys? Being raped herself?'

'He didn't say. There was a passing reference to her parents moving her to a different school so she wouldn't be reminded of Cill's disappearance, but that's all.'

Andrew clicked his fingers suddenly. 'Go back to the first paragraph where George has given a synopsis of the conversation about the girls,' he told Jonathan. 'Second line: "Mr Burton joked about his daughters' fiery hair and fiery tempers . . . said he'd pay to be rid of them."'

'And?'

'Red hair runs in families, but I'm damn sure the gene has to be on both sides to produce fiery red.'

Jonathan ran a thoughtful finger down his jawline. 'Go on.'

'You're hooked on the ginger-haired rapist, but what colour hair did Louise have?'

From: George Gardener [geo.gar@mullinst.co.uk]
Sent: Thurs 17/04/03 15:07
To: jon.hughes@london.ac.uk
Cc: Andrew Spicer
Subject: Louise Burton

Dear Jonathan and Andrew

The Bristol agency was very unhelpful, refusing to share any details of their investigation or divulge the Trevelyans' address. They cited issues of confidentiality, but they refused to phone the Trevelyans for permission. I'm afraid they thought I was a journalist. In the circumstances I decided against making them a free gift of Priscilla Fletcher, and re. Louise they simply referred me back to William Burton.

Our friend Fred Lovatt, has had no success with the archives, nor has he found any colleagues who were involved in Howard's case or Cill's disappearance. PC Prentice, who was mentioned in the newspaper clippings, retired in 1982 and is believed to have died of a stroke some time in the 1990s.

As I am reluctant to 'scare' William Burton away, I have decided to approach this from a different angle. The school the girls attended prior to Cill's disappearance was almost certainly Highdown Secondary Modern, situated in Wellingborough Road. It was reinvented during the 1970s as Highdown Community School and subsequently moved to new, larger premises in Glazeborough Road (*coincidentally* utilizing the site of the demolished Brackham & Wright factory where Wynne Stamp worked!) They only keep records of past staff and pupils who sign up for the OH (Old Highdowners) Register. However, I have the name and address of the headmistress who was in charge from 1968 to '73. It is: Miss Hilda Brett, 12 Hardy Mansions, Poundbury, Dorchester, Dorset.

I have made some enquiries and I understand that Hardy Mansions is sheltered accommodation for 'active' elderly – i.e. people who still have their marbles. This is very good news as Miss Brett *must* be the one who suspended Cill and should remember both girls. I am willing to talk to her on my own, though I would prefer Jonathan to come with me, not only because his status of research fellow and author will lend the questions academic authority – and may persuade her to be more forthcoming – but also because I am unsure how to structure the interview.

Do we say we're looking for Cill Trevelyan? For Louise? Do we mention Howard? None of them . . . just say we're researching Highdown of 1970 and were given her name by her old school? Help, please!

Best, George

PS If Jonathan can come I shall need some dates when he's free. On balance, I think we should just turn up, rather than attempt to book a meeting with her, as if she says 'no' we will lose this opportunity.

Twelve

THIS TIME Jonathan had opted for smartness, and he was relieved to see George had done the same when she met him at Dorchester South Station. 'What happened to the mobile filing cabinet?' he asked as he climbed into the car. 'I hope you didn't move it on my account.'

'I had a spring clean,' she told him, starting the engine. 'Everything's in its proper place at home.' She flashed him a smile. 'I decided Andrew's ex-wife is right: "Fine feathers make fine birds."'

Jonathan grinned. 'Except Andrew doesn't agree. He prefers, "Don't judge a book by its cover."'

'Me, too,' she said cheerfully, pulling away from the kerb, 'but we're in a minority, so I'm going for the two-second sound bite – smart car . . . smart home . . . smart clothes . . . *smart* mind.'

Jonathan laughed. 'How long will it last?'

'It depends how determined I am.' She turned right onto Weymouth Avenue before filtering left to head towards the western outskirts of Dorchester. She drove hunched over her steering wheel as if she couldn't see where she was going, and Jonathan closed his eyes to avoid flinching at every near miss.

'To do what?'

'Strike the right impression from the off. I realize I've only myself to blame that I'm never taken seriously.'

Jonathan had known it was a conversation that would come eventually. Unresolved issues never vanished of their own accord. 'If it's any consolation,' he said lamely, 'I said far worse things to Sergeant Lovatt. According to Andrew I called him a fascist . . . although I honestly don't remember it.'

'Oh, for goodness sake! I'm not doing this for you.'

'Who then?'

'Roy. He's been running rings around me because he thinks I'm a woolly headed spinster.' There was a hiatus while she manoeuvred between oncoming traffic and parked cars on her left. 'I've tucked a map of Poundbury behind your sunblind,' she told him, negotiating a five-way junction. 'We're looking for Bridport Road and then Western Crescent. I'm fairly sure of the way but it's two years since I was here and, what with all the new building, the layout of the roads has probably changed.'

He pulled out the map and spread it on his knee. 'What sort of rings?'

She sighed and took her eyes off the road to look at him. 'I didn't bring enough rigour to the information he's been giving me. Instead, I've wasted two years talking to people who were even more ignorant than I was about Howard.'

'Names supplied by Roy?'

'Mm. Mrs So-and-so who worked at Brackham & Wright in the 1960s and might have known what happened to Wynne. Mr So-and-so who used to buy newspapers from Roy's dad and might have known Grace. Ms So-and-so who was at St David's Primary around the time Howard was there. I must have spoken to about twenty people who had vague connections with the story . . . but none of them actually *knew* anything.'

Jonathan pressed his feet into the floor as they drew up six inches behind a juggernaut. 'Irritating!'

'I'd call it devious,' George said, mounting the pavement to bypass the lorry and pull left on to Bridport Road as Jonathan stared stoically ahead. She nodded towards a cream-coloured building ahead of them with a Germanic red-tiled spire. 'That's where Poundbury begins. Have you visited it before? Do you know what it is?'

'No.'

'Then you're in for a treat. It's Prince Charles's whack at modern architects and developers who build cheap estates full of identical red-brick boxes and expect people to be grateful. I mean, who wants to live in something *boring*?'

Roy Trent was promptly forgotten in her enthusiasm for the Prince of Wales's vision of how to build a new community. She insisted on making a detour into phase one of Poundbury which was less than ten years old but which, through its architecture and design – irregular roads, variety of building styles, use of local materials and housing arranged in mews, lanes, squares and courtyards – suggested history and permanence.

Jonathan was more impressed than he thought he'd be, although he doubted a similar estate would work in London. 'It would be difficult to translate to a city,' he said as she pulled out onto the main road again.

'I don't see why,' said George. 'The principle of local tradition and local materials would work just as well in Harlesden as they do in Dorset. It's the uniformity of cheap brick and reinforced concrete that people hate. A house should be an expression of its owner's individuality, not a clone of the one next door.'

'What about Victorian terraces?' he murmured ironically. 'They were built to off-the-shelf blueprints and you can't get more uniform than that. In a hundred years people may be as fond of red-brick boxes as we are of the nineteenth-century equivalent.'

George chuckled. 'Assuming the boxes are still standing in a hundred years. Victorian terraces were built to last . . . these days everything's obsolete within a year.' She slowed to read a street sign. 'Poundbury Close,' she announced.

Jonathan traced the map with his finger. 'Which makes Western Crescent the second on the right,' he told her, 'over there.' She flicked her indicator and pulled into the centre of the road. 'Tell me about Roy's deviousness,' he invited.

'What's to tell?' she said dispassionately. 'He's been sending me on wild goose chases because he doesn't want me finding out he was involved.'

'You can't be sure of that,' Jonathan warned. 'He may be quite innocent but keeps his ear to the ground because he knows it's important to you. The fact that he's never come up with anything valuable might be evidence that he's as ignorant as you and I.'

George gave a derisive snort. 'You don't believe that any more than I do. He's been playing me for a patsy. He wasn't remotely friendly until I mentioned an interest in Howard Stamp, then he became my newest pal. I should have smelt a rat then.' She was driving slowly up the road looking for house names. She came to a halt beside a large building built in Purbeck stone. 'Here we are . . . Hardy Mansions.'

*

They were both surprised by the ease with which they gained entry to the old woman. They expected to pass their request through a warden, but it took just the press of a buzzer with 'Hilda Brett' beside it, and George's mention of Highdown Secondary Modern into the intercom, for the door to swing open and a barked instruction to come to Flat 12. 'She's far too trusting,' said George disapprovingly as they followed arrows marked 5–12 down a corridor. 'We could be anyone.'

'Perhaps she likes living dangerously,' said Jonathan.

'I'm surprised it's allowed.'

'Then she's rebelling against living in a prison,' he murmured.

George pulled a face. 'It's supposed to be the exact opposite – liberation from care and worry.'

'Mm, but are undesirables being kept out or the inhabitants kept in? You can pay too high a price for freedom from care – fear of crime is more isolating than crime itself.'

George's protest against this slur on sheltered accommodation remained unsaid, because the door to Number 12 opened and a gaunt woman gestured them inside. 'Hello, hello!' she said happily. 'Come on in.' She leaned on a walking stick and drew back to let them pass. 'Into the sitting room on your right . . . my chair's the upright one with the cushions.' She closed the door and followed, examining her visitors brightly as she lowered herself into her seat. 'Sit down . . . sit down. Make yourselves comfortable.'

Jonathan folded his tall frame onto the sofa while George chose an armchair. 'This is very good of you, Miss Brett,' she said. 'We were given your address by the school, but as they didn't have your phone number we decided to take a chance on finding you at home.'

The woman was frail and looked well into her eightie s, but her faded eyes were full of intelligence. 'You'll have to help me,' she said. 'I'm afraid I don't recognize you at all. Obviously this young man was well after my time, but when were you there, my dear?'

George screwed her face into immediate apology. 'Oh, goodness, I didn't mean to suggest we were ever pupils of yours.' She watched disappointment cloud the old woman's expression. 'May we introduce ourselves? My name's Georgina Gardener and I'm a councillor for Highdown ward where your school still is, and this is Dr Jonathan Hughes – ' she gestured towards the sofa – 'who's an author and research fellow in European Anthropology at London University.'

Jonathan stood up and bent to shake her hand. 'This is a great privilege, Miss Brett. I've long wanted to meet a headteacher who had responsibility for steering a school into the comprehensive era. It must have been a difficult and stressful time . . . but exciting too, perhaps?'

She frowned slightly, as if doubting this was the purpose of their visit. 'All of those,' she agreed, 'but, of course, there was a strong crusading zeal at the time which carried us through. My staff and I had seen too many children relegated to what was effectively a second-class education because of their failure at the eleven-plus examination.'

'With little or no chance of going to university,' said Jonathan, sitting down again.

'Certainly. The direct route to higher education was through the grammar schools and private schools, which made it so pernicious that a child's future was decided at eleven.' She paused, glancing doubtfully from one to the other. 'Is this really what you came to talk to me about? I can't believe the opinions of a doddery headmistress – *long* past her sell-by date – add anything useful to the current debate on education.'

George looked guilty. 'Well . . .'

'In a way it is,' said Jonathan, hunching forward to address her more directly. 'We're doing a case study of troubled children in the decades after the Second World War. There are two from Highdown that interest us. Howard Stamp, who was convicted of murdering his grandmother, and Priscilla Trevelyan, who disappeared in 1970. Howard was certainly before your time, but I believe Priscilla was one of your pupils?' He raised an enquiring eyebrow which she answered with a nod. 'Would you be willing to tell us what you remember of her?'

She sighed wearily as her disappointments were compounded. 'If you're detectives, then you're wasting your time. As I told your predecessors, I have no idea what happened to the poor child.'

Jonathan took a card and security pass from his inside pocket and passed them to her. 'That's my photograph, name and title . . . and at the bottom of the card is my departmental telephone number. I am more than happy for you to call and verify that I am who and what I say I am. Councillor Gardener can be similarly verified through her office or by telephoning one of her colleagues at the Birches Nursing Home in Highwood.'

George promptly took one of her own cards from her case and offered it across. 'We aren't detectives,' she assured the woman, 'although I had the same response from Louise Burton's brother. I understand the Trevelyans have been trying to find their daughter for years.'

Miss Brett barely glanced at the cards before shifting herself forward, preparatory to standing up. 'I'm sorry but I can't help you. It was a devastating event . . . if I'd known anything useful I would have told the police.'

It was a clear dismissal but Jonathan ignored it. 'Georgina and I are approaching this from a very different angle,' he told her. 'We're more interested in why Priscilla became a statistic rather than where she is now. If her parents are to be believed from the press coverage, most of her problems stemmed from the fact that she was brighter than her peers . . . and that's not an unreasonable assumption. The links between truancy and delinquent behaviour are well documented, and boredom is a trigger for both. Do you agree – indeed *did* you agree at the time – with Mr and Mrs Trevelyan's assessment of their daughter? Would Priscilla have been a less disturbed juvenile if she'd won a place at grammar school?'

It was a question that was pitched at the educationalist in her, and it worked. She remained sitting. 'Truancy is commonly a symptom of *under*achievement Dr – ' she consulted Jonathan's card again – 'Hughes, while disruptive behaviour in class can be a symptom of an above-average IQ which is not being thoroughly tested. Priscilla certainly fell into the latter category . . . so in that respect I did agree with Mr and Mrs Trevelyan. But although her brightness made her a difficult and unruly child, I don't believe it was the cause of her truancy . . . or, more importantly, her disappearance.'

'What was?'

Miss Brett tapped her forefingers together. 'You must put that question to her father.'

Jonathan glanced at George, who stepped seamlessly into the conversation. 'William Burton told me she was knowledgeable about sex,' she said matter-of-factly. 'I know it was less understood in those days but – looking back – do you think she was sexually abused?'

'Yes.'

'By her father?'

'Yes.'

George reached for a notepad and pen. 'Is that something you told the police?'

There was a short silence. 'No,' said the old woman, then, 'it's a conclusion I've come to in the last ten years. For a long time I blamed myself – it's a devastating event in a teacher's career to feel responsible for a child's disappearance. I liked to think I was approachable – I *should* have been approachable . . .' She broke off abruptly.

George's inclination was to stretch out a sympathetic hand, but Jonathan spoke before she could do it. 'A student of mine was murdered in New York recently after I sponsored him to a scholarship out there,' he said evenly, 'and I'm left with "if onlys": if only he hadn't been black . . . if only America and the UK hadn't whipped up hysteria against world terrorism . . . if only the man in the street could recognize that Muslim and terrorist are not synonymous . . .' He smiled. 'I'm guessing your "if only" was to do with the rape? If only Priscilla had told you about it, you wouldn't have punished her for fighting with Louise, her father wouldn't have had an excuse to hit her . . . or *worse* . . . and she wouldn't have run away.'

Miss Brett nodded. 'That and more. She had a precocious, sexual vocabulary and didn't think twice about using it, particularly around the male teachers, but it never occurred to any of us that that might be a symptom of abuse.' She gave another sigh. 'I'm afraid it just made her unpopular in the staffroom and her punishments were always more severe because of it. I regret that deeply. One wonders where the poor child found kindness if she wasn't getting it at home.'

'There was so much ignorance then,' said George. 'It seems incredible now, but it wasn't until the Maria Colwell enquiry in '74 that the issue of child abuse really surfaced.' She caught Jonathan's eye. 'It wasn't until poor little Maria was dumped at hospital by her stepfather that the authorities recognized they should have protected her. He was her *murderer*, for goodness sake . . . he'd beaten a starving seven-year-old to death and he didn't think anyone would *object*.'

'Things haven't improved much,' said Jonathan, thinking of his own upbringing. 'The trouble is, there's a thin dividing line between child protection and eugenic experimentation. We object to children being forcibly removed from inadequate parents, but complain when the same children die of neglect and brutality. It's a catch-22 for the authorities.'

Miss Brett looked interested. 'First define inadequacy,' she said dryly. 'There were many other parents I came into contact with who would have fitted the description better than the Trevelyans. Who's to say which father is harming his child?'

'Or how?' said George thoughtfully. 'There's evidence that David Trevelyan hit Priscilla – even the mother seemed to admit it by talking about his strictness – but I'm less sure about the sexual abuse. William Burton's account of the rape suggests Cill was still a virgin. He said there was so much blood on her legs that Louise had to go home to find a pair of trousers to hide it. It may have been a period, of course, but I'm more inclined to think her hymen was broken . . . and that would make the rape the first time she was penetrated.'

'It doesn't mean she hadn't been introduced to sexual activity,' said Jonathan.

'I agree. And if her father was responsible it would explain why she didn't want him to know about the assault. He'd certainly believe she provoked it. It's how molesters and rapists excuse their behaviour – it's not their fault, it's the fault of the victim for arousing them.' She tapped her pen on her notepad. 'The same arguments would apply to her mother. I came across a case study that showed that as many as twenty-five per cent of sex-abuse offences are committed by women. Any number of dynamics might have been operating within the family.'

'Or *outside* it,' said Jonathan. 'A neighbour or relative might have been grooming her – perhaps her father was as troubled by her sexual precocity as her teachers, and didn't know how to deal

with it. He may have been guilty only of heavy-handed discipline.'
He looked enquiringly at the headmistress. 'What sort of man was
he? Did you know him well?'

'Not really. I spoke to him once about Priscilla's truanting and
once after she disappeared. On both occasions he was very angry.
There was no meeting of minds. On the first occasion he told me
it was the school's responsibility to ensure his daughter's attendance, and on the second he took me to task for suspending
Priscilla and not Louise. He said that had he realized that Louise
Burton was the other girl in the fight, he wouldn't have upheld
my punishment.'

'Why would he say that?'

She considered for a moment. 'Each set of parents thought the
other child was to blame for the truanting, but I believed then –
and *still* believe – that Mr Trevelyan was trying to shift the blame
onto me. If he could place on record that all he'd done was
reinforce a school punishment, then he could excuse whatever it
was that caused Priscilla to run away.'

'You didn't like him?' said George.

'Indeed I did not,' said the old woman firmly. 'He was an
overweight bully who shook his fist under my nose and expected
me to agree with him. I made it clear both times that I had no
responsibility for Priscilla when she was off the premises – other
than to report the fact to her parents and the relevant authorities
– so he promptly blamed the school for her difficulties.' She shook
her head. 'We'd held her back . . . she was bored . . . we weren't
challenging her enough . . . she was too bright to be at Highdown.
It was very depressing.'

'And all reported in the press?'

'Indeed.' Another sigh. 'And there was nothing we could say
in rebuttal. It would have been shabby to contradict their assessment of Priscilla, shabbier still to suggest the Trevelyans were – '
she canted her head towards Jonathan – '*inadequate*. It was very
much a case of: *de mortuis nil nisi bonum.*'

Jonathan eyed her curiously. 'Is that a figure of speech or did you believe she was dead?'

'Both. A missing child inspires intense emotion . . . we all grieved for her. Everyone expected a shallow grave to be found somewhere, and when it wasn't . . .' She broke off with an unhappy shrug. 'Her parents continued to hope, but no one else believed she could survive on her own.'

He nodded. 'So why did the police abandon the investigation?'

'I don't think they did. They kept the case open for years, but they were really just waiting for a skeleton to turn up. As one of the inspectors said, she vanished into thin air after she left her parents' house, almost certainly abducted by one of these monsters who prey on children. She could be buried anywhere.'

'Her father was questioned and ruled out,' said George. 'Do you know why? He seems the most obvious suspect.'

'He was working a night shift that week and her mother said Priscilla was still at home after he left for work. He reported her missing when he came home at six o'clock in the morning and found her bed hadn't been slept in, but his work colleagues said he hadn't left the factory all night.'

'What was his job?' asked Jonathan.

'He was a foreman at Brackham & Wright's tool factory. It closed a few years later and they used the site for the new comprehensive school.'

There was a long and thoughtful silence.

'What was that you said about linkage and synchronicity?' asked George, levelling her pen at Jonathan. ' "Don't be tempted by it . . . coincidences happen." Well, I *am* tempted.' She switched her attention back to Miss Brett. 'Do you remember Grace Jefferies' murder? Her body was discovered a week after Priscilla went missing.'

The old woman nodded. 'It was very shocking. You mentioned her killer earlier.'

'Howard Stamp,' said George. 'His mother, Wynne – Grace's

daughter – also worked at Brackham & Wright. It stretches the imagination to think a single workforce should be hit by an abduction and a murder within seven days of each other. Surely the two events must have been connected in some way? Did the police ever suggest that to you?'

'Not to me, although I do remember being surprised during the trial to learn that Mrs Stamp worked there . . . but that was a year after Priscilla vanished, of course.' Miss Brett fell into a brief reverie, staring towards her window as she sifted through memories. 'It seems an obvious connection to make with hindsight,' she said, 'but it wasn't obvious at the time. Brackham & Wright was a major employer in Highdown in the 1960s – at a rough estimate there were two thousand on the payroll – and a large number of my parents worked there. I believe Louise Burton's father was also a foreman, and many of our pupils went into their training schemes.'

'What sort of people were the Burtons?' Jonathan asked before George could speak.

'I don't believe I ever met the husband – there wasn't a great deal of contact with parents in those days – but I spoke to Mrs Burton about Louise's truanting. She was rather more amenable than Mr Trevelyan, accepting some responsibility for her daughter's behaviour, but she blamed Priscilla for it. She wanted me to separate the girls but, as I pointed out, it would achieve nothing while they continued living so close to each other.'

'How close were they? We know the Burtons lived in Mullin Street but we haven't been able to find an address for the Trevelyans.'

'If memory serves me right, they were in Lacey Street.'

'Two on,' said George, making a note. 'Do you know which number in Lacey Street?' she asked Miss Brett.

She shook her head regretfully. 'It was a long time ago.'

'Was Mrs Burton right?' Jonathan prompted. 'Was Priscilla the leader in the friendship?'

'Oh, yes. She was by far the stronger character. Also, it was she who started the truanting – afternoons at first, then whole days.'

'Every day? How long did it go on?'

Miss Brett considered for a moment. 'I can't be precise . . . perhaps once or twice a week during the spring term. Both sets of parents were given warnings when we broke up for Easter, but I do remember the girls were absent for much of the first two weeks of the summer term. It ceased abruptly after the rape, although we only learnt afterwards that that was the cause. I'm afraid I assumed the sudden improvement was because of a letter I wrote to their fathers, threatening immediate expulsion if the behaviour persisted.'

'When were the letters sent?'

'As far as I could judge from what the police told me, it was the same day as the rape. They failed to register again that morning, which is why I decided to take action.'

'And Louise just went along for the ride? She wasn't an instigator?'

Another pause for reflection. 'She was a strange child . . . rather deceitful. I felt she maligned Priscilla to the police. It was a damning picture she painted. A violent, promiscuous, out-of-control teen who hated her parents, truanted to have sex with boys and used threats to make other children do what she wanted. There may have been elements of truth in it – Priscilla was big for her age and she could retaliate strongly when she was teased – but she wasn't a bully, not by my understanding of the word, anyway. She was a magnet to smaller, shyer children, but I don't recall her being unkind to them . . . rather the reverse, in fact; she tended to protect them.'

'William Burton said the police questioning frightened Louise. Perhaps she was trying to win sympathy?'

'Indeed,' said Miss Brett with an ascerbic edge to her voice. 'It was certainly her character. She was prone to tears and fainting and wouldn't look you in the eye when she spoke to you – quite the opposite of Priscilla, who squared up and tried to battle her way out of it. It didn't mean Louise had no hand in the mischief, merely that her friend took the punishment for both of them.'

'As in the rape?'

'I would think so.'

'And the fight that caused Priscilla's suspension?'

'Yes. That was very typical of Louise. I was told by their teacher that she'd been whispering in Priscilla's ear all morning, but Louise insisted it was the other way round – that Priscilla had been trying to persuade her to truant again and attacked her when she refused.'

'What did Priscilla say?'

'Nothing,' said the woman regretfully. 'I warned her she'd be suspended if she didn't give me an explanation, I even suggested it was Louise who'd provoked her – ' she sighed again – 'but she wasn't prepared to lie.'

'Unlike Louise.'

'Mm.'

'Do you think with hindsight she was teasing Priscilla about the rape?' George put in.

'Oh, yes.'

'It would suggest a cruel streak, if she were . . . either that or a complete lack of imagination.'

Miss Brett thought for a moment. 'As to being cruel . . . well, possibly. She was certainly very pleased about Priscilla's suspension. But I've never met a deceitful child who lacked imagination,' she finished with a small smile. 'Telling stories against one's peers rather demands it, don't you think?'

Thirteen

BILLY BURTON had been sitting in his elderly Renault estate for over an hour watching the Fletchers' house for signs of life. It was getting on for two weeks since he'd passed the Bristol detective agency's address to Georgina Gardener, and he'd given up hope that she'd done anything about it. He wore a baseball cap over his thinning hair and a pair of cheap, black-rimmed reading glasses from Boots to break up his face. On the steering wheel in front of him was an open file of documents which he was pretending to study, but as time went by he became increasingly nervous that someone would mistake him for a thief and call the police.

The house was in a side street behind Panorama Road, where property prices were exorbitant because of the uninterrupted views of Poole Harbour and Brownsea Island but, even without a view, Billy would have been surprised if the Spanish-style, balconied villa he was watching was worth less than a million pounds. He'd read somewhere that the Sandbanks Peninsula commanded the fourth highest price per square foot of land in the world, with only Tokyo, Hong Kong and London's Belgravia coming in more expensive. But why this should be so was a complete mystery to him. Given the choice, he'd prefer a property on Malibu beach in California, where the weather was temperate all the year round.

He hunkered down in his seat as a car cruised past, his heart beating fiercely. This was crazy. Celebrities bought weekend retreats here – half the houses were empty for months on end. He'd probably been under surveillance from a CCTV camera. Who the hell was this Fletcher guy and how could he afford to live cheek by jowl with pop stars and footballers? It didn't make sense. Every enquiry Billy had made had come up blank. 'Never heard of him . . .' 'Sorry . . .' 'If he's on Sandbanks, he's out of my league, mate . . .' 'What does he do?'

Billy had been tempted to visit the Crown and Feathers and put some questions to Roy Trent, but had thought better of it. There were a number of adages governing ill-conceived action against animals like Trent, but 'beware of stirring up a hornets' nest' seemed appropriate. Trent had been a forgotten secret in Billy's brain for over thirty years and he cursed Georgina Gardener for resurrecting him.

Now he was trying to function on two hours' sleep in twenty-four, and driving his daughters mad by monitoring their every movement. He'd relived every minute of Cill's rape, but from the perspective of a grown man, not that of a naive, tipsy ten-year-old who hadn't a clue what was going on. He even knew what he was suffering from – post-traumatic stress disorder – because he'd been a firefighter long enough to recognize the symptoms. It was a disease of the job – the lingering trauma of dealing with car deaths and burn victims was devastating – although he could not account for the thirty-year delay in the onset – nor the intensity – of his guilt.

Why now? He'd dealt with detectives looking for Cill without blinking an eyelid, but a dumpy little stranger turns up, shows him a photograph and he promptly goes to pieces. The woman had told him too much, that was the trouble. *'It's more likely she was teasing Cill about the rape . . . It takes a lot of imagination to understand how devastating gang rape can be to the victim . . . the poor child was probably scrubbing herself raw every day in order to wash off their filth . . .'*

Thirty years on, he could work out what the blood on Cill's

legs had signified, and it made him sick even to think about it. In the way of dreams, it was his twins who wandered in and out of his nightmares, hymenal blood pouring down their thighs and puppy fat swelling their tiny breasts. Had Louise understood? She must have done. He recalled her smirk when she came back with some trousers and dropped them on the ground. 'Blokes can tell,' she'd said. 'You'll never get married now.' And he remembered Cill's tearful answer: 'At least I'm not a coward.'

He'd never spoken to Cill again. The friendship with Louise had ceased abruptly and Cill was gone within a month. There had been some weeks of unease until the family moved to Boscombe, and then the child had been excised from their minds. Billy had never asked his sister why she hadn't told the police he was a witness to the rape. At ten years old, he'd thought she was trying to keep him out of trouble and loved her for it. In his forties, he wasn't so sure.

'Grace's murderer had ginger hair . . .'

He remembered the day the police came to Mullin Street. He'd thought it was to do with Cill, until a uniformed officer rang their bell and said Mrs Jefferies was dead. His mother had been watching anxiously from behind a curtain as teams of coppers worked their way from house to house, then she'd ordered Billy upstairs to Louise's bedroom before she opened the door. Billy remembered her hands were shaking, and he remembered wondering why she was scared.

He'd stood just inside his sister's bedroom, listening to the conversation downstairs, while Louise's eyes grew huge in her white face. His mother's voice had been higher than usual as she said she'd never spoken to Mrs Jefferies and didn't know which house she lived in. The policeman pointed it out to her – Number 11 – and asked her if she'd seen anyone enter or leave during the week. No, said his mother, but then she hadn't been out much. She'd been looking after her daughter, who was Cill Trevelyan's best friend. The man was sympathetic. He had daughters of his own.

They'd never been troubled again. Howard Stamp was arrested

and charged within two days of Grace's body being found, and the 'Mullin Street murder' was as little visited in the Burton household as Cill's disappearance. 'Don't upset your sister,' had been the watchword for months. Billy's knowledge of both events had been gleaned from friends whose parents were willing to share information with their children. The accepted story on Cill was that she ran away to London. The accepted story on Grace was that Howard went berserk after she ticked him off for skiving.

It was a conclusion that had puzzled Billy when he was ten, because Howard hadn't seemed capable of hacking anyone to pieces. He was even afraid of Billy and Louise, sliding into shadow whenever he saw them because Louise giggled every time he passed and called him a spastic. She even tried to trip him up once and Billy remembered how frightened he looked. On one occasion, Mrs Jefferies came to their house and asked their mother to put a stop to it. She was a plump, grey-haired woman who wrung her hands nervously and had difficulty getting her words out. Billy remembered her saying please, all the time, as if she were the one at fault.

Their mother hadn't been particularly angry with them – '*Everyone knows there's something wrong with that boy*' – but she had warned them to leave Howard alone. '*According to his grandmother he's suicidal, and I don't want anyone saying you two were to blame when he does something silly.*' Afterwards, Billy assumed the 'something silly' was murder and that his mother had lied to the police about talking to Mrs Jefferies because she didn't want the family involved again. Their father was already furious that Louise had been questioned about Cill's disappearance. He kept talking about a terrible atmosphere at work where rumours were rife that if his daughter knew about Cill's rape, so must her parents.

It was a bewildering few months until they moved. Louise's fainting fits meant she stayed at home, while Billy was expected to go to school. He was suspicious and jealous of his mother's relationship with his sister and fearful of his morose father, who bit his head off every time he asked what was wrong. The

Trevelyans featured strongly in his parents' invective. When it wasn't that 'little tart Cill' who'd ruined Louise's life, it was 'that bastard David' who was forcing his father out of Brackham & Wright. Grace Jefferies was never mentioned at all, except in passing. *'The whole damn street wants to move since that bloody woman's murder . . .'*

When they transferred to Boscombe life settled down again. Their father took a new job, Louise changed her name to Daisy and wore her hair differently and Billy found new friends. Only their mother seemed to carry the baggage of Highdown with her, spying from behind the curtains every time the bell rang. Once in a while Billy thought he recognized a face in a crowd, but after a couple of years even that ceased to trouble him. In the great scheme of things, the events of three short weeks in the life of a ten-year-old – events he hadn't understood and couldn't control – became irrelevant. It wasn't his fault that Cill had disappeared or that Mrs Jefferies had been murdered.

'If they'd had DNA testing in 1970, Mr Burton, Howard wouldn't even have been charged, let alone sent for trial. It was someone else who killed Grace . . .'

'. . . someone with ginger hair . . .'

*

George retrieved the photographs of Priscilla Fletcher and Cill Trevelyan from her case and handed Priscilla Fletcher's to Miss Brett. 'Could this be Cill Trevelyan? Do you remember her well enough to say?'

The old woman studied the picture for a long time before shaking her head. She admitted to a vague sense of recognition, but it was over thirty years since she'd last seen the child and all she remembered was long brown hair and an overgrown body. George offered her the duplicate of Cill's photograph from the newspaper clipping and Miss Brett's response was the same as William Burton's. 'Oh dear, dear, dear! I'd forgotten how young she was. What a *terrible* tragedy.'

'Do you think they're the same person?'

She compared the pictures. 'I really couldn't say. Some of my ex-pupils have barely changed at all in adulthood, others are unrecognizable. There are strong similarities, of course . . .' She broke off with another shake of her head.

'We did wonder if it was Louise Burton,' said George.

The woman gave a surprised laugh. 'Goodness me, no. Louise was a ferrety little thing with a pinched face and sharp nose. It was why she latched on to Priscilla's coat-tails – I think she hoped some of the other child's appeal would wash off.' She stared at Cill's smiling face. 'It was rather pathetic, to be honest. She went through a phase of trying to ape Priscilla's looks and manner-isms and merely succeeded in turning herself into a Guy. It was an unbalanced friendship, of course. There was a lot of jealousy on Louise's side.'

'What colour hair did she have?' asked Jonathan mildly.

'She was a carrot-top,' said Miss Brett, returning to the photo-graph of Priscilla Fletcher. 'This certainly isn't her.'

*

A black BMW slowed as it came up behind Billy's Renault and he had a glimpse of a dark-haired woman in his rear-view mirror before the car turned left into the driveway in front of the Fletchers' house. He dropped the spectacles into his lap and lifted a pair of mini-binoculars to his eyes, using his hand to shield them.

He watched the car door open and the woman climb out. She was slim and smartly dressed in navy blue trousers and a pink polo-neck cashmere jumper with dark hair brushing her shoulders. He couldn't see her face because she had her back to him and, when she let herself into her house, he thought he'd put himself through the wringer for nothing. But she reappeared almost immediately, looking directly at him as she went to the rear of the car and released her boot. It was a trip she repeated several times in order to carry her shopping bags inside and, even if Billy hadn't recognized her the first time, he couldn't have failed to identify the way she walked. Quick, small steps that spoke of an impatient nature.

*

'The Burtons moved after Priscilla disappeared so that Louise could go to a different school,' George said. 'Do you know what became of her after that?'

'No. She went to Highdown's equivalent in Boscombe, but where she went from there . . .' Miss Brett shook her head. 'I did follow up with her new headmaster but I'm afraid he wasn't very flattering. I believe "unteachable" was the expression he used. Her parents changed her name and encouraged her to put the past behind her, but the headmaster said it was a mistake.'

'Why?'

'Oh, I imagine because it sent the wrong message. Changing one's name is such an easy way to wriggle out of one's difficulties, don't you think?' She was looking at Jonathan as she spoke, as if she suspected him of doing the same thing, and he felt his face heat up.

'What name did she take?' he asked.

'I believe it was Daisy.'

'Did she keep her surname?'

Miss Brett nodded. 'It was common enough not to worry about.' She paused. 'To be honest, I thought the Burtons over-reacted. It's true Louise was picked on when she returned to school the following week, but it would have passed. The other girls thought she was responsible for Priscilla being punished – and indirectly for the child running away – so she had a difficult two days. I urged her mother to take a tougher line, but I'm afraid she wasn't up to it. In the end it seemed sensible to compromise on a move.'

'You don't think it was Louise who was overreacting?'

'Without question,' said the old woman dryly, 'but, as I wasn't privy to what had gone on between the two girls, it was difficult to know how genuine she was being. I understood from her mother that her greatest fear was bumping into the Trevelyans, so clearly guilt played a part.' She gave a regretful shrug. 'It was desperately sad. None of us was immune. We all felt responsible.'

There was a wistful note in her voice as if her own guilt still lingered and George wondered if that was one of the reasons why she needed to paint David Trevelyan as an abuser. 'I'm sure you're right about it being trouble at home that caused Cill to leave,' she said gently. 'It's impossible to read her story without seeing her as a victim. Do you know if she had ever run away before? It tends to be a pattern of behaviour that's repeated until the child decides to leave for good.'

Miss Brett eyed her for a moment before leaning back to stare thoughtfully towards the window again. 'Do you know I've never considered that? How very interesting. I always put her absences down to truanting.' She fell silent for a moment or two. 'I think it's unlikely. On the one occasion when she was absent for three days in a row, Louise was also absent, and neither set of parents reported their daughters missing, which suggests they were going home at night.'

'Did the mothers work?' asked George. 'Perhaps the girls stayed in all day.'

'Oh, no, that wouldn't have been tolerated by either woman. I believe Mrs Burton had an office-cleaning job, but she was home at lunchtime. Mr Trevelyan worked nights, of course, so he'd have been sleeping during the day.' Miss Brett's mouth thinned with irritation. 'We had several persistent truants, particularly amongst the boys. It was an impossible problem, made worse when the leaving age was raised to sixteen. Short of tying them to their desks, there was little we could do if their parents wouldn't cooperate.'

'And ninety-nine per cent of teachers would rather turn a blind eye and be shot of the disruptive element, anyway,' said Jonathan lightly. 'The job's hard enough without having to cope with an illiterate Neanderthal dragging his knuckles along the ground.'

The old woman gave a grunt of amusement. 'Are you referring to the students or their parents, Dr Hughes? The more disruptive the child, the more ignorant and ill-disciplined the parents, I usually found. So many of the underachievers were lost causes before they ever reached Highdown. All one could ever do was pass the buck to the police and juvenile detention.'

'Was Roy Trent one of those lost causes?'

She studied him for a moment, a small frown creasing her forehead. 'I remember the name but I don't know why.'

'Dark-haired, medium height . . . his father ran a newsagent in Highdown Road. We believe Louise may have described him as one of Priscilla's rapists.'

Her eyes widened as memory surged back. 'Good heavens, you are well informed. Roy Trent, Micky Hopkinson and Colley Hurst.' She watched George make a note. 'In fact, Louise was insistent she didn't know who they were and could only give a vague description. It was the police who settled on those three because of their past history. They denied it, of course.'

'Were they on the school roll?'

'Not at that time. They had a history of expulsion and transfer to different schools but I don't know where they were registered in 1970 . . . if at all, frankly. I believe social services tried various supervision orders but it was an intractable problem. They should have been sent to approved schools to break the links with home – but there were too few specialist units left after the Government cut the funding.' She fell silent while she marshalled her thoughts. 'I don't remember Micky's or Colley's circumstances, but Roy's father remarried and wouldn't have anything to do with him. It was a cruel way to treat a child . . . did the poor boy no good at all.'

'We've been told that one of them had ginger hair,' said George.

'Colley Hurst,' she agreed.

'Where did he live?'

Miss Brett closed her eyes briefly as if looking back down a passage of time. 'I believe all three boys were in Colliton Way. It was a dumping ground for difficult families. Most of our under-achievers came from there.'

George glanced at Jonathan. 'I hope that rings some bells.'

He gave a doubtful shake of his head. 'Should it?'

'It's in your book,' she said mischievously, 'and it's another example of synchronicity. Wynne and Howard lived at 48 Colliton Way.'

Miss Brett was as intrigued by the coincidences as George was. 'One wonders why the police settled so quickly on Howard Stamp,' she said. 'As I remember it, he was taken in for question-ing almost immediately.'

'Several witnesses saw him running from Grace's house,' said George. 'He was a regular visitor, so everyone knew who he was, and when he confessed the police didn't need to look for anyone else.'

'But you don't accept the confession?'

'No. Dr Hughes and I believe it was coerced and that the story he gave in his defence fits the facts rather better. Do you remember it?'

'Only that he said his grandmother was already dead when he found her.'

George took a copy of *Disordered Minds* from her case. 'This is Dr Hughes's book, which includes Howard's case in Chapter 12. You might like to read it. It's a very well-argued rebuttal of the prosecution evidence.' She handed it across. 'He questions the pathologist's timing of the murder, the psychological profile of the murderer or murderers and whether that profile fitted Howard, as well as the forensic hair evidence which, along with the confession, persuaded the jury of Howard's guilt.'

'May I keep it?'

'Please. You have our cards and phone numbers. We'd be interested in any ideas you might have.'

Miss Brett reached for some spectacles. 'I remember Howard was a redhead,' she said, examining the cover, 'and if hair evidence was involved, that presumably explains your interest in Louise and Colley Hurst? You think one of them was the murderer?'

'It's a possibility. Colley fits the psychological profile, and Louise was living in the same road as Grace.'

'Mm.' She lowered the book to her lap and folded her hands over it.

'You're not even tempted by the idea?' asked Jonathan with a smile.

The old woman studied him over the rims of her tortoiseshell half-moons. 'I won't know until I've read it,' she said, 'but I fear you're clutching at straws . . . certainly where Louise is concerned. She would never have done something like that on her own – she was far too frightened – and if she had any knowledge of it she'd have spilled the beans immediately; that was her nature. She was a tale-teller.'

'Perhaps she wasn't asked?'

Miss Brett shook her head. 'She'd have found a way. Her favourite trick was to do what she did with Priscilla: needle away at whoever had annoyed her until they lost their temper, then plead innocence. I assume the aim was to get her own back on Priscilla for publicly breaking their friendship . . . but I never doubted that she was genuinely shocked by the poor child's disappearance.' She shrugged. 'You need to understand Louise's personality. She was a beastly little girl whose sole aim in life was to be the centre of attention – and telling tales on others was the only way she knew how.'

*

Priscilla Fletcher gave a frightened start as she slammed her boot and turned round to find a tall, well-built man in a baseball cap behind her. 'My God!' she snapped angrily. 'What the hell do you think you're doing?'

Billy removed the cap and smoothed his balding scalp. 'Hello, sis,' he said. 'I was about to ask you the same thing.'

Fourteen

CLOSE TO, Billy could see the tail-end of bruising under Louise's left eye, a yellow crescent, masked with make-up. He put a hand under her chin and lifted her face. 'Who's been hitting you?' he asked.

She pushed his arm away and pulled down a pair of dark glasses that had been holding back her hair. 'No one,' she snapped.

'I thought you'd done with all that, Lou. Never again, you said, the last time I saw you.'

She spun on her heel and marched purposefully towards the front door. 'You've got the wrong woman,' she called over her shoulder. 'My name's Priscilla Fletcher and I don't have a brother. I want you to leave.'

Billy followed her. 'And if I don't?'

'I'll call the police.'

He blocked her attempt to close the door. 'Don't be an idiot, sis. What would you tell them? That you've never seen me before in your life? All I'd have to do is phone the folks and get them to come up. Mum'll know you immediately. You've probably still got that mole on your thigh and the scald mark where you spilt boiling tea on your stomach.' He watched her shoulders slump in resignation. 'They've been worrying about you for twenty bloody years. We were told you'd gone to Australia.'

She stood irresolutely in the doorway, her head to one side as if she were listening for something in the farther reaches of the house. 'Look, you can't come in,' she said, touching a small hand to his arm. 'Nick's in his office and I don't need any more aggro. I'll meet you somewhere. When are you free?'

'Now. I'll take you for a drive.'

'I can't. He knows I'm home.' They both heard the sound of a door opening. 'Oh Jesus!' she hissed. 'I'll meet you outside Dingles at four this afternoon. Now, piss off quick, or I'll get my face smashed in again.'

He put his hand out instinctively to stop her closing the door. 'This is crazy. Tell him I'm your brother.'

But she was too fast for him. 'He won't believe me,' she whispered as the latch locked against him.

*

'I hate meeting women like that,' said George of Miss Brett as she unlocked her car door.

'Really?' said Jonathan in surprise. 'I thought she was incredible. Brain like a laser . . . memory like a computer. If I'm like that when I'm in my eighties I won't have any complaints.'

'Exactly,' said George, slinging her case onto the back seat. 'Life is so *bloody* unfair.'

He waited while she reached in to release the lock on the passenger side then stooped to face her across the seat. 'Loads of people beat cancer, George. There's no reason why you shouldn't make eighty if you do what your doctors tell you. You mustn't get hung up on genetic history – it's the curse of modern living. Just because your mother died of it doesn't mean you're going to.'

She settled herself on the seat. 'That's not why I don't like meeting women like Miss Brett. She's a *wonder*, Jonathan. She should have had *babies*. Imagine what they would have been like – intelligent, healthy, *wise*. It makes my heart bleed, it really does. What's *wrong* with men that they can't recognize a peach when it's under their nose?'

He wondered if she was she talking about herself. 'Genes aren't everything. Nurture's just as important. Miss Brett's role in life has been to mould other people's children, and that's a far harder prospect than thirty seconds' drunken copulation that produces a random selection of dodgy chromosomes. In any case,' he finished with a grin as he attached his seat belt, 'how do you *know* she hasn't had a child?'

'If she did, she wouldn't have been allowed to keep it . . . or talk about it. They'd never have put an unmarried mother in charge of a secondary school in the sixties.' She fed her key into the ignition and locked her own belt. 'It's a crazy world that helps the least able in society to go on reproducing but discourages intelligent career women.'

It was a surprisingly illiberal view for a woman who portrayed herself as the opposite. 'It's better than it was,' he murmured. 'At least women aren't stigmatized for having children out of wedlock these days.'

'Maybe not,' she said roundly, 'but you're certainly penalized for it financially. You try holding down a full-time job and paying for forty-plus hours of childcare on what remains of a single salary after taxes have been deducted. *That's* the disincentive. It's a ridiculous waste of good genetic material. If I were in government, I'd make it a requirement of law that every workplace had a crèche.'

'Too expensive and impossible to manage,' said Jonathan. 'Imagine the cost to a small company if only one female employee had a baby at any given time.'

'Then they form a cooperative crèche with other businesses in the area,' said George, starting the engine. 'What's the alternative? I read a report recently that said over thirty per cent of professional women are choosing to remain childless. That's a *disaster*. What happens if the rate reaches sixty per cent? What happens if we end up with a society produced entirely by *under*achievers?'

'That's a very bleak view.'

'I wish it were,' she answered, pulling away from the kerb and performing a three-point turn.

'It's just as hard for men,' said Jonathan.

'Except your clocks take longer to run down,' George said with a smile, 'and you can father a baby a week if you find enough accommodating women.'

'It's not that easy,' he said morosely.

She glanced at him as she drew to a halt at the junction with the main road. 'Then start making compromises,' she said bluntly. 'You're an attractive and talented man, Jonathan, and you should be a father.'

He gave a low chuckle. 'Thank you, George. Sadly, the more usual response to my clumsy efforts is: "I wouldn't have a baby with you if you were the last man on earth."'

'Then do something about it.'

'Like what?'

'Make compromises,' she repeated, waiting for a car to pass.

'Did you?'

'No. There was always something better round the corner . . . and by the time I realized what a flawed philosophy that was, I'd become redundant.' She flashed him a bright smile to quell any attempt at sympathy. 'Don't make the same mistake, Jon. There's nothing worse than living with regrets.'

In an uncharacteristic gesture, Jonathan put his hand on hers and gave it a quick squeeze. 'If it's any consolation,' he said, 'you're just as redundant if you *do* pass on your genes. Once a child is born – and barring the few years of nurturing that allows him to achieve independence – there's nothing you can add to him that isn't already there. It may be good, it may be bad, but by the third generation your genes will have become so diluted that your great-grandchild will carry only a tiny percentage of you. People's value is in their achievements, George, not in their ever diminishing gene pool.'

It was on the tip of her tongue to say achievements were empty when there was no one to share them with, but instead she gave a relaxed laugh. 'Then let's find somewhere to eat while we work out who really killed Grace,' she said, pulling left onto Bridport Road. 'That would be one *hell* of an achievement.'

*

She drove to the Smugglers Inn at Osmington Mill, to the east of Dorchester, which had been built in the thirteenth century, beside a stream, in a cleft between two swooping downlands that rose to meet the spectacular Jurassic cliffs of the Dorset coast. The car park overlooked the sea – a turbulent grey that April lunchtime, whipped by an easterly wind – with the thatched inn accessible via a steep ramp and a flight of steps. 'My treat,' said George firmly, leading the way. 'I had a pay cheque this morning so I'm feeling flush.'

Jonathan made a half-hearted protest. 'Why don't we go Dutch?'

'Because you're broke and I'm old enough to be your mother,' said George, pushing open the door. 'Also I'm starving, and I refuse to feel embarrassed about eating three courses while you pick away at some miserable little starter because it's all you can afford. Reason enough?'

He followed her inside. 'I suppose Andrew's been dishing the dirt on me again?'

'It depends how you define dirt. Most of what he said was highly laudatory.' She turned to look at him. 'What do you think?'

'That you're feeling sorry for me.'

'The *pub*, Jonathan. What do you think of the *pub*?'

'It'll do,' he said, taking in the impressive oak beams that criss-crossed the low ceiling, the open fireplaces with glowing embers and blackboards advertising local lobster and a healthy wine list. 'At least it's an improvement on the Crown and Feathers.'

'You're very difficult to please,' she said with a sigh. '*Anything*'s better than the Crown and Feathers. I hoped you'd appreciate some atmosphere.'

He laughed and steered her towards the bar. 'I was teasing, George. If you want to pass yourself off as my mother, you'll have to learn to take it.'

This sharing of a meal was so different from the first that Jonathan wondered whether George's remark about a bad beginning making a bad ending was true. If so, he blamed Roy Trent for it. However ill Jonathan had been feeling that day, it was the other man's use of 'black' and 'wog' that had really raised his hackles. 'Tell me something,' he invited when a natural lull came in the conversation. 'Did you phone Roy to tell him you were going to be late for the lunch in February?'

George paused with her fork, laden with steak-and-kidney pudding, halfway to her mouth. 'Of course I did. I said I'd be lucky to be there before twelve forty-five and asked him to take you up to the room. Why do you ask?'

'Just interested in why he was so aggressive. He left me standing at the bar for a good ten minutes before he put in an appearance, then the first thing he did was call me a wog, but he must have had some suspicion of who I was. The only other people there were a middle-aged couple and Jim Longhurst, so it's not as though there were droves of potential Jonathan Hugheses to choose from.'

George looked appalled. 'Did he *really* call you a wog?'

Jonathan nodded. 'Wog . . . black . . . darkie – the only thing he didn't call me was a nigger.'

George's face went through several gargoyle gyrations. 'Good *lord*! That's *outrageous*! No wonder you were so cross.'

Jonathan grinned as he cut into his fillet of salmon. 'I think he was trying to get rid of me before you arrived.'

'He'd have succeeded, too, if my neighbour hadn't come home when he did. I'd reckoned another half-hour on the charger before there was enough juice in the battery to give me a spark, then Barry turned up with jump leads and had me ticking over in a couple of minutes.' Her forehead creased in a frown. 'I phoned just after midday, and Roy said you were already there.'

'Then he was watching me through a spyhole,' said Jonathan bluntly, 'because he didn't emerge till twelve fifteen. I thought at the time it was a damn strange way to run a pub.'

'He has a CCTV camera above the till and a couple of monitors in the kitchen.' She chewed a piece of steak. 'I'm completely shocked. He told me the only racist remark he made was that he was expecting a white man and you took off like a rocket. Do you still think he isn't involved?'

Jonathan shook his head. 'I'd probably agree a ninety per cent certainty that he was one of Cill's rapists, but I can't see the connection with Grace unless the police missed a hell of a lot of evidence. Even if Colley Hurst was the murderer and bath-taker, there was nothing to indicate the other two boys were there.' He shrugged. 'I suppose Colley might have told them about it afterwards, but it doesn't explain why Roy would want to protect him now.'

'Perhaps we should ask him,' said George lightly.

'He'd laugh.'

'Not if we concentrate on Cill's rape,' she said. 'We know he was taken in for questioning about it and we know the names of his friends. It'll be interesting to see his reaction.' Impatiently, she pushed her plate aside and propped her elbows on the table. 'He's so smug, Jonathan. At least let's put him on the back foot.'

The idea was tempting. 'What good will it do if we can't link him to Grace?'

'It'll scare the bejabers out of him,' she said, 'particularly if we ask him who Priscilla Fletcher is and why she would want to steal your wallet. As far as he's aware, his ex-wife is completely unknown to us. In any case, I can't *believe* he called you a wog – it's so *rude.*'

*

The closer they came to Bournemouth the more Jonathan regretted agreeing to accompany her. Sticks and stones might break his bones but rudeness had never killed him. In one form or another, he'd lived with it all his life. It had turned him into a deeply repressed individual, but it was the sticks and stones that frightened him.

'*You're such a coward, Jon . . . it's embarrassing. When are you going to stand up for yourself?*'

'I'm not sure I can do this,' he said suddenly.

George, who had been prattling through his increasingly long silences, was unsurprised. A couple of glasses of wine had released his inhibitions long enough for him to accept the challenge, but the Dutch courage hadn't lasted the fifty-minute drive. 'He'll avoid any difficult confrontations for as long as he can,' Andrew had warned her. 'His expertise, as he'll tell you again and again, is researching documents. He'll want the longest paper trail you've ever seen before he'll tackle Roy Trent. It's a defence mechanism.'

'Against what?'

'Being in a situation he can't control . . . being found wanting . . . being afraid. I had the devil's own job persuading him down to Bournemouth to talk to you.'

'Why?'

Andrew shrugged. 'He didn't know who you were, or what to expect. He's a fish out of water with strangers.'

'Is it shyness?'

'Not entirely. He was badly bullied at school and it's left him paranoid about everything – rejection, in particular.'

'Like Howard.'

Andrew nodded. 'Except Jon's scars don't show, and I think that makes it harder for him. He doesn't have an obvious excuse to feel like an outsider – except his colour – which is why he portrays himself as a victim of racism. It's easier than admitting that what he's really afraid of is derision.'

George made no response to Jonathan's remark until she was able to pull off the main road and draw up behind a parked car in the first side street she could find. 'What don't you think you can do?' she asked, killing the engine.

'Talk to Roy,' he said, rubbing his face furiously with his hands.

'Why not?'

'We don't have enough information. What are we going to say to him?'

She watched him for a moment, not doubting that he was in a genuine funk. 'I'm planning to describe Cill Trevelyan's gang rape as told to me by William Burton,' she said unemotionally, 'then make it clear that I believe Roy was involved along with his friends, Colley Hurst and Micky Hopkinson.'

'He won't like it.'

'Should I *give* a damn?' asked George with an amused laugh.

'He'll deny it. You don't have any proof.'

'I'm not planning to arrest him, Jonathan, just let him know what I know and see where it takes us.'

He lowered his fists to his lap and banged them against each other. 'I can't see the point of putting him on his guard before we need to. Supposing he gets angry?'

'You should be more worried about me getting angry,' she said mildly. 'I hate rape with a passion, Jonathan, particularly gang rape of a child. If Cill had been *my* daughter – if *I'd* been Jean Trevelyan – I'd have camped on Roy's doorstep thirty-three years ago till he confessed, then I'd have ripped his head off. He should count himself lucky I wasn't.'

Jonathan stared at her in wide-eyed desperation. 'I really can't do it.'

She put a hand on his arm. 'What are you afraid of? That he'll hit me? I quite hope he does, as a matter of fact – I'll have him charged with assault – but he won't do it for that reason.'

Jonathan shook his head. 'You can't be sure.'

'No,' George agreed, 'but I'm damned if I'll let that stop me. In any case, I have a pepper spray in my bag. It's highly illegal – I bought it in America – but I'd rather be in prison for zapping a mugger than dead because he had a knife.' She paused to let him take the information in. 'I'm not easily intimidated, Jonathan. I may not be the fittest thing on two legs but my dad taught me to stand up for myself, and it was a good lesson. I'll tackle Roy alone, if necessary, but it won't help you if I do.'

He raised a mirthless smile. 'It'll do me more good than having my jaw broken.'

'Has that happened before?'

'Once.'

'By bullies?'

'*A* bully,' he said flatly.

'Did you report him?'

'No. I pretended I'd fallen off my bike.'

'Why?'

'Because he said he'd break it again if I didn't.' His smile became twisted. 'I didn't have a father like yours, George. The last thing you did with mine was stand up for yourself . . . unless you wanted more of the same, of course.'

*

There was no point telling him it was a variation on a theme repeated in every case study of physical abuse George had ever read. For Jonathan, and every abused child, their individual story was unique. A low-income family, struggling to survive. Secrecy, coupled with threats of retaliation if the abuse was exposed. A child who hid in the school lavatories because he was too frightened to go home. An angry father whose violent tendencies were aggravated by alcohol. A despised mother who allowed her son to be beaten in preference to herself. A dysfunctional parental relationship made worse by an elderly grandfather whose demands for attention increased the stress within the family. A skinny, fast-growing adolescent with ill-fitting clothes who was targeted by bullies because he wore his timidity too openly. A reinvention of history because lies were less painful than the truth. Repressed emotions, limited social skills, inability to commit to relationships, fear of criticism, fear of failure . . .

*

'Andrew told me you had a steady girlfriend until Christmas,' George said. 'What happened to her?'

'You're such a coward, Jon . . . it's embarrassing.'

This was not a story Jonathan wanted to narrate, and he wouldn't have done if George hadn't retreated into a deadening silence which became more insistent the longer it went on. He understood that hers was, a far more determined character than his, and he began to wonder if she and Andrew had cooked up this plot to persuade him to talk about Emma.

'Were you lying about wanting this meeting with Roy?' he asked angrily, as if George were party to his thought processes.

And perhaps she was, because she addressed his unspoken question. 'Is it really so hard to tell me about her?'

'There's nothing to tell,' he said harshly. 'It didn't work out so we split up. It happens every day.'

Again the silence drifted, nagging at Jonathan's nerves like a toothache. An interminable number of cars drove past while George sat calmly on, more prepared than he to wait it out. He wanted to despise her for her inquisitiveness, but he couldn't. An inquisitive woman would have pestered for an answer. He wanted to feel angry at her attempts to manipulate him, but he couldn't, for when he finally told the story it was because he wanted to.

Fifteen

BILLY BURTON took another look at his watch, then dropped his cigarette butt to the pavement and crushed it underfoot. He'd arrived early and had been standing close to the store entrance for forty-five minutes and, though crowds of shoppers had passed, Louise had not been among them. He was disappointed but not surprised. She'd failed to make several such rendezvous before the family lost touch with her, and the circumstances had been tediously similar.

At first, spurred on by his father, Billy had tracked her down each time she moved – always when her useless husband was given another stretch in prison – made an appointment to meet, only to hang around on a street corner waiting for her to show. In the end he became impatient, and he told his father to let her stew for a while. She'll call you when she's ready, he'd said confidently. But he was wrong. All contact with her had been lost, and they'd been out of touch for more than two decades.

There were no recriminations. Indeed, sometimes he thought they were secretly relieved to be shot of her. His father said he'd always expected it, his mother said Billy had tried his best, and, like a cracked record – never mind a whole river had passed under Lou's bridge – the parents returned to blaming Cill Trevelyan. Louise had never been the same since the 'little tart' had run away.

215

If they'd understood how much influence the beastly girl had wielded over their own naive Lou, they'd have strangled the friendship at birth.

Nevertheless, Billy had always felt guilty. Once in a while – usually under pressure from his wife – he would ask himself why his parents had never gone knocking on doors themselves in search of their errant daughter, but it wasn't an excuse that sat easily with him. Louise's prostitution and heroin addiction had been so inexplicable that on the rare occasions when she paid a visit home the Burtons' initial pleasure at seeing her had invariably degenerated into a blazing row, leaving Billy – no less puzzled by his sister's rapid descent from wife to hooker – as the only conduit of communication. The one thing he'd never told his folks was that amongst her various aliases was the name Cill.

Their mother was convinced she'd died in Australia, either from drugs or Aids, and there was endless speculation about children. Had she had any? Where were they? Who was looking after them? Councillor Gardener believed she'd had a baby by Roy Trent in her teens, and, while Billy knew that to be untrue, he was less sure about a marriage. Her name changes had been as hard to keep track of as her changes of address.

He took another look at his watch, toying with the idea of driving back to Sandbanks. Lou hadn't denied it when he suggested she was still on the game, but her remark about having her face smashed in *again* implied it was Fletcher who'd given her the black eye. God knows she'd had plenty in her time, from either her husband or customers, but what kind of pimp lived on millionaire's row and sent his wife out prostituting?

He lit another cigarette and promised himself he'd leave when it was finished. He couldn't make any more sense of Lou's situation today than he had twenty years before, but he'd give her another five minutes . . .

*

'It was *Guess Who's Coming to Dinner*, but without the happy ending,' said Jonathan. 'We lived together for a year before Emma allowed me to meet her parents – she insisted we wait until we were sure we wanted to get married.' He smiled painfully. 'So we invited them to the flat on Christmas Eve to give them the good news . . . and it was worse than anything I'd imagined. She warned me her father wouldn't like it, but she didn't tell me he'd call me a "dirty nigger" and then start lamming into her. I left the room when he slapped her . . . and she moved out on Christmas Day. She hasn't spoken to me since.'

'Where did you go?'

'I hid in the lavatory.'

'What did Emma say?'

'That I was a coward and I'd embarrassed her – nothing I didn't deserve. She was looking for a man who would stand up to her father, and I couldn't . . . so we split up.'

'Is she with anyone else?'

'I don't know.'

'Have you called her?'

'No.'

'Why not?'

He closed his eyes. 'Why do you think?'

'I don't know, Jon, but I can *guess*. Because suffering in silence makes you feel better about yourself? Because you've persuaded yourself Emma would rather have a relationship with a brutish father who abuses her than with a coward who hides in the lavatory?' George's tone was abrasive. 'Perhaps you're afraid he'll come round and hit you, and you've decided Emma isn't worth the thirty seconds of pain? Perhaps you *agree* with her . . . you *are* a coward and an embarrassment and she'll be better off without you? Or you're like Howard . . . and you hope that if you self-mutilate long enough someone like me will come along and rehabilitate you.'

He took to rubbing his face again. 'She'll refuse to speak to me,' he said harshly. '*That's* why I haven't phoned.'

'Oh, I see,' said George in mock surprise, 'you're afraid of rejection. Well, well, well! What a man of double standards you are, Jonathan. It doesn't matter whose feelings *you've* hurt . . . just so long as *yours* don't suffer. Are those the rules you operate by?'

'You know they aren't.'

'I don't, I'm afraid. You shared a bed with the girl and made love to her. At the very *least* you have an obligation to find out if she's all right.' She gave him an ironic smile. 'Or am I being very old-fashioned?'

*

'You look like shit,' said Billy, examining the new bruises under his sister's make-up. 'Are you all right?'

'Yeah,' she said, pulling her scarf over her mouth. 'Nick's got a fucking awful temper, but he doesn't mean to hurt me . . . not really. He's powerfully jealous, which I guess means he loves me.'

Billy took her arm and steered her towards a cafe in the alleyway opposite Dingles. 'You're such a tit, Lou,' he said, using a term he'd often called her in childhood. 'When are you going to learn that guys who love their wives don't beat them up?'

'Don't start,' she said crossly. 'I had enough of the lectures before. I wouldn't be here except I was afraid you'd come banging on the door again.'

He pushed open the cafe door and led the way to an empty table. 'What do you want? Tea? Coffee? Something to eat?'

'Black coffee,' she said ungraciously, 'but I can't pay for it because he took all my money.'

So what's new? Billy thought, as he went to the counter. The only difference between now and twenty years ago was that she was better dressed and lived in an expensive house. The beatings still happened . . . she was still having to touch her family for spending money . . . she still didn't want her brother knocking on her door. It was damn weird whichever way he looked at it.

He returned with two coffees and put one in front of her.

'So who's Nick Fletcher?' he asked, sitting down. 'What does he do?'

'He's a businessman,' she said.

'What kind of business?'

'He's a bookie.'

'Never heard of him.'

'No reason why you should.' She changed the subject abruptly. 'So what have you been doing with yourself, Billy? Are you married? Got kids?'

He nodded. 'Do you remember Rachel Jennings? Sister of Mark Jennings who was in your year? We got hooked up in 'eighty-five and had twin daughters two years later – Paula and Jules – they're sixteen now.'

'God!' said Louise. 'You mean I'm an aunt?'

Billy grinned. 'Of two redheads. What about you? Did you have any? Am I an uncle?'

She stared into her coffee cup. 'I had a miscarriage once but that's the closest I came. It's a bit of a bugger really. I'd have liked kids.'

There was too much regret in her voice for him not to believe her, and he wondered who'd told Councillor Gardener otherwise. 'I'm sorry.'

'Yeah. So how are the folks? Are they still in the old house?'

'No, Rachel and I bought it off them so they could move to Cornwall.' He gave her a potted history of the family's fortunes since 1980. 'Dad's supposed to have retired but he works as a jobbing gardener to avoid going stir-crazy at home, and Mum got born-again religion two years ago. She's a parish visitor or some-thing: calls on old people who can't leave their houses . . . then spends every Sunday in church. Dad can't understand it at all, keeps telling her she must have a lot on her conscience.'

It was seeing the smile vanish suddenly from Louise's face that made him think about what he'd said. He'd heard Robert Burton use the expression several times, but he'd always assumed it was a mild joke to account for Eileen's sudden obsession with Jesus.

Billy knew it annoyed his father, even made him jealous to have his pliant wife find an interest in life that excluded him, but he'd never taken the teasing seriously.

He watched his sister's gaze drop to the coffee cup again. '*Is* there something on her conscience?' he asked curiously.

'How would I know?' she snapped. 'I haven't spoken to her in years.'

'Then why are you looking so guilty?'

She didn't answer.

He stirred sugar into his own coffee. 'Do you want to know how I found you?'

'Not particularly, but you'll tell me anyway. It used to give you a hell of a buzz to prove how clever you were tracking me down. You were a real pain, Billy. The folks'd click their fingers and you'd come messing up my life again . . . and you never even asked yourself if I wanted to be found.'

'The first time I did, we lost touch with you,' he said prosaically. 'Was that what you wanted? I can't believe it. You couldn't take their money off me quick enough every time I turned up. You had upwards of a thousand quid in a couple of years . . . but you were damned if you'd come by and say thank you. That's all they wanted, to see you once in a while and know you were still alive.' He sipped his coffee. 'It was you got the buzz out of me traipsing around after you, made you think you were important. It's the same reason you let men hit you – you want the attention.'

'Cut the crap,' she said with a bitter edge to her voice, 'I'm not in the mood. I had a habit up to three years ago and it turned me into a zombie.' She raised her eyes again. 'Go on, tell me how you found me. I know you're dying to.'

'I had a visit from a woman councillor about ten days ago. Her name was George Gardener . . .'

*

Jonathan took out a handkerchief and blew his nose. He was still painfully thin, with wrists and hands protruding from his cuffs like paddles, and George wondered if he had ever developed beyond the bullied adolescent who grew too fast for his clothes. She recalled Roy's derisive comments about Howard Stamp's 'scrappy little beard' and 'sparrow chest', and wondered if Roy had spotted the same similarities between Howard and Jonathan as she had. It would certainly explain his attempt to see Jonathan 'off'. George doubted Howard had ever left his house without running a gauntlet of abuse, which raised the question, how did he find the courage to leave it at all?

'What would I say to her?' Jonathan asked. 'I'm sorry? It'll never happen again? It *will*, George. If her father slapped her twenty times, I'd still run away. I'm like my mother. I'd rather anyone had their jaw broken than me . . . *including* Emma. I'm everything she called me . . . I'm everything my mother was.' He drew a shuddering breath. 'And I *hated* my mother.'

'Therefore Emma hates you,' said George flatly.

'I don't blame her.'

'Except it's a grand example of transference, Jon – a cock-eyed view of the world where past relationships poison present ones.' She gave a small laugh. 'Let me put it another way – if you chose to play your mother, then what role did you give Emma? What did you want her to be?'

'Girlfriend . . . partner . . . lover. We didn't have any problems till her father showed up.'

'Are you sure?'

Jonathan had been watching an elderly man approach along the pavement. He had a tiny Yorkshire terrier on a lead and every time the dog showed an interest in a lamp-post, he yanked it away like a hairy yo-yo. It was obvious he resented the animal, either because it belonged to his wife or because he thought the red ribbon in its fringe reflected badly on him, but the harshly snapping lead was an easy cruelty.

'. . . *you can be so unkind, Jon. I'm not your keeper . . . nor am I responsible when things go wrong for you . . .*'

He shifted his attention back to George. 'I don't know,' he

said honestly. 'I was never that close to anyone before. I was a disappointment sometimes, but I didn't mean to be. I usually received a lecture when it happened.'

George looked intrigued. 'So you turned her into a nanny? How interesting. I'm not surprised she packed her bags. Women today don't even want to be nannies to their children, let alone their husbands.'

'I did not,' said Jonathan irritably. 'She may have acted like one sometimes, but that wasn't my choice. I wanted an equal.'

'Then your signals are confusing. We all get treated according to the reactions we provoke, Jon. I've known you half a second but it's obvious everyone nannies you . . . Emma, Andrew, me . . . even Priscilla Fletcher while she was stealing your wallet. I expect you have secretaries at work who do it.' She raised her eyebrows in enquiry. 'It's wonderful for your ego – means there's always nanny to blame when things go wrong – but quite incompatible with a mature relationship between equals.'

He turned away angrily to watch the old man. 'I didn't ask you to do this,' he said in a strained voice. 'I made a simple statement. I said I didn't want to talk to Roy. If you'd respected that, we wouldn't be having this conversation.' He paused briefly, as if wondering about the wisdom of saying anything else, before letting rip: 'You're like Emma . . . you go *on* and *on* . . . pick, pick, pick . . . and for what? So that I'll stand up to some *fucking* bastard I hardly know, just because you don't like the way he treats you.'

'We all have transference reactions of some degree or other,' George countered mildly. 'My father blighted my life.'

Jonathan glared at her suspiciously. 'That's not the impression you give. You always talk as if you were fond of him.'

'I was. No other man came close. Why do you think I've never married?'

*

Louise looked very shaken by the time Billy had finished the account of his meeting and telephone call with George Gardener.

Her hands were trembling so much that she couldn't lift her cup without spilling the coffee. 'If you knew it was me, why the hell did you tell her to go to the Trevelyans?' she hissed.

'Because she was going to go anyway . . . maybe not immediately, but she'd have got round to it eventually.' He lit a cigarette and offered it to her. 'I thought it was quite clever of me,' he said with as much artistry as she used in her lies, 'so a thank you wouldn't come amiss.'

Tears glittered on her lashes as she fumbled the cigarette into her mouth. 'What's clever about it? I'll have a sodding detective on my doorstep next.'

'So? You can prove you aren't Cill Trevelyan. I'm sure the folks still have your birth certificate.' He lit a cigarette for himself and leaned forward. 'The reason it was clever is that, by being helpful, I persuaded this Gardener woman that Priscilla Fletcher isn't Louise Burton. That's not to say she won't find out, but at least it gives you time to come up with an explanation.'

She stared at him with suspicion. 'For what?'

'For a kick-off, why you've turned yourself into Cill's clone. Why *have* you, as a matter of interest?'

'None of your business.'

'Is it guilt? Did something happen to her?'

'She was raped.'

'Other than that.'

She wouldn't look at him. 'Why did it take you so long to find me? You said your meeting with George was ten days ago.'

'I've been on days for a while, so I haven't had time. And you're ex-directory. I had to persuade a mate at the post office to give me your address.' He took note of the way she said 'George'. 'Do you know this woman, Lou?'

'No.'

'All right, do you know *of* her? She seems pretty clued up about you . . . or rather Priscilla Fletcher. She told me you live in Sandbanks, that you were married to Roy Trent and that you had a son by him when you were in your teens.' Billy's heart sank as he watched fear widen his sister's eyes. 'Oh Christ, Lou!' he muttered, lowering his voice. 'What the hell did you get into? Was she right about Roy? Were you lying when you said you hadn't had kids?'

He could read her expressions as easily as when she'd been a child, and he watched her face as her mind manufactured alternative versions of history, only to discard them. None was convincing enough to persuade him that she wasn't in trouble. 'I wasn't lying about kids,' she said finally, 'but Roy had one. A boy. He's grown up now and lives in London – courtesy of Wandsworth prison – but he stayed with us for a while when we first married. That'll be where the nosy cow got the son bit from, I should think, though I'd bloody well like to know who told her. The kid was a nightmare . . . always on the take, always in trouble with the cops . . . he's the one caused me and Roy to split up.'

'Who was his mother?'

'One of Roy's tarts. I told him he didn't need to take the boy on, but he had a thing about his own dad dumping him, so he wouldn't listen. The kid ended up in prison – ' her mouth twisted – '*surprise, surprise* – he was sixteen when we took him on and nineteen when they banged him up – and in three years he managed to ruin everything Roy and I had going.'

'When was this?'

She wiped the glowing end of her cigarette around the sides of the ashtray, then took another drag before squashing it. 'We got married in 'ninety-two, split up after nine years of me being told his bloody son's problems were my fault and divorced last year. It was a fucker, Billy. Roy and me would have done OK – he still fancies me something chronic – it was the bloody kid caused all the trouble.'

There was too much information and Billy wasn't practised enough to sort the wheat from the chaff. Why had Louise married Roy at all? Had she been one of his tarts? What had she done to make his son's problems her fault? What happened after the divorce? When did she marry Nick Fletcher? How did she know

Roy still fancied her? Was he the reason for her black eye and swollen lip?

In the end he asked the question that troubled him the most. 'Did you ever go inside Grace Jefferies' house?' he demanded, gripping her wrist between his strong fingers. 'I want the truth, Lou.'

The change of expression was too obvious. This was an explanation she'd rehearsed. 'Don't be an idiot!' she said scornfully, wriggling her hand free. 'You know damn well I didn't. I was barely thirteen years old and I'd had my head done in because my best friend went missing. Ask Mum if you don't believe me. She stood guard over my door in case I did something stupid.'

'I said *ever*, Lou. I didn't say, "Were you in there the day she was murdered?"'

Louise reached for his pack and lighter and took another cigarette. Her hands were trembling again. 'I never went in Mrs Jefferies' house. *Satisfied?*'

'No.' Billy shook his head. 'I think you and Cill hid out with her when you truanted. I remember you telling me once that she had a bigger telly than ours.'

Her mouth started working fiercely and she lifted her scarf to hide it. 'You haven't changed much, have you, Billy?' The tears glimmered on her lids again. 'You always were a fucking nuisance.'

Sixteen

25 Mullin Street, Highdown, Bournemouth
Wednesday, 23 April 2003, 5.00 p.m.

GEORGE'S HOUSE was a 1930s semi, with white pebble-dashed walls and anachronistic mock-tudor features in contrasting black. There was an embossed petal motif beneath the eaves, diamond leaded panes in the windows and two skimpy wooden beams set at right angles to each other to suggest a structural wooden frame. 'It's typical of its period,' she said with irony, when Jonathan made no comment.

He smiled back. 'Rather like Poundbury, then – relatively new but pretending to be old.'

'Just good old pre-war sham,' she said, leading the way up a short path to the front door, 'but at least it was built to last. I'm not a big fan of the outside either but the inside's all right.' She turned her key in the lock. 'According to the neighbour who saw Howard's arrival, it's an exact replica of Grace's house.' She nodded towards a block of flats fifty yards down the road. 'That's where it was before it was pulled down.'

'Where did the Burtons live?'

George swung the door open and held it ajar with her knee. 'Number 18,' she said, pointing to a terrace of brick houses opposite the flats. 'They used to be council-owned but they were sold to the tenants in the eighties.'

She took him into her sitting room and dropped her case onto

226

a chair. It was a big, open room with a French window to the garden and an archway through to a dining area and kitchen. George clearly liked clutter, because every available surface was covered with knick-knacks and curios. Her taste in colour was interesting, thought Jonathan, while wondering if he liked the combination of mustard yellow walls and chocolate brown carpet. Very baked earth, and not always complimentary to the paintings on the walls, but the whole feel of the room was a good reflection of George's personality. Warm, full of ideas, but not entirely comfortable to be around.

'The phone's in the kitchen,' she told him, shrugging off her suit jacket and folding it over her arm. 'I'm going upstairs to change, and it'll take me about half an hour. The coffee's by the kettle and there's an open bottle of wine in the fridge. Help yourself to whatever you want.'

'What if I don't do it?'

George shrugged. 'You'll never know what the next chapter might have been.' She pulled a wry face. 'But don't do it to please me. Dad always said I was far too curious for my own good. Do it because you want to, Jon.'

He waited until he heard her footsteps on the stairs, then walked through the archway to look for the telephone. It was on the wall at the end of an L-shaped worktop that split the kitchen area from the dining table. He put his briefcase on the table and took off his jacket, automatically removing his wallet and tucking it into the case. Even as he did it, he recalled performing the same routine in the Crown and Feathers, right down to the brush of the briefcase lining against the backs of his fingers. He raised his eyes to stare through the lead-paned windows at George's unkempt garden. He was certainly curious about that chapter. Why had Priscilla Fletcher taken his wallet if she hadn't wanted to draw attention to herself?

With a sigh, he moved to the worktop and took the receiver from the hook. In the pit of his stomach he knew the call would end in tears, but he also knew that George was right. He couldn't live in an emotional vacuum for ever. Not without going mad.

*

Louise flung Billy's hand off her arm as she stormed out of the cafe. 'If you don't leave me alone, I'll start screaming,' she hissed under her breath, 'and I'll tell anyone who asks that you gave me the bruises.' Her pale, obstinate eyes raked him. 'You know I'll do it.'

He did. She'd always been ready to lie about his involvement if it meant getting off scot-free herself – except on the one occasion of Cill's rape. 'Go ahead,' he said, with mirrored obstinacy in his own eyes. 'Scream your head off . . . and when the police arrive, I'll tell them I was a witness to Cill Trevelyan's rape, that I can name all three of the bastards involved and that Howard Stamp wasn't the only person with ginger hair who spent time in Grace Jefferies' house.'

Louise gave a shuddering laugh. 'You wouldn't do it,' she said. 'You're too like Mum. You'll worry about what the neighbours'll say and keep your mouth shut.'

'Don't rely on it, Lou.'

There was a tiny hiatus before, with an unexpected show of affection, she touched a hand to his cheek. 'It's forgotten history,' she told him, 'and you can't re-open it without hurting your wife and kids. Do you think they'll thank you for dragging their name through the mud? It's never the guilty who suffer, Billy.'

She turned away and this time Billy let her go, fear rising like a sickness in his throat. '*Your mother has a lot on her conscience . . .*'

*

Jonathan was in the garden when George returned downstairs. He was picking his way rather aimlessly about her overgrown patch of lawn, head determinedly down, hands crumpling a handkerchief. She knew he'd made the call because she'd heard his voice through her bedroom floorboards.

'Oh, *bugger*!' she muttered to herself as she took the wine from the fridge. 'Bugger! Bugger! Bugger!' She poured a couple of glasses and took them outside. 'Chin up,' she said with false cheer, handing one to Jonathan and clinking it with hers. 'Try thinking of it as a beginning . . . when a door closes behind you it means you can move on. And that's healthy. It's how it's supposed to be.'

'Your grass needs cutting,' he said, scuffing his foot across the lawn. 'Do you have a mower? Do you want me to do it for you?'

'Wouldn't you rather go home? I can give you a lift to the station.' She lowered her wine glass. 'I can finish this when I get back.'

Jonathan put a slender finger under the stem and pushed it up. 'Drink away. Andrew lent me thirty quid, so I'll take a taxi when the time comes.'

She waited for him to continue, and when he didn't: 'Do you want to talk about it? What did Emma say?'

'Nothing, I didn't speak to her.' He smiled wryly at her expression. 'Her father answered her phone. He said he'd "*rip* my black nuts off" if I ever called again. I presume she's living with them, or he's confiscated her mobile.'

'What did *you* say?'

He played his foot across the grass again. 'That I'd be round tomorrow morning to rip his white ones off if he didn't put Emma on immediately.'

George gave a surprised laugh. 'Oh, well done! And?'

'He doesn't think I've got the nerve. He hung up.'

She let a beat of silence pass while she watched his fidgeting toe. '*Do* you have the nerve?'

'Maybe . . . if I do a trial run first.'

'Who with?'

'Roy Trent,' he said with a smile, 'because the way I'm feeling at the moment, I'll rip *his* nuts off if he makes a remark I don't like.'

From: wandr.burton@compuline.com
Sent: Wed 23/04/03 17:31
To: robandeileen.burton@uknet.co.uk
Subject: Louise

I know its rachel or the twins usually does this but I can't ring
because I'm angry and I don't know how to say this without getting
in another row about the strikes Ive found louise and she's living
with another abuser plus there's stuff going on here that's doing my
head in lou looks like cill trevelyan and she was married to one of
cills rapists for a while she says there's things mum kept to herself
to save the family embarrassment and I want to know what they are
  There's a woman councillor saying Howard stamp didn't kill grace
jefferies and I remember mum lying about knowing her when the
cops came round I always knew something bad happened round
that time because you were both mad with worry this woman says
it was someone with ginger hair killed grace but it wasn't Howard I
know you both know lou was in grace's house every time she
skived so is that the only thing mum kept quite about why do you
keep saying mums got things on her conscience

I need some answers dad otherwise Im thinking of going to the
cops.

Billy

From: Rob Burton [robandeileen.burton@uknet.co.uk]
Sent: Wed 23/04/03 18:40
To: wandr.burton@compuline.com
Subject: Louise

Dear Son,

I've had great difficulty trying to make out what on earth you're talking about. I wish you'd learnt to use punctuation when you were younger. Spellchecks can only do so much. As to rows, you know my feelings. The strikes are unpatriotic, son, and browbeating will not make me change my mind.

As to this ridiculous nonsense you've written, I can only presume Louise has been filling your head with lies again. Obviously, it's the drugs talking and I'm afraid you're even more foolish than I thought if you pay any mind to her.

I don't know who this woman is you're referring to or why you say your mother lied about knowing her. Nor do I understand what you mean by 'Lou looks like Cill Trevelyan'. Of course Howard Stamp killed his grandmother, he confessed immediately and was convicted, and if your mother and I were 'mad with worry' at that time, it was because David Trevelyan was making life difficult for me at work. He accused the family of spreading lies about Cill, saying there was only Louise's word the rape had happened. According to him, if both girls were together then they would both have suffered the same fate, and he was angry with Louise for suggesting his daughter was 'easy' and 'asked for it' while Louise was left alone. Unfortunately, his thinking was muddled. Another accusation he made was that if the rape had happened, Louise must have told your mother and me because she was so quick to tell the police. The implication was that we failed to pass the information to him, and instead allowed Cill to be punished for the fight with Louise while knowing that Cill was in a vulnerable state. By some rather twisted logic, that made us responsible for his wretched child running away.

I should say, we were never convinced about the rape, although we certainly believed Cill had had sex with some boys in front of Louise, and your sister had misinterpreted what was happening. From your mother's and my point of view, it was a friendship made in hell, with your sister being introduced to things she shouldn't have known at 13. I'm afraid we had our doubts about David Trevelyan from the beginning. He was unnaturally keen to thrash the girl, particularly after she started to develop, and neither of us was comfortable with it. If your mother has anything to regret it is certainly that. She has said many times that she should have found the courage to speak out and accuse him of abuse. I should add that we have often wondered if some of Louise's problems stem from the fact that he may also have abused her. She spent a lot of time in their house, and there's no doubt she became very frightened of him after Cill went missing. We tried to keep an open mind but that became increasingly hard when David started drumming up sympathy at work by making my life difficult. He was under a lot of pressure from the police because, despite an alibi, he would certainly have been charged had Cill's body ever been found. Yet he was able to deflect attention from that amongst our colleagues by accusing your sister of lying. On two or three occasions Jean had a screaming match in public with Mum on the same subject, and your mother found it embarrassing and stressful. It was this as much as anything that turned Louise into a frightened little mouse and persuaded us to move.

Re. your mother's 'conscience': I have no idea what secrets she keeps in her heart but I am quite certain she had no knowledge of Louise 'skiving' in Grace Jefferies' house because it wasn't true.

Who put that idea into your head? And as to Louise marrying one of Cill's rapists, where did that piece of nonsense come from? Louise herself didn't know the names of the boys and the police never revealed which ones they questioned. As a matter of fact, I believe several were taken in because Cill was rather too easy with her 'favours', but there was nothing to connect any of them with the alleged rape or the disappearance. If Louise is your source, then I ask you to remember how drugs affect her brain. She was never able to be truthful about anything once she was caught in the cycle of addiction and prostitution, and I doubt much has changed if she's with another 'abuser'. It's a terrible waste of a life, but I'm out of sympathy with her now. Your mother and I couldn't have done more to get her away from it, but she made it clear she preferred the squalor of selling herself for heroin-induced stupors to behaving like a mature adult.

I have no problem with you giving her our address and phone number, though I doubt she'll bother to call. I expect, as usual, she left you in the lurch with threats of doing something silly if you interfere again. It's all so predictable, and not something I will ever understand. Mum is out at the moment but should be back by 7.00 p.m. If you want to talk to either of us, feel free to call, though I'd prefer it if we didn't have a row. Louise has caused so many in the past, and I don't have the energy for them these days. Your mother is well, as I hope are Rachel and the girls.

Dad

From: wandr.burton@compuline.com
Sent: Wed 23/04/03 18:55
To: robandeileen.burton@uknet.co.uk
Subject: Louise

Dear dad   it wasn't just lou saw the rape it was me too   roy trent
was part of the gang   he's the one lou married   there were three in
the gang and one had red hair   he was called colley hunt or
something like that   roy was the worst and now I find lou married
him and has turned herself into a cill trevelyan clone   looks just like
her   plus lou did go into grace jefferies house   cill too   I watched
them sneak out the back a couple of times   ask mum   she knows
its true   grace came round one time to complain about the way me
and lou teased Howard and she said shed tried being nice to lou to
get it to stop by letting her in to watch tv   I need you and mum to
talk this over and see what you remember   at the moment I don't
know what to do for the best   I'll call later but I don't want you telling
me to keep my mouth shut   I feel really bad about not saying
anything before   but seeing cills photo the other day makes me
realize she could never have looked after herself   I reckon her dad
killed her and got away with it and I think lou knows he did   that's
why she went so peculiar   plus I always thought it was weird that
Howard killed his gran because he was so frightened of everything
he cried once when lou called him a spastic
Billy

Roy flicked Louise a brief stare of dislike when she sidled into his kitchen and told him George Gardener had been asking her brother about Cill Trevelyan's disappearance. 'I told you she'd find out about it, but you wouldn't listen to me.'

He was sitting at the table, eating his supper and watching the CCTV monitors. He concentrated on his food and didn't bother to answer.

Louise's eyes flashed angrily. 'Don't ignore me, Roy. You think you can control everyone . . . but you can't. George knows my name, she knows I was married to you and she's showing my picture around and one of Cill just before she went missing. Billy let her think I'm Cill by giving her the number of the last detective agency that came snooping, but the minute the Trevelyans see my photo, they'll tell her Priscilla Fletcher's Louise Burton. Then what are we going to do?'

He pushed his plate away and lit a cigarette before tilting his chair back and propping his feet on the table. 'More to the point, what are *you* going to do, my darlin'? *I'm* not the one pretending to be someone else. Maybe I'll just wash my hands of you the way I should have done the day you took my son to bed.' He blew a smoke ring into the air and watch it drift and expand towards the ceiling. 'What say I throw you to the wolves, eh?'

She moved behind him to rest her cheek against his hair and link her wrists over his chest. 'You'd never do it. Nick'd kill you first.'

He stroked the soft down of her forearm. 'Has he been hitting you again,' he asked, squinting up at her bruised lip, 'or was that for Billy's benefit?'

She smiled as she dropped a kiss on the top of his head. 'Billy's putty in my hands when he's feeling sorry for me. I always got more money if he told Dad I was being done over.'

Roy dropped his feet to the floor. 'What are you up to?'

'Nothing.'

He shook her off abruptly and stood up. 'I should never have helped you get off the white stuff. You were halfway controllable when you were stoned, a sodding nuisance since you started thinking for yourself. I wouldn't mind so much if you didn't have sawdust for brains. You act before you think, Cill, that's always been your trouble.' He moved away to put some distance between them.

'Don't call me that,' she said irritably. 'You know I hate it.'

Roy shrugged. 'It's what you've been called for most of your life.' He watched her expression sour. 'You're carrying too many ghosts, darlin'. They come back to haunt you every time you feel sorry for yourself. You should have kept your clothes on and left the lad alone, then maybe I wouldn't have been so keen to let Nick take his turn in the queue.'

She lifted her scarf to hide her mouth. It was an automatic gesture, learnt from long experience of avoiding inquisitive eyes, but it was a waste of energy with someone who knew her as well as Roy. 'Billy told me Mum's got religion,' she said with a sudden little giggle, 'and when he asked Dad why, Dad said she had things on her conscience. That's pretty funny, isn't it?'

Roy eyed her thoughtfully. 'What else did Billy say?'

'That George knows about the rape and thinks you and me had a baby when we were in our teens.' She flicked him a sly glance. 'She's confused because she thinks I'm Cill – which makes the kid the product of rape, and you its daddy.'

Roy's jaw tightened. 'And?'

'I told Billy he was your son by one of your tarts and I mothered him as best I could in the circumstances.'

'What circumstances?'

'That he took after his dad,' she said lightly. 'A highly sexed, out-of-control teen with a habit, who couldn't keep his hands to himself and ended up in prison.'

'My *God*!' he said with loathing. 'You really *are* a bitch, aren't you?'

She raised an indifferent shoulder. 'It's as near the truth as damn it.'

Roy had a momentary understanding that he had never controlled her – *even when she was on her knees, begging for a hit* – but the idea was too radical to hold for long. 'You're one sick bitch, Lou.'

She let the comment go. 'So what am I going to say to Billy? He'll come back, he always does.'

Roy squeezed out the glowing tip of his cigarette and let it drop to the floor. 'Not my problem,' he said harshly. 'You've brought this one on yourself. You should have left George to me, like I told you.'

Louise wrapped her thin arms around herself. 'Maybe I didn't want to,' she said, with a catch in her voice. 'Maybe I hoped she'd find out about Cill . . . maybe I can't live with ghosts as easily as you can, Roy.'

He gave an angry laugh. 'Don't do this,' he warned. 'It might work on your brother but it never worked on me. There's the phone.' He jerked his chin towards a receiver on one of the worktops. '*Use* it. Call her. See how well the damaged-little-girl act works on a woman. Better still, call the cops. If you're lucky, they won't believe you—' He broke off as she leaned forward to stare at the monitor. 'What's up?'

'You've got visitors,' she said in a remarkably steady voice, all pretence at sympathy-seeking forgotten.

He followed her gaze and saw George and Jonathan talking to the barmaid. 'Bloody hell!' he growled, as the girl lifted the trapdoor and gestured towards the kitchen. He manhandled Louise out of the door. 'Upstairs and stay put till I tell you,' he ordered, crushing her arm in an iron fist, 'because I'm warning you . . . if Hughes catches even a glimpse of you, I'll drop you in it so fast your feet won't touch the ground.'

Louise glanced at him scornfully as she placed her foot on the first step.

Seventeen

The Crown and Feathers, Friar Road, Highdown
Wednesday, 23 April 2003, 7.35 p.m.

GEORGE HAD predicted that Roy would be affable, at least at the start, so his hostile demeanour when they entered the kitchen worried her. She wasn't much of a psychologist, she realized, as she glanced at the CCTV monitor showing the bar. Forewarned was forearmed, and a man like Roy would always favour attack as the best form of defence. As usual, the second monitor was dead, and, not for the first time, she wondered why he needed two. Jonathan reacted to the animosity immediately, jutting his jaw and clenching his fists at his sides, instinctively bracing himself for assault. It was reminiscent of their first meeting, but this time there was no coerced apology from Roy to oil the water.

The man was facing the door, bottom propped on the table, a beer mug in his right hand which he was carelessly wiping with a tea towel. But he held it by its handle, as if polishing were not the aim of the exercise. He appeared very relaxed and, owing to where he'd stationed himself, George and Jonathan were unable to move out of the doorway into the room. They were too close together and it put them at a disadvantage, not least because it made them look comical.

Roy grinned. 'Well, well, well . . . if it isn't the Odd Couple. What can I do for you?'

'We wanted a chat,' said George lightly.

He stared at her for a moment, his expression unreadable. 'It's not a good time. If you come back tomorrow morning, I'll see what I can do.' He shifted his attention to Jonathan. 'Not you, mate, you're barred.' His eyes narrowed threateningly. 'I don't like people who accuse me of lying, and I sure as hell don't want them in my pub.'

'Jon never—' George began.

'Let him speak for himself,' Roy cut in. 'He's got a tongue, hasn't he? Or is he too scared to use it?'

Jonathan didn't say anything.

'That figures. I sussed you as a jessie the first time I saw you.' He pushed himself upright and took a step forward. 'End of conversation. Now sling your hook before I phone the cops and have you arrested for causing a nuisance.'

George was the first to retreat. 'Come on,' she said, plucking at Jonathan's jacket. 'He's within his rights, unfortunately. A licensee can exclude anyone he wants from his premises and he doesn't have to give a reason for doing it.'

But for the first time in his life, Jonathan stood his ground. 'Then I'll have to change his mind.'

Roy dropped his right hand and took another step forward, holding the glass at his side. 'And how are you planning to do that?'

'Not by fighting you,' said Jonathan mildly, relaxing his clenched fists. 'In the first place I'm not armed and in the second place it would give you an even better excuse to exclude me.' He indicated the courtyard. 'There's a black BMW parked in the road, registration number R848 OXR. It was there when I met George – I saw it when I left – and again in the evening when Andrew Spicer drove me back here to collect my wallet. Is it yours, Mr Trent?'

'None of your business.'

'Do you know what car he drives, George?'

She frowned, remembering a reference to a BMW but unable

to recall why. 'As far as I know, it's a van. He keeps it in a garage at the back.'

'The ticket clerk at Branksome Station said the woman who went through my briefcase drove away in a black BMW. I think it's your ex-wife's car, Mr Trent. She said she'd seen me here and knew who I was, and she was certainly here when my agent came for my wallet.' He glanced towards the stairs. 'Is she upstairs now? If so, we'd like to talk her.'

Roy raised his left palm and shoved it against Jonathan's chest. 'Out!' he ordered. 'Now! Go on! Piss off, the pair of you!'

Jonathan backed away immediately. 'There's no need for violence, Mr Trent.' He raised his voice. 'Tell Priscilla Fletcher we'll wait by her car till she comes out. We'd like to ask her about Cill Trevelyan's gang rape by Roy Trent, Colley Hurst and Micky Hopkinson.'

'Keep your voice down,' Roy snarled. 'There's customers can hear you.'

Jonathan ignored him. 'We also want to ask her about Grace Jefferies' murder,' he called. 'We know Roy Trent lived in the same road as Howard Stamp, and Louise Burton lived opposite Grace. We think Priscilla can tell us the connections. We're prepared to wait as long as it takes. She can't leave her car out there for ever.'

It was George who thwarted any attempt Roy might have made to shut Jonathan up. She used her briefcase to block his upswinging arm. 'How *dare* you do that?' she squeaked, her face turning brilliant red. 'You can't intimidate us the way you intimidated those defenceless children. What happened to Cill? What happened to Louise? How many other little girls did you rape?'

Roy might have reacted if his barmaid and one of his regulars hadn't appeared in the corridor behind Jonathan. They stood open-mouthed, listening to what George was saying. 'In the kitchen,' he told George and Jonathan tersely. 'And *you –* ' he pointed to the girl – 'back behind the bar. It's a private argument . . . none of your business.'

But Tracey wasn't inclined to go that easily. 'It didn't sound very private. Everyone could hear it. Should I phone the police?'

'No.'

Tracey turned to George, her expression alight with curiosity. Perhaps she felt a sisterhood with the other woman after the remarks about 'rape', or perhaps she didn't like her boss much. 'What about you, love? Are you OK? Has someone been hurting you?'

George shook her head. 'I'm all right for the moment, Tracey, but if there's any more shouting, I believe you should call the police. We haven't come for a fight, but things get out of hand very quickly when people lose their tempers.'

'That's for sure,' said the girl with feeling. She took a last look at Roy and there was a hint of derision in her eyes, as if things had been said that struck chords with her. 'I'll see you later then.'

Roy gave an abrupt nod and shut the door on her, but it was a while before he said anything. He stood with head bowed, staring at the floor, and it was obvious to both George and Jonathan that he was working out what to do. Jonathan, buoyed up by success, wanted to seize the advantage, but George put a finger to her lips and persuaded him to stay quiet. Every so often, the boards creaked on the floor above, although whether from the natural contraction and expansion of wood or under the weight of an eavesdropper's stealthy footsteps it was impossible to tell.

When Roy finally spoke, it was without heat. 'By rights, I should put a lawyer on to you,' he said, looking up. 'What you've done is slander me in front of my customers and staff. It's true that I was taken in for questioning about Cill Trevelyan's rape, along with Colley and Mick, but we denied it and there was no evidence to connect us with it. The girl who gave the information, Louise Burton, didn't know the names of the boys and didn't identify us – ' he shrugged – 'so the cops ended up questioning if a rape had even happened.'

He moved away from the door and reached for his cigarette pack on the table. 'I'm not going to say we weren't wild, because we were. Everyone despaired of us, including ourselves. We were never in school . . . couldn't read . . . always on the make.' He bent his head to the lighter. 'About the only thing that made life bearable was alcohol and, when we couldn't get it, we'd be thinking of more extreme ways to top ourselves. In that respect, we were no different from Howard.' He fixed his attention on Jonathan. 'You talked the other day about him having nowhere to go except inside himself. Well, we were no different. We did similar stuff . . . not to ourselves so much, though it happened – ' he flexed his fingers – 'Mick was the worst, always carving spirals on the back of his hands – but mostly we targeted other people.' His mouth twisted cynically. 'This isn't easy to say, and you probably don't want to hear it, but we felt good when someone else was hurting. It meant we weren't the only people living shit lives.'

He fell into a brief silence while he took a drag on his cigarette. 'We were awful to Howard,' he said abruptly. 'It went on for years . . . started when we were nippers and he was in his teens. He lived down the road from us and we were at him all the time. Mick used to prod him in the back with his knife . . . drew blood quite often till Howard got himself a leather jacket. It was too damn easy. He was such a miserable little wimp.' Again he focused his attention on Jonathan. 'I guess we hoped he'd fight back – show a bit of spirit – but he never did. Too much common sense, perhaps.' His eyes hardened as if he were making the point for Jonathan. 'Like George said earlier, things get out of hand when people lose their tempers, and Howard was really scared of Mick's knife.'

Jonathan leaned his hands on the back of a chair. 'There were three of you and one of him,' he said matter-of-factly. 'What kind of odds were those?'

'Not good,' Roy admitted, 'which is why he showed sense by ducking and weaving. The trouble is, it made us worse. Most days he hid – either in his house or at his gran's – but we were always on the lookout for him. You both keep saying he didn't kill his gran. Well, he *did*. And the reason I know is because we wound him up for it. Mick was always on his back, jeering at him because he didn't have a weapon, and one day Howard pulls a sodding great carving knife and starts slashing at Colley. They said at the trial he went berserk and slashed his gran . . . well that's what he did with Colley. He was completely out of it . . . mad as a bloody hatter and so wild Mick and me couldn't get close. He cut Colley on the arm a couple of times before we legged it, and our next stop was the hospital. Far as I remember, Colley had twenty stitches, and he was still carrying the scars five years later.'

He turned to George. 'I'm not proud of it, which is why I didn't want you finding out. We were scared Howard was going to blame us for turning him into a raving lunatic, but the cops never came near us even though most of the street knew we'd been bullying him. The strange one was Wynne. She used to hiss at us every time she saw us, but she didn't say anything, not even at the trial.' He flicked ash to the floor. 'I've never understood why not. If they'd gone with diminished responsibility, he'd have been sent to Broadmoor and given some psychiatric help. Instead they banged him up in Dartmoor, where he was never going to make it.'

George pulled out a chair and sat down, clearing a space for her case. 'He pleaded not guilty,' she said, flicking the catches, 'therefore your treatment of him was irrelevant to his defence. You know that as well as I do, Roy. Rather more interesting is why the prosecution didn't quote this episode with the carving knife to strengthen their case.' She took out her notepad. 'Did Colley report it? What explanation did he give the hospital?'

'He said he'd been in a fight but didn't give any names.'

'Why not?'

Roy shrugged. 'We spent all our time avoiding the cops. No point getting involved if we didn't have to.'

'When did it happen?'

'A month or two before Grace was murdered. I don't remember exactly.'

Jonathan stirred. 'How well did you know her?' he asked.

'Not at all.'

'Then why call her Grace?'

There was a small hesitation. 'Everyone did. It's how she was labelled in the newspapers.'

'You said you couldn't read.'

Irritation flickered briefly in the dark eyes. 'So? It was the main topic of conversation in my dad's shop. He read every damn newspaper . . . told anyone who wanted to hear what the latest update was.'

Jonathan reached over to flick back a page of George's notepad. 'According to our information, you were estranged from your father. Your parents' marriage failed and you went to live in Colliton Way with your mother. Your father remarried and refused to have anything more to do with you.' He looked up. 'Presumably your stepmother had children of her own and didn't want an illiterate thug for a role model?'

Roy's jaw tightened. 'What's the big deal? George always refers to her as Grace, and so do you in your book, Dr Hughes.' He smiled grimly. 'And before you jump on me for that, I learnt to read in a young offenders' institution when I was sixteen. I did twelve months for burglary . . . and it taught me a few things – mostly that prison was a mug's game.'

Jonathan straightened and took out his own cigarettes. 'The big deal is that I don't believe you, Mr Trent,' he said, flicking his lighter. 'Howard going berserk with a knife a month before Grace was murdered is a little too convenient, don't you think? It's quite impressive if you managed to concoct it in the last few minutes, but it sounds more like a story you and your friends invented at the time.'

'Why would we do that?'

'In case you were questioned.'

Roy shook his head dismissively. 'We wouldn't have been. We were never in the frame. Call me a liar as much as you like – it's water off a duck's back – but you're trying to prove a negative.

Our patch was Colliton Way and the rundown buildings on the industrial estate at the back of it. We didn't know Grace from Adam, never went near her house and wouldn't have wanted to. It was when we strayed outside our boundaries that we got into trouble . . . sticking close to home meant we were left in peace. And that's how we liked it.'

Jonathan stared him down. 'The only reason you weren't in the frame was because Howard confessed. If he hadn't, you'd have been high on the list of suspects. The police had questioned the three of you only five days before about the rape of a missing girl who lived just two streets away from Grace. You matched the description given by that girl's best friend, Louise Burton, who lived *opposite* Grace. You were well acquainted with Howard Stamp, knew that he had a grandmother, knew that he took refuge in her house and knew that he bought goods for her at your father's shop. One of your gang, Micky Hopkinson, regularly carried a knife. Another, Colley Hurst, had red hair, as did Louise Burton, who was truanting regularly and was certainly associated with you.'

'Then why couldn't she identify us?' Roy snapped.

'*Didn't*, is the word you're looking for, Mr Trent. Why *didn't* she identify you?'

'Because it wasn't us.'

George looked up from her note-taking. 'It's easily proved, Roy. Her brother, William, witnessed the rape and, if you're agreeable, I'll show him a photograph of you and see what he says. Do you have any from when you were a teenager? Better still, do you have a group picture of yourself with Colley and Micky?'

This time the hesitation was a long one. 'No,' said Roy at last. 'It's a period of my life that I'd rather forget.' He crushed the butt of his cigarette into the ashtray and moved to look at the monitor. 'Have you any idea how difficult it is to try to make something of yourself after the kind of childhood I had? You have to cut yourself off from everyone you know and start again. I've no idea where Colley and Mick are now . . . what happened to them . . . if they're still alive.' He gave a grunt of amusement. 'I don't think there *were* any pictures – you'd have to know someone with a camera to have your photo taken – and *we* didn't. Only the rich sods went in for that kind of crap.'

It was an excuse that might have appealed to Jonathan – there was hardly any record of his childhood either – but George just laughed. 'Oh, *please*! Spare us the violins. I bought a little Brownie in 1960 for about three and fourpence . . . which is under 20p in today's money. It was hardly a rich man's pastime. There must be some snaps of you. Anything from your late teens or early twenties would do. You wouldn't have changed much. What about a wedding photo?'

'The wife took them.'

'Priscilla Fletcher?'

'First wife . . . mother of my kid.'

George eyed him for a moment. 'How many wives have you had?'

'Two,' he said harshly. 'Not that it's any of your business.'

'What was the name of the first one?'

He didn't answer.

'Not my business?' she asked with a smile. 'Well, you're probably right.' She removed a digital camera from her case, then eased back her chair preparatory to standing up. 'If you've no objections, I'll take a photograph of you now. There's a function on my computer that allows me to airbrush out the signs of ageing, so I should be able to produce something that approximates to what you looked like in 1970.'

Roy turned his back immediately. 'Don't even think about it,' he warned, 'not if you want your camera intact when you leave.'

'It's to your advantage,' she pointed out mildly. 'If you had nothing to do with the rape then William Burton will exonerate you.' She placed the camera on the table in front of her and shuffled through her case. 'Let me show you a photograph of Cill Trevelyan just before she went missing . . . see if that jogs your memory at all. She bears a striking resemblance to your second wife.' George slid the copy across the table towards his rigid back and paused to see if he'd bite. 'I also have one of Priscilla, taken by Jim Longhurst at a barbecue here.' She lined the second picture up beside the first. 'The ticket clerk confirmed that she was the dark-haired woman who went through Jonathan's briefcase at Branksome Station.'

Roy lit another cigarette but wouldn't look at the photographs. 'What's the point you're trying to make? That I married Cill Trevelyan?'

'Did you?'

He gave an angry laugh. 'Of course I bloody didn't. The kid vanished. If the cops had done their job properly, they'd have put her father in the dock.'

'He had an alibi,' said Jonathan. 'He was at work all night.'

Roy half turned. 'There was only his wife's word he didn't do it before he left. The cops didn't believe Mrs Trevelyan any more than anyone else did. She was protecting her husband.'

Jonathan watched George scribble notes across a page. 'Why would she want to?' he asked.

'Because she was just as guilty. She should have taken better care of the girl.'

'In what way?'

'Kept her out of harm's way. That's what mothers are for.'

It was a remark that begged a number of questions, thought Jonathan, recalling his own situation. How far was any mother responsible for her child's victimization – unless she was the abuser? What if she were being abused herself? Where did responsibility to others end and the drive for self-preservation take over? What was anyone's duty in life when terror was an all-consuming emotion? How far was Roy projecting his mother's neglect of him onto Mrs Trevelyan? How far was he simply trying to divert attention from his own involvement?

'What harm are you talking about?' Jonathan asked bluntly. 'The rape?'

'The beltings her father used to give her . . . that'll be how he killed her.'

'Was it Cill who told you about them?'

Roy flicked him a withering glance. 'Couldn't have been, could it, as I never met her. It was in the newpapers, mate. It was given to me second-hand, like everything else, till a halfway decent screw decided I needed an education.'

George intervened. 'If David Trevelyan killed her, then when and how did he get rid of the body?' she asked matter-of-factly. 'According to Miss Brett, he reported her missing as soon as he reached home on the Saturday morning, which means he had to kill her and bury her between the time she was sent home on the Friday afternoon and before he started his night shift. That's a tall order. The body would have to be deep enough – and far enough away from his house – to prevent it ever being found . . . or, if it *was*, to make it feasible that she'd been killed by an abductor.'

Neither man said anything.

'The only Trevelyan who had all night was *Jean*,' George went on slowly, 'and a woman would have to be Myra Hindley to dispose of her daughter and appear normal afterwards.'

'It happens,' said Roy.

'Except the psychology's wrong,' George protested. 'I should have thought this through before. Look – ' she tapped her pencil on the newspaper clippings – 'first Mrs Trevelyan told the police that there were difficulties at home and that her husband had had a row with Cill, *then* she gave an interview to the press about her regret and anguish that they'd both been so strict with her.' She turned a perplexed face to Jonathan. 'But she'd have said the opposite if she knew the child was dead. She'd have stressed what a *good* relationship she and her husband had had with their daughter.'

'Perhaps she was being clever.'

'The kid was always in trouble with her dad, and everyone knew it,' said Roy. 'If her mum had pretended different, there'd've been even more eyebrows raised.'

'A person would have to be psychopathic to work that out after a night's digging and no sleep,' said George sarcastically. 'Not to mention cleaning the house of every shred of evidence that a murder had been committed.'

'All I know is what people said at the time,' Roy countered stubbornly. '*He* killed the kid and *she* was protecting him. It forced them out in the end.'

Eighteen

9 Galway Road, Boscombe, Bournemouth
Wednesday, 23 April 2003, 8.00 p.m.

ROBERT BURTON picked up the receiver after a single ring and Billy pictured him in the cramped hallway of his bungalow, standing, waiting for the call to come, then pouncing on the telephone before it disturbed his wife. Billy had always had an easy, if distant, relationship with his father, but suspicion corroded trust and he didn't bother with pleasantries. 'I want to talk to Mum,' he said.

'She's not here.'

'You said she'd be back by seven.'

'She's on one of her parish visits. It's obviously taking longer than she expected.' There was a ten-second hiatus as his hand muffled the receiver, but not before Billy had heard his mother's voice in the background. 'Sorry, son, the cat was after the wire. Why don't I ask Mum to call you when she comes in?'

'No thanks,' Billy responded curtly. 'I'd rather you put her on now. I know she's there. I heard her.'

'She doesn't want to talk to you.'

'Then tell her I'll drive down tomorrow.'

Another brief pause. 'Why aren't you at work?' his father asked. 'You know what I think about these twenty-four-hour strikes. You're letting the country down, expecting the army to cover for you while they're trying to fight a war in Iraq. It's unpatriotic, son.'

Billy stared irritably at the wall. It was the sort of diversionary tactic his father always used. 'Give it a rest, Dad, I'm not in the mood. I'm between shifts . . . back on days from Friday. Now, put Mum on, please. I really do need to talk to her.'

'I'll try, but I don't think she'll come.'

The receiver was placed beside the telephone and Billy heard his father walk into the sitting room. He couldn't make out what was being said because his parents spoke in whispers, but his mother's lighter tread returned. 'Hello, dear,' she said in her usual inexpressive tone. 'Dad says you've found Louise again. How is she?'

'Hasn't Dad told you? I sent him an email.'

'He said she was back to her old tricks.' His mother sighed with what sounded like a genuine regret. 'There's nothing to be done about it, Billy. I pray every day that she'll be given back to us but Jesus can only work miracles with people who have faith.'

Billy wasn't interested in metaphysical solutions. 'There's a woman asking questions about Grace Jefferies' murder,' he said baldly. 'According to her, Howard Stamp didn't do it, and I remember you lying to the police about knowing Mrs Jefferies. You said you didn't know where she lived and had never talked to her . . . but you did and you had. So why did you lie, Mum?'

He expected her to deny it, or say she didn't remember, but she surprised him with honesty. 'Because I was worried for the family,' she said. 'We were already connected with one scandal and I didn't want us dragged into another. You were so young you've forgotten how awful it was – everyone was terrified – we thought it was going to happen again until Howard Stamp was arrested.'

Billy refused to be diverted from the lie. 'You were worried even before the police came to the house,' he said. 'I was watching you. Your hands were shaking.'

Eileen hesitated, as if debating the merits of truth. 'I thought it was to do with Cill,' she said after a moment. 'I was afraid they'd found her body and the whole thing was going to become even more of a nightmare.' She made a small noise that sounded like a laugh. 'It was such a relief when they said Mrs Jefferies was dead. I thought, oh, thank goodness, no one can say *we* had anything to do with that. It was a small lie, Billy, and I wasn't the only one,' she went on. 'No one admitted to knowing her. It was bad enough what happened, without being singled out for questioning. We all just wanted it to go away, and it did, of course, as soon as the wretched grandson confessed.'

Billy stared at the wall again. 'Why would you think Cill's body was in Mullin Street?'

More hesitation. 'I didn't mean it to sound like that. I just meant I was afraid they'd found her body . . . not *where* it might be, just that it was somewhere. I'd been thinking about nothing else for days . . . when were they going to find the poor child's body? And with all those policemen around . . .' She petered into silence.

Billy wanted to believe her. Even at ten years old, it had been his first thought – that the police had come to Mullin Street because of Cill Trevelyan. 'Cill and Lou used to go into Mrs Jefferies' house to watch her telly. I know you knew that because I heard Mrs Jefferies tell you.'

Eileen didn't answer.

'Did you never think Cill might have gone there when she ran away? You should have told the police, Mum. So should Lou.'

A tiny edge of malice entered his mother's voice. 'And what do you think the Trevelyans' reaction would have been if I'd suggested Cill was involved in a murder? Jean was already screaming at me like a fishwife every time she saw me.' She took a breath. 'It's all very well criticizing, Billy, but I had two seconds to make up my mind and I'm still sure I did the right thing.'

Perplexed, Billy rubbed his head. 'I'm not saying she had anything to with the murder,' he protested, 'I'm just saying she might have gone there when she ran away.'

'Well, if she did, it was nothing to do with us.'

'Except everyone was trying to find her. Why didn't you or Lou say something when Lou was questioned about the rape?'

There was a catch in his mother's voice. 'She wasn't asked, neither was I . . . and I don't understand why you're being so beastly to me—'

The receiver was taken by his father. 'You're upsetting your mother, son. What's the point you're trying to make? Because if you're suggesting *she* had something to do with that bloody woman's death, you'll have me to deal with. Understood?'

Billy thought of his mother's long, red hair which he used to fumble into loose plaits whenever she let him. It had been an intimacy they shared until she dyed it a deep auburn when they moved. After that he was never allowed so close again, and the intimacy was reserved for Louise, who, at the same time, became a brown-haired urchin called Daisy. Until now he'd forgotten how jealous he'd been. 'Did she have anything to do with it, Dad?' he asked harshly. 'Councillor Gardener said it was someone with ginger hair killed Mrs Jefferies . . . and Ma sure as hell had ginger hair before you made us cut and run from Mullin Street. So did Louise. You called them "the terrible twins". Remember?'

The line went dead immediately.

The Crown and Feathers, Highdown, Bournemouth
Wednesday, 23 April 2003, 8.15 p.m.

George was intensely sceptical. 'That would mean three people were all suspected of murder in the same place, at the same time – ' she ticked them off on her fingers – 'Howard Stamp, David Trevelyan and Jean Trevelyan – and with *two* different victims. Don't you think that's a trifle unlikely, Roy? It's not as though murder's a common crime in this country. Manslaughter, maybe, but not *murder*. There wouldn't have been more than three to four hundred during 1970, and to have two of them happen a couple of streets apart and within days of each other is a statistical improbability.'

'Unless they were connected,' said Jonathan.

'We don't even know if Cill's dead,' George pointed out, levelling the tip of her pencil at the photograph of Priscilla Fletcher. '*That* might be her.'

Jonathan watched Roy's gaze stray towards the picture. 'Is it, Mr Trent?'

'No.'

'Do you mind telling us who she is?'

The other man shrugged. He was growing more relaxed as each minute passed, and Jonathan wondered why. *Because they'd strayed from Howard Stamp?* 'She was calling herself Priscilla Curtis when I wed her.'

'Then how can you be so certain she wasn't Cill Trevelyan? She looks just like her.' He watched for a reaction, but Roy's expression remained deadpan. 'You can't have it both ways, Mr Trent,' he went on. 'If you never met Cill, then you have no way of knowing if she *was* the woman you married.'

Roy stared at George's busily writing hand. 'You're on the wrong track, mate,' he said, allowing irritation into his voice. 'I don't deny I was caught up in a bad crowd when I was a lad, but I wasn't involved in murder and I don't know what happened to Cill Trevelyan – ' he jabbed a finger at the table top to reinforce his next sentence – 'and *neither* does my ex. Now you can take my word for that or you can go to the cops and run this crap past them, because I've had enough. I may not have told George precisely how I knew Howard – I wasn't proud of teasing the poor little bugger – but everything else I've said is true.' He stood up and moved towards the door in clear dismissal. 'Take it or leave it, because this conversation ends now.'

Jonathan exchanged a glance with George. 'Then you won't object if we ask Priscilla to corroborate this,' she said to Roy.

He eyed her with some amusement. 'Go ahead, but you'll have

to find her first.' He nodded at the monitor. 'I watched her sneak out about ten minutes ago.'

George frowned at the screen. 'Why does that please you?' she asked. 'I'd be mad as a hatter if the only person who could prove I was telling the truth left me in the lurch.'

'She'll back me up when you find her.'

'Depending on how well you prime her,' said George sarcastically. She shook her head. 'You haven't done much of a job so far, Roy. She seems to drop you in it more often than she helps you out. I presume it wasn't your idea to steal Jonathan's wallet . . . you didn't need to, you'd already seen him off. So why did she do it?'

'You're plucking at straws,' he said dismissively. 'There was no crime committed. Your friend got everything back intact.'

George made an abrupt decision. 'I think we'll go with your second option and take what we've got to Sergeant Lovatt,' she said, gathering her bits and pieces together and cramming them into her case. 'Neither Jon nor I believes that Cill Trevelyan's disappearance and Grace Jefferies' murder weren't connected, and if the sergeant suspects that Priscilla's Cill, then he'll certainly want to talk to her . . . and to you.'

Roy opened the kitchen door and stood back. 'Feel free,' he told her, 'but you'll be making idiots of yourselves. You've got nothing at all if Priscilla can prove she wasn't Cill – which she can – and the cops won't resurrect Howard just so you can make money out of a book. They had him bang to rights at the time, and everyone knows it – ' his lip curled – 'except you two.'

Jonathan took the case and gestured to George to precede him. 'I'm sure they said the same about James Watson and Francis Crick,' he murmured, 'and look how right they proved to be. The discovery of the double helix was a conceptual step, but Watson and Crick were the only two who believed it at the beginning.'

The other man's jaw jutted aggressively. 'You should learn to speak English, mate. I don't know what you're talking about.'

Jonathan halted in front of him. 'Of course you don't, but that's not my problem – *mate* – it's yours. You're an ignorant sociopath.'

Roy made a grab at his arm but Jonathan was ready for it. He wrapped his fist around Roy's in a surprisingly gentle gesture and pushed it away. 'I'm talking about the three-dimensional structure of the DNA molecule, Mr Trent. If the police haven't destroyed all the evidence from Grace's murder, then it may be Watson and Crick's discovery that sends you to prison.'

*

George tut-tutted severely as she wedged herself behind the steering wheel. 'You're lucky he didn't hit you.'

Jonathan grinned. 'He was afraid you were going to scratch his eyes out.'

She smiled automatically, but her mood had turned to despondency. 'So what do we do now? He's right about the police, you know. It wouldn't be fair to waste Fred Lovatt's time with this. We haven't anything concrete – it's all just speculation. We don't even know who Priscilla Fletcher is, let alone if she was in Highdown in 1970. She might have grown up in Sydney for all we know.'

'She speaks with a Dorset accent.'

'That's not proof of anything.'

Jonathan was on top of the world, buoyed up by adrenalin, so her sudden depression took him by surprise. 'What's up?'

'We're no further forward than we were an hour ago.'

'Did you expect to be?'

'Yes,' she said wearily, leaning her elbows on the wheel, per-versely worn out by the excitement. 'What was the point of doing it otherwise?'

To triumph over a phobia, thought Jonathan, wondering if that was his single, most powerful reason for doing anything. He felt better than he had for months and he couldn't understand why George was being so negative.

'I can't see how we move on,' she continued. 'I suppose we can corner Priscilla Fletcher but even if she agrees to speak to us, it won't get us anywhere. All she has to do is tell us her name was Mary Smith and we won't be able to prove any different. We haven't the authority to insist on a birth certificate.'

'What about her husband? He must know as much of her history as Roy does.'

George gave an impatient sigh. 'And how do we approach him? If we go knocking on the door, it'll certainly be Priscilla who answers, and she'll slam it in our faces. I don't know anything about him, except that he's some sort of bookie, and even that's a bit doubtful.' She nodded towards the pub door. 'My source was Tracey and she had it second-hand off Jim Longhurst. I don't even know the man's Christian name.'

'Well, we can't do anything tonight,' said Jonathan firmly, consulting his watch, 'so let's just sleep on it. I need to be at the station by nine, otherwise I won't be home till after one thirty. If you can drop me at Branksome, I'll take a taxi into town.'

George wouldn't hear of it. 'Don't be ridiculous,' she said, starting the engine and pulling away from the kerb. 'Andrew would be furious if you spent borrowed money on a cab. I'm sure he meant you to buy food with it.'

'Probably.'

'Then buy a sandwich on the train and start taking care of yourself.'

He wasn't listening. 'What about William Burton?' he suggested. 'I'd say he's worth another shot, particularly if we can persuade him to come to the police station with us and name the boys who raped Cill. Lovatt can hardly ignore that, not if we show him your two photos. He's bound to interview Priscilla Fletcher in those circumstances . . . Roy, too, if he's one of the three that Burton accuses.'

George cheered up immediately. 'Do you think he'll do it?'

'I don't know,' said Jonathan, 'but it has got to be worth a try.' His mind worked through the possibilities. 'We also need to find the Trevelyans. If they didn't have anything to do with Cill's disappearance, then they'll be ahead of us in the queue, piling on the pressure. I need to listen to the tape because I'm guessing Roy told us a lot more than you think he did – it's just a question of isolating what's important.'

'Did you get it all?'

'I hope so.' He took a recorder from his pocket and pressed 'rewind', letting it run for five seconds before touching 'play'. Roy's jeering tones broke into the silence inside the car. '. . . *you'll be making idiots of yourselves. You've got nothing at all if Priscilla can prove she wasn't Cill* . . .' Jonathan cut the voice short. 'That's the first thing that needs sleeping on,' he murmured.

'You think he's lying?'

'No,' said Jonathan regretfully.

George was promptly downcast again. 'That's what I thought when he said it.'

'So?'

'There's no point looking for Cill's parents.'

'Wrong,' said Jonathan affectionately. 'It makes it even more important. How would you feel if someone was masquerading as your daughter? You'd want to know *why*, wouldn't you?'

George glanced at him in surprise. 'Is that what she's doing?'

'It's as plausible as my transference theory. One's conscious, the other's unconscious . . . I guess it depends whether you think the lights are on and no one's at home or if there's method in her madness.'

George was doubtful. 'What's the point?'

'Of a masquerade? Perhaps she's doing an Anna Anderson – re-emerging as the Grand Duchess Anastasia in order to lay claim to the Romanov fortune. Cill was an only child, don't forget, so there might be some money to be made out of it.'

'Priscilla lives on Sandbanks,' protested George. 'Her husband must be rolling in it.'

Jonathan shrugged. 'Perhaps Fletcher doesn't own the house . . . perhaps he insisted on a prenuptial agreement.'

'Yes, but . . . it's *absurd*,' she said forcefully. 'Even if the Trevelyans managed to buy a house in the West Country, it'll be worth a pittance. They were living in council accommodation when they were in Lacey Street, so the best they could have done was make an exchange, then buy whatever property they ended up in . . . and council property's never that valuable.'

'It'll still be worth something.'

'Then why isn't she calling herself Cill Trevelyan? Why hasn't she made herself known to the parents? It's the most far-fetched theory I've ever heard,' she finished indignantly.

'OK, OK,' said Jonathan with a small laugh. 'It was just an idea. The only other theory I've come up with is coincidence – that a woman called Priscilla looks just like a Priscilla who went missing and happened to marry her rapist, Roy Trent – but that seems equally far-fetched. And you know how much I hate coincidences.'

George concentrated on her driving for several minutes. 'Anna Anderson led a comfortable life,' she said, breaking her silence. 'I saw a documentary on her a while back and there were a number of people who believed she was Anastasia. She lived on their charity for years, then ended up marrying a rich American who treated her like royalty.'

'She was a fraud,' said Jonathan. 'They used DNA samples to prove she was a Polish factory worker.'

'That wouldn't worry her . . . not once she was dead. It's living like a princess while you're *alive* that's important.' There was a gleam in her eye. 'Put it this way, if she was Anastasia, then she was robbed of her inheritance, but if she was a Polish factory worker, then she did extremely well out of the deception. But it wasn't the Romanov *family* who kept her in clover – they refused to recognize her – it was the people she *conned* . . .'

From: Dr Jonathan Hughes [jon.hughes@london.ac.uk]
Sent: Thurs 01/05/03 11:16
To: geo.gar@mullinst.co.uk
Cc: Andrew Spicer
Subject: Roy Trent

Dear George

Herewith some thoughts re. the tape. As agreed, I have conferred
with a psychologist colleague and we have divided Trent's
statements into four categories.

Category 1 (statements that we both believe to be true)

1. The gang bullied Howard with a knife.
2. Howard subsequently acquired a knife and went berserk.
3. The gang experienced similar suicidal thoughts to Howard's.
4. Their stamping ground was Colliton Way.
5. They got into trouble when they left it.
6. Trent detested prison and did not want a repeat.
7. He regrets his behaviour.
8. Priscilla Fletcher is not Cill Trevelyan.

Category 2 (statements that we are undecided about)

1. Trent and his gang did not know Grace.
2. David Trevelyan killed his daughter.
3. Jean Trevelyan told lies to protect him.

Category 3 (statements that may not be true but that Trent himself
believes)

1. Howard killed Grace Jefferies.

2. He did so as a direct result of being bullied by Trent, Hurst and Hopkinson.
3. Wynne Stamp could have helped her son's defence by citing the gang.

Category 4 (statements that we both believe to be false)

1. Trent did not know Cill Trevelyan – *he did.*
2. Louise Burton did not know the names of the rapists – *she did.*
3. She did not identify them because they weren't involved – *they were.*
4. Trent has not seen Hurst or Hopkinson since they were youngsters – *he has.*
5. His ex-wife knows nothing about Cill's disappearance or Grace's murder – *she does.*

I should stress that *our conclusions may be wrong* – deciphering content and tone of voice is not an exact science by any stretch of the imagination (!) – nevertheless, Trent's responses were interesting. My colleague was impressed by the way he dealt with questions about himself, his gang and Howard Stamp, less impressed by his answers about Cill Trevelyan. As you will see from Category 4 above, most of the 'lies' are associated with Cill and the rape.

Despite this, my colleague made the point that Trent was prepared for questions about Cill, viz. his calm response after you and I accused him of it. 'It's true that I was taken in for questioning . . .' etc. This suggests he knew we'd found out about it. Yet only two people were aware of that – William Burton and Miss Brett. It is highly unlikely that Miss Brett reported the fact to Roy Trent or anyone who knew him, but quite probable that William Burton passed it on, either directly to Trent or to Priscilla Fletcher.

Had our accusation come out of the blue, my colleague believes

Trent would have postured and protested rather more strongly while he tried to collect his thoughts. In addition, he employed some fairly aggressive diversionary tactics at the beginning in order to prevent us asking anything at all. Since he seemed fairly comfortable talking about Howard, it was questions about Cill Trevelyan and/or Priscilla Fletcher that he wanted to avoid.

Of particular notice is that he shifts the conversation very quickly to Howard – where he feels on stronger ground – and only becomes comfortable talking about Cill when he knows Priscilla Fletcher has left the building. In light of what's on the tape and also Trent's attempts to keep you away from the Cill Trevelyan story, it seems reasonable to make the following assumptions:

1. William Burton repeated details of your conversation with him.
2. Priscilla Fletcher knew Cill Trevelyan well enough to copy her look.
3. Trent does not want us to talk to Priscilla.

I am left with the conviction that Trent was not involved in any way with Grace's murder – and genuinely believes that Howard was guilty. However, I have an equal conviction that he (a) raped Cill; and (b) knows what happened to her. If those conclusions are right, then Priscilla Fletcher was party to the crime(s), and my best guess at the moment – whatever Miss Brett may have said to the contrary – is that Priscilla Fletcher is Louise Burton, that William Burton knows it and that he almost certainly alerted his sister to your interest in the story.

Where that leaves us on Howard, I don't know. I won't abandon his 'miscarriage of justice' lightly, but I am concerned about the 'slashing and stabbing' incident described by Trent. When I wrote Howard's chapter in *Disordered Minds*, there was nothing to suggest a history of 'manic' behaviour against others. But if the

episode happened – and we find proof of it through hospital records/
Hurst/Hopkinson and/or their families/neighbours – then we will
have to *rethink*. It indicates that Howard had a breaking point, was
ready to ignore injury to himself and had a knife. You can't blame
him – he had a miserable existence – but it makes our job harder.

For the moment I suggest we concentrate on bearding William
Burton in his den and attempt through him to gain access to Priscilla
Fletcher. I'm afraid it may turn out that the two stories are
unconnected, as the police decided at the time, but we need to
establish this for our own satisfaction.

Best wishes, Jon

PS Am sending a copy of the tape by snail mail.

From:	George Gardener [geo.gar@mullinst.co.uk]
Sent:	Sun 04/05/03 14:29
To:	jon.hughes@london.ac.uk
Cc:	Andrew Spicer
Subject:	Conclusions

Oh dear! Snail mail delivered, and I do rather agree with you. It's so disappointing. I set such high hopes on Louise Burton or Colley Hurst and it's wretched to have them dashed. If you remember, I was depressed on the way to the station because, even while Roy was speaking, I thought what he said about Howard and his gang sounded like the truth. I was especially struck by Roy's references to 'suicidal tendencies' and 'shit lives', both of which are well documented in literature about alienated youth.

I shall email some possible dates tomorrow, but at the moment I'm questioning the sense of wasting any more time on Cill or Louise. I fear it's what you said at the beginning — coincidences are seductive — and if the police didn't make a link in 1970 then it's doubtful there was one.

Best, George

PS What happened with Emma's father?

From: Andrew Spicer [Andrew@spicerandhardy.co.uk]
Sent: Mon 05/05/03 10:46
To: jon.hughes@london.ac.uk; geo.gar@mullinst.co.uk
Subject: Earning advances

Dear both,

I am in the middle of negotiating a delicate – but healthy – deal
which is based on a presumption of Howard Stamp's innocence.
While I have listened to a copy of the tape and also been mildly
entertained by your hand-wringing emails on the subject of whether
or not Roy Trent was telling the truth about his revoltingly
unpleasant behaviour as an adolescent, may I remind you that the
object of the exercise is to make him tell you *everything* he
remembers about the Stamp family.

Personally, I couldn't give a monkey's toss how suicidal he felt in his
teens. If it's of any interest to you, I experienced identical feelings at
fourteen when I contemplated my pre-ordained fate of gaining huge
amounts of weight like my mother, failing to score with attractive
women like my father, then taking on the family firm in order to deal
with authors who *keep* changing their minds.

Despite these miserably unappealing prospects, I did *not* go out and
rape a 13-yr-old because I enjoyed watching people hurt; *nor* did I
provoke a sad young man with a harelip and learning difficulties into
producing a knife because my psychopathic friend had sliced his
back whenever he felt like it. Should I now be worrying about you,
Jon, because you stood up to Trent and called him a sociopath?
Was that a 'manic' incident? And what about your 'berserk' episode
on Bournemouth Station? Does this mean none of us is safe any
more?

You know Howard had a knife because he was a self-mutilator, and there was no point going against Trent and his gang without it. Give the poor chap credit for finding some courage at last, instead of assuming that one desperate attempt at gaining self-esteem led to an automatic downward spiral of murderous behaviour. In your shoes, I'd be looking for evidence that his confidence improved in the wake of the incident. Find Wynne. Talk to her. Ask her why Howard agreed to go job-hunting on the Monday and Tuesday before Grace was found. Whose idea was that? Hers or his?

Meanwhile, go back to George's neighbour's testimony which states that Howard could not have committed the murder on the Wednesday because he did not arrive at Grace's house until 2.00 p.m. Then reread Jon's chapter on Howard where the defence pathologist argued that the murder happened on the Monday while the above job search was happening. If the knife-wielding episode worries you so much, then concentrate on *opportunity*. How and when could Howard have done it?

I hate to be a Victorian parent, but get *real*, for God's sake! Anthropologists who invite pretentious colleagues to listen to a tape over a cup of tea and councillors with politically correct leanings are persuadable enough to make me weep. Of course Roy Trent was convincing. He's had years of practice . . . he even persuaded one of his victims to marry him, if Jon's theory about P. Fletcher being Louise Burton is correct. *Plus* he's managed to keep George at arm's length from this story ever since he met her, by allowing her free access to his pub for 'surgeries' in order to woo voters.

Next time you see him ask him how the Crown and Feathers survives without customers. Who owns it? Where's the money coming from? These are the interesting questions, and if either of you had ever run a business, you'd know it. You were a tax inspector, George. Trent's finances should be grist to your mill. The man's a crook, so of course he doesn't want to go back to prison. Name me one who does!

Best,

Andrew Spicer

PS OK, pal, give us the dirt. What *did* happen with Emma's father?

From: Dr Jonathan Hughes [jon.hughes@london.ac.uk]
Sent: Thurs 08/05/03 14:33
To: geo.gar@mullinst.co.uk; Andrew@spicerandhardy.co.uk
Subject: Emma's father

The bastard called me an asylum seeker, punched me in the gut and manhandled me out the door. And yes – *pal* – much as I hate to admit it, you're right! One swallow doesn't make a summer, so unless Howard had better luck than I did the next time he stood up to someone, he probably went back to carving his initials on his arm. *However*, the odds are high that the 'next time' was Grace, and the poor little sod lost it when she didn't run away. My pretentious colleague says there's no going back after the first cut, unless you're clear-headed enough to realize what you're doing . . . and that's well-nigh impossible when there's a red mist in front of your eyes. 99% of murders are committed in anger, and the reason the cases are tried as murder, not manslaughter, is because the culprits try to cover their tracks afterwards. Be warned! If Jenny or Greg test your patience too far, and you bop one or other of them on the head with a crowbar, phone the police immediately and plead provocation. You may get five years if the judge recognizes what a saint you've been towards a couple of shysters . . . but you won't get life.

Nevertheless, I have taken on board your Victorian strictures. You always were a bully, Andrew. I think it comes from being small and fat . . . although galloping baldness clearly isn't helping. The real mystery is why you have so much self-esteem. Considering what you look like, and the fact that beautiful women ignore you, it *ought* to be zero. J.

PS To avoid further emails on the subject of my love life, Emma wasn't there and I haven't heard from her. According to her mother, who followed me out, she is getting married on 9 August to a white Anglo-Saxon Protestant with a double-barrelled name. I have written to congratulate her.

Nineteen

RACHEL BURTON moved the cursor to 'send', then hovered her finger over the mouse. 'Are you sure about this, sweetheart?' she asked her husband, looking up from the monitor. 'Once it's gone there's no bringing it back.'

Billy rested a hand on her shoulder and leaned forward to stare at the message on the screen. 'It's not my choice. It's what you think that matters.' He sighed despondently. 'I just wish to God that stupid Gardener woman had done something, instead of making us do the dirty work.'

'OK, then we send it.' Rachel pressed the mouse button and watched the email vanish. 'I'd rather have a husband with a clear conscience than a galloping insomniac, and if you change your mind, you don't have to give them her address.' She reached up to squeeze his hand. 'Look, it may not be as bad as you think. Louise could be squeaky clean . . . your mother's conscience might only be troubled by a few white lies. Blame your parents for refusing to talk to you . . . blame me and the twins for forcing you into it.'

He dropped a kiss on the top of her head. It hadn't taken much forcing once he came clean about what was worrying him, because her attitude was the same as his. Neither of them was confident that George Gardener would let the issue of Priscilla Fletcher drop, and if there were skeletons in the Burton closet, then it was better to open the door themselves than wait for a stranger to do it. They wouldn't have a leg to stand on if the press arrived on their doorstep demanding to know why Billy had failed to recognize his sister, was Rachel's argument, so the best solution was to make Louise tell her story herself.

'And how do we do that?' Billy had asked gloomily. 'She's never 'fessed up to a damn thing in her life.'

'Tell the detective agency where she is,' suggested Rachel. 'You've got their card. Persuade *them* to ask the questions. That way, the police won't be involved . . . or not immediately.'

'She'll lie.'

'At least they might find out why she's pretending to be Cill.'

'How's it going to help us if they don't report back?' Billy said. 'We'll be just as much in the dark as we are now.'

Rachel had a more positive character than her husband. 'Then we need to find a way of making them.' She stroked his face. 'You can't go on like this, love. Right's right and wrong's wrong, and you'll have a breakdown if you don't do something pretty damn quick. You were ten years old. Whatever happened wasn't your fault.'

'Perhaps it wasn't Louise's either. Perhaps that's why she went the way she did.'

'Then the truth won't hurt her,' said Rachel, with a minimum of sympathy. Her own knowledge of Louise was confined to a brief period at school when the older girl had singled her out for spiteful attention. Chubby, freckle-faced, copper-haired, and very unsure of herself, Rachel Jennings had been teased mercilessly by dark-haired Daisy Burton who revelled in calling her a 'fat ginger-bread freak'. Her hatred for Daisy had made her avoid Billy for years, and it wasn't until he admitted that his sister's name was Louise, that she was a redhead herself, and, better still, had probably died of a drug overdose, that Rachel had discovered the eternal truth – siblings are rarely alike.

Nevertheless, it was no surprise when Billy explained his pre-occupation of the last few weeks on Louise's resurfacing. Rachel had always feared it would happen one day. She'd asked him why he hadn't told her that he'd recognized the photograph Councillor Gardener had shown him, and he'd answered, 'Because I hoped I was wrong. Nothing good ever came from Louise. She's been easier to live with since I thought she was dead. At least that way, I could feel sadness for her.'

From: wandr.burton@compuline.com
Sent: Sat 10/05/03 21:10
To: info@WCHinvestigations.com
Subject: Cill Trevelyan

Dear Sir

I am Louise Burton's brother. One of your detectives came looking
for her three years ago and gave me your card. It was in connection
with Mr and Mrs Trevelyan's search for their daughter, Cill. I can
supply you with Louise's name and address. However, I have only
recently found her again and am concerned about her welfare. If
you decide to talk to her, then I would appreciate a follow-up
meeting with you afterwards in return for me telling you where she
is. I am finding it difficult to speak to her and hope you will have
more success, but I would need some guarantees before I release
the information. It might be of interest to you to know that she is
calling herself Priscilla and styling herself to look like Cill Trevelyan.
I understand that all dealings are confidential.

I wait to hear from you.

Yours sincerely

William Burton

Peckham, London
Saturday, 10 May 2003, 9.30 p.m.

When his doorbell rang, Andrew looked up from the manuscript he was reading with a frown of irritation. Off the top of his head, he couldn't think of a single acquaintance who would be so crass as to visit unannounced at nine thirty on a Saturday evening. As his daughters were asleep upstairs, he didn't immediately leap to the idea that it was the police, but waited to see if the bell rang again. When it did, he rose reluctantly from his seat.

One of the downsides of living in a poky mews cottage, where every window faced forward and table lamps threw his shadow against the curtains, was that whoever was at his door certainly knew he was there, and he was too courteous a man to pretend otherwise. But he wasn't pleased about it. He was wearing scruffy corduroy trousers and an old denim shirt with soup stains down the front, and he had a sinking feeling that he was going to find Jenny and Greg outside, dressed to the nines for a party and hiding their smiles at his sad old man's appearance.

He slipped the Yale latch and opened the door, and if he hadn't recognized his visitor immediately as the woman he'd seen at the Crown and Feathers, he would certainly have known her from George's photograph. Priscilla Fletcher. He was quick-witted enough to see that he had two choices – to acknowledge her or pretend ignorance – and he rapidly assessed the advantages of each while hiding his astonishment behind a polite smile. 'Can I help you?'

'Do you know who I am?' she asked bluntly.

Andrew prevaricated. 'I believe so. You're Jonathan Hughes's mystery woman. I saw you at Roy Trent's pub in February.'

Close to, she looked nothing like the black-and-white snapshot of plump, unlined Cill Trevelyan. Her face was thin and drawn, with signs of ageing around her eyes, and Andrew was surprised at how dyed her hair looked. She reminded him more of an anorexic Wallis Simpson playing at being queen to a vacillating Edward VIII than she did of a vibrant thirteen-year-old on the threshold of life.

'Do you know my name?'

Andrew chose to play it straight. 'It depends which one you're answering to,' he said dryly. 'Priscilla Fletcher . . . Cill Trent . . . possibly Daisy Burton or Louise Burton? Which do you prefer?'

'Louise,' she said. 'I never really got used to the others.' She jerked her chin towards the room behind him. 'Are you going to let me in?'

He examined her face for a moment, then pulled the door wide. 'As long as you're not planning to steal my wallet. I'm even poorer than Jonathan, so it won't do you any good.'

'I didn't steal it,' she said, walking past him. 'I borrowed it for an hour to see what I could find out about him.' She looked critically about the small, open-plan room that had a kitchen at one end, stairs rising out of the middle and a couple of armchairs and a coffee table at the other. 'It's not much of a place, is it? I guess being an agent doesn't pay.'

Andrew closed the door. 'Who told you where I lived?'

She drew some business cards from her pocket and handed them to him. 'These were in your friend's wallet. Yours has your home address written on the back of it.'

Andrew flicked through the cards, most of which carried New York zip codes, until he came to his, dog-eared, at the bottom. He could even remember the fit of loneliness, shortly after he moved, that had prompted him to jot the number and street in Peckham on the back of it. He'd spun the card across a restaurant table at Jonathan and asked him to drop by one evening when he had nothing better to do. He never had. 'Did you take anything else?'

'No. It was Hughes's address I wanted, but he didn't have any cards of his own.' She glanced towards the stairs as if wondering if there was anyone else in the house. 'He's a bit of a weird bastard, isn't he? His eyes were rolling the whole time I was talking to him . . . I thought he was a junkie.'

'He was ill.'

She wasn't interested enough to pursue it. 'Do you mind if I sit down?'

'Be my guest.'

She took off her jacket and dropped into one of the armchairs. 'How about offering me a drink?'

He opened a kitchen cupboard and took out some wine glasses. 'Red or white? I've a halfway decent Margaux or an excellent Pouilly-Fumé.'

'What about vodka?'

'Wine's my limit, I'm afraid.'

'Jesus!' she grumbled. 'It's not much of a life, is it? I thought people made a fortune out of books.' She eyed the two bottles that he held up for her. 'OK, give me some of the red.' She watched him cut the foil from the neck and insert the corkscrew. 'Aren't you going to ask me why I'm here?'

'Do I need to?' he murmured, sniffing the cork to make sure it wasn't tainted. 'Aren't you going to tell me anyway?'

She scowled at what she clearly thought was a piece of effete snobbery. 'Not if you're gonna act like a ponce.'

He poured some wine into one of the glasses and held it briefly to his nose before filling them both. 'This isn't a particularly expensive Margaux,' he said mildly, 'but it still costs around twenty pounds a bottle.' He took the glasses in one hand and the bottle in the other and brought them to the coffee table. 'How much is vodka these days?'

'Twelve . . . fifteen quid, but you'd have to be an alky to drink that much every night.'

'Mm. Well, corked wine's about as disgusting as drinking sour milk,' said Andrew, handing her a glass and lowering himself into the other chair. He raised his glass to her. 'Cheers.'

She took a tentative sip. 'I guess it'll do,' she said churlishly. 'I prefer vodka and lime, though. Are you going to let me smoke?'

'Do I have a choice?'

She gave an abrupt laugh. 'Not if you want to hear what I came to say.'

Andrew rose to his feet again and fetched an ashtray from one of the cupboards. 'Feel free,' he said, handing it to her. 'I'll open the window.' He pulled the curtains back and unlatched one of the panes, glad of the excuse to make his affairs public. He didn't think she was going to pull a knife on him, but at the back of his mind was what happened to Grace.

'You're a strange bloke,' she said, lighting up. 'Don't you ever say no?'

He resumed his seat. It wasn't a question he'd ever been asked before and he was surprised by its perspicuity. 'Not often,' he admitted. 'I turn down manuscripts fairly regularly, but those are business decisions.'

'So what are you? A soft touch . . . a bit lonely?' Her gaze travelled about the room again and came to rest on the soup stains on his shirt. 'You're not married, that's for sure. Are you gay?'

Andrew shook his head. 'Heterosexual and divorced. My two daughters are in bed upstairs.'

She glanced towards the ceiling. 'How old?'

'Old enough to phone the police if I raise my voice,' he said good-humouredly. 'Young enough to stay asleep if this encounter remains peaceful and legal.'

She gave a small laugh. 'What do you think I am?'

He tilted his glass to the light and gently turned it, watching the Margaux run legs down the curved inside. 'I don't know, Louise. I'm waiting for you to tell me. Your old headmistress, Miss Brett, says you're a liar . . . Jonathan Hughes says you're a thief . . . and both he and George Gardener think you witnessed Grace Jefferies' murder.' He watched her for a moment before savouring a mouthful of wine. 'Does anyone have anything good to say about you?'

He expected her to take offence, but she didn't. 'I doubt it. I've been a fuck-up most of my life. What did Billy say?'

Billy. 'Is that your brother?'

Louise nodded.

'Nothing much,' said Andrew, recalling George's transcript. 'I believe he said you were married and your family thought you were in Australia. But he didn't recognize your photograph . . . or claimed he didn't.'

She drained her glass at one swallow and put it on the coffee table, leaning forward to stare at the floor. 'He's OK, is Billy, except he only sees what he wants to see . . . wouldn't notice a fucking elephant if it sat on his bed unless it flattened him in the process.' She dedicated herself to smoking her cigarette.

Strange expression, thought Andrew, reaching for the bottle and topping her up again. She didn't seem to notice.

'I hated that bitch,' she said suddenly. 'She was always hauling Cill in for a lecture, but it never amounted to much – everyone knew she liked her. It was me she dumped on. People think an up-front punishment's a bad thing, but it's the drip-drip stuff that's worse. She'd tell Cill she was too bright to hang around with the likes of me . . . then tell me I was thick as pig shit and only good for bringing other kids down. It wasn't true. Cill was a maniac – stubbed a cigarette out on my arm once when I told her to get stuffed.'

Andrew guessed the 'bitch' was Miss Brett. 'What did Miss Brett say to you after the fight?'

'The usual,' she said cynically. ' "You're a nasty piece of work, Louise Burton, and one day you'll get your comeuppance. You provoked that fight deliberately to get Cill into trouble." Bloody old cow! I'm sure she was a dyke.'

'Was she right? Did you provoke it?'

Louise looked up, a gleam of amusement lighting her eyes. 'What do you think?'

'Yes.'

She gave an indifferent shrug. 'It served Cill right. I took so much shit off her about the rape – why hadn't I jumped them? . . . why hadn't I screamed? . . . why didn't Billy do something? . . . why did I keep telling her to forget it?' Her small, glittering eyes held Andrew's for a moment before sliding away. 'It wasn't even that bad . . . three puny fourteen-year-olds who couldn't keep it up for five seconds. OK, she had a bit of a kicking, but that was all.' Louise jammed her cigarette into the ashtray and immediately lit another one. 'She was shit-scared she was pregnant but even that was a no-no. She had a period ten days later and rammed it down my throat because she knew she was in the clear.' She lapsed into silence, revisiting memories.

'What happened to her?'

There was barely a pause for reflection. 'Her dad thrashed her for the fight, so she hid out with Grace.' She smiled sourly at his expression. 'That's what you wanted to hear, isn't it? It's where we went when we couldn't think of anything better to do. Grace let us watch telly all day as long as we could show her some bruises.'

Andrew waited for her to explain. 'Try running that past me again,' he encouraged, after another silence. 'You lost me between the telly and the bruises. At the moment I don't see a connection.'

She rolled up the sleeve of her shirt. 'Like this,' she said, showing him a naked forearm with blue weals striping the flesh. 'Enough of them and you could lounge around on her settee till the cows came home . . . if you had a mind to it, of course.' She licked her finger and rubbed a white line through the stripes. 'Eyeshadow,' she said laconically. 'Pretty effective, eh? I put it on in the car before I came in. Grace fell for it every time.'

Andrew took another slow mouthful of Margaux. 'Why?'

'She was a moron . . . just like her stupid grandson. Me and Cill could run rings around the pair of them.' She paused, waiting for him to react. 'It was Cill started it,' she went on when he didn't. 'She knew Howard hung out there all the time, doing eff all, so she rang the bell one day and told Grace her dad had been beating up on her. It worked a treat.' She lifted a shoulder in a disdainful shrug. 'We couldn't understand a word she said – she was worse than Howard like that – but she let us watch telly and gave us something to eat.'

Andrew showed his scepticism. 'Why?' he asked again. 'What did she have to gain by it?'

'I don't know. She just did.'

'Bullshit,' he said without emphasis. 'Grace may have had speech problems, but that wouldn't have affected her IQ. Your parents lived across the road. Why would she make enemies of them by letting you truant at her place?'

'She let Howard.'

'He was her grandson. She felt sorry for him.'

'Then maybe she felt sorry for us. Cill's dad had beaten her black and blue that first time. It was only afterwards we used the eyeshadow.' Louise took a curl of smoke into her mouth and stared at him with dislike. 'You reckon you know it all, don't you? So when did your dad take a stick to you?'

'Never.'

She pointed towards the ceiling. 'How many times have you beaten *them* within an inch of their lives?'

'Never.'

'Then don't tell me what Grace would or wouldn't do. She knew about people's lives being fucked. Why do you think Howard was the way he was?'

'He had a disability.'

Louise shook her head. 'His mother used to thrash the living daylights out of him. She was a right bitch. He was so scared of her, he kept running away to Grace.'

Andrew remembered a couple of lines from a letter Jonathan had received. '*Sometimes his mother dragged him in by his ear . . . she wasn't a nice woman . . . she was always hitting him.*' 'Did you know Howard well?'

'Well enough,' she said dismissively. 'He had a thing for Cill.'

'Was he in the house when you were there?'

'Sometimes. Cill used to let him feel her tits whenever his gran was out of the room. It got him really excited.'

Andrew looked towards the window, quelling a prudish distaste. 'It's hardly unusual,' he said. 'Adolescents explore each other all the time.'

'Yeah, but he wasn't an adolescent, was he? He was twenty years old.' The pale eyes fixed on Andrew again. 'Actually, it was pretty funny watching him. He'd get a hard-on just looking at her, and when he touched her he'd start juddering as if he was having an orgasm.' Another scornful shrug. 'He probably was, too – he was a sad little git . . . shot his load early every time, I reckon, assuming anyone let him get that close.'

It wasn't just the remarks but the brutal way she said them that set Andrew's teeth on edge. Perhaps she thought shock tactics would make her more believable. 'Who instigated it? Cill or Howard?'

'Cill, of course. She was a right little tart.'

'What about you? Was Howard interested in you?'

'Like hell he was,' said Louise bluntly, taking up her glass again. 'I was the gooseberry so his gran wouldn't ask questions. He'd have gone the whole way with Cill if he could've got rid of Grace. He was always pressuring the silly old cow to go to the shops, but she never did because she hated leaving the house.'

Andrew watched her drain the glass. It wasn't hard to see where she was going with this. 'So because he was sexually obsessed with Cill, he killed his grandmother?'

'Had to've done,' she agreed. 'He was a dirty little pervert.'

'*Had* to have done?' he queried. 'You don't know?'

'Oh, I know all right,' she said confidently. 'I just can't prove it.'

Andrew let a silence develop. 'What was the point of coming here?' he asked at last. 'I may be a soft touch in some areas of my life, Louise, but I'm not entirely stupid. Were you expecting me to believe this rigmarole?'

'What's not to believe?'

'That Grace would have allowed Cill to stay in her house once the police became involved. They were appealing for sightings on the Saturday morning. Grace wouldn't have hidden her in those circumstances.'

Louise shrugged. 'Maybe she was already dead.'

'She can't have been,' he said with conviction. 'There was a debate over time of death at the trial, but the disparity between the two sides was twenty-four to forty-eight hours. If Cill disappeared on the Friday evening, then Grace would have had to have died on the Saturday in order to be ignorant of police involvement . . . which would have meant her body lying for nearly a week before it was found.' He shook his head. 'And that isn't possible. Decomposition would have been well into the second and third stages.'

'Not my problem,' she said indifferently. 'I'm telling you how it was. It's up to you to work out how it fits.'

He gave an abrupt laugh. 'Then it's a pity you didn't make your story match the facts before you brought it to me. Let's start with Cill. If you knew where she was, why didn't you tell the police?'

'She'd have killed me.' She reached forward to stub out her second cigarette. 'Like I said, she was a psycho. If they'd hauled her kicking and screaming back to her dad for another larruping, she'd have got me in a corner, first opportunity, and scratched my eyes out.'

'So why tell them about the rape?'

'Because they wanted to know what the fight was about. Plus, I reckoned that if the police knew she'd been raped and got social services involved, her dad wouldn't be able to take her apart for it.' Her expression became almost rueful. 'I was trying to do her a favour, though you wouldn't think it the way things turned out. It's no good looking at it with twenty-twenty vision, you have to picture what it was like then. Far as I knew, Cill'd sneak home when she got bored and that'd be the end of it. I didn't know she was going to vanish and Grace was going to die. No one did.'

It was a fair point, he thought. 'How did you know she was in Grace's house?'

'Soon as her mum phoned to see if she was round our place, I went and checked. We used to go through the gate in the fence at the back and in the kitchen door. I watched her through the window, stuffing her face with ice cream.'

'Did you talk to her?'

'No chance. She'd have gone for me. It was my fault that cow Brett suspended her.'

'What about Grace?'

'Didn't see her.'

'Howard?'

She shook her head.

'What time was it?'

Louise shrugged. 'Nine o'clock or thereabouts.'

'Morning? Evening?'

'Morning. I was down at the nick two hours later, being quizzed by the cops.'

It sounded convincing, but Andrew wasn't much of a judge in these matters. Women had always run rings around him. He couldn't forget that, at the period Louise was describing, she was only thirteen years old – and, if her ex-headmistress was to be believed, not very bright. 'Had you had dealings with the police before?' he asked. 'I can't imagine withholding information at thirteen.'

Her eyes glittered scornfully, but whether in contempt for Andrew's boyhood fear or impatience with his questioning, he couldn't tell. 'It was my mother did most of the talking, and she was mad as hell that anyone'd think we knew where Cill was and wouldn't tell.'

'But *you* knew.'

'Right.' She lit another cigarette. 'That's why I talked about the rape.' She forestalled his next attempt at a question. 'Oh, come on, lighten up, for Christ's sake! What was the big deal? I wasn't going to rat on Cill, even if I did think she was a little bitch. All she'd done was take herself off for the night . . . hundreds of kids do it every day. In any case, I didn't want the cops finding out we'd been truanting round there because I didn't know what they'd do to Grace. Or *me* for that matter,' she added reflectively. 'My plan was to go round as soon as I got home and give Cill a bollocking, but Mum got fired up about the rape and wouldn't let me out of her sight. After that it all went pear-shaped.'

'How?'

'How do you think?' she said morosely. 'When I next went round, it looked as if a bloody war had broken out.'

Twenty

IT WAS LIKE watching a battery-operated toy run down. Whatever had stimulated Louise to come to Andrew's house and tell her story was rapidly being neutralized by the wine and exhaustion. She rested her head against the back of the chair and stared at the ceiling.

'Did you go inside the house?'

'I was too damn scared.'

'Why?'

'Everything was on the floor.'

'Where?'

'In the kitchen . . . in the sitting room . . .'

'What sort of things?'

'*Everything*. Drawers, broken bottles, plants. It looked like a bomb had hit it.'

Andrew flicked her a sideways glance. 'How could you see into the sitting room? I thought the curtains were pulled.'

'Not at the back they weren't. There were some French windows onto the garden. I looked through them.' She flicked ash onto his carpet before taking another drag on her cigarette. 'It did my head in as a matter of fact. I knew something bad had happened. There was blood on the pane . . . right in front of my eyes. I thought it was Cill's.'

'Why?'

She turned her head towards him. 'Because Grace was a loony,' she said flatly, 'and I always knew she'd turn nasty one day. Cill used to tease her something chronic about the way she spoke and I reckoned she'd gone too far and made Grace flip.'

'So what did you do?'

'Ran home, kept my mouth shut and refused to go out for weeks.' She gave a faint smile at his expression. 'I thought the cops'd come down on me like a ton of bricks for not telling them where she was on the Saturday. I should have done . . . *would* have done if my stupid mother hadn't stuck her oar in first.'

'Which day was this?'

She thought for a moment. 'It had to be the Tuesday. I ducked in on my way back from school because I was hacked off with everyone asking questions about Cill. Come the Wednesday I had a fit, and the folks kept me back till we moved to Boscombe.'

Andrew filed that piece of information away. 'Why didn't you tell your mother what you'd seen?'

Louise didn't answer immediately but returned to staring at the ceiling as if wisdom could be found in its matt white paint. 'What makes you think I didn't?' she asked then.

'There's no record of her going to the police.'

'That doesn't mean I didn't tell her.' She bent forward abruptly to kill the cigarette. 'She went off like a rocket, so did my dad. How could I let the family down? What were the neighbours going to say? Didn't I understand what a dreadful position I'd put them in? First a rape . . . then keeping quiet about where Cill was . . . now telling stories about blood on Grace's windows . . .' She gave a hollow laugh. 'They never liked me much so I'm sure they thought I was involved in some way.'

Andrew placed his glass on the floor to avoid looking at her. '*Were* you?'

'Course not,' she said without heat. 'I hadn't a clue what was going on. Even when they arrested Howard, it didn't make any better sense. I kept asking Mum what had happened to Cill, till she boxed my ears and told me never to mention her again. It was a weird time . . . I couldn't make head or tail of anything. In the end I worked out that Howard'd killed Cill, too, as being the only thing that made sense . . . but it was way too late to say anything. The cops would've crucified the folks for keeping quiet.'

She was very believable, thought Andrew. Everything dovetailed neatly until he thought about the questions she hadn't answered. 'He couldn't have done,' he said evenly. 'He didn't have a car and there was only one body in the house. So how did he get rid of her?'

'Who knows?' she said glibly. 'Promised to take her home? Took her for a walk? He was a right little paedophile . . . if he'd got away with Grace's murder, he'd've been picking kiddies off the street. It suits you to think he was innocent, but it doesn't mean he was. I was *there*, I *knew* him.' She flashed him another contemptuous look. 'He was a slimeball.'

Andrew propped his elbows on the arms of his chair and steepled his hands under his chin. 'Except there was no evidence anyone else had been in Grace's house,' he told her. 'Why weren't Cill's fingerprints all over the place? Why weren't *yours*? Even if the police couldn't identify them, they'd have questioned why two unknown sets were in there. Grace was a known recluse. The first thing everyone said about her was that she didn't have visitors.'

'Not my problem,' she said again. '*You* explain it. I can only tell you what I know. She was always cleaning up after us.'

It was a clever tack – a challenge of belief – and he wondered fleetingly why her headmistress had thought her stupid. 'Howard couldn't have killed anyone on the Monday or Tuesday, Louise. His movements were accounted for all day . . . which is why the prosecution pathologist argued strongly that the murder took place on the Wednesday.' He lifted a cynical eyebrow. 'But that's not your problem either, I suppose?'

She flashed him a mischievous smile. 'Right.'

'So why pick on Howard? Nothing you've said so far proves he was even there.'

'Who else could it have been?' she said with a shrug. 'There was no one else went near Grace, except us and him.'

'How about Roy Trent, Colley Hurst and Micky Hopkinson?'

She was ready for that, he thought. Her answer was too quick. 'Dream on,' she said scornfully. 'They never left Colliton Way. What the hell would they be doing at Grace's?'

'Looking for Cill,' Andrew suggested. 'They'd raped her once, maybe they fancied another go.' He watched her mouth turn down. 'Perhaps they were looking for you?'

'What for?'

'To teach you a lesson for giving their description to the police.' For the first time lines of indecision appeared around her eyes. 'I should think they were mad as hell to have a two-bit kid rat on them.'

'I didn't name them.'

'You didn't need to. They must have been so well known to the police that saying there were three of them was probably enough.' He watched her for a moment. 'If you added in the bonus of Colley Hurst's red hair, then you might just as well have named them.'

'It wasn't them,' she said dismissively, 'and I should bloody well know. I married one of the bastards.'

Andrew smiled. 'That's hardly proof of innocence.'

'You think I'd marry a murderer?'

'No reason not to. They don't have "M" tattooed on their foreheads.'

She considered for a moment. 'Meaning he might have done it, but I didn't know.'

'That's one interpretation.'

'What's the other?'

'That you could marry him safely because no one else knew he was a murderer.' He watched a look of amusement crinkle her eyes. 'So why *did* you marry him?'

'Why does anyone marry anyone? He was like Everest . . . he was *there*.'

'Didn't it worry you what he did to Cill?'

'Not particularly. He was a damn sight better prospect than the bastard I had before. At least Roy had a place to live with some money coming in.' She shrugged. 'Name me a man who hasn't gone in for a bit of rough sex at some point in his life. It's natural, isn't it? You're all just Stone-Age types under the suits.'

Andrew gave an abrupt laugh. 'So that's where I've been going wrong. I had no idea sex was supposed to be painful. I thought it was about pleasuring women.'

'Oh, *sure*,' she murmured sarcastically. 'And you can tell when a woman's having an orgasm, I suppose?'

He'd always thought he could, until Greg moved into his bed. 'No,' he confessed. 'I wouldn't be divorced otherwise.'

'Jesus!' Louise wasn't used to honesty in men. 'You shouldn't admit to things like that.'

'I'm not very good at lying.' He grinned as she pulled a face. 'And I don't have the kind of personality that measures itself by the length of its penis.' He tapped the side of his head. 'I'm more interested in this. What makes people tick? Why are some of us a success and others a failure?' He let a moment pass. 'How does Roy make money when his pub doesn't have any customers?'

Louise reached for her jacket. 'Not my problem. It was fine when I was there.'

'Who owns it?'

'Maybe Roy does.'

Andrew shook his head. 'No chance. It's prime development property. He'd be under siege from potential buyers . . . and one of them would have persuaded him to sell by now.'

She threaded her arms into the sleeves of her jacket. 'How come you know so much? I thought it was your mate who was writing the book.'

Andrew looked amused. 'He consults with me . . . so does George Gardener. Is that a disappointment? Did you choose me because you thought I was too ignorant to ask questions?'

'Apart from George's, yours was the only address I had,' she told him matter-of-factly, 'and I wasn't going to talk to George. She'd have spilled the beans to Roy, and I don't need that at the moment.'

'Why not? You said he wasn't involved.'

'Different stuff,' she said rather bleakly, 'nothing to do with Cill or Grace.' She pushed herself forward in the chair. 'Are you going to tell George and your friend what I've said?'

'It's why you came, isn't it?' He took her silence for assent. 'They'll want to talk to you themselves, though. If what you've told me is true, then you're only guessing that Howard took his obsession with Cill too far . . . but you know for a fact that Roy and his friends did. You were *there*,' he said in a conscious echo of what she'd said earlier, 'and gang rape is a better indication of sociopathic behaviour than a bit of clumsy groping on a sofa.'

'She'd been geeing them up to it for weeks,' she said with an edge of malice in her voice. 'They were drunk as skunks and she talked dirty for half an hour to get them excited. I told her she was asking for trouble, but she wouldn't listen to me.' Her mouth thinned as she remembered. 'She was an arrogant little cow. She thought she knew everything. It drove me mad sometimes.'

Andrew watched her eyes smoulder with irritation. 'Then why try to look like her?'

This was another question she was prepared for. 'If she was beside me, you wouldn't think there was any similarity, except for the hair. And you can blame my mother for that. She was the one who dyed it to avoid difficult questions after we moved. Now no one knows me as anything other than a brunette – ' she gave a small laugh – 'and I'm too vain to let the grey show through.'

'You've been calling yourself Priscilla,' he reminded her.

She stood up and buttoned her jacket. 'Yeah. Shouldn't have done, should I?' she said ingenuously. 'George wouldn't't've kept digging if I'd stuck with Daisy.' She tucked her cigarettes into her pocket. 'I changed to Priscilla when I was married to my first loser.'

Andrew pushed himself out of his chair. 'Why?'

'It sounded glamorous,' she said with a strange wistfulness, 'and that's crazy when you think what happened to Cill.' She moved towards the door. 'I guess Miss Brett was right, eh?'

He moved ahead of her to turn the latch. 'In what way?'

' "Louise Burton acts before she thinks",' she said with a twisted smile. 'Story of my life.' In a surprisingly warm gesture, she offered him her hand. 'I'm hoping you're one of the good guys. Otherwise I'll end up regretting this, too.'

He took the hand in his. 'Are you safe to drive?'

'Better be.'

She didn't give him time to respond, but turned away and headed up the mews. As she rounded the corner at the end she glanced back at him, her pale face lit by a street-lamp. It was impossible to read her expression from that distance, but there was no mistaking the small wave she gave him. He had no idea whether anything she'd told him was true but, as he returned the farewell courtesy, he was surprised at how much he wanted to believe her.

*

Jonathan was working through some student essays in bed when the telephone rang at eleven thirty. He had a surge of hope that it was Emma, until he picked it up and heard Andrew babbling excitedly about 'something important'. It was so out of character that he assumed his friend was drunk and told him to call back in the morning, but Andrew insisted on giving him bullet points of the conversation while they were still fresh in his mind. 'She was pretty convincing.'

'Who was?'

'Priscilla Fletcher. Larger than life in my house and calling herself Louise Burton.' He heard Jonathan's intake of breath. 'Right! So get your pencil out, you lazy sod, and take some notes.'

'Why can't you write them yourself?'

'Because I'm only getting a tenth of your earnings and I'm bored with doing all the work.'

'You don't sound bored,' said Jonathan dryly, pulling a notepad forward. 'What did she do to you?'

'Charmed me,' said Andrew succinctly.

Jonathan remembered the Good Samaritan act on Branksome Station. 'And what's she stolen?'

'Belief.'

*

'If Cill was in Grace's house, then she's the obvious suspect for the murder,' said Jonathan thoughtfully, running his pencil down his notes. 'She was big for her age, she was there, she was a disturbed adolescent . . . recently raped with a possible history of sexual abuse. Put that with a volatile cocktail of hormones, and God knows what might have happened.' He tapped the pencil against his teeth. 'I can imagine a scenario where Grace tried to make her leave because she was worried about police involvement and Cill lost her temper and lashed out. The timing would work. She hid with Grace over the weekend, killed her on the Monday, then took herself off that night. It would explain why there were no sightings of her at the beginning . . . although it's odd she wasn't spotted afterwards.'

Andrew yawned at the other end. 'Who took the bath and left ginger hair behind?'

'Pass.'

'What about Howard fancying Cill? That sounded fairly convincing. She was an attractive girl.'

'She was thirteen.'

'Oh, come on! What's age got to do with anything? He was a retarded adolescent himself, so a grown woman's expectations would have terrified him. Maybe that's why he lost his rag when his grandmother told him to put himself about a bit. If he was besotted with Cill, he wouldn't have been interested in anyone else. More to the point, it would explain why he haunted Grace's house. Men'll do anything if there's half a chance of a shag at the end of it.'

'Speak for yourself,' Jonathan said tartly.

'I am,' said Andrew with a laugh. 'I abase myself regularly before beautiful women, and they all think I'm a comedian.' He paused to take what sounded like a drink. 'You should run this past your psychologist friend, but I'll put money on Louise being honest when she descibed Howard as a pervert. I'm not saying he *was*,' he went on when Jonathan attempted to break in, 'I'm saying that was her perception of him. She called him a "slime-ball", and it sounded too strong to be a latter-day invention. I think it's what she genuinely felt at the time.'

*

Jonathan leaned his head against the pillows and rubbed the grit of tiredness from his eyes. 'I need to sleep on this,' he told Andrew. 'I still don't understand why she came to you instead of me or George.'

Andrew explained about his business card and the handwritten address. 'I wouldn't think that was her reason, though. I'm guessing she expected me to swallow it whole without asking questions . . . either that, or it was a practice run.'

'For what? She can't change the details now, not without eyebrows being raised.' He looked at his notes again. 'What was the punchline, anyway? Which bit were you supposed to believe?'

'Presumably that Howard was guilty and Roy and his gang weren't involved.'

'Then she was sent by Roy,' said Jonathan matter-of-factly. 'He told us she'd back him up.'

'Not very successfully. If Grace was already dead on the Tuesday, that exonerates Howard.'

'There's only Wynne's evidence that he didn't go out on the Monday night,' Jonathan warned. 'It's not something we can prove. She was never cross-examined in court because the prosecution plumped for the Wednesday.'

'Whose side are you on?' Andrew demanded. 'Howard wouldn't have gone back if he knew Grace was dead . . . or if he did, he wouldn't have run away like a bat out of hell and refused to tell anyone. This is a gift, for God's sake! It's precisely the piece of evidence you and George have been looking for.'

'That's what's making me suspicious,' said Jonathan gloomily. 'Why would Roy Trent tell Louise to say Tuesday? It doesn't make sense if he's read *Disordered Minds*.'

Twenty-One

THE WELL-ENDOWED young woman from WCH Investigations was nothing like Rachel or Billy's idea of a private detective. She was young and rather nervous and they both thought she resembled an Eskimo, with her sallow skin, heavy black hair, flat cheekbones and narrow eyes. She gave her name as Sasha Spencer and began by explaining that her firm's contract with David and Jean Trevelyan had long since expired, but that she had been interested enough by William's email to look up the file, as it was the second approach on Cill Trevelyan that the firm had had in four weeks.

'Who was the first?' asked Rachel.

'I can't answer that, Mrs Burton. We take confidentiality seriously.'

'Georgina Gardener,' said Billy. 'She's the one who put me on to Louise, although she doesn't know who she is . . . just spotted a similarity to Cill that wasn't real. Why didn't you respond to her approach? Why wait for ours?'

Sasha glanced uncertainly at her notes as if to confirm the name. It was a reverse-psychology technique that usually worked for her. Signs of indecisiveness and nerves persuaded interviewees that they knew more than she did, and it encouraged them to set her straight by telling her more than they intended. 'I didn't speak to the person in question, but I understand they were trying to discover the Trevelyans' address.' She looked up again. 'It's not the sort of information we can reveal, so the meeting ended fairly rapidly.'

'Meaning you didn't tell her anything?'

The young woman nodded. 'We couldn't take it any further at that stage, because we were given no details about why the person was interested in Cill or her parents. However, when we received your email I called Mr Trevelyan and explained that we'd had two approaches from two different sources in under a month and asked him if he wanted me to pursue either of them. He told me he did.'

Rachel leaned forward with a frown. 'Are you saying that because your contract's with him, you won't be able to report back to us?'

'Not necessarily. I explained there was a quid pro quo – in return for divulging a name and address, one of the sources was asking for information for themselves. When I pointed out that it might be the only way to progress the search, Mr Trevelyan instructed me to proceed as I thought best.' She looked from one to the other. 'I could, of course, approach the other party – whose contact details I have – and that person might give me the name and address for free, but I doubt they can give me the sort of background information that you can.'

'Not if it's Georgina Gardener,' Billy agreed. 'I think she only came across Cill by accident when she was looking into Howard Stamp's story.'

Sasha Spencer eyed him for a moment, then took a mini-cassette player out of her case and placed it on the coffee table between them. 'Do you have any objections to my recording this? I'll be taking notes at the same time but it's useful to have a back-up.'

Billy looked unhappy. 'Who are you going to play it to?'

'No one. It's just a memory aid.'

But Rachel shook her head firmly as she reached for the

recorder and tucked it under a cushion. 'Sorry, love,' she said, 'but it's more than Billy's life's worth. His folks'll kill him if it ever gets out that he talked on tape about family secrets. Plus, there's no guarantee he's right, so he'll spend another few months tossing and turning because there's a cassette somewhere with his voice on it.' She nodded to the notepad. 'Let's stick to the old-fashioned way.'

'No problem,' said Sasha cheerfully, recognizing that the wife was tougher and cannier than the husband. 'I tend to concentrate better on what people are saying if the tape's running, but it's no big deal.' She sent Rachel a laughing smile that went all the way up to her eyes, deliberately courting her, while working out ways to persuade her to leave the room.

*

Listening in Robert and Eileen's old sitting room to Billy's account of his sister's upbringing gave substance to Louise in a way that hearing the same story in an office might not have done. There was an album of childhood photographs in a sideboard, items of furniture which had moved with them from Highdown and passed on to Billy when his parents left for Cornwall, even a china doll that Rachel said had once belonged to his sister.

Nevertheless, there were glaring holes in Billy's picture of the girl he grew up with. He claimed his mother was very protective of her after Cill's disappearance, but couldn't explain why – 'I used to think she was worried Lou would abscond as well, but I'm not so sure now . . .' He said his father allowed her to behave like a prima donna – 'He hardly ever told her off' – but again couldn't explain why – 'I assumed he shared Mum's fear of frightening her away . . .' Nor was he able to give a clear sense of Louise's character, vacillating between describing her as a lying bitch – 'She was always telling stories about people . . .' – and as being scared of her own shadow – 'She'd go catatonic at the drop of a hat'. When he went on to describe her descent into prostitution and drugs, his clear implication was that her life had been wrecked by her parents' sudden relaxation of her moral boundaries when she was thirteen.

Sasha looked up from her notes. 'I'm not sure I understand,' she said carefully. 'Are you saying they backed off after Cill vanished because they knew Louise was involved in some way?'

Billy exchanged a glance with his wife.

'It just seems odd,' said Rachel. 'When you look at what became of her, you have to ask yourself why. It didn't happen with Billy. He turned out OK, but only because his folks never let up on him.' She put a supporting arm through Billy's, hugging him close. 'So why didn't they do the same with Louise instead of making excuses for her all the time?'

'It doesn't necessarily follow,' said Sasha. 'Siblings' characters vary hugely because of the different dynamics that operate inside families.' She paused to consolidate her thoughts. 'It's interesting, though, particularly as you're both suggesting it was Louise who was in control. It may have been straightforward emotional blackmail – "Lay off me or I'll run away" – or you were right at the time,' she told Billy, 'they were afraid she'd imitate Cill.'

He flicked another sideways look at his wife, as if seeking permission to be more forthright. 'Maybe she had something on *them*,' he muttered uncomfortably.

'What sort of thing?'

'I don't know.'

Sasha frowned. 'You must have *some* idea.'

Billy stared at her rather helplessly for a moment, then hunched forward and concentrated on the floor. 'It all happened together. The rape . . . Cill vanishing . . . Lou being questioned . . . Grace's murder . . .' He lapsed into silence.

'We don't think it's coincidence,' Rachel put in. 'I mean, if Eileen lied about Louise going to Grace's house, then she probably lied about other stuff.' She moved her hand to her husband's back and rubbed it gently. 'It's what we want you to find out. Billy's worried there's things he was never told, and it's driving him bananas.'

Sasha watched them both for a long moment then sculpted an ironic 'T' with her hands. 'Time out?' she suggested. 'I'm quite good at what I do, but I'm not a policeman. My forte is tracking down missing people – mostly children – and I succeed more often than I fail. Murder is something else entirely.'

'It was a long time ago,' said Billy.

'It makes no difference. If you think you have information about a murder, you should take it to the police.' She closed her notebook. 'Apart from anything else, you're putting me in a difficult position. Withholding evidence is a serious crime and I can't be a party to it.'

Billy would have abandoned it there and then but Rachel gave a disparaging laugh. 'No wonder none of you has ever found Cill. How can you go looking for a girl and not know there was a murder on her doorstep a few days later? OK, I don't know how old you are, or if you were even born then, but David Trevelyan bloody well ought to have mentioned it. If it hadn't been for Grace's death, the police would have spent more time looking for Cill. Didn't he tell you that?'

'Are you saying the two events were linked?'

Rachel shrugged. 'All we know is that Lou was questioned about Cill going missing, then Eileen lied about knowing Grace.' She gave Billy's back another comforting stroke. 'And we don't know why, since Lou and Cill spent time in Grace's house . . . and Eileen knew it.'

Sasha pondered for a moment, then reached into her case for a file. 'I think you should read the Trevelyans' statements.' She took out a file and extracted some papers. 'These are copies of the ones they made to the police.' She passed them across. 'Jean's is a factual account of sending Cill to bed on the Friday night and waking up in the morning to find her bed empty. David's is more interesting, because it was made in response to some tough police questioning.'

She watched Rachel split the copies and pass one to Billy. 'Last night I listened to tapes of the interviews my predecessor had with both of them. They mention the names of numerous children and adults that Cill was friendly with – I have a list in here – ' she tapped the file on her lap – 'but there's no one called Grace and there's no mention of murder.' She jerked her chin at the papers. 'As far as I'm aware, those statements represent the limit of their knowledge.'

INCIDENT REPORT

Date: 30.05.70

Time: 09.30

Officers attending: PC Lawrence Reed and PC Paul
Prentice

Incident: Missing child — mother, Jean
Trevelyan, interviewed at home

Mrs Jean Trevelyan reported her daughter missing at
09.17. Officers Reed and Prentice responded
immediately. After taking and transmitting details
of Priscilla (Cill) Trevelyan's description, the
officers questioned Jean Trevelyan (mother). She was
extremely upset and not very coherent. However, she
dictated the following statement and agreed it was
an accurate and chronological record of events:

Cill was sent home from Highdown School yesterday
afternoon [Friday, 29.05.70] at about two o'clock.
She told me she'd been suspended for a week because
she'd had a fight with another girl. The girl's name
is Louise Burton and she was Cill's best friend until
they fell out at the beginning of this month. They
haven't talked to each other since, and my husband
and I were pleased about it because Louise was a bad
influence on our daughter.

Cill refused to tell me what the fight was about and I
warned her that her father would be angry about the
suspension. She lost her temper and stormed off to

her bedroom, saying it wasn't her fault. I understood from something she said that Louise Burton had not been punished in the same way. As this seemed unreasonable, I telephoned Miss Brett at Highdown School and asked for an explanation. She told me Louise had said the fight started when Cill tried to persuade her to truant again, and Cill had not denied it. In the circumstances, she felt it proper to punish Cill.

The last three months have been a big worry to us. For no obvious reason Cill started truanting, and the school warned us a few weeks ago that she would be asked to leave if her poor attendance continued. She was encouraged to truant by Louise Burton, who struggles with schoolwork and finds lessons difficult. Both my husband and I have spoken to Miss Brett about moving Cill into a more challenging class. We have also asked Mr and Mrs Burton on two occasions to address Louise's behaviour. Nothing has come of either approach.

My husband, David, works the night shift at Brackham & Wright's tool factory. At the time Cill arrived home he was asleep, and I decided to keep her in her room until he left for work at 8 p.m. I knew he'd be angry and felt it would be better to tell him about the suspension this morning [Saturday]. However, Cill was making so much noise that she woke him up. When he demanded an explanation, she swore at him and said she didn't have to say anything if she didn't want to.

Cill is our only child and David worries about her a

great deal. She's well developed for her age and brighter than average, but she's easily led. We never had any problems with her until she went to Highdown School. Cill has accused David many times of being too strict, citing other children's parents as examples. She is angry that she isn't allowed to go out in the evenings or wear provocative clothing, and this has led to arguments with her father.

When she refused to say why she'd had a fight with Louise, he gave her three lashes of his belt. David has always taken the view that school punishments should be upheld and he ordered Cill to stay in her room until she was ready to explain and apologize. She went upstairs immediately and slammed her door again.

I knocked on her door shortly after David went to work and asked her if she wanted something to eat. She didn't answer but I could hear her crying. Her radio was playing pop music in the background. I decided against going into her room but spoke to her for several minutes through the door. I can't remember exactly what I said, because I was angry myself, but I did urge her to show some sense in the morning and to apologize to her father at the first opportunity.

When I went to bed at ten thirty there was no light under her door and the radio had been turned off. She certainly did not leave the house while I was downstairs, because I would have seen her. I am a light sleeper and I remember waking during the night. I believe the time was about twelve fifteen.

I assume now that it may have been the front door closing, although I can't be sure.

When David returned from work this morning [Saturday] at seven thirty I got up to make breakfast. We discussed Cill for about an hour in the kitchen before he asked me to call her down. We both agreed that confining her to the house and insisting she did chores was the best way forward. However, she was not in her room and her bed hadn't been slept in. A small rucksack is missing from her wardrobe along with her nightdress, two skirts and some T-shirts.

I immediately telephoned the parents of Louise Burton and three of her other friends [Rosie Maine, Ginny Lawson, Katey Cropper] but none of them knows where she is. I decided to call the police after David set off in his car to see if he could find her. She has never run away before and we cannot think of anywhere she could go at twelve fifteen in the morning. If she was with a friend, the parents would have alerted us. We are desperately worried that she's put herself in danger by hitching a lift with a stranger.

It has been made clear to me by Officers Prentice and Reed that runaways are treated differently from abductions. I understand that in most circumstances children who leave home after a row with their parents return within twenty-four hours.

Jean Trevelyan

WITNESS STATEMENT

Date:	02.06.70
Time:	11.30
Officers interviewing:	DC Williams and PC Prentice
Witness:	David Trevelyan
Incident:	Disappearance of Priscilla (Cill) Trevelyan on 30.05.70

Mr David Trevelyan was invited for interview at Highdown Police Station. He presented himself voluntarily but was hostile to many of the questions that were put to him. The following statement was dictated and signed by Mr Trevelyan.

I know nothing about my daughter's disappearance. You can call ours a love-hate relationship if you like, but it wouldn't be true. I have never hated Cill from the moment she was born. If I thought it would have done her any good, I'd have spoilt her rotten and given her everything she asked for. Instead, I put pressure on her to work because I know she is bright enough to do better than her parents. We had few problems with her until she reached puberty, but her difficult adolescence is putting a strain on the family.

I was upset when she didn't make it to grammar school. She has a good brain, but she was let down by her primary school. There's so much rubbish talked about the eleven-plus. It's supposed to be a test of IQ, but

the more you practise the skills the better you are at
them. Anyone can bump their level up by ten points
when they know what's expected. Cill sat it blind and
missed by a point, and you're not going to tell me
that's fair. There's people I work with whose sons got
through on lower scores. The system's rigged in
favour of the middle classes.

I am strict because I want the best for her. The world's
changing and women should have as good an education as
men. I don't want her to be a packer at Brackham &
Wright's or a lowly-paid hairdresser. I want her to find
a decent job in London where she'll meet a good man who
earns enough to buy his own house. My greatest fear has
always been that some boy will take advantage and get
her pregnant before she's sixteen.

It has caused a great number of arguments between us.
My daughter developed early and thought she could
look after herself. I have told her many times that
she doesn't understand how vulnerable young girls
are, and when the truanting began last term I felt I
had no option but to take a sterner line. My wife and I
have tried everything from delivering and collecting
her from school ourselves to enforcing a curfew after
six o'clock at night, but the only discipline that
seems to work is physical punishment.

I object strongly to any suggestion that I take
enjoyment from this. My relationship with my daughter
has never strayed beyond a parental one with all my
efforts geared to ensuring her future success. I
recognize that my ambitions for her may exceed her

own, but my hope has always been that she would never suffer my frustrations. If this has led me to be too severe on a child I love, then I am deeply sorry, but my intentions are good.

I was horrified to learn that Louise Burton made a statement on Saturday saying my daughter was gang raped at the beginning of May, and 'brought it on herself'. I understand that Louise blames my strictness for the fact that Cill was unable to tell my wife and me that it happened. We are deeply upset about this as we have long had concerns about Louise's truthfulness and fail to understand why this story of rape is believed when she could neither name the perpetrators nor identify the three suspects who were brought in for questioning. Nor do I understand why Louise failed to tell her own parents at the time. The Burtons take a relaxed view of their daughter's behaviour and I cannot believe they were unaware of the rape if it happened. In summary, there is no evidence to support Louise's allegation and I am angry that it has been given credence when it reflects so badly on our daughter.

In reference to the argument I had with Cill on the afternoon of Friday, 29 May, it was no different from the ones that had gone before. She and I are forceful people and there was a lot of shouting. My recollection is that she swore profusely and called me a 'Victorian parent', 'Hitler', 'Methuselah', and accused me of 'playing God'. She then turned on her mother and called her a 'tell-tale creep' and a 'snivelling bitch'. She also accused us of trying to

live her life, and of caring more about what the other
parents at school would say than we did about her.

I insisted on an explanation for the fight with Louise
Burton. When she refused, I asked her if Louise's
version was true — namely that she'd tried to persuade
Louise to truant again. Cill began throwing things
about the room and I felt I had no option but to give
her three lashes of the belt. I then sent her to her
room and instructed her mother to make sure she
remained there. It was an unhappy experience for all
of us, but I was confident that the outcome would be
the same as usual: Cill would apologize in the morning
and her behaviour would improve in the short term. Our
difficulty, as ever, was how to deal with her behaviour
in the long term, specifically the truanting.

I left for work at eight o'clock [Friday] and at that
time Cill was in her bedroom. As a foreman in the
engineering department at Brackham & Wright's, I
oversee a night workforce of approximately fifty.
Louise Burton's father, Robert, has similar
responsibilities in the packing department. A female
work colleague of mine, Deborah Handley, noticed that I
was upset on arrival and asked me if something was
wrong. Deborah has two daughters in their late teens
and I've regularly asked her advice about Cill's
behaviour. During the shift I explained what had
happened and told Deborah that Jean and I were at our
wits' end. She suggested I talk to Robert Burton and find
out what the fight was really about. I believe her words
were, 'If Cill was too worked up to invent a reason,
then I bet there's more to it than meets the eye.'

I approached Robert in the canteen at approximately
one o'clock in the morning. He was unwilling to talk
to me, claiming the school's punishment showed that
Cill was at fault, not Louise. I pointed out that
Louise's version of events was very convenient, since
she knew how worried we and Miss Brett had been about
Cill's truanting. He asked me if I was accusing his
daughter of lying, and when I said it was a
possibility, he became abusive and a fight broke out. I
did not do this to draw attention to myself and create
an alibi or to disguise any bruises from a previous
encounter with Cill. It happened as a result of my
deep concern and anxiety for my daughter's welfare,
which boiled over when Robert Burton referred to her
as 'a cheap little tart who deserved what she got'.

I have no idea why he made this remark unless Louise
had already told him about the alleged rape. If so, he
had a responsibility to pass that information to
myself and my wife.

In conclusion, I have accounted for my movements
during the night of Friday, 29 and Saturday, 30 May
1970. Also, my fifty-minute drive on the morning of
Saturday, 30 May when I went to Branksome Station and
Bournemouth Central in the hope of finding my
daughter. I confirm that I know nothing about Cill's
disappearance and that I am ignorant of her current
whereabouts.

David Trevelyan

By the time Billy had finished reading and laid the pages on the coffee table, his hands were shaking. 'God!' he said with feeling. 'Do you think Mr Trevelyan's right? Do you think my folks *did* know about the rape?'

Assuming he was addressing her, Sasha Spencer demurred. 'David's never been convinced the rape happened,' she said. 'He thinks your sister was lying to shift attention away from her part in Cill's suspension. Jean believes it, though, and she beats herself up regularly for being a lousy mother. It's a very sad situation. Rightly or wrongly – and for different reasons – they each hold themselves responsible.'

Billy lowered his face into his hands. 'It certainly happened,' he muttered. 'I was there, I saw it. They took it in turns . . . kept kicking her . . . she had blood all down her legs. It makes me sick just thinking about it.'

Rachel saw the distaste on Sasha's face. 'He was ten years old and they'd filled him with vodka,' she said, leaping to Billy's defence, 'so he didn't understand what was going on. He thought it was a fight. If the police had included him in the questioning, it would have been different, but no one knew he'd been with Cill and Louise that day.'

'Cill was that scared of her dad, she said she'd kill us if we ever breathed a word,' Billy went on unhappily, 'so I never did. And it wasn't until a bloke at school told me his mum had read it in the newspapers that I found out Louise had told the police . . . I didn't even know what rape meant – he had to explain it to me . . . and that was a good two months after Cill vanished. It wasn't mentioned in our house. *Nothing* was.' He dropped a hand to David Trevelyan's statement. 'I didn't know Mr Trevelyan cared about his kid that much . . . I didn't know my dad and him had a fight . . . I sure as hell didn't know Dad was calling Cill a tart *before* anyone knew she was missing.'

There was a long silence.

Sasha opened her notebook again. 'Why is that important?' she asked.

'He said Cill "deserved what she got". I think it means he knew about the rape.'

Sasha eyed him with a frown. 'I still don't understand why it's important. It may not reflect well on your parents, but it doesn't mean they had anything to do with Cill running away.'

Billy took a printout of his father's email from his shirt pocket. 'Read this,' he said harshly, 'then ask yourself what else he's been lying about. You don't tell a man his kid deserves what she gets if you think he's abusing her . . . and you damn well talk to the police if you think that man's been after your own daughter as well.'

Twenty-Two

25 Mullin Street, Highdown, Bournemouth
Thursday, 15 May 2003, midday

JONATHAN SUGGESTED they sit in the garden so that he could inspect the rear of George's house, but she told him there was only one chair and no table. She seemed depressed, and he thought it sad that she had no one to share her garden with. He said the day was too glorious to miss and insisted on moving furniture out from the kitchen. Puffs of high cloud drifted across a turquoise sky and the scent of wisteria on her neighbour's wall was heavy on the air. He collected a cushion from the sitting room and tucked it behind George's back, worried about the signs of pain and weariness that were showing round her eyes. 'What's wrong?'

'Nothing,' she said. 'I'm just aching a bit.'

He took the chair next to her. 'You look tired.'

'It goes with the job. I'm on nights again.'

'I hope you're not playing the martyr,' he warned her. 'I'm investing a lot of time and energy into this book.'

She gave a faint smile. 'You're *such* a bully.'

'I've been taking lessons from Andrew. Have you been to the doctor?'

'I'm going tomorrow.'

He didn't press it. Instead he produced a printout of Andrew's bullet points which he'd emailed George at the beginning of the week. He began with what could be proved. If, as George's previous neighbour had told her, her house was an exact replica of Grace's, then Louise could certainly have seen into the sitting room through the French windows. Jonathan was less convinced about the girls entering through a gate in the fence at the back in order to truant. He nodded at George's rear boundary. 'Their only access would have been through other people's gardens,' he pointed out, 'so why were they never seen by Grace's neighbours?'

George sorted through a folder that she'd asked him to fetch from her sitting room. 'I think I've solved that.' She drew out a photocopy of a street map and spread it on the table. 'I found this in the library. It's from an early *A–Z* of Bournemouth, printed in 1969.' She took up a pencil and placed the tip on Mullin Street. 'This is where the houses were demolished to make the apartment block and, as near as I can get it, *this – *' she drew a small circle – 'was Grace's house. If I'm right, then there was a narrow cul-de-sac at the back which was reached from Bladen Street.' She ran her pencil up a road at right angles. 'The alleyway doesn't exist any more, because these two houses adjacent to Bladen Street appear to have extended their gardens, and the flats have garages along the boundary . . . but it was obviously there in 1970.'

Jonathan gave a nod of approval. 'Good stuff.'

George pulled a face. 'It doesn't prove anything. What about fingerprints? The police would have found some if Cill had been there for any length of time. Children's fingers are smaller than adults' so, if juvenile prints had been there, the police *couldn't* have missed them. Particularly Louise's. Miss Brett said she was a skinny little thing. Even if she didn't go inside, she'll have touched the windows when she looked in. It's the natural thing to do.'

'Did Lovatt have any ideas?'

'He said eyebrows would have been raised by children's prints. He also thinks there would have been a comparison set on file as Cill's would have been lifted from her bedroom in case a body was found.'

'So Louise is lying?'

'That's his view.'

Jonathan linked his hands and stretched them towards the sky, cracking the joints at the back of his neck. 'Louise told Andrew he'd have to explain it himself,' he murmured, 'which was very clever of her, because he's a competitive little man and he loves winning.'

George tut-tutted. 'You shouldn't keep drawing attention to his height. You'll give him a complex.'

'Fat chance!'

'He thinks that's why his wife left him.'

Jonathan relaxed again, dropping his arms to the table top and favouring George with a grin. 'I did what you told me to do and went to see her a couple of days ago. She's bored with the parasitic stud, stressed to the eyeballs with work and kept asking me if Andrew had a girlfriend.'

'What did you say?'

'That she didn't deserve a second chance because she was a two-timing bitch.'

'You *didn't*!'

'Bloody did.'

'No, you didn't.'

He laughed. 'OK! I may not have used those exact words, but I did say Andrew was a prince among men and if she had a blind bit of sense she'd recognize the fact. I also said he'd never had a bad word for her and was eating his heart out because she and the children were the best thing that ever happened to him.'

George's eyes sparkled with delight. 'What did she say?'

'That both girls had told her he'd had a woman in the house on Saturday, and the place stank of smoke on Sunday morning.' He smiled at her deflated expression. 'What's wrong with that? It means he's desirable.'

'I hope you explained.'

He shook his head. 'I said the ladies were queuing up for him so she'd better get a move on.'

'Do you think it'll work?' she asked, her soft heart visible in the pleasure that showed in her face.

'Should do, assuming he hasn't been seduced by Louise.'

'Don't be silly!'

Jonathan tapped the bullet points. 'He's very keen to believe her. His theory is that the house was cleaned either after Cill left it or after Grace was murdered.'

'Who by?'

'Anyone you like. If it was after Cill left, then it might have been Grace herself. If it was after Grace died, then it was her murderer.'

George pondered for a moment. 'Why weren't Howard's prints wiped away at the same time?'

'They would have been, but he left enough on the Wednesday to satisfy the police. There's a clear suggestion in the prosecution case that part of his attempt to cast the blame elsewhere was to clean his prints from anything that looked suspicious – such as the bathroom taps – but that he was too stupid to do a thorough job.'

She looked doubtful again. 'It would have meant him using the lavatory after he found Grace's body. Do you think that's likely?'

'Very likely,' said Jonathan dryly. 'He probably vomited into it.'

'What about Grace's prints?'

Jonathan eyed her with approval. 'What about them?'

'If her murderer had cleaned up, there wouldn't have been any.'

'Go on.'

'Wouldn't the police have noticed?' she asked with a frown. 'I mean, if they were arguing that Howard wasn't thorough enough to remove all of his, then Grace's should have been all over the place. Do you see the point I'm making? It would have been very peculiar if the only prints found were Howard's. The defence team would have picked up on it straight away because it would have supported his story.'

Jonathan pulled a letter from his briefcase. 'That's more or less what I thought, so I wrote to Howard's solicitor first thing Monday morning and this is his reply. I'll read the relevant paragraph . . . it's quite brief: "By recollection, the main sets were Grace Jefferies' and Howard's. In addition, policemen touched objects in the hallway and kitchen before the house was sealed. These prints were accounted for. Two or three unidentifiable sets were found on objects in the sitting room, which was considered unusual (most houses contain many more) until it became clear that Grace was a recluse. These sets were not considered suspicious. There were a number of partial prints about the house, which were thought to be Grace's, but they were too degraded for comparison."' He looked up. 'The rest is a diatribe about my suggestion that the defence team was negligent.'

'Oh dear!'

He consulted the letter again. '"We made every effort to substantiate our client's story, but I remain in no doubt that the verdict was a correct one."' He pushed the letter across the table. 'So unless they were even more negligent than I painted them,' he said lightly, 'which will be hotly disputed by my friend here, then Louise is lying and Cill was never there *or* – and this is Andrew's view – Grace cleaned the house of Cill's presence herself.'

'Why?'

'Because someone told her she'd be for the high jump if the police discovered she'd been harbouring a runaway.'

'Who?'

Jonathan shrugged. 'Anyone you like,' he said again, 'but Andrew's guessing Mr or Mrs Burton.'

*

It was only when Rachel asked Billy to make a pot of tea that Sasha Spencer found out what he really believed, and she made a mental note never again to make assumptions about protective wives. Rachel waited until the door closed, then leaned forward and spoke urgently into the silence. 'He's not going to tell you this because he's trying to convince himself he's imagining it. He's been surfing the Net researching recovered-memory syndrome. Half the sites talk about it being a recognized psychological phenomenon, the other half say the memories are invented . . . and he doesn't know which is the case. I keep telling him the false stuff comes out of dodgy therapy sessions, but he doesn't want to believe me. He's off his head because he can't sleep, and he's worried he's developed a thing about his dad because Robert keeps lecturing him about the firemen being on strike . . .'

*

George closed her eyes and lifted her face to the sun while Jonathan explained Andrew's theory. 'It's in bullet points again,' he said, extracting another sheet of paper. 'Cill took refuge at Grace's on the Friday night . . . Louise saw her there on the Saturday morning . . . she told her parents about it – probably on the Saturday afternoon—'

'I thought she told them on the Wednesday,' George broke in.

Jonathan put a finger on the line and looked up. 'Andrew says she never specified a day, only *implied* the Wednesday. Now, he thinks it's more likely she owned up after the police questioning because her mother had been so insistent the Burtons didn't know where Cill was.'

'OK. Next point.'

He returned to the page. 'One of the Burton parents went round to Grace's . . . read Cill the riot act and told her to go home . . . put the fear of God into Grace about harbouring truants and runaways . . . became anxious when Cill remained missing . . . started to lose it when Louise reported the state of Grace's house on the Tuesday or Wednesday . . . and lost it completely when Grace's body was found. Result: withdrawal of Louise from school in case she said anything, total clampdown on the story in the Burton household and enormous effort to distance themselves from Mullin Street and the Trevelyans.'

'So what does he think happened to Cill?'

'Pass.'

'Who killed Grace?'

'Pass.'

George shielded her eyes from the sun and squinted at him. 'They'd have known by the Monday morning that Cill hadn't returned home,' she pointed out, 'so why weren't they worried about Louise spilling the beans at school that day?'

'They told her not to.'

She eyed him with amusement. 'Did she always do what she was told? They couldn't stop her truanting, don't forget.'

'They threatened her with the police. Billy said she was frightened of them.'

George shook her head. 'I've never heard such a half-baked theory. There's only one explanation for why she wasn't confined to the house until the Wednesday: she didn't tell her parents she'd seen Cill in Grace's house until after she saw the blood on the window.'

Jonathan gave his head a thoughtful scratch. 'Maybe,' he mused.

'What other explanation is there?'

'The parents were worried someone would come asking questions if Louise didn't turn up on the Monday . . . she was threatened with a thrashing if she didn't keep her mouth shut . . . they told her she was to blame for not telling the police where Cill was . . . she was a fluent liar and was used to keeping secrets, so they were confident she'd keep that one.'

'What sort of secrets?'

Jonathan shrugged. 'The rape? The reason for the fight?'

'Why didn't they make her go in on the Wednesday? All the same reasons apply.'

'The circumstances had changed. The blood on the window was a secret too far and she threw a fit.'

'Assuming she's telling the truth,' said George cynically. 'I'm not as easily seduced as Andrew.'

'She's an incredible flirt.'

'Oh dear!' George sighed. '*Please* don't tell me Andrew fell for her.'

'Probably,' said Jonathan. 'He's a randy little beast – short-arses always are – but I meant, she flirted with information. She told him it was Howard who did it, but what she was really doing was hooking him into her father and Roy Trent.'

*

Rachel pulled nervously at her hair. 'This isn't easy,' she said. 'I've known Robert for ages and I'd never have thought . . . Billy's saying now that he doesn't want the girls anywhere near him. He's even wondering if his dad had a go when they were younger. I keep telling him he can't have done because they never stayed overnight with the folks, and his mum was always around in the daytime. But it's funny, looking back. It was Billy who insisted they had to come home before bedtime . . . and I never really thought about it till now. I asked him the other day if it was because of all this – ' she made a vague gesture towards Robert's email – 'and he said, no, he'd forgotten. He just needed to know his kids were safe with me while he was on night shifts. He thought it was because he was afraid of fire breaking out . . . now he thinks it was these unrecovered memories working like instinct. That's weird, isn't it?'

She didn't expect a reply because she wasn't even looking at Sasha. Instead, she twined a strand of hair about her fingers and concentrated determinedly on the carpet. 'The trouble is, there's nothing specific. Billy never *saw* anything – it's just stuff he heard and things that Louise said . . . like she hated her mother's cleaning job because it meant their dad had to get them ready for school. Eileen did offices from six to ten in the morning and the kids'd be left to sleep till Robert came off his night shift around seven. Billy was never woken till eight, but Louise was always up and her dad'd be giving her breakfast and laughing with her. He didn't do it with Billy . . . just whacked some food at him and told him to get a move on.' She paused. 'You could say it was a daughter–dad thing – opposites attract and all that – but a few times Billy woke early and heard his dad talking to Louise in her bedroom. As a kid, it made him jealous because Robert never bothered to talk to him, but now . . .' She lapsed into a troubled silence.

Sasha watched her for a moment. 'It doesn't prove he was an abuser, Rachel. The daughter–dad thing is just as likely.'

The woman sighed. 'I know, that's the trouble.' She clasped her fingers in her lap. 'It's why Billy keeps surfing the Net. There are other things that are just as vague – but nothing that proves abuse. They just look suspicious when you put it all together.'

'Try me.'

Billy returned with a tray of cups while Rachel was talking and resumed his seat without interrupting her. He appeared relieved that she'd taken a lead and after a while began to interject memories himself. To Sasha, watching him, it was clear that some of these memories were coming back to him even as he was speaking. Did that make them true? She had no idea, but the picture he painted of his childhood was a disturbing one.

'You try to make sense of things when you're a kid,' he said at one point, 'so I thought Dad only liked ladies. He called Mum and Louise his "beautiful girls", but it was always Lou got the attention . . . never Mum. She used to make me plait her hair in front of him, then push me away the minute he left the room.' He smiled rather crookedly. 'She said if I got a taste for it, I'd turn into a pansy. I thought she was talking about flowers.'

On another occasion: 'It was Lou started the Cathy McGowan thing. Dad slipped her some money and she came back with a miniskirt and loads of make-up. She was prancing around the sitting room in front of him, and Mum went completely crazy. Lou had this black eyeliner all round her eyes and pale pink lipstick, and Mum called her a tart and started hitting her. Dad just laughed . . .

'. . . he gave Cill money as well, so she could buy the same stuff as Lou. He called them his princesses. That's when Lou started getting uppity and saying she didn't want to be friends with Cill any more. She was really jealous. I mean, she was skinny as a rake. You'd have to be blind not to see that Cill looked better than she did . . .

'. . . I don't know if my father abused Cill. You don't think about things like that when you're a kid. All I know is he liked her. He'd sit her on his lap when Mum wasn't around and play with her hair.'

'Why did your mother go out if she was worried about him?' asked Sasha.

Billy buried his head in his hands for the hundredth time that morning. 'I don't know if she was. I don't even know if I'm imagining all of this.'

Rachel squeezed his hand. 'Eileen worked in the evenings as well – four to eight. She was only at home when the kids were at school and her husband was asleep.'

'She hated being a mother,' said Billy. 'It was Dad looked after us.'

'Perhaps they needed the money,' said Sasha.

'Then why didn't she work in a supermarket? That's what Rach does.'

'Perhaps it was the only job available,' the woman said. 'Did Louise have any other friends who came to the house?'

'A few.'

'Did your father sit them on his lap?'

'Sometimes, but Cill was the only one who'd let him play with her hair. I think she did it to make Lou jealous.' He shook his head. 'He can't have done anything really bad to her because I'm sure she was a virgin when those bastards raped her. There was too much blood on her legs.'

'He may have been grooming her. That's usually how child molesters work.'

Billy stared at her with a sick expression in his eyes. 'It was never talked about in those days. There were kids like Cill who were given a larruping by their dads every time they stepped out of line, but this other stuff . . .' He shook his head. 'There was Ian Brady and Myra Hindley, but they were psychopaths and went for other people's children. It's as if sex in families only started in the last ten–fifteen years.'

'It's been going on for centuries,' said Sasha, who'd researched the subject in depth. 'It's society's attitude that's changed. We know now that if a child's forced into a relationship where the balance of power is unequal, the damage is irreparable. They tend to replicate that imbalance in future relationships, which is what Louise seems to have been doing.'

*

Jonathan shielded his own eyes against the sun. 'Louise persuaded Andrew not to look at it with the benefit of hindsight, but to keep in mind that no one knew Grace was going to die. In those circumstances, the only thing the Burtons were guilty of was failing to ensure that Cill returned home. They'd have been as shocked as anyone when the police continued to report her missing.'

'Why didn't they say something then?'

Jonathan shrugged. 'They were worried about what the neighbours would say.'

George pulled a disapproving face. 'I can't believe any parent would behave so irresponsibly.'

'You're looking at it with hindsight again. As far as they were concerned, it was perfectly straightforward. Cill was alive, she was streetwise, her house was round the corner, she promised to go straight back to it. They probably thought she'd be spotted before she even reached the end of the road.'

'Why wasn't she?'

'Pass.'

'Dear, dear, dear! You're expecting me to swallow more coincidences than I ever offered you. It's complete nonsense, Jon. You must see that.'

He held up his hands in mock surrender. 'I'm simply playing

devil's advocate on behalf of the fat controller. I said I'd run it past you and I have.'

'Do *you* believe it?'

Jonathan considered for a moment. 'Andrew's looking for anyone other than Howard to be guilty . . . and he prefers Mr Burton or Mr Trevelyan because he likes the symmetry of child abuse running through the story.'

George pulled a face. 'You're supposed to be bringing a critical eye to bear on the evidence.'

He grinned. 'Then I'll tell you what I do believe. When Louise told Andrew she looked through Grace's window on the Tuesday, it was done deliberately to implicate Roy and his friends.'

George squinted at him again. 'Why?'

'I don't know . . . unless it's the truth . . .'

*

'She always picks blokes who're violent,' Rachel said. 'The one she's got at the moment gave her a black eye a few weeks ago. That's why Billy's worried about her. You could argue it's bad luck, except that, for a while, she was married to one of the boys who raped Cill. We don't understand that at all, because she must have known what she was getting into. She'll tell you she didn't know their names and couldn't identify them, but she'll be lying.'

'It wasn't an accident that we all hooked up on the the day of the rape,' said Billy. 'Cill and Lou knew where to find them, so they must have been with them before. There's no way she wouldn't have recognized Roy when she saw him.'

'Who's Roy?'

'Roy Trent . . . manages a pub in Highdown. He's the one Lou married.' Billy shook his head. 'He's a right bastard . . . raped Cill twice then kicked her. So why would Lou want to marry a man like that? I can't get my head round it at all.'

Sasha smiled slightly. 'Better the devil you know?' she suggested. 'She'd have had more power in a relationship where she held a bargaining chip. Secrets are powerful weapons. You made that point yourselves in reference to the way your parents treated her.'

'Then why leave him for someone she *can't* control?' asked Rachel. 'It doesn't make sense.'

'Only because you're assuming a rationale behind her behaviour which probably doesn't exist. If Roy was an inadequate lover, she'd move on to a man who was better.'

'She can't go on doing it for ever,' said Rachel with a moue of disapproval. 'She's no spring chicken any more.'

'I shouldn't think age has anything to do with it but, in any case, you said she's trying to look like Cill at thirteen, so perhaps she wants to act thirteen as well.'

'That's pathetic.'

'Yes,' Sasha agreed soberly, 'but, if your husband's right about his father, then she's a very damaged woman. Louise would have learnt at ten or eleven that orgasm equals relationship . . . so how can a relationship exist without it? It would explain why she cut Billy out of her life, and why she isn't interested in you or your children. She lacks the skill to handle non-sexual relationships.'

'She hasn't spoken to Dad in years,' said Billy, 'just took money off him.'

'I expect she felt she'd earned it.'

There was a brief silence while Billy and Rachel digested this.

'God!' said Rachel abruptly. 'I hope we're not wrong about this. It's a hell of an accusation against a seventy-year-old.'

Billy looked at Sasha. 'What do *you* think?'

She hesitated, wondering how blunt she could be. 'I'm no expert,' she warned, 'but you've described a common background for abuse. Absent mother, touchy-feely father, secretive behaviour, taboo subjects – he certainly had the opportunity.'

'Is that a yes?'

'I'd certainly like to talk to him about Cill. As far as I know, he wasn't interviewed at the time of her disappearance.' She watched Billy's expression turn to anxiety. 'It's what you suspect, isn't it? That he knows what happened to her? Your mother, too?'

He looked devastated, as if he'd wanted her to say the opposite. 'Yes,' he admitted. 'And Louise.'

'It certainly sounds as if he was using your sister as a procurer, although I wouldn't think she understood what role she was playing until she brought Cill into the house. You said she was jealous and uppity, so I'm guessing she realized that your father was getting bored with her.' She paused. 'As a matter of interest, how did she react when the boys paid more attention to Cill on the day of the rape?'

'She teased them about being virgins. It's what got them steamed up.'

'So she contributed to what happened?'

Billy covered his eyes again. 'She made Cill come back to help her, and that's when they jumped her.'

'What did Louise do?'

'Curled into a ball,' he said harshly. 'Me, too, if it comes to that. Neither of us did a damn thing . . . just let it happen.'

Sasha exchanged a glance with Rachel. 'What happened after the boys had gone?' she asked. 'How did Cill clean herself up?'

'She didn't, not then. Lou sneaked off and got her some clothes so she could cover up, then the girls left.' He paused. 'I've never been so scared in my life. I tried to go after them, but Lou said she'd drop me in it if I did.'

'Did they say where they were going?'

'No.'

'What time was it?'

'Afternoon . . . two-ish.'

'What did you do?'

He raised his head. 'Hid in the park till school ended, then went home. I felt ill from the vodka, but no one noticed. Dad was in the garden, so I went to my room and stayed there till Lou came back. I was shaking like a leaf . . . kept thinking Cill had died or something and the police were going to come. Then Lou waltzes in as if nothing had happened – it was weird.'

'Did you ask her where she and Cill had gone?'

'I didn't need to,' said Billy flatly. 'I guessed where she got the clothes from, because she couldn't go to Cill's house or ours in case she was caught. Grace Jefferies,' he explained. 'Had to be. She came back with some trousers that were way too big for Cill. She had to bunch them at her waist to stop them falling down.'

*

The sun was so strong that George decided they needed hats. Her face had turned the colour of beetroot and she reappeared from upstairs with a pink straw confection on her head. 'Friend's daughter's wedding,' she said succinctly. 'Total waste of money. They were divorced two years later. Here!' She plonked a cap on his head. 'This was my father's postman's hat. At least it'll keep the sun off your face.'

Jonathan turned it round so that the peak was shading his neck. 'It's the boiling brain that's the problem. The face was bred for this sort of weather.'

She giggled as she sat down. 'You look as if you've got a saucepan on your head.'

He eyed her with amusement. 'And you look *great*, George! I've always thought red and pink were the perfect combination.'

She giggled again. 'Wasn't it a terrible choice? Some wretched shop assistant told me it suited me, and I *believed* her!' She tapped the table. 'Here's a question. I was thinking about it upstairs: why did Grace allow the girls to truant in her house? I don't believe that nonsense Louise told Andrew about bruises. Grace was a mature woman. If she was concerned about the girls, she would have phoned the NSPCC, or social services, or the school, even the police . . . and she could have done it anonymously. So why didn't she?'

'For the same reason she didn't rat on Howard.'

'And what reason was that?'

'She felt sorry for him.'

George pondered for a moment. 'Any normal grandmother would have bust a gut to find him some help, particularly when he was younger.'

'Perhaps there wasn't any to be had.'

George ignored him. 'The only person who did anything for him was Wynne. She may not have been very effective, but at least she had a go. She dragged him to school by his ear, beat him up to make him stay there, went out to work to support him, took a two-day sickie to help him find a job, tried to get help from the GP.' She raised her eyebrows. 'Don't you think it's interesting that as soon as the two-day job search was over, he went straight back to Grace's house?'

'Not really. It's where he always went.'

George wagged a finger at him. 'Exactly.'

'So?'

'Grace kept undermining Wynne's efforts. Every time Wynne got him up to the mark, Grace seduced him back again.'

'She wouldn't have needed to seduce him. He preferred it there.'

'Then she should have made it uncomfortable for him. It explains why Wynne never went to see her. They probably rowed all the time about Grace ruining Howard's chances. *I'd* have blooming well rowed with my mother if she'd kept my son from school.' She smiled at Jonathan's continued scepticism. 'Oh, come on! At least try to be objective. She did the same with Louise and Cill . . . reinforced their truanting against their parents' wishes. But none of us volunteers for anything unless it works to our advantage. Grace was a recluse. She hardly ever went out, didn't have a job, rarely saw her daughter, couldn't socialize with her neighbours because she had a speech impediment. What does that tell you?'

He shrugged. 'She was difficult? Unlikeable? Divorced from reality?'

'Probably all of those things . . . but why did children like being with her?'

'She let them watch her television.'

More finger pointing. 'Right. And why did she do that?'

Jonathan shook his head. 'Pass.'

'She was *lonely*, Jon. I'll bet Louise could have had a party in there, and Grace would have baked the biscuits.'

He stared thoughtfully down the garden, more taken by one of her earlier points. 'Howard was supposed to be starting a job at the local dairy that Wednesday afternoon,' he murmured. 'Perhaps he was intending to do it until he found Grace's body.'

'Why go to her house at all?'

'To see if Cill was there?'

Twenty-Three

SASHA SPENCER drew up outside the Fletchers' house in full view of a CCTV camera on a lamp-post and reached into the back seat for her briefcase. Whether she was being monitored or not, she could see no point in pretending to be anything other than she was. She stepped out of the car, smoothed her skirt and took stock of the adobe facade before opening the gate. She had taken the trouble to consult an estate agent before she drove onto the peninsula and had discovered not only that Palencia was a rented property but also that the present tenant had announced his intention not to renew the lease. Was Ms Spencer interested in taking it on?

There were no cars in the driveway and no answer to her persistent ringing of the doorbell. A garage to the left of the house was also empty. She looked for cameras but, if they existed, they were well hidden. Ostentatiously consulting her watch, she followed a path down the right-hand side, looking in windows as she went, before knocking loudly on the kitchen door. There was no response. Indeed, the only sign that the house was inhabited was a sun lounger on the lawn with a towel over it.

According to Billy Burton, Louise had said her husband was in his study the day Billy called, but Sasha had seen only a sitting room and a small dining room. With another quick scan for

328

cameras, she moved past the kitchen and peered through the next set of windows, shading her eyes to cut out the glare of the sun. This room, too, was unoccupied but she could see the back of a computer console on the desk and a large flat-screen television on the wall behind it. Light flickered across its surface and she wondered if it was active until she realized it was a reflection from the computer monitor. She narrowed her eyes to see if she could make out the image but, even as she watched, the reflection vanished.

It was a moment or two before she questioned why. Then she straightened abruptly and stepped back. The monitor had shut down automatically because the computer hadn't been used for a preset number of minutes, usually fifteen. Someone was in the house, and a reactive prickling between her shoulders told Sasha she was being watched. With a look of annoyance, she consulted her watch again, then retraced her steps to the front. She took a business card from her pocket, scribbled, 'FAO Louise Burton. Please call me. Need to speak to you urgently re. Cill Trevelyan' on the back and pushed it through the door. As she left, she had a strong suspicion that, even though she hadn't seen any cameras, all her movements had been recorded.

25 Mullin Street, Highdown, Bournemouth
Thursday, 15 May 2003, 3.30 p.m.

George opened the door and smiled enquiringly at the visitor on her doorstep. 'How can I help?' she asked, assuming the young woman was a constituent.

Sasha took in the bizarre hat and red face without flinching. 'Are you Councillor Georgina Gardener?'

'Yes.'

Sasha produced her operating licence. 'I'm Sasha Spencer. I work for WCH Investigations. You visited our offices a month ago asking for information on Mr and Mrs Trevelyan. My colleague took your details but was unable to assist you for confidentiality reasons. I was wondering if you'd be willing to give me a few minutes of your time now.'

George was too surprised to say anything for several seconds. 'Well, well, well!' she then declared. 'And Jonathan doesn't believe in coincidences!' She chuckled at Sasha's expression. 'You'd better come in. We're in the garden.'

Sasha felt at a distinct disadvantage as she was shepherded outside, introduced to Dr Hughes, whose head attire was even more peculiar, and given a kitchen chair to sit on. She had no idea who he was, didn't take greatly to his amused smile and wasn't given a chance to run through her spiel before Councillor Gardener piled in with her own comments. She was better informed than Billy Burton realized and canny enough to recognize that Sasha wouldn't be there unless the Trevelyans had authorized it. She asked the young woman bluntly what had decided them to do it. 'It can't have been my approach to your colleague, because I didn't explain why I was there. And you wouldn't have driven all this way just to find out why I asked for their address.'

'I'm afraid the issues of confidentiality remain the same, Councillor Gardener. I'm not at liberty to say.'

'Has someone else contacted you?' She took the woman's silence for assent and looked at Jonathan. 'It must have been William Burton. Interesting, eh? Why does he want his sister investigated?' She turned back to Sasha. 'Have you spoken to her?'

'Who?'

'Priscilla Fletcher.'

There was a pronounced pause before Jonathan took pity on Sasha. In a funny sort of way, she reminded him of George. A little on the chubby side, inappropriately dressed for a warm day in Bournemouth and certainly no beauty. Her mouth kept reaching nervously for a smile, as if she'd been trained to defuse difficult situations by offering a symbol of good will, but it wasn't something that came naturally to her. As usual, he failed to take into account the effect his intense gaze had on people and decided she hadn't been long in her job.

'Why don't you let Ms Spencer tell us why she's here?' he suggested to George. 'At the moment she's looking a trifle shell-shocked . . . which was rather my experience the first time I met you.'

George promptly pulled an apologetic face. 'I'm so sorry, dear. I thought it would be simpler if we just got on with it . . . but Jonathan's right. Please – ' she made an inviting gesture – 'go ahead.'

Sasha wondered what to say. She had been taught to go through certain formalities, but she was more used to the nervous responses she'd had from the Burtons than to this amused impatience. She played for time by opening her briefcase and taking out her notebook. 'If I may, I'll begin by explaining my company's policy with regard to your rights and the rights of my clients. You are under no obligation to answer my questions, however—' She broke off as Jonathan cleared his throat. 'Who *are* you?' she demanded abruptly. 'Why are you so interested in Cill Trevelyan?'

Jonathan gave a nod of approval. 'How prepared are you to share information?' he asked. 'We're fairly well informed on her story, but there are gaps in our knowledge that you might be able to fill.'

'I can't breach client confidentiality.'

He exchanged a glance with George. 'Then there's no incentive for us to help you,' he said. 'We've put time and effort into researching Cill's story, and you wouldn't know Priscilla Fletcher was worth investigating if Councillor Gardener hadn't paid a visit to William Burton.'

Sasha tried another smile. 'Do you know where Cill Trevelyan is?'

'No.'

'Do you know if she's still alive?'

'No.'

'Then what *do* you know that's worth my breaking company rules?'

'Enough to give you a helping hand,' said George. 'Have you spoken to Priscilla Fletcher?'

Sasha shook her head. 'I've just come from her house. I'm pretty sure someone was inside but they refused to answer the door. I've no idea if it was her or her husband.' She hesitated. 'Her brother says you have a photograph of her as she is now. May I see it?'

'As long as you show us one of Cill as a child,' said George. 'The Trevelyans must have given you one, but all we have is a black-and-white newspaper cutting. Trade for trade? We'll tell you something . . . you tell us something.'

Sasha wasn't as naive as Jonathan thought, so she played with her pencil and pretended to think about it. They'd be freer with their own information if they thought hers had to be enticed out of her.

As if to prove her point, Jonathan leaned forward. 'Live dangerously,' he encouraged her, 'otherwise George'll psychoanalyse you . . . and that's a nightmare.'

*

Louise spotted the card the minute she entered her front door. It lay on the carpet a metre from the doormat as if a current of air had wafted it from the letter box. She picked it up and read it, then thrust it hurriedly into her pocket. If she gave any thought at all to the cameras and tapes that ran in twenty-four-hour loops in Nick's office, it was only in relation to her own arrival. She retreated through the door, her busy mind already working out excuses for her rapid turnaround, and left as quietly as she'd arrived.

*

Jonathan passed David Trevelyan's statement to George and bent his head to read Jean's. The noise of an occasional car filtered through from the road outside, but otherwise the only sounds were a distant motor-mower and the hum of crickets in the grass. Sasha sat patiently waiting, wishing there was an umbrella. Her skin was reddening in the sun and sweat was running down her back.

'Why don't you take off your jacket?' said Jonathan suddenly. 'You'll fry if you're not careful.'

Sasha gave her automatic smile. 'I'm fine, thank you.'

'Have a hat,' said George, whipping off the pink straw creation and offering it across.

'No . . . I'm all right . . . thank you.'

Jonathan came to the end of the page and pushed it away. 'Very interesting.' He turned his attention to Sasha again. 'Have you met either of them? What are they like?'

'No, it was a predecessor who interviewed them. He noted down his impressions afterwards.' She sorted through her brief-case, looking for them. 'I've listened to the tapes and spoken to Mr Trevelyan on the phone, but that's all. Here we are.' She read from the page: ' "David Trevelyan: Big, impressive man with easy manner. Did most of the talking. Clearly blames himself for what happened. No sense that he was keeping anything back. Jean Trevelyan: Slender, good-looking woman. More subdued than her husband. Spent most of the interview in tears. Also blames herself. No sense that she was keeping anything back. Some disagreement between them over the rape. Jean believes it happened. David can only focus on the way it allowed Cill to be portrayed as a tart. This still makes him angry." ' She looked up. 'That's it.'

'Does he talk on the tapes about the argument with Robert Burton?'

'All the time. He's convinced the Burtons set out to blacken Cill's name deliberately.'

'Why?'

'He's not very sure. He keeps talking about the end result –

that the police decided she was promiscuous, probably had a boyfriend she'd never told anyone about, and therefore wrote her off as a runaway.' She paused to collect her thoughts. 'He accuses Louise of lying about everything, including the rape. He says she was diverting attention from something she'd done and accuses the Burtons of backing her up to avoid the police taking too close an interest in their own daughter.'

'That last bit is probably true,' said George thoughtfully, mulling over what Sasha had told them. 'They wouldn't want *anyone* taking an interest in Louise if William's right about the abuse.' She folded her hands over David Trevelyan's statement. 'I wonder how much the mother knew.'

'She enabled it to happen,' said Sasha.

'Mm.' George pursed her lips in thought. 'Except she couldn't know about the abuse *and* the rape. One or other, perhaps . . . but not both.'

'Why do you say that?' asked Jonathan.

'Because she'd have told Louise to keep her mouth shut at the police station. There was no guarantee they'd accept Louise's story. If they'd had her examined to see if she'd been raped as well, then her father's abuse might have shown up.'

There was a short silence.

'So what do you think happened?' asked Sasha.

'God knows,' said George despondently. 'There's too much to take in . . . I can't see the wood for the trees.'

'It's not that bad,' said Jonathan reassuringly, reaching for a clean sheet of paper. 'Let's start with what we know to be true.' He jotted them down as he spoke. 'The rape. The names of the rapists. Cill and Louise's connection with Grace. Mrs Burton's knowledge of it. Her readiness to lie to the police.' He glanced from one to the other. 'Anything else?'

'Abuse,' said Sasha.

'We'll come to that in a minute. I'm after anything that's supported by an independent witness.'

'The fight between the girls,' said George, 'presumably also the fight between Robert Burton and David Trevelyan . . . and Robert Burton's remark about Cill deserving what she got. The fact that Cill didn't disappear until after her father left for work.' She gestured towards Sasha. 'The Trevelyans' known commitment to trying to trace their daughter. The Burtons' willingness to let theirs go. Louise's troubled history – marriage to one of the rapists . . . *remarriage* to a man of the same type—'

'Do we know that for a fact?' Jonathan broke in.

'She had a black eye when William saw her,' said Sasha.

'We don't know it was given to her by her husband – ' he tapped Andrew's bullet points – 'and it may not have been real, anyway. She turned up with fake bruises when she went to see our agent.'

'What do you know about her husband?' Sasha asked. 'William tells me his name's Nicholas Fletcher and he's a bookie, but he hasn't been able to find out anything else.'

George shrugged. 'We haven't done much better. He had a fight with Roy Trent over Priscilla on one occasion – ' she pulled a wry face – 'assuming you believe my not very reliable source at the Crown and Feathers who got the information second-hand off a customer. The barmaid,' she explained. 'She told me the other day after Jonathan and I had a set-to with him.'

Sasha looked interested. 'Did Mr Trent report it? I might be able to find out Fletcher's details if he did.'

'I shouldn't think so. He gives the police a fairly wide berth.'

'When was this?'

'Two years ago. It was before Tracey started working there, which is why it's hearsay.'

Sasha consulted her own notes. 'Didn't you say Priscilla was at the pub in February when she stole Dr Hughes's wallet?'

George nodded.

'Does her husband know she's still seeing him?'

'No idea . . . and it may not be relevant, anyway, if she's still working as a prostitute and her husband's her pimp.' Her mouth turned down disapprovingly. 'It's all very murky, whichever way you look at it. My father would be spinning in his grave if he knew the antics people get up to these days. What's wrong with being loyal to one partner? It always used to work.'

Sasha caught Jonathan's gaze and a flicker of amusement shivered between them.

George pretended not to notice. 'If she isn't in her house now, then she may well be at the Crown and Feathers. She's like a bee to a honeypot where Roy's concerned. I never noticed her car before, but now, almost every time I pass the pub, it's there in the road. You'd think she'd be worried about Nicholas seeing it. I mean, if *I've* noticed it, why hasn't he?'

'What sort of car is it?'

'Black BMW,' said Jonathan. 'We can even give you the registration number.'

Sasha eyed him thoughtfully. 'What about Nicholas? What does he drive?'

'Pass.'

'Then perhaps the BMW's his. It's worth a try.' She took out her mobile telephone. 'There were no cars at the house when I was there,' she explained, 'but I'm sure there was someone in the house.' She punched in a number. 'Can you write out the registration?' she asked Jonathan. 'This is a check I can run quite quickly through the office.'

*

Louise slid through the kitchen doorway and watched Roy peeling potatoes. He was working at a chopping board near the monitor, and he had his back to her. It was funny how he reminded her of her father. They had similar builds and similar ways of speaking, but she didn't think either of those triggered memories of Robert. It had more to do with the fact that Roy was always preparing meals. 'I don't know why you bother,' she said into the silence. 'Who's going to eat them?'

He'd known she was there. Just like her father, he always heard her come in. 'Private room's booked out till midnight,' he told her. 'Card game.' He wiped his hands on a towel and turned round. 'What's up?'

She walked round the table to give him Sasha Spencer's card. 'That bitch George must have told them. What should I do?'

Roy squinted at the writing on the back. 'How did you get it?'

'It was posted through the letter box.'

'Did you tell Nick?'

'Don't be an idiot!'

Roy jerked his head towards the monitor. 'I've been watching him. He was waiting by the letter box when this Spencer woman poked it through.' He tucked the card back into her pocket. 'You'd better start working out how to tell him who Louise Burton is. He'll probably kill you for it . . . but I'm past caring.'

She raised her mouth to his and teased him with her tongue. 'Nick I can handle. What do I do about Sasha Spencer?'

He stared into her eyes before pulling her into a rough embrace. 'What you always do,' he said with a grim smile. 'Tell her it was someone else. Cill'll not stay buried this time. There's too many people asking questions.'

*

When George went inside to make a pot of tea, Jonathan suggested moving the table to a spot further down the garden where a neighbour's tree offered some shade. Sasha accepted gratefully. He tucked her chair well under the tree, then retrieved the other two, placing his in the sunshine, at an angle to the table, and stretching his long legs in front of him. 'Do you mind if I ask you a personal question?'

She gave a slight smile, predicting the question which had been asked so many times before. 'Mongolian grandfather,' she said. 'He came to England as a bareback rider in a circus and married my grandmother. All his genes passed virtually intact to me. My sister's an English rose.'

'Strange things genes,' said Jonathan nonchalantly. 'My father was a Jamaican road sweeper and my mother was a Chinese maid.'

Sasha glanced at his card. 'You've done well,' she said. 'They must be proud of you.'

Perhaps they were, he thought. 'So what got you into tracing children?' he asked.

'An ad in the local newspaper,' she admitted honestly. 'I thought it sounded more interesting than my previous job.'

'Which was?'

'Office work.'

'What sort?'

'I worked for the Inland Revenue.' She laughed at his expression. 'Now you know why I wanted to leave.'

'It's not that,' he said. 'George used to be a tax inspector in London.' He laughed. 'You'll be telling me you have degrees in psychology and behavioural science next.'

'I wish I had. They'd be more useful in this game than medieval history.' She paused. 'She's an interesting person. Have you known her long?'

'Not really.' He rearranged the postman's hat so that the peak settled more comfortably on his neck. 'It just seems as if I have.' He smiled at Sasha's expression. 'That was a compliment. She has a disproportionate effect on the people she meets . . . her influence on them is stronger than theirs on her.'

'Some people are like that. Louise Burton, for example.'

'Do you think so?' Jonathan asked curiously. 'To me, she has all the attributes of a loose cannon.'

Sasha shrugged. 'Then why does everyone protect her? Her brother . . . Roy Trent . . . possibly even Nicholas Fletcher. Why does your agent want to believe she's telling the truth? There must be something about her that attracts people. You said yourself you felt comfortable with her until you discovered your wallet was missing.'

'It's a man thing,' he answered cynically. 'Miss Brett wouldn't agree with you. She didn't like her at all.'

'But she didn't punish her the way she punished Cill,' Sasha pointed out.

George picked up the tail end of the conversation as she brought out a tray of cups and a teapot. 'Cill went back to rescue her before the rape,' she reminded Jonathan as she resumed her seat, 'which suggests she perceived Louise as more vulnerable than she was. Weakness can be a strength in certain situations, particularly if it's used to manipulate emotions.'

'It didn't work for Howard or Grace,' he said.

'No,' she agreed, 'but they weren't manipulators.'

'And Louise is?'

'She was very successful at persuading you to let her look through your briefcase . . . and Andrew into feeling sorry for her.' She wagged a finger at him. 'She had a good teacher, Jon. There's no more manipulative personality than an abusive father . . . and no one with less moral sense. It's an appalling role model for an impressionable child. You should know that better than anyone.'

'Are you saying I'm manipulative?'

George chuckled. 'You could write a book on it, my dear.'

*

Louise lit a cigarette. 'Don't tell me what to do, Roy. You're not my bloody keeper. Never have been. You all think you own me because of what happened, but you *don't* . . . *I* own *you*!' She moved away from him. 'You're so like my dad, darlin', you wouldn't believe. Love you, love you, love you, baby . . . now gimme what I want or I'll thrash the living daylights out of you.' Her eyes flared disparagingly. 'I used to think he was God till he started feeling up Cill . . . then I realized what a dirty little creep he was . . . and I hated him. It was OK when he told me he loved me better than Mum. It wasn't OK when he said Cill was his favourite.'

Roy had heard it all before. Every time she was stoned or drunk the shabby family secrets poured out, contaminating her, contaminating him. He wondered sometimes if he would ever have been drawn into this suicidally symbiotic relationship if she'd told him the truth at thirteen, but he was honest enough to recognize that he would. The sort of madness that had possessed them all that fatal May in 1970 was generated by drink and self-loathing, and the problems of a skinny child who held no attraction for them wouldn't have been heeded, much less understood.

She was right about ownership. She had held their fate in her hands for thirty-plus years, and the only thing that had kept her alive was heroin. Stumbling from one fix to another, she had been a threat to no one. Clean, she was a walking time bomb. 'Take care, Lou,' he warned. 'I can't protect you for ever.'

She blew a lungful of smoke in his direction. 'You're so arrogant,' she said scornfully. 'Did you never think I might be protecting you? You're the one Nick's worried about, darlin'. You know what he's like – gets a bee in his bonnet and there's no shifting it. I told you months ago he didn't like you buddying up to George, but you wouldn't listen.'

'That's crap.'

She gave an indifferent shrug. 'Why do you think he lets me come here? He doesn't trust you . . . wouldn't trust Micky either if he was still alive. It's him told me to go through the wog's briefcase. He's round the bloody twist . . . sees ghouls and goblins everywhere.'

It was partially true. The bits of Nick's memory that remained intact had fused into a looped tape of events that bore little resemblance to reality. Somewhere in the regions of his mad mind, it was only Grace's death he remembered.

*

Sasha closed her palm over her mobile's mouthpiece. 'The car's registered in the name of Priscilla Fletcher Hurst.' She frowned at George. 'Where does the Hurst come from? I thought you said her previous husband was Roy Trent.'

'Colley Hurst,' said George slowly. 'How very stupid of me. It's an old-fashioned abbreviation of Nicholas.' She sorted through her folder for the transcript she'd made of her conversations with Billy Burton. 'Her brother said her first husband was called Mike,' she said, looking at Jonathan. 'Could that have been Micky Hopkinson?'

'Wouldn't he have recognized him?'

'He said he was in prison so he never saw him.'

Jonathan hunched forward in his chair. 'What kind of a data-bank are you accessing?' he asked Sasha. 'Is it worth telling your colleague to feed in Nicholas Hurst – maybe Michael Hopkinson, too – and see if he comes up with anything?'

'We'll give it a try but I wouldn't think so, not unless they've been convicted in the last ten years.' She spoke into the phone again, giving both names, then hung up. 'He'll call back in a couple of minutes with a yea or a nay.' She pondered for a moment. 'We have a sister company of enquiry agents who can find out anything you want to know – bank account details, family details, employment and car history, even medical and social service records – but, as most of that information's privileged, the costs are higher, to cover the company's risk. I know for a fact that Mr Trevelyan can't afford it, but if either of you can, it might be worth a try.'

'How much?' asked George.

'Upwards of five hundred pounds.'

George pulled a face. 'Is it ethical?'

Jonathan exchanged another amused glance with Sasha. 'Absolutely not,' he said. 'I should think it breaches every privacy law that's ever been written . . . but *bloody* interesting, George. We could use some of this famous advance Andrew keeps promising us.'

'What about your debts?'

He bared his teeth at her. 'Don't keep reminding me.'

'*Someone* has to. You'll be grateful—'

She broke off as the mobile rang and Sasha put it to her ear. 'Yup,' she said, 'go ahead.' She wrote fast in shorthand across her pad. 'Got that. What about Michael Hopkinson? OK . . . thanks.' She laid the phone on the table. 'Nothing on Hopkinson, but three years ago the Metropolitan Police was ordered to pay

Nicholas Hurst two hundred thousand in compensation for brain damage, wrongful arrest, wrongful imprisonment and loss of earnings. At the time of his injuries he was managing a William Hill betting shop in the East End. He was in and out of hospital for three years and returned to Bournemouth in 2001 when the compensation came through. Last known address – ' she raised her head – 'the Crown and Feathers, Friar Road, Highdown.'

'Good lord!' exclaimed George. 'How very incestuous it all is. Do you realize that if Mike was Micky Hopkinson, then she's been married to all three of them at one time or another? Why aren't the men jealous of each other?'

'Because they have no more feelings for Louise than they do for each other,' said Jonathan.

'There used to be a law that said wives couldn't testify against their husbands,' put in Sasha. 'I don't know when it was repealed, but perhaps they think it still applies.'

Jonathan shook his head. 'They're a tribe,' he said. 'Marriage is just a device to keep Louise within the fold.' He paused. 'The interesting question is why she goes along with it . . . unless she has more to gain than they have.'

'Like what?'

'Security?' he suggested. 'It's a primary tribal instinct.'

From: Sasha Spencer [S.Spencer@WCHinvestigations.com]
Sent: Wed 21/05/03 10:02
To: jon.hughes@london.ac.uk; geo.gar@mullinst.co.uk
Subject: Report on Roy Trent, Crown and Feathers, Friar Road, Highdown

Dear George and Jonathan

Re. the report from Bentham Enquiry Agents

Bentham's agent has given me a verbal account of his investigation into Roy Trent. Copies of the full report will be posted on to you as soon as they're ready, but in the meantime the following is a summary of his findings:

1. Roy Trent has ownership of the pub until his death. His first wife, Robyn Hapgood, was the daughter of the previous owner. She OD'd on heroin in 1988, leaving the property to Trent for his lifetime, and after that to their son, Peter (12 years old at the time of her death). The property's heavily mortgaged – possibly to pay inheritance tax at the time of Robyn's father's death (1984) – but Trent keeps up the repayments. The debts will be cleared in 2009.

2. Peter Hapgood, now aged 28, has a criminal record and a history of drug abuse. He was first sentenced in 1994 and is currently in the second year of a 5-year term for aggravated burglary.

3. Trent has received numerous offers on the pub and has rejected them all. It is not clear why as he has *insufficient* funds to develop it himself. There may be a clause in the will preventing him from selling it – but this is unlikely as such clauses can be challenged. Bentham's view is that he is holding on until the property's free of debt.

4. He married Louise Burton aka Daisy Burton aka Priscilla Hopkinson in 1992.
5. Michael Hopkinson OD'd in 1986 after several terms in prison. He and Louise married in 1974 (she was 17). She became chronically drug-addicted (heroin/crack cocaine) and maintained her own and her husband's addictions through prostitution.
6. Following their marriage, Trent made some attempts to wean her off drugs (e.g. obtained a placement in a rehab centre where she lasted 6 weeks before relapsing). One source, not corroborated, says she had an affair with Peter while he was under his father's roof. The same source suggests it was Louise who got the boy (a) addicted and (b) into crime to supply them both.
7. Trent offered Nicholas 'Colley' Fletcher Hurst free accommodation in 2000 and applied for a 'quickie' divorce which came through in June 2001.
8. Louise began an affair with Nicholas while he was at the Crown and Feathers and they moved into rented accommodation on Sandbanks in August 2001. Hurst's compensation came through in October 2001 and he and Louise married in November 2001. Louise has been 'clean' since she hooked up with Hurst.
9. Louise continues to be a regular visitor to the pub.
10. Trent is well regarded by the local community (cf. George's initial impressions). The consensus view is that he has not jumped on the 'leisure bandwagon' but continues to provide a service for the poor of Highdown who can't afford expensive prices. He has a reputation for being anti-drugs.
11. Full details of Trent's bank balance and mortgage history are in the report. Also, Peter Hapgood's criminal record. Trent himself spent 6 months in a juvenile institution for 5 counts of theft.

The Bentham agent suggests you look very closely at the drug connections. Despite Trent's publicly expressed views on the subject, there's been a high level of abuse amongst the people he's associated with. The main source (ex-prostitute who claims Trent was her pimp in the late '70s) claims she was buying class-A drugs off him until 1985 when she quit. No evidence that he's still dealing, but there are question marks over the profitability of the pub and Trent's apparent ability to make repayments on the loans.

There's a garage at the back which the agent was unable to investigate without blowing his cover, but it's heavily alarmed, has a CCTV coaxial cable supply and a hatch that faces onto an alleyway. (He obtained some digitally enhanced photographs from his car which are supplied with the report.) It would be possible to mount a surveillance operation from one of the neighbouring houses to establish if it's being used for dealing, but the operation would be extremely expensive in manpower and fees, with no guarantee of success, and would be better done by the police. The agent's words to me were, 'There may just be a Ferrari in there.'

Re. Robert and Eileen Burton

After discussing the Burtons with my senior colleague, I have decided to put them on hold until I/we've had a chance to talk to Louise. It would, of course, be a great advantage to interview her from an informed position but, as Robert Burton's email to his son and the conversation William had with his mother both suggest that they will deny everything, no advantage would be gained. A premature meeting would only alert them to a possible police investigation, which in turn might prejudice future cooperation, particularly from Eileen Burton.

Re. Louise Burton/Priscilla Fletcher

I can confirm that her initial contact last Friday, 16 May, was followed up yesterday with a proposal to meet at her house on

Monday, 26 May at 11.00. In this first instance, I suggest I meet with her alone and allow her to set the agenda. Assuming you're both free, I will report to you at George's house afterwards.

Hoping this meets with your approval,

My best wishes

Sasha Spencer

From: Dr Jonathan Hughes [jon.hughes@london.ac.uk]
Sent: Wed 21/05/03 17:06
To: S.Spencer@WCHinvestigations.com
Cc: geo.gar@mullinst.co.uk
Subject: Playing safe

Dear Sasha

Thank you for this, but I question the wisdom of holding the meeting in the lions' den. I urge you to go back to Louise and suggest neutral territory. N.B. Colley Hurst is a brain-damaged rapist who may have been party to Grace Jefferies' murder.

These are not sane people you're planning to confront, Sasha. George and I may have agreed to fund a rather dodgy investigation into Roy Trent. We did not authorize ill-considered interviews with possible murderers.

Please do something, George! You're the psychologist. Is this sensible?

Best, Jon

From: George Gardener [geo.gar@mullinst.co.uk]
Sent: Thurs 22/05/03 08:41
To: S.Spencer@WCHinvestigations.com
Cc: jon.hughes@london.ac.uk
Subject: Playing safe

Dear Sasha

Written in haste. Jonathan is right. At least question why Louise would let you into her house when her brother's experience was the exact opposite – no entry under any circumstances. Please reconsider. Everything we know about Colley Hurst suggests he's a violent man. Best, George

From: Sasha Spencer [S.Spencer@WCHinvestigations.com]
Sent: Thurs 22/05/03 12:07
To: jon.hughes@london.ac.uk; geo.gar@mullinst.co.uk
Subject: Trust me

Dear Jon & George

I'm over 21. I don't need nannies!

Sasha

Twenty-Four

Palencia, Frean Street, Sandbanks, Bournemouth
Monday, 26 May 2003, 11.00 a.m.

As ANDREW SPICER had found, the close-up reality of Louise was nothing like Cill Trevelyan. She was finer boned, smaller featured and her eyes were the wrong colour. She was also prettier and younger looking than Sasha had expected, with only a vague resemblance to the scowling, sulky child in William Burton's album. She answered the door in a crisp, well-fitting jade green dress that accentuated her slim figure. Sasha, bulky in an overtight brown suit and wearing unattractive spectacles, felt fat and gauche by comparison, and showed it by tugging her jacket down to cover her hips. With an amused smile, Louise led her across the hall to the sitting room.

Sasha would have known it was a rented house even if she hadn't been told by the estate agent. It was painted throughout in standard cream with unexceptional furniture and framed prints of Impressionist paintings and Dorset scenes on the walls. There was very little of a personal nature and the only point of interest in the sitting room was a large television screen similar to the one in the study. It was showing a horse race but the sound was muted. Louise noticed Sasha looking at it.

'My husband's an Internet gambler,' she said, gesturing to an armchair before lowering herself to the sofa. 'We have wall-to-wall racing off the digital channels.'

Sasha went into her smiling routine as she took the chair. 'I didn't know there were meetings in the morning.'

Louise glanced at the screen. 'It'll be a recording. There's a video link to his study that means I have to watch whatever he's watching. Is it bothering you? Do you want me to turn it off?'

Sasha listened to the silence. 'No, it's fine. I wouldn't want to upset him.'

'He won't know unless he joins us,' said the older woman, reaching for the remote and killing the picture. 'Turning one off doesn't affect the others.' She crossed a neat leg over the other and looked encouragingly at the younger woman. 'How can I help?'

Sasha went nervously into her preamble about confidentiality, while recognizing that she might easily have been persuaded that William's story was fantasy if Louise had opened the door twelve days ago. The woman was composed, charming and elegant, and there was nothing to indicate a violent husband or a history of drugs and sexual abuse. Her voice was more educated than William's rough Dorset burr, although Sasha wondered how natural it was.

Louise allowed Sasha to finish her presentation without interruption. 'You mentioned Cill Trevelyan on your card,' she said then. 'Does that mean David and Jean are your clients?'

Sasha nodded. 'Do you remember them, Mrs Fletcher?'

'Of course,' she said easily. 'Cill was my best friend ... as you know, or you wouldn't have written "FAO Louise Burton" on your card.'

Sasha ran her tongue across her lips. 'I did, yes.'

Louise was watching too closely not to notice the signs of nerves. 'So how are the Trevelyans?' she asked. 'I often think of them – it must be desperate to lose a child like that.'

It was a very different start from the one Sasha had been expecting – more like the opening courtesies at a social function – but she went along with it, explaining that Jean hadn't been well recently. Louise produced several amusing memories of visiting the Trevelyan home in Highdown, then spoke of her shock when she learnt that Cill had run away. 'We were incredibly close,' she murmured, before lapsing into an abrupt silence and waiting for Sasha to continue.

There was a sliver of sound from somewhere in the house and this time Sasha's nervousness was genuine. 'I expect you're wondering how I found you.'

'Not really,' said Louise. 'I'm hardly in hiding. You can't get more high profile than Sandbanks.'

Sasha fixed her automatic smile to her face. 'In fact it was your brother who passed your details to us, Mrs Fletcher, because he knew we were acting for Mr and Mrs Trevelyan. I gather he re-established contact with you a month or so ago?' She was watching equally closely and saw the sudden narrowing of Louise's eyes. 'As you'll appreciate, David and Jean have never given up hope of finding Cill and we periodically reactivate the investigation when new information comes our way.'

She retrieved her file and notebook from her case and placed them on her lap. 'You may not be aware that various agencies have tried to locate you over the years without success,' she went on. 'Presumably because of your various name changes.' She bent her head to her notes, holding her glasses in place with a finger. 'First Louise Burton, then Daisy Burton, then Daisy Hopkinson, then Cill Trent, now Priscilla Fletcher Hurst.' She looked up again, inviting Louise to respond. 'I'm a little puzzled why you chose to take Cill's Christian name and marry her rapists, Mrs Fletcher.'

Louise answered readily enough. 'Not that it's any of your business,' she said mildly, 'but I've known all three of them since I was a youngster. I'd have stayed with Michael if he hadn't died . . . and with Roy if Colley hadn't come back. There's nothing sinister about it. Sensible people always marry their friends. That way, you know what you're getting.'

Sasha held her gaze for a moment. 'Except that, in this case, you knew you were getting three violent young men who gang raped your best friend. It traumatized your brother – he's still having flashbacks thirty years after the event. Were you not similarly affected . . . especially as Cill vanished into thin air three weeks later?'

'Billy reinvents history to make his life more exciting,' Louise said dismissively. 'I expect you would, too, if you'd married the most boring person you'd ever met, always done what your father told you and only ever lived in one house. He was ten years old and he was drunk. Whatever he remembers is bound to be distorted.'

Sasha made a note. 'You make him sound too unimaginative to reinvent history,' she remarked. 'He certainly believes his flashbacks are real.'

The classy accent began to slip a little. 'It was hardly a rape. Cill was gagging for sex with Roy, couldn't lift her skirt quick enough . . . and it was only when Micky and Colley piled in on top that she started complaining. They were fourteen-year-old virgins, drunk as skunks on vodka, and at least two of them ejaculated before they even got in.' She shrugged. 'I'm not saying it's fun to have three teenage drunks wank over you, but Cill was as big as they were and gave as good as she got.' She paused. 'It's not what made her run away either. That was her dad taking the strap to her. She'd been saying for weeks she'd bugger off if he tried it on again.'

Sasha refused to be sidetracked. 'Your brother remembers it differently, Mrs Fletcher. He describes a sickening level of brutality that was inexcusable whatever the age of the participants.'

'Then you'll have to choose which of us you want to believe . . . though I can't say I'm happy about having my brother slander my husbands. The only time he spoke to any of them was that day, and he was so paralytic he could hardly string two words together.'

Sasha removed copies of the newspaper clippings that George had found and extracted Jean Trevelyan's interview. 'You told the police at the time that it was a gang rape,' she said, handing her the page. 'Jean Trevelyan refers to it as such in this article.'

Louise glanced at the headline, then laid it on the coffee table without reading it. 'How could I use a phrase I didn't know?' she countered. 'All I did was describe what happened. Gang rape was what the police called it . . . and it's probably why Billy's embroidering his memories now.' She took a breath and went on in a more conciliatory tone. 'Look, is this really necessary? It's not going to help the Trevelyans to have Billy's version accepted. The boys were questioned at the time, but they weren't charged because it wasn't considered serious enough.'

'No charges were brought because Cill was missing and you refused to identify the culprits.'

'It wasn't a refusal. I *couldn't* . . . not then. It was only later we became friendly, when Micky and I started going together. I never remembered he was one of them until I saw all three together and twigged who they were, and by that time Micky'd persuaded me they were OK.' She smoothed a hand down the crisp cotton of her dress. 'Maybe you should ask Nick?' she suggested. 'He'll tell you it's true.' She tilted her head to one side. 'Do you want me to fetch him?'

Sasha quelled a nervous tremor in her stomach. 'That would be helpful,' she said. 'Thank you.'

Louise gave an abrupt laugh and reached for her cigarette packet on the mantelpiece. 'I wouldn't advise it. He suffered brain damage a while back and doesn't take too kindly to being quizzed about his past . . . mostly because he can't remember it and hates being made to look a fool.' She lit a cigarette. 'It's weird the way the brain works. He's forgotten whole chunks of his life, but he can remember the form of all the horses back to 1980 and still work out odds in half a second flat. On a good day he can make ten grand just by sitting at his computer.'

'Does he remember the rape?'

'I don't know,' said Louise, with a malicious glint in her eye. 'I've never been stupid enough to ask. Feel free, though. His study's past the kitchen.'

'Does he remember you?'

'What's that supposed to mean?'

'Are you part of a chunk that he remembers?'

Louise didn't answer immediately, as if fearing a trap. 'I've known him for years,' she said. 'He'd have to've forgotten his whole fucking life to cut me out completely.'

'Interesting,' remarked Sasha idly, thinking that Louise's language and accent were falling apart by the second. 'So what does he call you, Mrs Fletcher? Louise? Daisy? Cill? Priscilla? It would be a very good indication of which . . . er . . . *chunks* . . . he remembers.'

'Priscilla,' she said, watching the younger woman through the smoke from her cigarette. 'The same name I've had for twenty years.' She smiled cynically. 'And, before you ask why, I was stoned when I chose it, so any thoughts of Cill were in my subconscious. I used to think it was classier than Louise or Daisy . . . probably because the Trevelyans were such snobs.'

Sasha let a pulse of silence pass. 'Why didn't you tell the police that Billy was a witness to the rape? He knew the names of the boys.'

'I was protecting him. The folks didn't know he'd been truanting.'

'Why didn't the school notice his absence?'

'I phoned in for him, pretending to be Mum. Said he was sick.'

'Why?'

'To get him off the hook, of course.' She took a pull at her cigarette. 'It was his one and only time . . . he was so scared he never did it again. He should be grateful for small mercies instead of turning it into a drama.'

Sasha smiled again. 'I'm not sure he'd agree with you, Mrs Fletcher.' She paused to push her spectacles up her nose. 'I meant, why did you want him with you that day? He told me the meeting with the boys was pre-planned, and that you and Cill talked sex non-stop to get them excited. I can't see the point of having a ten-year-old tagging along in those circumstances.'

'That's rubbish,' retorted Louise angrily. 'There's no way it was pre-planned . . . couldn't have been. We'd never seen them before. We went down the arcade and bumped into them by accident, and Cill promptly got the hots for Roy. The only reason we were stuck with Billy was because he couldn't go into school without being quizzed and he couldn't go home because the folks were there.'

Sasha flicked back a few pages of her notepad. 'I understood it was Cill who persuaded him to go with you, and you were furious about it.'

There was a pronounced hesitation. 'I don't remember, but it's probably right,' she said. 'It made Cill feel better about herself if she could get the rest of us to bunk off with her.'

'Billy's interpretation is different. He says Cill wanted him along because she wasn't as keen to meet the boys as you were. He says you contributed to the rape . . . and may even have ordered it because you were jealous that Roy fancied Cill more than he fancied you.'

'Dream on,' said Louise scornfully. 'If I'd ever wanted Roy that much, I'd still be married to him.'

Sasha located the page she wanted from a follow-up interview with Billy. 'Your brother doesn't buy into the idea that you were protecting him, Mrs Fletcher, so he's looking for reasons why you didn't tell the police he was there. His childhood experience of you is that you got him into trouble at the drop of a hat to save your own skin.' She ran her finger down the lines of the notepad. 'These are some of the explanations he's offered. The boys were friends of yours and, as you didn't want them arrested, you couldn't afford to have Billy name them.' She briefly raised her eyes. 'No? Then perhaps you wanted a free hand to malign Cill because you knew how much your father liked her, and you didn't want Billy standing up for her?'

Louise squashed her cigarette into an ashtray. 'Dad couldn't have given a shit. It was Mr Trevelyan got excited about it. How *dare* Louise Burton suggest his daughter was a slut? It was quite funny, really. Everyone knew it was true except her tight-arsed parents.'

Sasha let that go. 'How about this one? You knew where Cill was but you didn't want to be asked questions about it, so you diverted attention onto something that had happened three weeks earlier. If Billy was involved, he might have mentioned Grace Jefferies' name, and you didn't want that.' She deliberately echoed some of Louise's own words to Andrew Spicer. 'It was no big deal. Cill was alive . . . she was safe while she was with Grace . . . and as far as you were concerned she'd go home as soon as she was bored.' She looked up again and met the pale gaze.

'Billy never told you that.'

'No,' Sasha agreed, 'but he's not the only person I've spoken to, Mrs Fletcher. Let's go back to the rape for a moment. Billy says you went to Grace for replacement clothes because Cill's were torn and bloody. What happened then? Did you take her to Grace's house so that she could have a bath and clean up?'

Louise's expression hardened, but she didn't say anything.

'Should I take that as a yes?' She looked for a reaction which she didn't get. 'Clearly, you couldn't tell the police about going to Grace's house,' she went on evenly, 'otherwise they'd have put two and two together and gone straight round to interview her about Cill's disappearance. And for some reason you didn't want that. Why not?'

'Because she'd have killed me for ratting on her. We'd had one fight already – I didn't want another one.' Louise's lips twisted into a bitter smile. 'Everyone pictures her as this poor little girl who ran away because she was unhappy, but she wasn't like that . . . she was a bully. You didn't cross her unless you wanted your head caved in.'

'What did you and she fight about?'

'What girls always fight about. Who's more attractive, me or you?' She shook her head at Sasha's expression of incomprehension. 'Oh for *Christ's* sake! What planet are you from, sweetheart? Lose some weight . . . get your hair done . . . talk dirty once in a while. You'll be a spinster all your life, if you don't. *Sex* – darlin' – *men*! She kept boasting that she was more fanciable than me, so

I said I'd tell her folks about the rape if she didn't shut up. It was getting on my wick something chronic.'

Sasha concentrated on her notes. 'So you did know it was a rape?'

'Figure of speech,' Louise said scornfully. 'Who the hell cared what it was? As far as Cill was concerned, it was a walk in the park ... proof that she was attractive enough to be fucked.' She watched a look of distaste cloud Sasha's face. 'Don't fret yourself. It'll never happen to you. You're not the type to get jumped. You have to show a bit of flesh if you want guys to be interested.'

Sasha's fingers fled automatically to her spectacles, but she stuck gamely to her interview plan. 'If Billy had been questioned, he'd have mentioned Grace. Is that the real reason you didn't want him involved?'

Louise lit another cigarette, then leaned her head against the back of the sofa and stared at the ceiling. 'If you got all this off Andrew Spicer or his tame author, then I might as well save my breath. None of it would have mattered if the stupid girl had gone home. I was trying to do her a favour – give her an excuse for a bit of sympathy. Instead, she landed me in it by vanishing. She'd've been mad as hell if I'd let Billy name the boys, because she still fancied Roy. She'd have milked her mum's heart and thrown a wobbly if the police had tried to take it any further. That's the way she worked.'

'You, too?' Sasha asked curiously. 'Your mother became very protective of you afterwards.'

Scorn sparked in her eyes. 'Protective of herself, you mean. She wet herself every time she thought of what the neighbours'd say when they found out I'd seen Cill at Grace's on the Saturday. The whole bloody family would've been hung out to dry.'

'When did you tell her?'

'About Cill being at Grace's?' She lifted an indifferent shoulder. 'Can't remember.'

'It's important, Mrs Fletcher.'

Louise lowered her gaze. 'Why? What difference does it make?

Mum'll tell you I'm lying. She's like Billy – been rewriting history for years.'

'So you told her on the Saturday?'

A brief nod.

'Before or after you went to the police station?'

'Before.'

It was like pulling teeth, thought Sasha, as a silence developed. She wondered how contrived the strategy was, and who had instigated it. 'How exactly?'

'It was a Saturday. She didn't work on Saturdays.'

'And?'

'We were in the kitchen when the phone rings. It was Jean Trevelyan wanting to know if Cill was at our house. Mum says no, and hangs up, then gives me the third degree. What had I done? Why would Cill run away? What did I know? So I go looking round Grace's place. By the time I got back Dad was home, and he was in a right schiz because David Trevelyan had thumped him at work. Mum said it'd serve them right if Cill stayed away for good, so I told them she was holed up with Grace.'

'Your mother told the police she had no idea where Cill was.'

'Only because Dad was pissed off with David Trevelyan. He said it'd do him good to worry a bit. Then the cops turned up saying I had to go down the nick for interview because I was Cill's best friend. That *really* fired Dad up. He wanted them to talk to me at home, but they quoted the rules about questioning kids and Dad jumped to the idea that David had grassed him up about their fight. Dad's the one wanted me to tell the cops about Cill having sex, so the Trevelyans would know what a slut their daughter was.'

'Your parents knew about that?'

A curl of smoke drifted out of Louise's mouth. 'Dad did,' she said curtly. 'I don't know about Mum.'

'Who told him?'

'Who do you think?'

'You?'

'Like hell!' she said dismissively. 'There was nothing in it for me. Why would I want to give him a reason to get worked up over her? You seem to have worked out that he liked her.' She regarded the other woman cynically. 'It was Cill. That's how she operated. As long as men were fighting over her, she had what she wanted. It drove Dad crazy to think she'd let Roy have a bit of the action. It drove *David* crazy the amount of time she spent round our place.' She gave a mirthless laugh at Sasha's shocked expression. 'Oh, come on! You weren't born yesterday. Why the hell do you think the bastard kept thrashing her? It wasn't because he needed the exercise. It was because his wife was frigid and he creamed every time he lammed into Cill's arse.'

Shock tactics were effective, thought Sasha, as she stared at the photocopy of Jean Trevelyan's interview on the table – 'Mother's anguish over missing teen' – and remembered David's forceful voice on the taped interviews. 'Did Mr and Mrs Trevelyan know that you and Cill truanted at Grace's house?' she asked.

Louise shook her head. 'Not unless Cill told them.'

'But your parents knew?'

'Only after we'd stopped it. Howard kept pestering me about Cill, so I told him to fuck off and he went whining to his gran. Next thing I knew, Grace was on our doorstep wanting to know what was going on, and Mum sussed the whole thing in half a second flat. She gave Grace a right drubbing, told her she was lucky she wasn't going to report her for harbouring truants just so her useless grandson could drool over a couple of teenagers.'

It was like the pieces of a jigsaw slotting together. Every snippet of information that Sasha had been given, directly or indirectly, was finding its place. She pondered for a moment. 'What was your father doing while you and your mother were at the police station?' she asked.

'No idea. Sleeping probably. He'd been at work all night.'

'Was he in the house when you got back?'

'I presume so. We had to keep our voices down on Saturday mornings, and I don't recall that day being different.' She paused.

'He was there in the afternoon. I remember watching *Grandstand* with him, because he kept talking over it to ask me what the police had said.'

'Where was your mother?'

Louise took a drag of her cigarette. 'No idea,' she said, with an amused smile. 'Probably round at Grace's giving her another bollocking.'

'Do you know that for a fact?'

'Of course not!' she said disparagingly. 'The only facts I know are that Cill was there on the Saturday morning and was gone by the time the police found Grace's body.'

'What about the Tuesday evening?'

'I didn't see her, but it doesn't mean she wasn't there.' Another teasing smile. 'Maybe she was upstairs, slashing at poor old Grace.'

'Unlikely,' said Sasha. 'Her fingerprints weren't found any-where in the house.'

'Jesus!' Louise said with an abrupt return to scorn. 'It wasn't a serious suggestion. How the hell would I know where she was? I kept my mouth shut because the folks got twitched when the silly bitch was still missing on the Monday. Maybe one of them went round to see what was going on, but if they did, they didn't tell me . . . and come the Friday, none of us fancied owning up to anything.'

'You must have thought about it, though. What do you think happened?'

'What does it matter what I *think*? What I *know* is, it was a fucking nightmare.'

'I'd be interested.'

Louise looked towards the door into the hall. 'All right,' she said abruptly. 'Howard went to Grace's on the Saturday afternoon, found Cill there, persuaded Grace she was mad to be hiding her and told her he'd take her home. Whatever happened after that wouldn't have been good, because Howard was a pervert. I'm guessing Cill wound him up by telling him about having sex with

Roy, and he probably said he wanted it too. They got into a fight and she ended up dead.'

Sasha felt the same prickling sensation between her shoulders as she'd felt the first time she came to this house, but she forced herself not to look at the door. 'Why weren't they seen?'

'Because it was dark. If they'd left in daylight, everyone would've known Grace was involved.'

'Where did he put the body?'

'How would I know? Somewhere close to where he killed her, I guess. It depends where he took her. He lived down Colliton Way and there was a lot of waste ground at the back of it.'

'Her body would have been found.'

Louise shrugged. 'It's an industrial estate now, so maybe she ended up in someone's foundations. They were building the new Brackham & Wright's factory around that time, and Howard was always going on about it because they were putting in state-of-the-art automation and his mum was scared there'd be redundancies.'

So neat. *Too neat?* 'What happened then?'

Louise frowned. 'He went home.'

'No, I meant, what happened with Grace?'

'Howard took a carving knife to her. Had to've done. I expect she kept asking him why Cill hadn't gone home. She was on his back all the time to get himself a girl, but she wouldn't have wanted him having a go at a thirteen-year-old. She married a guy who was much older than her, so that's what she wanted for Howard . . . someone motherly who'd give him confidence but wouldn't expect sex. It wasn't what *he* wanted. Sex was the only thing he ever thought about.' She smiled at Sasha's expression. 'Just because a person's disabled doesn't make them pleasant, you know. They were both bloody strange, and they both thought it was everyone else's fault they were lonely. They rowed about it all the time.'

Sasha pointedly returned to her notes. 'It's difficult to see when he could have done it, Mrs Fletcher. His mother gave him an alibi for the Monday and Tuesday, but you say you saw blood on Grace's window on the Tuesday afternoon. That suggests someone else killed Grace.'

'Don't see why. What was to stop Howard doing it Monday night?'

'His mother alibied him. She said she was awake all night worrying about his job prospects.'

'You talking about Wynne?'

'Yes.'

'She was lying through her teeth.'

'The prosecution didn't think so. That's why they argued that Grace died on the Wednesday.'

'Not my problem,' Louise said frankly, reaching forward to stub out her cigarette. 'You asked me what I thought and I told you. Wynne was a lush – put away half a bottle of gin a night because she couldn't stand Howard and she couldn't stand her job – and I've never heard of a chronic alky lying awake worrying. Everyone at Brackham & Wright's knew. Her shift followed Dad's, and she was so hungover sometimes, she'd collapse over her bench with her head in her hands. Why do you think she was so worried about getting the chop?' Her pale eyes flashed with sudden humour. 'Ask David Trevelyan. He'll tell you it's true. Everyone knows the whole Howard thing did her a favour. She ended up with the money from the sale of Grace's house and got shot of her useless son.'

Sasha rested her pencil against the arm of her spectacles and stared at her notepad.

'Is that it? Are you done?'

'Just a couple more questions, Mrs Fletcher. You said it was Cill who told your father about the rape . . . yet, according to your brother, you and she fell out so badly that she stopped coming to your house.' She looked up with a smile. 'When did she have an opportunity to talk to him?'

Louise didn't answer immediately. 'Probably on the phone when Mum was at work. It's the kind of thing she did.'

'Not easy if she was at school all day. There were no mobiles in 1970.' No answer. 'And if it wasn't Cill, there were only two other people who could have told him: you or Grace.'

'Why not Billy?'

'He wouldn't have said that Cill deserved it, Mrs Fletcher, but Grace might have done if you fed her your version first when you collected the clothes.' She paused in face of Louise's incomprehension. 'I'm trying to understand why your father encouraged you to tell the police about the rape on the Saturday morning, when David Trevelyan had punched him only a few hours earlier for saying Cill was a cheap little tart who deserved what she got. Most men – particularly men with unhealthy passions for little girls – don't do that. They damp down police interest as fast as they possibly can.'

Out came another cigarette. 'He always called her a tart.'

'Only after the rape. Before the rape he wanted her on his lap all the time. That must have made you jealous.'

'Why should it?'

'He was an abuser, Mrs Fletcher, and you were his little princess. Did he show his disappointment too obviously when Cill stopped coming to the house? What did you tell him? That she preferred rough sex with Roy Trent to letting a dirty old man grope her?'

It was a second or two before Louise could bring the flame into contact with her cigarette. 'What if I did? It doesn't change anything.'

'It changes everything, Mrs Fletcher. It says you're a liar and that you were jealous of your friend. And that lends credence to your brother's version of events.' She paused. 'It must have made you very angry that everyone you ever met – male or female – preferred Cill.'

Twenty-Five

THERE WAS so much hatred in the pale eyes that Sasha moved warily to the edge of her seat. On paper, there was no contest. She was taller, heavier and younger, but she didn't know how crazy Louise was and she certainly didn't fancy her chances if the woman seized on the heavy glass ashtray as a weapon. 'I'm sorry if I offended you,' she said, reaching down to put her notepad in her case. 'It was a flippant remark and I apologize.'

Louise watched her suspiciously. 'What are you doing?' she demanded.

'I've taken up enough of your time.'

'You haven't finished yet,' she snapped. 'Aren't you going to ask me how my father reacted when he heard I'd told the police Cill had been raped?'

This time there was no pretence when Sasha ran her tongue across her lips. There was too much emotion in the room and she lacked the experience to deal with it. 'Certainly. If you want to tell me.'

'The usual. Said he'd have me the minute Mum was out of the house.'

'And did he?'

The cigarette trembled violently in Louise's fingers. 'He sent Mum and Billy shopping, then buggered the life out of me in front of *Grandstand*. I even remember what was on – a horse race. I hate the fucking animals and they're on every television screen in this house.' She gave a harsh laugh. 'You're all obsessed with Cill's rape. What about *mine*?'

364

'*Leave,*' said Sasha's boss in her ear. '*Trevor's watching her . . . says she's about to blow.*'

It was true. Anger flared in the woman's eyes again like a forest fire fanned by wind. 'Why don't you say something? What sort of damage do you think a grown man does to a skinny little kid? Why do you think I've never had babies?'

Sasha fluttered a hand to her mouth. 'I'm trying to find some . . . *words*. I'm not qualified for this, Mrs Fletcher. You should consult a lawyer or someone who works in the field of abuse.'

Louise's derision was colossal. 'How often have you been buggered, darlin'? Have you even had sex? Maybe you consult a lawyer every time a man looks at you, just so your fat little arse remains intact. *Cill* never got buggered – rogered by a trio of clowns, maybe, but never buggered. She should have been. It would've taken some of the heat off me.'

'*Humour her . . .*'

'I'm sorry,' said Sasha inadequately. 'Have you ever thought about having your father prosecuted? There's no time limit on this sort of case . . . and I'm sure your brother would support you. He's the one who first suggested to us that your father abused you.'

The woman stared at her. 'Dad paid me and Micky a small fortune in blood money to keep quiet.'

'About what?'

'Micky had a knife . . . said he'd chop my dad's dick off if he didn't pay for what he'd done.' She fell silent, looking back down some dark corridor of time. 'He was *so* scared . . . couldn't look at me without shaking. I reminded him of Cill. It gives you a buzz when you get that kind of reaction.'

Sasha ignored her boss's voice in her audio-specs telling her to leave. 'Did he kill Cill, Mrs Fletcher? Your brother says you know what happened to her.'

The woman stirred. 'It was Howard,' she said automatically.

'Is that what Roy Trent told you to say?'

Louise's mouth twisted into a cynical smile and, for a moment, she looked as if she were about to agree.

'Don't be an idiot, Lou,' said a man's voice from the doorway. 'There's no harm done except your pride's been dented. Let's cool it, eh?'

Sasha's heart leapt in her chest. *Colley Hurst?* She flicked a rapid sideways glance at the newcomer, but he had dark hair flecked with grey. '*Leave now,*' said her boss's voice in her ear. She reached for her briefcase again.

The woman looked murderously towards the visitor. 'This is my house, Roy. I'm the one who says what happens in it.'

'Except you're making a fool of yourself,' he said harshly, before jerking his head at Sasha. 'Get your stuff together, girl, and I'll see you out.'

There was a pulse of time in which Louise seemed ready to accept his authority. A look of resignation crossed her face and she leaned forward to abandon her cigarette in the ashtray before pushing herself to her feet. But something happened. Perhaps Roy was too insistent. Perhaps Sasha drew attention to herself by moving. Perhaps Louise heard the tinny voice in the spectacle-arm. The end result was the same – a manic fury that was beyond anything Sasha had ever imagined or witnessed.

It happened so fast she could only watch in horrified paralysis as Louise swamped Roy with a burst of energy, battering at his head and eyes with the ashtray, kneeing, kicking, forcing him to the floor. 'It's always about *you* . . . protect *you* . . . keep *your* fucking secrets.'

At the back of Sasha's mind was a bizarre hope that it was a performance put on for her benefit, and she was only halfway to her feet when Louise brought the heavy glass weight crashing down on Roy's temple. She lurched forward in a panic, sending the coffee table crashing onto its back. 'Mrs Fletcher! MRS FLETCHER! For God's sake, STOP! You're killing him.'

Either the woman didn't hear her or Sasha was too insignificant to worry about, but there was no time to debate the rights and wrongs of any particular action. Sasha's instinctive response was to stop the terrible battering and she lunged forward to grab at Louise's wrists. It was like being caught up by a tornado, a whirling frenzy of movement as Louise turned on her, knocking her to the floor. Sasha felt her shoulder glance off a coffee-table leg before the underside rim slammed into her spine and knocked the wind from her lungs.

If a sensible thought about tactics entered her head, she had no recollection of it. She just gritted her teeth and clung grimly to the other woman's hands, thwarting every attempt to bring the ashtray in contact with her face. Flat on her back, and unable to gain an advantage because she was trapped between the legs of the table, she fought a desperate, sweaty struggle to hold the other woman at bay.

She remembered thinking her boss would be furious because the audio-specs were somewhere beneath her, broken. She remembered thinking she needed to lose weight, as she felt the back of her jacket rip. She remembered thinking her mother had taught her that nice girls never got into fights. Most of all, she remembered thinking that if she got through this she would hand in her notice immediately. Fear grew as Louise's knee jammed into her midriff and made the struggle for breath even harder. Why hadn't she heeded George's and Jonathan's advice?

After how long she decided to bullshit the woman, she didn't know. Hours? Seconds? 'You don't . . . need to do this,' she grated out of half-starved lungs. 'We *know* . . . what happened.'

Louise released her left hand from the ashtray. 'No one does except me and Roy,' she snarled, thrusting her hands apart and slamming Sasha's arms against the sharp edges of the table legs to break her hold. 'Micky's dead and Nick can't remember.'

'Then *you* . . . tell us,' Sasha managed despairingly.

Louise dragged her hands together again, preparing to repeat the exercise. 'Nick'll kill me.'

Sasha exerted all her strength to hold her wrists together. 'Not if we . . . can *prove* it,' she grunted.

There was the briefest relaxation of pressure, and this time it was Sasha who whipped her arms out, gasping from the pain as the sharp edge of the wood cut into the flesh of her arm in the same place as before. As a tactic, it worked spectacularly. The shock of the impact catapulted the ashtray to the far side of the room and, by luck rather than judgement, toppled the smaller woman off balance, pulling Sasha into an ungainly roll. As the table legs gave way beneath her weight, she took a lungful of air and then flailed a leg across the writhing woman, pinning her to the ground.

'ENOUGH!' she roared. 'I am NOT Cill Trevelyan.'

POOLE POLICE STATION

CIVIC CENTRE   POOLE   DORSET BH15 2SE

INCIDENT REPORT

Date:	26.05.03
Time:	12.23
Officers attending:	PC Alan Clarke, WPC Mary Chambers
Incident:	Disturbance at Palencia, Frean Street, Sandbanks.

The disturbance was reported at 12.23 by Duncan Bartholomew of WCH Investigations. An ambulance was requested at the same time. Officers Clark and Chambers arrived at Palencia within ten minutes. Five persons were in the house: Mrs Priscilla Fletcher (tenant/occupier), Mr Roy Trent (visitor), Mr Duncan Bartholomew (partner with WCH Investigations), Ms Sasha Spencer (WCH Investigations employee), Mr Trevor Paul (Bentham Enquiry Agents employee). Bartholomew, Spencer and Paul are licensed operators.

Ms Spencer reported a fight between Mr Trent and Mrs Fletcher, and subsequently between herself and Mrs Fletcher when she tried to intervene. Mr Trent had been hit on the head several times by a heavy ashtray but was sitting up by the time the officers reached the scene.

Paramedics arrived within five minutes. Although Mr Trent initially refused medical assistance, he was persuaded to go in the ambulance and receive treatment at Poole General Hospital. He had difficulty focusing and standing, and severe concussion was diagnosed. He was asked to remain at the hospital until Officers Clarke and Chambers could take his statement. His address – Crown and Feathers, Highdown – was supplied by Mrs Fletcher.

Mrs Fletcher agreed that Ms Spencer had come to her house by invitation and that Mr Bartholomew and Mr Paul had come to Ms Spencer's assistance when the fighting got out of hand. They deny trespass. Mrs Fletcher admitted that she left her front door open when Ms Spencer arrived, which is how Mr Bartholomew and Mr Paul gained entry. She thanked them for their assistance.

Mrs Fletcher said that she had taken her husband Mr Nicholas Fletcher for a check-up at Poole General this morning. She expressed considerable fear of both him and Mr Trent and said she couldn't remain in the house in case either of them returned. She refused to give a statement at this time, asking instead to be taken to Poole police station to make a written statement there.

After escorting everyone off the premises, Officers Clarke and Chambers secured the house and drove Mrs Fletcher to Poole police station. A statement was subsequently taken from Mr Trent at the General Hospital. On his advice, Officers Clarke and Chambers allowed him to inform Mr Fletcher of the incident. Mr Fletcher reacted angrily but accepted Mr Trent's offer to stay at the Crown and Feathers in Highdown until the matter is resolved.

POOLE POLICE STATION

CIVIC CENTRE   POOLE   DORSET BH15 2SE

WITNESS STATEMENT

Date:	26.05.03
Time:	16.30
Witness:	Priscilla Fletcher aka Priscilla Fletcher Hurst aka Louise Burton aka Daisy Hopkinson aka Cill Trent
Officers present:	DS John Wyatt, DC Peter Hughes
Also present:	Ms Sasha Spencer (at the request of the witness)
Incident:	The murder of Priscilla 'Cill' Trevelyan on the night of 30/31 May 1970.

This statement was written from notes made during an interview with Priscilla Fletcher. She agrees that it is a true and complete record of what she said, and she has signed it accordingly.

My father started abusing me when I was eleven years old. I believe my mother knew what was happening, although the subject has never been discussed between us. When Cill and I became friendly, I tried to keep her away from our house because I knew my father liked her. She was unhappy at home and preferred spending time in other people's houses. When we bunked off school we usually went to Grace Jefferies', where we spent time with Howard Stamp.

I became jealous of Cill because she was popular and I wasn't. I had few girlfriends at school because none of them liked the way my father behaved towards them. Howard didn't like me because I'd teased him in the past. Our teachers blamed me for leading Cill astray, and Cill's parents reported me to my parents, saying that Cill's problems were my fault. The fight we had at school on Friday, 29 May was sparked by my jealousy.

After Mrs Trevelyan phoned on the Saturday morning [30 May] to say that Cill had not slept in her bed the previous night, I went round to Grace Jefferies' house. Cill was eating ice cream in the kitchen. I thought it was funny because my mother had said how upset Jean Trevelyan had sounded. That is what decided me not to say anything to my parents or the police. This decision was reinforced when my mother became angry after the police suggested we might know where Cill was. I couldn't contradict her without being punished.

I told the police about the rape to get Cill into even more trouble with her father. He always said he'd wash his hands of her if he found out she'd had sex with a boy. I was still angry about our fight the day before when she had punched me and pulled my hair. It seemed a good revenge to make her life even more difficult.

I hadn't told my father that Cill had been raped because I didn't want him feeling sorry for her. Instead, I told him she'd had consensual sex with three boys. He became upset and started referring to her as 'a tart'. When he told Mr Trevelyan that 'she deserved what she got', he was referring to a possible pregnancy, as I'd told him that Cill had missed a period. This wasn't true, but my father was pleased about it because he thought the Trevelyans were snobs. After Cill went missing, he told me to

repeat the story to the police so that David Trevelyan would
know the sort of daughter he had.

Soon after my mother and I returned from the police station on
Saturday, 30 May, my mother ordered me to go to my bedroom
so that she could tell my father what I'd said to the police. I
disobeyed. Instead, I went to the public telephone in Bladen
Street to call Roy Trent. I had made friends with Roy Trent,
Micky Hopkinson and Colley Hurst after Howard kept
complaining to Cill and Grace about the way they bullied him.
Even at the time I understood that I had more in common with
alienated teens than I did with losers like Howard Stamp and
Grace Jefferies. Now I realize that I was looking for anyone who
shared my sense of unhappiness and lack of worth.

It is true that I sought out Trent, Hopkinson and Hurst and
asked them to give Cill Trevelyan a fright. It is also true that
I engineered the meeting and was angry when Cill insisted on
bringing my brother along. At no point did I suggest rape.
I asked them to pretend to like her, then treat her unkindly
afterwards. My feelings about the rape were mixed. I was glad
that Cill was violated but I became obsessed with the idea that
Trent, Hopkinson and Hurst only did it because they fancied her.

This made me angry. Although I didn't name the boys, I
described them well enough to be identified. They were well
known to the police at that time as persistent truants, petty
thieves and vandals, and they were regularly taken home in a
drunk and disorderly state from Colliton Park and the waste
ground behind Colliton Way (now Colliton Industrial Estate).
I hoped Trent, Hopkinson and Hurst would be scared and
embarrassed by being taken in for questioning. I hoped the same
would happen to Cill when she went home.

I spoke to Roy Trent at his mother's house at approximately
12.30 p.m. on Saturday, 30 May 1970, and told him what I'd
said to the police. I did this because I wanted him to know how
angry the rape had made me. He told me I was a fool because
Micky Hopkinson carried a knife and would cut me at the first
opportunity. I said they should deny they were the boys involved
because I hadn't named them and wouldn't identify them. I had
also kept secret from the police that my brother, William, had
been a witness. Roy said none of that mattered because Cill
would identify them.

He asked me where Cill Trevelyan was, and I said she was at
Grace Jefferies' house. He told me to go back to Grace's and
persuade Cill to go to Howard Stamp's house in Colliton Way.
I said she would never agree because she knew Trent, Hurst and
Hopkinson also lived in Colliton Way. Roy accepted that.
Instead, he told me to persuade her to go home by leaving the
house via the alleyway at the back. He asked me to wait until it
got dark at around 8.30 p.m.

I refused, saying I didn't care if Cill never went home again and,
in any case, I wanted Mr and Mrs Trevelyan to suffer. The
money ran out before the conversation ended. I did not
understand what Roy Trent intended to do. I believed he wanted
to threaten Cill to make her keep her mouth shut. If neither of us
identified Trent, Hurst and Hopkinson as the boys who
committed the rape, then the police would let the matter drop.

I had no intention at that time of doing what Roy Trent asked,
but my mother had told my father that I'd described the incident
to the police as a gang rape. He was angry with me because of
what he'd said to David Trevelyan the night before. By way of
punishment, he sent my mother and my brother shopping and

anally raped me in front of the television. All I could think about was that it was worse than anything Cill had suffered. My bottom bled for days but I couldn't tell anyone. On Wednesday I started having fainting fits. My mother made my father call the doctor, and though I didn't tell the doctor what was really wrong, my father was frightened.

I became very upset in the wake of this incident on Saturday afternoon. I realize now that I was deeply confused and frightened, but I believed that I would be blamed for everything: the rape, the fight, Cill running away, my failure to tell the police that I'd seen her at Grace's. I was also afraid that Trent, Hurst and Hopkinson would take revenge on me if Cill identified them. I see now that I directed all my hate at Cill when I should have been directing it at my father, but I was too disturbed to understand this at the time.

At 8.15 p.m. on Saturday, 30 May I told my parents I was going to bed. They were watching television with my brother and weren't interested in me. I shut the sitting-room door and let myself out into the street. I was absent for approximately half an hour, but I do not know if either of my parents was aware of this. They have never mentioned it.

I ran down Mullin Street to Bladen Street and turned into the alleyway at the back of Grace's house. Trent, Hurst and Hopkinson were waiting there, even though I'd told Trent I wasn't going to do what he'd asked. They said they planned to give Cill a fright so that she wouldn't name them to the police, and I believed them. They threatened me similarly if I changed my mind about identifying them. I said I wouldn't.

I had no trouble entering Grace's house because the kitchen door was open. She and Cill were watching television in the sitting room with the curtains closed. Cill wasn't pleased to see me, but Grace was. She was worried about news coverage of Cill's disappearance and had already told her that she must go home. I told Grace that I'd been questioned that morning, and that the police were saying that anyone found harbouring Cill would be arrested. Grace was so concerned that she became angry with Cill and ordered her to leave. Cill burst into tears and refused, so I helped Grace drag her through the kitchen into the garden. Grace locked the door behind us.

I knew Cill would lash out at me so I ran straight to the fence. I saw Trent, Hurst and Hopkinson in the shadow of Grace's garden shed. I did not speak to them, nor did I hear them speak to Cill. I let myself out through the gate and ran home. I expected to hear the following morning that Cill had returned home.

I remember very little of the next few days because I was so frightened, by both my anal bleeding and Cill's continued disappearance. I attended school on the Monday and Tuesday but spent most of the time hiding or crying. I was shown no sympathy by the teachers or students because they held me responsible for Cill's suspension. On Tuesday afternoon I began to wonder if Cill was still in Grace Jefferies' house, so I sneaked into her garden on my way home from school.

I looked through the French windows into the sitting room. There was blood on one of the panes and the room had been vandalized. I was too scared to try the kitchen door and went straight home. From this point on, my fainting fits and convulsions became so serious that I was taken out of school and my family was eventually rehoused.

I had no contact with Trent, Hurst and Hopkinson until after Howard Stamp had confessed to Grace's murder. I was aware that they had been questioned and released about Cill's rape, but I wasn't confident enough to phone Roy Trent until it became clear that Stamp had killed his grandmother. Roy set my mind at rest immediately. He said they'd threatened Cill with a beating if she named them, then sent her home. He and his friends had no idea what had happened afterwards, but they believed she'd gone looking for Howard Stamp and he'd lost his temper with her in the same way he'd lost it with Grace. He described Howard as behaving like a lunatic in the days between Cill's disappearance and his arrest. However, none of us could report it because of our own involvement.

This is the extent of my first-hand knowledge and involvement in the murder of Cill Trevelyan. Anything else I know was told to me by my first husband, Michael 'Micky' Hopkinson, many years afterwards.

Micky was always more troubled by his conscience than either Roy Trent or Colley Hurst. He stifled it with drugs and alcohol. He was chronically addicted to heroin by the time he was seventeen and he remained addicted until his death from overdose in 1986. We were married for twelve years and he was thirty when he died. During that time he persuaded me into drugs, forced me into prostitution to fund our habits and had several prison sentences for possession and theft. He also blackmailed my father to buy my silence about the abuse.

I realize now that my relationship with Micky was just another form of abuse. It's a pattern I repeated in my subsequent marriages to Roy Trent and Nicholas 'Colley' Fletcher Hurst.

We were bound together by our knowledge of what happened on 30 May 1970, but I had no idea how dangerous my knowledge was to them until Micky confessed to Cill's murder shortly before he died.

The story he told me was as follows:

Trent, Hurst and Hopkinson had caught Cill as she was leaving Grace's garden and Colley Hurst put his hand over her mouth to stop her screaming. Because she struggled, Micky showed her his knife and said he'd use it if she didn't do as she was told. She allowed Roy to put a handkerchief in her mouth and tie her hands behind her back, then they walked her to Colliton Way waste ground. Roy and Colley draped their arms over her shoulders, and Micky walked behind with his knife in her back. He said she cried the whole way there but, even though some pedestrians and cars passed them, no one noticed that anything was wrong.

They hadn't intended to kill her, but everything got out of hand when Roy and Colley decided to rape her again. Both boys had been drinking heavily since my phone call to Roy at lunchtime, and Micky thinks she died of suffocation because they didn't untie her or remove the handkerchief in case she started screaming. He said it was similar to the first rape and they only realized she was dead when she hadn't moved for several minutes. He never said whether he raped her, but I think he must have done.

He told me they put her body in one of the test pits that had been dug during the construction of the new Brackham & Wright factory. They shovelled rubble in on top of her, then went home to get some clean clothes. Roy had sobered up enough to realize that if the police took them in for the first rape, they'd find Cill's blood and hair on what they were wearing that night. Micky said he made them change and then slog across town to dispose of the clothes in someone's dustbin.

They never expected to get away with it, but all the test pits were filled in a few weeks later without being examined. Micky told me that Cill's body is under the grassed area where the factory workers eat their lunch in the summer.

I have no knowledge of the murder of Grace Jefferies. Micky never spoke about it, and Roy has always denied any involvement in it. I can only assume that Howard learnt from Grace that Cill had been in her house and became angry because she hadn't told him. His interest in Cill was perverted, which may explain why he never mentioned the connection at his trial.

My life has been regulated and controlled by Roy Trent since 30 May 1970. My dependence on him was fuelled for many years by my addiction to heroin. While I was married to Micky, he was our main supplier. After Micky's death in 1986, Roy took over as my pimp in order to retain control. He had a stable of prostitutes, one of whom was his wife, Robyn Hapgood. Roy married me in 1992 when I was at a low ebb in my life and close to suicide. At the time I was grateful to him.

When Colley Hurst suffered brain damage because of his treatment at the hands of the Metropolitan Police in 1998, Roy recognized that the damages would be high. He invited Colley to stay with us at the Crown and Feathers in order to access the money when it came through. Colley's life expectancy was low and he had no surviving relatives. Roy's idea was to take power of attorney during Colley's lifetime and to construct a will that made him sole beneficiary.

I had been calling myself Priscilla for some time, although Roy always shortened it to Cill because it amused him. Colley is a very sick man with extensive amnesia, but he has a lasting memory of Cill Trevelyan. He has no recollection of killing her but he does remember that she was important to him. He believes I am Cill Trevelyan because Roy was calling me Cill when he first arrived at the Crown and Feathers, and he recognized me as someone he knew.

Since the assault, Colley finds contact with people frightening and it brings on his violence. During his stay with us, he and Roy came to blows regularly over Colley's fear of the customers. In the same disturbed way that he remembers Cill as someone he loved, he remembers Roy as someone to fear and distrust. Roy was the leader when they were a gang, and I'm sure part of Colley remembers that he led them into trouble. During these outbursts I was the only person who could control him, and Roy conceived the idea that I should marry Colley and move to a secluded house where contact with people would be minimal. In return, he promised to watch over me via webcams which would be connected twenty-four hours a day to a monitor in the Crown and Feathers kitchen.

I freely admit that I went along with this plan. As Colley's wife I would inherit everything automatically, and it is an indication of Roy's arrogance and controlling nature that he never questioned my willingness to return to him once Colley was dead. Colley and I moved into Palencia on Sandbanks in August 2001 (initially paid for by Roy) and we married in November 2001, subsequently calling ourselves Mr and Mrs Nicholas Fletcher.

This was the first time in thirty years that I was truly free of Roy Trent's influence and I used the opportunity to kick my drug habit by going cold turkey. It was made easier because Colley's paranoias meant I had to keep him tied to me all the time. He may be a violent and dangerous man, but he understood the pain I was going through and helped me in a way that no one else has ever done.

I also freely admit that I have planned for the last two years to 'out' Roy Trent, Colley Hurst and Micky Hopkinson as Cill Trevelyan's murderers. I also admit that by doing this I will secure Nicholas 'Colley' Fletcher Hurst's money for myself. It has been suggested to me that it is convenient that one witness to Cill's murder is dead (Micky), and the other is an amnesiac (Nick/Colley). I can only answer that I was afraid of being killed in the same way Cill was if I'd told my story earlier.

I believe Roy has been suspicious of me ever since I came off drugs. One of his reasons for placing webcams about Palencia was to monitor anyone who came to the house. He knew, for example, that my brother had visited me before I told him. He also knew that Ms Sasha Spencer had left her card. I told him about both incidents in order to allay his suspicions, but I did not tell him that I'd agreed to an interview with Ms Spencer.

I hoped that by turning off the computer at my end he would think it was a glitch, but it merely made him suspicious. He has had keys to the house since August 2001 when we first moved in and he entered via the back door because he was suspicious of WCH Investigations' van in the road. I heard him come in, which is why I gave Ms Spencer the version of events involving Howard Stamp that Roy instructed me to tell after Councillor Gardener and Dr Hughes discovered Cill's story. However, when he attempted to remove Ms Spencer, I realized I would be severely punished for stepping out of line.

Had I known that Ms Spencer's colleagues were monitoring our conversation, I might have found the courage to tell the true version. They believed my husband was in the house and were ready to intervene because of his violent nature. While I understand that I have certain rights in law relating to privacy and security of information, I do not wish anyone to be prosecuted as a result of this morning's intervention by Mr Duncan Bartholomew and Mr Trevor Paul. I am grateful for their assistance in calling the police and the ambulance service.

I am relieved to have finally cleared my conscience.

I confirm that everything I have said in this statement is true.

Priscilla Fletcher

POOLE POLICE STATION

CIVIC CENTRE POOLE DORSET BH15 2SE

WITNESS STATEMENT

Date:	27.05.03
Time:	17.00
Witness:	Roy Trent
In the presence of:	DS John Wyatt, DC Peter Hughes
Also present:	n/a (Witness refused a lawyer)
Incident:	The alleged murder of Priscilla 'Cill' Trevelyan on the night of 30/31 May 1970.

Mr Roy Trent presented himself voluntarily at Poole police station in order to answer allegations made against him by Priscilla Fletcher on 26 May 2003. This statement was written by him and he agrees that it is a true and complete record of what he said. He has signed it accordingly.

Priscilla Fletcher's story is a complete fabrication. I deny absolutely that I, Micky Hopkinson or Colley Hurst had any involvement in or knowledge of the alleged murder of Priscilla 'Cill' Trevelyan on the night of 30/31 May 1970.

It is almost thirty-three years, to the day, that Cill Trevelyan went missing and it is impossible to prove or refute these allegations when so many witnesses are dead or, as in Nicholas 'Colley' Hurst's case, severely brain damaged.

I do not deny that we raped Cill in early May 1970, nor that we bullied Howard Stamp mercilessly until he pulled out a knife and attacked us. I cannot recall precisely when this incident happened but I believe it was some time in late March or early April 1970.

Priscilla Fletcher is a deeply damaged woman who suffered appalling abuse at the hands of her father when she was a child. She has been a prostitute and a drug addict, although I deny that I ever pimped for her or supplied her with class-A narcotics.

I cite my reputation in Highdown for being anti-drugs and the attempts I made when Priscilla and I first married to put her into rehab. I would also ask for my son, Peter, to be interviewed, who will testify on my behalf re. Priscilla's corrupting influence. By the time he was seventeen years old she had ensnared him into the drug culture, with all that that entails.

We became inextricably linked with Louise Burton aka Priscilla Fletcher long before Cill Trevelyan's disappearance and Grace Jefferies' murder. Louise gravitated towards us because of her own unhappiness at home, and because she knew we had a similar ill-feeling towards Howard Stamp as she had. In her case it was fuelled by jealousy of Cill.

In the wake of the above two events, she became a natural ally because of her refusal to name us to the police. None of the secrets we shared were so bad that we couldn't have revealed them at the time, but we weren't bright enough to understand that.

I have no explanation for why she is now accusing us of murdering Cill on the night of 30/31 May 1970 unless it is to rid herself of the nuisance of looking after Nicholas 'Colley' Fletcher Hurst. She genuinely loved Micky Hopkinson and was married to him for twelve years. I allowed her to move in with me after my first wife died because I felt some responsibility for her as Micky's widow. I became fond of her and we married in 1992 on the understanding that she would kick her habit. She didn't.

We had been living apart for six months when I offered to take on the care of Nicholas 'Colley' Hurst in 2000. Louise immediately saw an advantage in marrying him. I made no objection because he was difficult to manage at the pub. In exchange for a percentage of the inheritance, I agreed to monitor them via webcams in case he became violent. He carries a mobile telephone which I have trained him to answer. In this way I can defuse difficult situations before they happen. His 'violent' episodes are rare.

Contrary to what Louise has told you, Colley readily responds to me, but is easily roused to anger when she becomes impatient with him. I cite yesterday's example at the hospital when he agreed to come home with me, as witnessed by two police officers.

I went to Palencia yesterday because the webcam link had failed and I wanted to check it. I deny that I ordered Ms Sasha Spencer from the house to prevent Louise talking to her. I did it because I could see that Ms Spencer's unwise remark about Cill Trevelyan's popularity had fired Louise into a temper. Cill Trevelyan is an obsession with her. I believe it comes from guilt. She needs to be told all the time that it wasn't her fault Cill vanished.

I agree that Nicholas 'Colley' Hurst believes that Louise is Cill

Trevelyan. I also agree that neither she nor I has attempted to correct this assumption. I have no explanation for why he retains a memory of Cill unless the rape remains on his conscience.

I have never raised a hand to Louise, although I threaten it from time to time when she attacks me as she did yesterday. She has an aggressive nature and is willing to provoke fights. I cite the fact that I could easily have defended myself, but chose not to because I would have done more damage to her than she did to me.

I believe now, as I have always done, that Howard Stamp was responsible for the murder of Grace Jefferies and the probable murder of Cill Trevelyan. I have no knowledge of either crime, but I have always wondered why Stamp never mentioned Cill's connection with Grace to the police or his defence team. If he was innocent of Grace's murder then he would have given the names of anyone remotely connected with her in order to shift police attention away from him. For example, he would have named myself, Hurst and Hopkinson, since he would have known about the rape. If Cill didn't tell him herself because they were friends, then Grace would certainly have done after Cill used her bathroom to clean up.

I admit that we lived in fear of this happening. I admit, too, that we made a pact to deny everything as the safest course of action. There have been many times in the past thirty-three years when I have wanted to come clean about the events of May 1970, but it wasn't my story to tell. Whatever Louise may say now about clearing her conscience, she has always been the main instigator in keeping the truth suppressed.

In conclusion, I repeat the point made above. If Howard Stamp had been innocent of Grace's murder, then he would have told the whole story. If he was guilty of two murders, then he would have selected the pieces that best suited his defence.

I confirm that everything in this statement is true.

Roy Trent

Twenty-Six

25 Mullin Street, Highdown, Bournemouth
Friday, 30 May 2003, 2.30 p.m.

DUNCAN BARTHOLOMEW, a lean, grey-haired man in his fifties, reached forward to switch off the tape recorder as Sasha's voice called out, '*Mrs Fletcher! For God's sake, stop! You're killing him.*' 'We lost sound a few seconds later, but you get an idea of Louise's mood in the lead-up to the attack. Not quite the reasonable individual that she presented at Poole police station when she made her statement.'

'I *do* find that odd,' said George. 'Why did she want Sasha listening in?'

'So that we'd know the allegations against Trent,' said Bartholomew. 'I imagine she wanted us to do exactly what we have done. Report them to Mr and Mrs Trevelyan and, with their permission, repeat them to you and William Burton. The police are unlikely to mount an investigation unless there's considerable pressure put on them. At the moment it's just Louise's word against Trent's.'

'Have the police heard the tape?' asked Jonathan.

Sasha, who was sitting beside her boss on the sofa, shook her head. 'They're wary of compromising a prosecution – illicit gathering of information,' she explained. 'But I made it clear in my statement that I thought Louise was stringing me along until Roy arrived. I'm sure she'd have given me twenty anecdotes of her visits to the Trevelyan house if she hadn't heard the back door open. *I* certainly heard it.'

'So what was it all in aid of?' asked George. 'Why didn't she tell you straight out what she told the police?'

It was Duncan Bartholomew who answered. 'If you believe Mrs Fletcher, then it was because Roy Trent was listening and she was too afraid to stray from the version he'd taught her. If you take Sasha's view that she was playing a game, then she wanted to engineer a confrontation that would involve the police being called. She said afterwards that she'd expected Sasha to dial 999 immediately instead of weighing into the fight.' He folded his hands in his lap. 'Her statement *is* very convincing.'

'I know,' said George with sigh, 'and you can understand how reluctant she might have been to make it without some strong guarantees that it was taken seriously. Talking to a private detective agency, or a couple of amateurs like me and Jon, wouldn't have got her anywhere. Even talking to the police without support from people like you would have been a gamble.'

Bartholomew nodded. 'Trent denies it, of course.'

'He sent George a copy of his statement,' said Jonathan. 'Did he send you one?'

'Yes.'

'It's a spinning war. You pays your money and you takes your choice. Roy makes a good point at the end when he questions why Howard never mentioned Cill in his defence. I checked it with Howard's solicitor. He was astonished to discover that two schoolgirls were regularly truanting in Grace's house. He said that if they'd known there was a disturbed adolescent in the house on the Saturday, they'd have concentrated their efforts on her. According to him, Cill was the reasonable doubt that might have swung the jury in Howard's favour.'

'Assuming he didn't kill her,' said Bartholomew dryly.

'Oh dear!' sighed George. 'It's *so* depressing. Fred Lovatt says it's stalemate. He pointed to the fact that Louise's hearsay evidence came from a dead heroin addict with a history of criminal behaviour who probably fantasized his life to make himself more interesting. He says the CPS will drop it for lack of evidence and Howard will go down in the annals of crime as a serial killer.' She pulled a comical face. 'Which is the exact opposite of what Jon and I set out to do when we first embarked on this wretched story.'

Jonathan stood up and walked to the kitchen area to plug in the kettle. 'Is there anything going for Howard?' he asked.

Sasha took out her notepad. 'There's one small discrepancy,' she said. 'Louise authorized Nicholas Hurst's consultant to give me whatever information I requested. He vouched for his patient's brain damage, catastrophic amnesia and unpredictable aggression. He also paid tribute to Mrs Fletcher for her care of a man who's greatly disabled.' She looked up. 'That's why she wanted me to talk to him. He couldn't praise her enough . . . said that if she hadn't stayed with him, Nicholas would have died a year ago. As far as the consultant's concerned, whatever she inherits is cheap at the price.'

Bartholomew's thin face broke into a smile. 'He was very insistent about it, apparently . . . says he's known grizzly bears with more charm. He's never understood how Louise put up with it.'

'She didn't have to,' said George cynically, propping her chin on her clasped hands. 'She watched him on the monitor at the Crown and Feathers.'

Sasha moved to the next point on her pad. 'The consultant also confirmed some old knife-wound scars on Hurst's right arm. The scars healed well, so he clearly received treatment for them, which I believe is what Roy Trent told you.'

George nodded. 'They took him to hospital.'

'I also checked with David Trevelyan about Wynne Stamp's drinking. That's true, I'm afraid – apparently she was quite notorious – so the alibi she gave Howard for the Monday night isn't reliable.'

'Does he know what happened to her?' asked Jonathan, spooning tea leaves into the teapot.

'He said her drinking spiralled out of control in the lead-up to Howard's trial, so Brackham & Wright's paid her off and she was rehoused somewhere along the south coast – possibly Weymouth. We've made enquiries there, but we haven't found a Wynne Stamp or a Wynne Jefferies.'

'It's the name that's the problem,' Bartholomew put in. 'If she changed it, we've virtually no hope of locating her. We've tried the Public Record Office at Kew to see if she registered a new one, but they have no record of anyone called Stamp changing his or her name between 1963 and 1983. It doesn't mean she didn't do it, of course – it's not compulsory to place it on public record. Her most likely course was to do it free by adopting a new one through usage . . . but that makes tracing her impossible.'

'Is that legal?'

'Perfectly legal. You can't alter your birth certificate, but you're entitled to call yourself anything you like. You can change your name every other day if you want to. Louise Burton's been doing it for years. That's why she remained hidden for so long.'

Sasha moved down her pad. 'I've tried the Dorset crematoria in case Wynne died,' she said, 'but I've had no success there either. No Wynne Stamps or Jefferies have been cremated in the time frame we're looking at. I wondered if the housing department might have kept her details.'

George shook her head. 'They were the first people I went to when my neighbour told me Grace's story, but they'd shredded their files from the 1970s long before I arrived.'

'If you really want to find her, then the best course is to advertise in the local newspapers,' said Bartholomew, 'but I wouldn't pin your hopes on her coming forward.'

Jonathan nodded. 'What about Robert Burton?' he asked. 'Did he agree to see you?'

The man nodded. 'He did . . . heavily chaperoned by his wife. Very strange characters, both of them. We don't have a tape because they refused to be recorded, but they were in bullish denial for half an hour.' He gave an abrupt laugh. 'How dare we believe anything their drug-addicted daughter said about her wholesome, upright father? How dare we suggest that a good Christian woman like Eileen would lie to the police?' He jerked his head at the tape recorder. 'When we got bored, we played them that interview with Louise.'

'And?'

'Robert went to pieces,' said Sasha, 'but Eileen continued to deny everything. It was interesting. She's a tough woman – there's no way she's going to take responsibility for anything her husband did. She described Louise as a compulsive liar and was adamant they never knew Cill was with Grace.' She turned to George. 'She latched onto your point immediately: why would they have sent Louise to school on the Monday if they'd known where Cill was? She says Louise could never have kept the secret because all the children were firing questions at her about the fight on the Friday.'

'So why did they take her out from the Wednesday?' Jonathan asked.

'For the reasons that Louise and William gave. She kept throwing fits. Her father called a doctor, who diagnosed delayed shock and put her on sedatives. The idea was to wean her back to school gently but, what with Grace's murder and Cill's continued disappearance, the doctor's advice was to start again somewhere else. He even helped them by putting a recommendation for a move to the housing department.' Sasha shrugged. 'I asked Mrs Burton about the hair dyeing and the name change and she said they were done to give Louise courage. She dyed her own hair to make the child comfortable. She was completely immovable on the subject of abuse. As far as she's concerned, it never happened ... Louise invented it to excuse her prostitution and drug addiction.'

'What did Mr Burton say to that?'

'Very little,' said Bartholomew. 'I don't know if he realized she was hanging him out to dry if Louise makes the abuse allegations public ... but he managed to pull himself together enough to bluster a bit. It wasn't very convincing. He went white as a sheet when Sasha repeated what William had said about his visits to Louise's bedroom. He obviously thought he'd kept it secret from his son.'

'The chances are he'd react the same if he were innocent,' George said fairly. 'It's a terrible accusation . . . and very frightening if both your children are making it.'

'The abuse isn't in question,' said Bartholomew. 'He had no answers for anything . . . couldn't explain why he visited her bedroom and not Billy's . . . why he wanted her in provocative clothes and make-up . . . why he encouraged her to bring her friends home so that he could sit them on his lap. If we'd had him on his own he'd have given us chapter and verse, but Sasha's right – Eileen's a different kettle of fish entirely.'

'Was she telling the truth?' asked George.

'About what?'

'Anything.'

'I'd say she was being truthful about what she knew at the time,' said Duncan. 'Whether she's worked out since that things were happening behind her back – and has chosen to close her mind to it – I don't know.'

'Then Louise lied about telling her Cill was at Grace's?'

'We think so.'

'What about Robert?'

'He denied it very strongly. It's the only time we believed him.'

'Then there's only Louise's word that Cill was ever there?'

'I'm afraid so.'

'And that's not enough to convict Roy Trent?'

'No. He can draw on the evidence from the time that the only fingerprints found were Grace Jefferies' and Howard Stamp's.'

There was a short silence.

'So what's this small discrepancy?' asked Jonathan.

'The scars on Nicholas Hurst's arm,' said Sasha. 'He's right-handed and they're on his right forearm – on the ventral surface – and there's some muscle wastage and loss of mobility in his hand. He can't touch his fifth finger with his thumb. This is characteristic of median nerve damage and it takes a long time to repair, apparently. Sometimes, as in Hurst's case, minor losses of function can become permanent.'

Jonathan was ahead of her. 'And it can't be attributed to the brain damage?'

'Unlikely. The arm's not paralysed or semi-paralysed. It's just the hand that's affected. One thing the consultant was very clear about was that anyone with the sort of scars Hurst presents would have been in considerable pain at the beginning and his hand would have been seriously – and *visibly* – disabled for months.' She smiled. 'William Burton didn't notice anything wrong on the day of the rape, he even says Hurst had charge of the vodka bottle. Yet, according to what Roy Trent told you about the fight with Howard, his hand should have been a useless claw.'

Jonathan gave a small whistle. 'I'm surprised Roy forgot that.'

'How does it help us?' asked George. 'He'll just say he made a mistake on the dates.'

'Except the details are in Hurst's medical records,' said Sasha with a grin, 'and when I asked the consultant when the damage occurred, he told me the treatment was dated 1972 – the year after Howard was convicted.'

Extracts from a report compiled by Sasha Spencer,
on the instructions of Mr and Mrs Trevelyan, requesting
that Priscilla Trevelyan's disappearance on Saturday,
30 May 1970 be re-opened as a murder enquiry

WCH INVESTIGATIONS

REPORT

Subject
Priscilla 'Cill' Trevelyan, aged 13

Incident
Went missing from her parents' home in Lacey Street,
Highdown, Bournemouth on the night of 29/30 May 1970

Present whereabouts
Believed buried under the Colliton Way industrial estate

Circumstances
Murdered by Roy Trent, Nicholas Hurst and Michael
Hopkinson (deceased) on the night of Saturday/Sunday 30/31
May 1970

The full details of WCH Investigations' examination of Cill
Trevelyan's disappearance are available on request. Much of

the evidence is circumstantial. However, WCH Investigations is confident that if the case is re-opened as a murder enquiry, further proof will be found. It is without the scope of WCH Investigations to carry out searches, trace witnesses who have left the area, fully substantiate medical evidence or locate police files from 1970. Nevertheless, the case for murder is a compelling one.

(Attachments include transcripts of interviews and statements made by: Louise Burton, William Burton, Robert Burton, Eileen Burton and Roy Trent, and additional material supplied by Councillor George Gardener and Dr Jonathan Hughes.)

. . .

IN CONCLUSION

It is clear that Roy Trent and Louise Burton have conspired for many years:

1. to suppress any connection between Cill Trevelyan's disappearance and the murder of Grace Jefferies
2. to protect Trent, Hurst and Hopkinson from accusations of rape
3. to maintain the fiction that Cill Trevelyan ran away and vanished
4. to throw blame for that onto David and Jean Trevelyan
5. *when that failed*, to involve Howard Stamp by painting him as a 'pervert'.

The remit of this investigation was to 'find the present whereabouts of Priscilla "Cill" Trevelyan'. As demonstrated, we believe her body is buried in or around the Colliton Way industrial estate. However, questions have been raised about the murder of Grace Jefferies and the conviction of her grandson, Howard Stamp. While we have no evidence to dispute the jury's verdict, we believe the following facts should be considered:

1. At Stamp's trial the prosecution convinced the court that Grace Jefferies' murder happened on Wednesday, 3 June. The time of death was disputed by the defence.
2. Louise Burton claims to have visited Grace's house on Tuesday, 2 June 1970 and seen blood on the windows.
3. Robert Burton, Eileen Burton, William Burton and Louise herself all testify that she had a fit on the morning of Wednesday, 3 June and refused to go to school. William Burton has testified that his sister threw fits, curled into the fetal position or became catatonic whenever she was frightened. Her GP was called and she was prescribed sedatives. This record, giving the date, may have survived.
4. Grace Jefferies was fond of Cill Trevelyan, and regularly harboured her and Louise Burton. If either of them came to her door late at night, she would have admitted them. Roy Trent, Nicholas Hurst and Michael Hopkinson knew this, and might have used one or both girls as a means of entry to Grace's house.
5. Councillor George Gardener has a signed and notarized statement from Grace Jefferies' neighbour (now deceased) that Howard Stamp did not arrive at Grace's house on Wednesday, 3 June 1970 until 2.00 p.m. – allowing only half an hour for him to commit a vicious murder *and* take the bath that condemned him.

It is the contention of WCH Investigations that Stamp's conviction was unsafe and should be re-examined.

At Stamp's trial he failed to give a convincing explanation for why he chose to visit his grandmother on Wednesday, 3 June

1970 instead of following up on a job at the local dairy (Jannerway & Co). There was a suggestion that he became angry when she took him to task for shirking work. We believe a more likely explanation is that he made a detour via Grace Jefferies' house on his way to Jannerway's in order to ask her if she knew what had happened to Cill Trevelyan. *This suggests he was ignorant of her fate.* Finding Grace dead, he was too shocked to do anything other than run home.

The transcript of Roy Trent's interview makes much of the fact that Stamp did not cite his friendship with Cill Trevelyan in his defence. Yet, despite their questioning by the police, Trent, Hurst, Hopkinson and Burton never mentioned it either. Stamp's excuse is that he was never asked about the missing girl.

There is no such excuse for Trent, Hurst, Hopkinson and Burton, whose questioning related *only* to Cill Trevelyan.

Bournemouth Evening News – *Friday, 27 June 2003*

New Evidence in 33-Year-Old Mysteries

Police announced today that they have re-opened the investigation into the disappearance of Priscilla Trevelyan who vanished from her parents' home in Highdown in 1970. 'New evidence has come to light,' said DS Wyatt, the officer in charge of the case, 'and we now believe Priscilla was murdered.'

No one has been arrested for the crime but three Bournemouth residents who were teenagers in 1970 are thought to be implicated. 'We've been given a possible site where Priscilla's body was buried,' said DS Wyatt, 'and we hope to excavate it within the next few weeks.' He refused to say where the site was, although he agreed it was somewhere in the Highdown area.

Mr David Trevelyan, father of the missing girl, said, 'My wife and I have lived with this tragedy for over 30 years. It will be a relief to have closure at last.' He thanked Councillor George Gardener of Highdown for her efforts in bringing the case to public attention. 'Without her persistence, Priscilla would have remained a statistic.'

Councillor Gardener came across the story while she was researching a book on Howard Stamp. Stamp was charged with the murder of his grandmother nine days after Priscilla Trevelyan went missing, and the police now believe the two cases may have been linked.

Councillor Gardener described Stamp's conviction as a terrible miscarriage of justice which couldn't happen with today's DNA testing. 'I am optimistic of clearing his name,' she said, 'even though he isn't alive to see it happen.' Tragically, Howard Stamp committed suicide in prison in 1973.

The police are asking for witnesses from the time to come forward. 'We are keen to talk to anyone who was living in Colliton Way during the first half of 1970,' said DS Wyatt. 'They may have information that will lead to an arrest.'

From:	Dr Jonathan Hughes [jon.hughes@london.ac.uk]
Sent:	Tues 15/07/03 19:23
To:	Andrew@spicerandhardy.co.uk
Subject:	George

Dear A, This is a PS to the previous email which I'm not copying to George. The bad news is she's developed secondary cancer of the bone – in the ribs. The good news is it doesn't seem to have spread anywhere else. She's on some hefty hormone therapy and starts a course of radiation next week to deal with the pain. I've invited myself to stay with her for the duration of the summer vacation in order to act as chauffeur and get the book written. She seems happy about it. There shouldn't be a problem with the meeting next week as her radiation appointments are in the mornings, but she'll certainly be tired. She's a remarkable lady, refuses to give in to anything, although I've finally managed to persuade her to take some sick leave from the nursing home. I shall tell her I've told you, but I suggest you don't dwell on the sympathy too much. She's willing to talk about it, but won't tolerate pity!

Best, Jon

Twenty-Seven

Spicer & Hardy's offices, West London
Wednesday, 23 July 2003, 2.30 p.m.

JONATHAN WAITED for George to take a seat, then dropped into the spare visitor's chair and surveyed his friend with amusement. 'You look like the cat that's got the cream,' he said. 'Let me guess. You've managed to double the advance?'

'Bugger off,' said Andrew.

'Don't tease,' said George as she settled herself in the other chair.

Jonathan's eyes gleamed wickedly. 'Then it must be the clash of the Titans. Tall, glamorous actor-stud with full head of hair loses out to short, fat, bald bloke with embarrassing parents.'

George wagged a finger at him. 'Embarrassing *friends* more like. I don't recall you rushing to talk about your love life.'

'Mine's non-existent.'

'That's not what I've heard,' said Andrew. 'Who's this Mongolian bareback rider that George keeps talking about?'

'Oh, for goodness *sake*!' said George crossly. 'You're like a couple of children.'

Andrew dropped her a wink. 'How's the radiotherapy going?'

'Fine,' she said, 'apart from Jon's chauffeuring skills. I'm not at all convinced his licence is genuine. We spend most of our time reversing.'

'It's worse than driving Miss Daisy,' groaned Jonathan. 'Yack,

yack, yack from the back seat – and me expected to tug my forelock so the nurses'll treat her like royalty. I wouldn't mind if we weren't using that miserable old rust-bucket of hers.' He levelled his forefinger at Andrew. 'I'm not just the official chauffeur, you know, I'm also the resident gigolo. The neighbours are having a field day.'

George's eyes sparkled. 'That's *such* a lie. He's told everyone he's my son.'

'Except they don't believe it. They're much happier thinking their upright local councillor has moved a black toyboy into her mock-Tudor semi. It's doing her reputation no end of good.' He pulled a face, as if living with George had taught him to ape her mannerisms. 'It's like sharing a house with a Mexican bean. She gets zapped with X-rays in the morning and bounces around all afternoon. When she's not on the phone, tracking down witnesses, she forces me onto the streets to get a sense of location. It's wearing me out.'

Andrew watched spots of pleased colour brighten George's cheeks. 'I can't let you do everything,' she protested. 'I have to earn my fifty per cent.'

'Less Andrew's ten,' Jonathan reminded her, 'which he seems to think he earned by entertaining a mad woman for half an hour . . . and swallowing everything she told him hook, line and sinker, not to mention being charmed out of his socks.'

Andrew grinned. 'Some of it was true.'

'Such as?'

'There was blood on Grace's windows by the Tuesday evening.'

'There's only her word for that. Roy Trent denies it.'

'The police believe her. Otherwise he wouldn't have been charged.'

Jonathan bared his teeth. 'I'd rather believe Roy. At the moment Louise looks like washing her hands of both murders.'

Andrew looked enquiringly at George.

'She's squeaky clean,' she agreed with a sigh. 'All she's admitted to is persuading Grace to unlock her door on Monday, then running away once the boys gained entry. Roy's been under the microscope since they found poor Cill's skeleton with the remains of the balled gag still in her mouth. They're being very cagey about the chances of recovering any DNA off it – probably vanished now – but it supports the version that Louise gave.'

'Then perhaps she's innocent,' said Andrew. 'It makes sense that she went back to Grace's house on the Tuesday to check that everything was all right . . . and only started throwing fits and fainting when she realized it wasn't.'

'It's not credible,' said Jonathan irritably. 'Why would Roy and his friends want to murder Grace? Even Louise says they were hiding behind the shed – so there's no evidence Grace ever saw them. *Louise* is the one with the problem, because she took Cill out of the house.'

'I'm playing devil's advocate,' said Andrew mildly. 'However much you dislike Louise, you must at least weigh her innocence in the balance. You're the one who'll be complaining when Jeremy Crossley accuses you of "flawed analysis".' He tapped his fore-fingers together. 'How does Louise explain it?'

'By playing the abused-child card. She was a damaged thirteen-year-old with rectal bleeding . . . confused about why Cill hadn't returned home . . . turned to her only friends, the boys, who told her the police would give them another grilling if they didn't persuade Grace to keep her mouth shut as well. Of *course* she worried that they'd killed her when she saw the blood on the window . . . but then Howard was arrested and she realized they *couldn't* have done.' He arched a sardonic eyebrow. 'The DS in charge finds her very convincing.'

'What's Fred Lovatt's view?' Andrew asked George.

'Deeply sceptical – but he's prejudiced in our favour. Poole police are milking her for all she's worth because it's her testimony that will convict Roy. She's very cunning,' George finished with reluctant admiration. 'Each new statement gives the police a little more of what they want while Roy's are so full of holes you can drive a coach and horses through them.'

'Mm.' Andrew looked from one to the other. 'So what's the problem? Why are you here?'

'We want to name her in the book as the main instigator in the murder of Cill Trevelyan and the only murderer of Grace Jefferies,' said Jonathan.

'Can you prove she murdered Grace?'

'No. The police have lost or destroyed the physical evidence from Grace's house.'

'Then she'll sue,' said Andrew.

'That's the idea,' murmured George. 'As things stand at the moment she'll get Colley Hurst's damages, compensation from the state for the abuse she suffered in childhood and a small fortune off the newspapers for selling her story. It's *so* unjust.'

Andrew shook his head. 'And another small fortune off your publisher when she wins. They'll never go for it.'

'Then find us a publisher who will.' George urged him. 'She might just as well have persuaded Roy to murder Howard as well. The end result was the same.' She leaned forward. 'Do you know what I find most appalling? The way she uses her father's abuse to excuse all her actions. He was a *disgusting* man – and I would *never* condone what he did to her – I even have sympathy for her when I consider her objectively – ' she sighed – 'but hundreds of children a year are abused by their parents, and they don't become murderers. Look at Roy. He was as damaged as she was, but he's not claiming his father was responsible for what he did to Cill.'

'Are you feeling sorry for him, George?'

She pulled one of her gargoyle faces. 'Yes,' she admitted. 'Whatever Louise says, I don't think Roy and his friends murdered Grace. Only *one* person took a bath in Grace's tub that day and only *one* pair of gloves was recovered. There'll be as gross a miscarriage of justice the second time round as there was with Howard. At least Roy tried to *learn* from his mistakes. He didn't abandon his son. He honoured Robyn's wishes to keep the pub and pass it on to the boy. His garage is a storeroom for Peter's possessions. He gave Louise a home . . . gave Colley a home. He's watched over everyone in one way or another. Me, too, when I first got cancer. What he hasn't done is continue to *destroy* people.'

'And Louise has?'

'Yes.'

Andrew exchanged a glance with Jonathan, who knew as well as he did that no publisher would countenance a potential libel suit. 'What do you think?' he asked his friend.

'She's guilty as sin,' said Jonathan. 'Her nature is pathologically jealous and deceitful. She loses her temper at the drop of a hat and provokes fights when it suits her. She's the only one who had anything to lose if Grace spoke to the police about Cill's continued disappearance. She wielded the knife herself and enjoyed watching Grace die. She took a bath afterwards and got a buzz from doing it because the last time she was in that room was when Cill was washing hymenal blood off her legs.' He shrugged. 'The only thing we might be able to prove is a negative: if all she did was gain entry for Roy and his friends, then why did the police find no evidence of them?'

'What are you waiting for?'

'Advice,' said Jonathan. 'Neither of us has yet worked out how to prove a negative.'

Twenty-Eight

Winchester Prison
Tuesday, 29 July 2003, 3.00 p.m.

GEORGE WAITED with DS Wyatt in a side room off the entry corridor of Winchester Prison for ten minutes before Roy was brought from the remand wing. The sergeant had been more open to persuasion on this project than George had expected, and she wondered if Fred Lovatt had dropped a word in his ear. Or perhaps Louise's charm was beginning to wear thin. Unable to repress her curiosity indefinitely, she asked him why he'd agreed to do it, and he told her he was beginning to find both her and Dr Hughes's arguments persuasive. But he warned her that they undermined the case for Howard Stamp's innocence.

'You'll never persuade a jury that a skinny thirteen-year-old was capable of slashing an adult to death on her own,' he said.

'She had no trouble pinning Roy and Sasha to the floor,' George reminded him, 'and she isn't much bigger now.'

When Roy finally arrived, he showed immediate antagonism towards George. 'What's she doing here?' he demanded, taking a seat on the other side of the table and looking at Wyatt. 'I was told it was another police interview.'

The sergeant offered him a cigarette. 'I've agreed to let Ms Gardener ask the questions.'

'What if I refuse to answer them?'

406

'I'll put the questions for her. It'll take a lot longer, Roy, but you aren't going anywhere.'

Grudgingly, he accepted a light. 'Where's the wog?' he said with a sneer for George. 'Why isn't he part of this jolly little party?'

'Dr Hughes is waiting outside,' she told him. She wasn't surprised Roy was angry, but she did wonder whether he felt the same kinship for her as she did for him. Their friendship had had its lighter moments and there was a sort of recognition in his eyes as if he remembered them. No man was so evil, she thought, that he had no redeeming qualities, and Roy had been kind to her. 'He didn't think you'd talk in front of him.'

Roy watched her for a moment. 'Too damn right,' he said bluntly, 'but I'm not going to talk in front of you either, girl, so you've wasted your time coming. I should have given you your marching orders the first time I saw you.'

'Why didn't you?'

'Because that stupid old fool Jim Longhurst told you I knew Howard, and I thought you'd be suspicious if I didn't show some interest.' He propped his elbows on the table and stared belligerently from one to the other.

'Ms Gardener's on your side, Roy,' said DS Wyatt mildly. 'She doesn't believe you killed Grace.'

'More fool her. If it wasn't me and Colley, then it was Howard, and she's been scraping the barrel for years trying to prove *that* little wanker innocent.'

Wyatt gave a faint smile. 'I've explained that to her, but I'm still interested to hear how you respond to her questions. This isn't a formal interview so you aren't obliged to talk to her . . . but I suggest you do. You've nothing to lose by it.'

'I've got everything to lose if she twists my words so she and her tame author can claim Howard was innocent.'

'That's why I'm here, to ensure fair play.' The sergeant tapped his forefinger on the table. 'You're on remand because the magistrates agreed you pose a threat to a witness – Mrs Fletcher. But that threat only relates to Grace Jefferies' murder.'

'She's lying through her teeth,' said Roy angrily. 'We never went near Grace's house after the Saturday evening.'

'Then persuade us of that and there's a possibility the remand order will be revoked. We wouldn't have opposed bail on Cill Trevelyan's manslaughter. You've already said you won't contest the charges, and your clean record since 1974 and the fact that you were a juvenile when the crime was committed work in your favour.' He paused for emphasis. 'But I need something more convincing than denials, and "she's lying through her teeth", if you expect a review on the Jefferies' murder.'

Roy stared him down. 'If I had anything more convincing, don't you think I'd have told you? How am I supposed to prove the bitch is lying when Micky's dead and Colley can't remember a damn thing? She can say what the hell she likes . . . and you'll believe her.'

George leaned forward. 'Negatives are such difficult things to prove, Roy. In your favour is the fact that the police found no evidence that there was more than one person in Grace's house when she died. Against you are Louise's testimony that she engineered your access to Grace . . . that you had a motive . . . and that you'd already committed one murder.'

He refused to look at her, not out of anger or resentment, she decided, but out of shame. 'It was an accident,' he said. 'Mr Wyatt's accepted we didn't mean to kill her.'

'The end result was the same,' said George.

'I'm not denying that,' he said curtly, 'which is why I'm holding my hands up to manslaughter.'

'Do you regret it?' she asked.

Anger sparked in his face again. 'Of course I bloody regret it,' he snarled. 'The poor kid would have lived if she'd listened to her father and steered clear of the likes of us.'

'You were quite happy to smear David Trevelyan when Jonathan and I spoke to you,' she reminded him. 'Why should any of us believe that you aren't doing the same to Louise? Her story holds water. Yours doesn't.' She watched his fingers clench involuntarily round his cigarette. 'Perhaps whoever killed Grace didn't mean to do it either, but she was still dead by the time they left ... and at the moment you and your friends are the only people apart from Louise and Howard who had any close connection with her.'

He took a breath. 'We – never – had – *any* – connection – with – Grace,' he said with painstaking emphasis. 'We knew her name from Howard, and we knew where she lived, but the *only* time we came anywhere close to her was when she shut the door behind Cill on the Saturday night.'

'Then help me prove it,' she urged. 'If it wasn't you who killed her, who was it?'

'Howard,' he said.

'What about Colley Hurst or Micky Hopkinson?'

Roy shook his head. 'We were always together. One of us couldn't have done it without the others knowing.'

'Then why is Louise saying you did?'

He raised impatient eyes to hers. 'To get me banged up in here and Colley confined to a loony bin. It's like Mr Wyatt says, we'd rip her miserable heart out if we had the chance. She only came up with this stuff when I looked like making bail on Cill.'

George pulled a wry expression. 'So your only regret is being caught? As long as no one ever found out about Cill, you could pretend to yourself her death was just an unfortunate accident.'

He pressed his thumb and forefinger into the corners of his eyes. 'Don't lecture me,' he warned her, with a dangerous edge to his voice. 'You haven't lived my life. You don't know what I regret and what I don't.'

'Was Grace another unfortunate accident? Did it start as a joke and end up as a murder because Micky pricked her with his knife and she started squealing the way Howard did?' She moistened her mouth in face of his naked anger. 'You said it yourself,' she went on. 'If Howard didn't commit the murder, then it had to be the three of you. You were the only other people with a motive.'

Roy glared at Wyatt. 'I *told* you. She's stitching me up.'

'It's a reasonable inference,' the sergeant said. 'If Grace knew you were in her garden when Cill left, then you certainly had a motive.'

Roy arched forward, stabbing his cigarette at the other man. 'I've told you a thousand times, she *couldn't* have done. There was no way she could have seen us. Even Lou's saying we were hiding behind the shed.'

'Perhaps Louise told her you were waiting,' said George.

'Oh sure!' he said scathingly. 'And you think Cill would have come out if she knew her rapists were planning to jump her.' He took a pensive drag on his cigarette. 'We'd have been mad to go near Grace after the grilling we had on the Monday morning. All we could think about was putting distance between ourselves and anyone who'd known Cill. If we'd seen Howard, we'd have run a mile in case he guessed what we'd done.' He paused, remembering. 'We were scared out of our wits the cops had only let us go to follow us back to the body. We were a mess for months . . . shat bricks every time we saw bulldozers on the waste ground.'

'Then why lie about Howard attacking Colley with a knife?' she asked reasonably. 'It was so easily disproved, and it makes everything else you say suspect.'

'Because I was sick to the back teeth of you and that damned author bleating on about Howard's innocence. I knew he was guilty . . . *everyone* knew he was guilty. About the only thing Lou's said that's true is that he was a pervert. He was always creeping around the kids in Colliton Way.'

'That's tantamount to saying all perverts are murderers, Roy. On that basis, Louise's father could have murdered Grace.'

He shrugged. 'She'd go for it if there was a shred of evidence to support it. He didn't think twice about destroying *her*. She hates him with a passion.'

George nodded. 'She certainly flew that kite when she talked to Andrew Spicer.'

Roy showed a reluctant interest. 'When did she talk to him?'

'Nearly three months ago.'

That surprised him. 'She never told me.'

'It was also the first time she mentioned seeing blood on Grace's window on the Tuesday,' George said. 'It suited us, of course, because it pointed towards Howard's innocence . . . but it didn't suit you or your friends. Jonathan believes she started trying to set you up from the minute he arrived on the scene.'

Roy frowned. 'She told Sasha Spencer it was Howard. I heard her. She even gave chapter and verse on how he did it . . . by sneaking out when his mother was drunk. *That* was the truth. It's this garbage about getting us into the house that's the lie.'

'She only named Howard to give the impression that she was frightened of you.' George watched a frown draw his heavy eyebrows together. 'She wanted the police involved. It's probably why she stole Jonathan's wallet and passport. She's a sexy woman and she's *bored* with playing nurse to a mental cripple.' She pulled a face. 'To be honest, I don't think she cares who gets dragged into the net, just so long as she can walk away and start again. She doesn't have your loyalties . . . or your conscience.'

'What's that supposed to mean?'

'Has she ever expressed remorse for delivering Cill into your hands?'

He squeezed the glowing end out of his cigarette and dropped it into the ashtray. 'We don't talk about it.'

'What did you say at the time? How did you explain the fact that Cill was still missing?'

He thought back. 'I said she'd run away from us when we left the alleyway.'

'And Louise believed you?'

'I didn't ask.'

DS Wyatt leaned forward. 'When did you speak to her?'

'On the Monday afternoon. She called from a payphone on her way home from school wanting to know if the police had questioned us about the rape. I said they had and they'd let us go.'

'What else?'

'I told her to keep her mouth shut about Saturday night, otherwise the police'd know we'd been lying about the rape.'

'Did you threaten her?'

Roy nodded.

'What with?'

'I said we'd tell the cops it was her idea.'

'The rape, or abducting Cill from Grace's house?'

'Both. It was Lou delivered the poor kid to us each time.' He stared bleakly at the wall behind Wyatt's head. 'I don't know why we went along with it now, except we knew Howard liked her. It was him we were really after.' He shook himself suddenly as if to rid himself of phantoms. 'It was Lou's big mouth that was the problem. I told her we'd have her if she made it any worse for us.'

'Are we talking about the lunchtime conversation on the Saturday or the Monday afternoon one?'

'Saturday. She'd already dropped us in it by describing us.'

'Is that when she said Cill was at Grace's?'

He nodded.

'And?' asked Wyatt.

'She came up with the idea of giving Cill a scare. Problem solved if she didn't name us.'

'What about Grace?' put in George. 'She must have known about the rape, and almost certainly knew, or could guess, that you were responsible. Why didn't you think it was necessary to give her a scare as well?'

Roy's eyes narrowed suspiciously. 'We weren't that bloody thick. If Cill denied it was us, then it didn't matter what Grace said.'

'Did you consider the idea at all?' Wyatt asked mildly.

Roy hesitated. 'I'm not answering that,' he said then, jerking his chin at George. 'I'll have my words twisted if I do.'

'Fair enough. Let me put it another way. Did Louise suggest for the Saturday night what she's now claiming happened on the Monday – that she engineered entry for you, Micky and Colley in order to scare Grace into keeping quiet?'

A tic started working violently at the side of Roy's mouth. 'I'm not answering that either.'

'Grace couldn't have died on the Saturday,' George told him, 'otherwise Cill's fingerprints would have been found.' She saw incomprehension in his eyes. 'No one's saying you killed Grace on the Saturday,' she explained. 'All we're asking is if Louise suggested you go into the house with her.'

He didn't answer.

'Should we take that as a yes?' Wyatt asked. 'Presumably you'd be denying it if she hadn't?'

Roy gave a terse nod. 'We didn't go in, though.'

'Because you didn't want Grace to see you?'

Another nod.

'But you didn't have a problem if she saw Louise?'

He shrugged. 'It was her idea. She'd have talked her way out of it. We didn't have much of a say except to be waiting in the alley at the back by eight thirty.'

'But all this was before Cill died,' Wyatt pointed out. 'How did Louise react on the Monday when you said you'd take her down with you if she ever talked about the events of Saturday night.'

'She got uppity and we had a row. I told her not to ring again. I was scared witless the police were going to find out we knew each other.'

'What was the relationship between you?' George asked. 'Was she keen on you?'

'Must have been,' he said. 'She was always on the phone, wanting to talk to me. I didn't feel the same way about her – not then – she was nothing to look at in those days. More of a joke, really.'

'So you dumped her?' said Wyatt.

Roy shrugged. 'It was for her sake as well as ours. She'd been acting pretty damn crazy since the rape – kept accusing us of fancying Cill. It was driving Micky round the bend, and he was never too stable at the best of times.' He paused. 'I'm not saying it's fair, but we all blamed her for what happened. If she hadn't told us where Cill was, we'd never have done it.'

'Weren't you worried she'd take revenge?' Wyatt asked. 'She was disturbed enough.'

Roy shook his head. 'She couldn't – not without getting herself into trouble.'

'Until Grace was murdered,' said George. 'She was the only other person who knew Louise was involved.'

There was a short silence.

'Whoever killed Mrs Jefferies had red hair,' said DS Wyatt. 'It was someone she was willing to open her door to . . . and someone who was deeply disturbed.'

Roy flicked a wary glance between the two of them.

'Louise was in a dangerously unstable mood after that weekend,' George said. 'Far more unstable than Howard, for example, who was looking for a job and was given one by Jannerway's Dairy. She was being blamed at school for provoking the fight that led indirectly to Cill running away . . . being accused by the Trevelyans of telling lies. She hated her father for what he was doing to her, hated you for abandoning her, and most certainly hated Cill. By the Wednesday, a doctor was prescribing tranquillizers to control her panic attacks.'

'How could she have done it? She was a skinny little kid.'

'Who was wielding a carving knife against a woman who tried to escape upstairs. She was slashing at her legs as she went after her.'

Roy ground his fists into his eyes. 'What was the point? Lou didn't know Cill was dead. The kid could have returned the next day, and the heat would have been off.'

George shook her head. 'She wouldn't have been thinking as rationally as that, but are you sure she didn't know Cill was dead . . . or at least guess? If she was watching while you walked away up Bladen Street, she'd have known Cill didn't run away when you left the alley. Perhaps you said something on the Monday that allowed her to put two and two together?'

He stared at her. 'Are you saying she did it after she spoke to me?'

'We think Tuesday's more likely. If she was ostracized for a second day at school – which she was – then it's probable her resentments spilled over in the evening. Everyone was blaming her. Her mother was furious because Jean Trevelyan had screamed at her in the street, and her father was angry because David Trevelyan was souring the atmosphere at work. She may even have gone to Grace's for sympathy and lost her temper when she didn't get it.'

Wyatt offered him another cigarette. 'You described her as "uppity",' he prompted. 'What did she say?'

Roy dredged his memory. 'I know she kept on about me fancying Cill, because that's what got me riled,' he said. 'The kid was already dead but she wouldn't let it drop. Lou was obsessed with her even then. Did I think Cill was prettier? Did I think Cill was sexier? I told her I'd kill her if she didn't shut up.' He fell into a morose, brooding silence.

'She gives a great deal of detail in her statement,' said Wyatt. 'She claims it all came from Micky Hopkinson shortly before he died but it's very accurate for a story that was told her fifteen years after the event. She knew about the handkerchief . . . Cill's hands being tied . . . Micky holding a knife to her back . . . Cill crying the whole way to the waste ground . . . burial in one of the test pits . . . you getting rid of your clothes in a dustbin on the other side of town.'

Roy lowered his head into his hands. 'She'd have to've followed us to know all that for herself . . . and she didn't. I'm not *thick*, Mr Wyatt. Do you think I wouldn't've caught her out by now? Do you think I'd've let her call the shots all these years if there was a chance she'd murdered Grace?'

'Did she have Micky or Colley's number?'

He hesitated. 'She might have had Colley's. Micky's family didn't have a phone.'

'Would she have called Colley?'

'Maybe . . . but it's not something you can prove. He's forgotten the whole thing now.'

'When did you next see her?' asked George.

'After she and Micky hooked up. I recognized her immediately. She'd changed everything else, but she couldn't change her eyes.'

'Was she calling herself Priscilla?'

'Not then. She was Daisy at that point. She changed to Priscilla about three years after she married Micky.'

'Did she explain why she chose it?'

He stirred the dirt in the ashtray with the end of his cigarette. 'She liked it better than Daisy or Louise.' He pondered for a moment. 'Actually, I think she said *Micky* liked Priscilla better than Daisy or Louise, and she probably meant it that way, too. She never believed any of us liked her for who she was . . . you could say Colley's proved it by forgetting Louise completely.'

'Did she ever mention Grace's murder or Howard's conviction?' Wyatt asked.

'Only since George came on the scene and started asking questions.'

'What did she say?'

'That if George ferreted around too much she'd find out about Cill.'

'Anything else?'

'She was worried about DNA evidence.'

'In what connection?' asked George. 'Cill's murder or Grace's?'

Roy eyed her for a moment. 'Grace's,' he said slowly. 'She read Dr Hughes's book where he mentioned that if some of the physical evidence had been kept, it would clear Howard. She was frightened that if that happened, the police would re-open the case and almost certainly look at Cill's disappearance again – ' he paused – 'and that would put her, Colley and me in the firing line because we were all questioned at the time.'

'What was your answer to that?'

He didn't speak for a moment, and George could almost hear his brain working. 'That you'd already told me the physical evidence had been destroyed and there wasn't much chance of anyone else being put in the frame.'

George frowned at him. 'I never said that, Roy. Even the police don't know if the evidence still exists. Fred Lovatt's looked through the archives and he hasn't found anything . . . but I live in hope. The Black Museum in London still has bits of evidence from the Ripper murders.'

Roy's mouth twisted into a cynical smile. 'She was acting paranoid. I wanted her out of the pub before she drew attention to herself. Bloody joke, eh? I wouldn't be here if I'd kept my stupid mouth shut.'

Wyatt exchanged a questioning glance with George.

'Two hours later she stole Jonathan's wallet and passport,' George said. 'That's the only reason we became interested in Cill Trevelyan.' She pulled a wry expression at Roy's dawning disillusionment. 'I did say she didn't have your loyalties, Roy, and perhaps, after all, we should blame her father for it. If he hadn't made her the whipping boy for his frustrations, and forced her to lie about it, she wouldn't have learnt how easy – or *pleasurable* – it was to see someone else punished for *hers*.'

From: wandr.burton@compuline.com
Sent: Tues 29/07/03 15:23
To: robandeileen.burton@uknet.co.uk
Subject: Louise

Dear Robert and Eileen

I'm writing to you without Billy's knowledge because he's forbidden
me and the girls to talk to you, but someone has to say something
before this awful situation gets any worse. You can't be so stupid
that you'd go on lying for Louise when she's lining up Eileen as
Grace's murderer if Roy Trent can wriggle out of it. Maybe you think
you owe her something because of Robert's abuse. Maybe you
think that by giving her an alibi, you're helping her. You're not.
You're just accusing YOURSELVES. I'm guessing you're sticking to
a story you invented years ago, but all you're doing is digging a
bigger and bigger hole for yourselves because the police haven't
told you what Louise has been saying.

Billy KNOWS that Eileen went to work on the Monday and Tuesday
afternoons as usual, which means she COULDN'T have got home
until after Robert clocked on at Brackham & Wright's. It wasn't until
the Wednesday, when Louise started her fainting fits, that she gave
up work. Robert, you know this too, so why are you lying about it?
The police keep asking Billy the same questions over and over
again. What time did his mother come home on the Tuesday? Was
Louise there? Did his mother go out again later?

Eileen's already under suspicion because she said she collected
Louise from school on the Monday afternoon and kept her at home
for the rest of the day. That's contradicting Louise's OWN story
about phoning Trent from a call box after school, then helping him
and his friends gain access to Grace that evening. Because of that,

they're now questioning whether Eileen collected Louise on the Tuesday. If you've been lying to protect the family, then you're MAD. At the moment, Eileen's next in the firing line. If you're guilty of Grace's murder, Eileen, then I have no sympathy for you, but if you're NOT, then you must tell the truth.

The worst I think you might have done is cover for Louise afterwards. I'd know if either of my girls had done something bad. I bet she came home in a state on the Tuesday, long after you'd got back from work, probably in something of Grace's because she'd left hers on the bathroom floor. I expect she lied and said Grace was already dead when she got there. So what did you do? Go back for the clothes? Was it you who wiped the taps? It's the sort of thing you'd think of. I wonder why you didn't clean the bath as well, but maybe the blood and hair didn't show when it was wet. You must have been very frightened, of course, so perhaps you felt too sick to do the job properly. Was it you who vandalized the house to make it look like a burglary?

I'm not surprised you were shaking when the police came door to door. I bet you couldn't believe your luck when the police didn't find any fingerprints. I wonder if it was you who picked up the bloodstained gloves and carried them away to a bin. You probably hoped Louise wouldn't have been clever enough to wear them, so you left them where they could be found in case they proved someone else was responsible.

I don't know what I would have done in your shoes, Eileen, but I hope I'd have had the courage – and sense – to do the right thing. You didn't solve anything for her, or for yourselves, by closing your mind to her guilt. I'm sure the whole idea of it was unbearable, particularly because you KNEW that only a very disturbed person could have murdered Grace in that way. Perhaps you even understood why Louise was disturbed – or at least guessed – so you share some of her guilt. Robert carries the most blame, though, because he treated her like a plaything that could be discarded when he got bored.

Then Howard confessed and you were able to persuade yourself that Louise had been telling the truth. Poor little bloke. He didn't have a mother who was prepared to cover and lie for him. Wynne just made his situation worse by saying he cut himself because he thought he was ugly. Billy's been having dreams about Cill. Well, I've been having them about Howard Stamp. I can't get out of my mind that, in his whole life, no one except his gran and Cill was ever kind to him. But, when he needed them – when he was at his most lonely – they weren't there.

Louise has no conscience, Eileen, because you and Robert taught her that it's OK to lie. Half of me thinks it would be natural justice for you to take the blame for her this time – you SHOULD have spoken out in 1970 – the other half revolts at it. She's already sent one innocent person to prison for this. Can't you see how WRONG it would be to let her do it again. Louise is not your only child. You are BILLY'S mother, too.

Rachel

Twenty-Nine

Winchester Prison car park
Tuesday, 29 July 2003, 4.00 p.m.

JONATHAN WAS standing by the car listening to the radio through the open window when George and DS Wyatt emerged through the judas gate in the huge oak doors that formed the entrance to Winchester Prison. He watched them walk the two hundred yards to the car park while a commentator talked about a forthcoming enquiry into the events surrounding the mysterious death of the Iraqi arms expert Dr David Kelly.

'Campbell and Blair to give evidence to Hutton Enquiry . . . Government stands accused . . .'

To Jonathan, still as sceptical as he'd been in February, the idea that an enquiry could get at the truth when the major player was dead was laughable. There were no absolute truths. Only half-truths and interpretations that begged to be spun by anyone strong enough – or *determined* enough – to force his opinions on everyone else. It was single-minded zealots who ruled the world – politicians, religious leaders, terrorists, media and business moguls – and most of them were too arrogant or stupid to see that their beliefs were flawed.

He cocked an eyebrow as George and DS Wyatt drew close. 'Any luck?'

'Nothing we can use as yet,' said George, 'but at least he's started thinking for himself.' She gave a small giggle. 'I shouldn't laugh – not after what he did to poor Cill – but he was huffing and puffing by the end. He can't *believe* what a fool he's been . . . he swallowed everything Louise ever told him and never thought for one *minute* that she had anything to hide.'

Jonathan reached into the car and switched off the radio. 'His memories won't help us,' he warned her. 'He'll come up with a stream of them if it gets him off the hook. We need something we can prove if we're going to name her.'

'Oh, don't be so miserable,' she said cheerfully, tapping his wrist. 'Mr Wyatt's very optimistic. He tells me persistence is everything. If he keeps asking questions, Louise will trip herself up. She's not bright enough to do anything else – *none* of us is.' Her wise eyes smiled into his. 'She's already handed us a wealth of ammunition because of the numerous different versions she's produced. It's the tangled-web syndrome, Jon. Roy fell into it the minute he tried to sex up Howard's guilt. Lies always unravel under pressure. *You* know that.'

He gave her a fond smile. 'But I wasn't fully committed to mine, George.'

She clucked like a mother hen. 'Of course you weren't, my dear. You're far too honourable . . . and Emma wasn't worth the heartache it caused you. Sasha's a much better prospect. There are no sides to her . . . probably because her Mongolian blood is so obvious. It's not the sort of thing you can hide, is it?'

Jonathan opened his mouth to protect what little mystery he had left, but Wyatt forestalled him with an outrageous wink. 'Never argue with a lady, Dr Hughes . . . particularly when she's right. Ms Spencer's a fine young woman, and I *am* optimistic. Mrs Fletcher's never been questioned about Grace's murder and she's already contradicted her original statement where she claimed ignorance. It's just a matter of time before she ties herself in knots.'

Jonathan looked into George's face. 'You'd better not start feeling sorry for her,' he warned.

'She was only thirteen.'

He held up a finger. 'I'm a man, George, and I can't cope with any more emotion.'

'But—'

With a fond smile, he pulled her into his arms. 'She's my mother,' he told Wyatt over her head. 'She had a one-night stand with a Jamaican road sweeper thirty-five years ago and she's been regretting it ever since. I wouldn't mind so much but she keeps trying to pass me off as her toyboy.'

The policeman gave a doubtful smile.

THE END